THINGS I
FORGOT ABOUT

KELSEY HUMPHREYS

THIS BOOK IS FOR...

the woman who always does everything herself,
because she's always had to.

THE CANTONS

Jon Canton

Jonny + Dr. Sandra Canton

Susan Canton-Bell, 36
+ Adam Bell

Sadie Canton-Riggs, 33
+ Shep Riggs

Skye James, 30
+ Matthew James

Samantha Clark, 28
+ Emerson Clark

Sally Canton, 22

Robert + Heather Canton

Katherine Canton, 25

PLAYLIST

Listen while you read!
kelseyhumphreys.com/thingsiforgotabout

1

"Mommy, look! Aunt Sadie is in the peoples magazine again," my eight-year-old calls to me from the kitchenette. I brace myself and plaster on a smile. *I will not give Lucy a complex about this.*

I love my cousin, I do. And I am rooting for her massive, continued success. But boy howdy, it is not a blast to be related to famous people. How much of our lives revolves around the other Cantons?

Still, right now that's *my* issue, not Lucy's. She just thinks it's amazing that Aunt Sadie is getting yet another movie deal.

I almost chuckle as I walk from the tiny bathroom out into our studio apartment. *Not passing down my own baggage.* That is mothering a daughter, in a nutshell. Why wasn't that in any of the parenting books I skimmed back when she was tiny?

My fake smile perks up as I cross into the space where she sits at our tiny breakfast table. Her big, teal-blue eyes are wide with excitement. I point at the magazine.

"Lucile S. Canton, where did you get that?"

She deflates a bit. "Gramma's. But Aunt Sadie lost."

I frown. "Lost what?"

"The top of the page says 'who wored it better' and has Aunt Sadie and some other lady in the same blue dress. And then there are some numbers, and her number is small, and she got the red thumbs down sign. So I think that means she lost because the other lady got a green thumbs up so Aunt Sadie lost, right?"

I clench my jaw shut. I will have to text my mother about these magazines *again*. After a deep breath, I put my smile back on.

"It's wore. 'Who Wore it Best.' And this is why we don't read these magazines, Luce. Because if we make one person feel better by making another person feel bad, is that kind or is that mean?"

"Mean." She nods once and furrows her brow. She puts down the magazine with disgust that I know will only last a few seconds before she'll be itching to pick it back up again.

"Right." I start gathering my things as I walk around the table. "Aunt Sadie always looks awesome, and even if she looked like yesterday's roadkill, would we care?"

"No."

"Nope on a rope. Go get your shoes on please. Time to go open up."

"Okay!" She jumps up from the table.

I let her skip cleaning up her cereal bowl this time because we're running a few minutes behind schedule. Also, I know I only have a few more years before opening the restaurant with me becomes lame. I'm in that sweet spot of time where she still thinks following me around for adult chores is amazing, but thank the good Lord, she can wipe her own a—*butt*. Not a toddler anymore, but not yet a tween obsessed with tween-y things.

So, I'll get her cereal bowl for her, just this once.

"Ready."

"Bed, sister." I nod behind her.

She turns to pull up her comforter and straighten up her stuffed animals.

I'm not a neat freak by nature, but with this tiny space, I have to be more of a drill sergeant than I'd like. The bunk bed, love seat, tv, breakfast table, and kitchenette barely fit in here. Add in her toys and stuffies and crafts and... I close my eyes. *Only a few more years, Kat. You can do it.*

As if they can sense we were just talking about them, my cousins—more like sisters most days—start blowing up my phone.

Susan: It's already time to plan your Fourth of July travel!

I grunt.

Susan, the oldest of five sisters, and the first Canton grandchild, is the leader, the organizer. Even after the difficult year she's had. Her Type A tendencies worsened about a decade ago with the loss of Aunt Sandra, their mom.

Skye: Suze it's months away.
Sam: We'll be there, OBVS!!!
Sadie: Wouldn't miss it.
Sally: What Skye said.
Sally: Also what Sam and Sadie said.

I can't help but smile. When I got pregnant at seventeen, Susan and Sadie, the now-famous romance author who apparently wore it worse, stepped up when my mother couldn't. Or wouldn't.

Skye, introverted artist and queen of snark, also showed her support. She, Samantha, and Sally are closer to me in age, and they all flew in together when Lucy was born, joining the others who were already here.

It's why Lucy's middle initial is S. For all five of them. I couldn't pick one.

Samantha, crazy lovable extrovert, used to be my closest friend out of the sisters, but she went and got married.

So, it's Sally, the quirky genius with the perfect MCAT score, who I have spent the most time with lately. I know she'll be the one who asks me to chime in.

Sally: Kat?

I wince. Fourth of July weekend is their big Canton Family Fireworks Festival in Tulsa, but it's a huge week for the Roadside. It'll be hard to get away.

Kat: I'll try but you know the Fourth is busy here.
Sam: Boooooo!!!
Sadie: Tell your boss you need a break!
Kat: I just took a break with Sally in Park City!
Sally: That was a year ago.
Susan: Well, it won't be as fun without you, but we know you have to do what's best for you and your Lucyloo!

My phone explodes with heart emojis as I tuck it away.

Lucy bounds back to me. "Can I get the switches today, pleeee-ase?" She begs me as we reach our door.

"Okay, no chair duty today."

"Yessssss!" She runs past me, out into the short wood-pan-eled hall that connects the Roadside Inn to the back office and then finally the Roadside Grill area.

"Hey, slow down. You know sometimes there are slick spots." I call after her, cringing at how much of a *mom* I am, but sure enough, she slips on an oily spot by the first set of light switches. I hold back a snort, watching her straighten up quickly and try to play it off. She even looks over each shoulder dramatically, as if there is someone here other than me. Eight is a fun age.

As she hums to herself and literally skips around, incapable of simply walking, the restaurant comes to life. Twinkle lights, spotlights, neon beer logos, and funky road signs light up one after the other across the wood paneled walls. Spotlights highlight Arkansas photos, flags, and of course anything and everything Razorback Football.

"Morning Bullwinkle," she chirps as a spotlight flickers on above a huge Moose head. Shortly after, faint classic rock music fills the space. "Morning fam!" she adds, as she passes the sign Shep, Sadie's husband, gave us in the corner.

It's a large, framed family photo from my cousin's wedding, including all the Cantons. Above the photo, large print states, "Sooners Welcome But Not Encouraged."

Shep and Adam, Susan's husband, played Sooner football at OU, so they have to give me a hard time.

Lucy loves opening up the restaurant, and I don't mind it. There's something hopeful about mornings here, especially when she is with me. Which she always is.

I flip the chairs down and give everything a once over as I go.

Ruthie will be here shortly, and she'll give me what-for if I miss anything. Last night was a Sign Night, so I need to triple check for tiny glass shards or spilled condiments left over from the madness.

Speak of the angel herself.

"You still flippin' chairs? She's gonna be late for school, Kat!" The Roadside Grill's robust head chef and general manager breezes in. She's like joy and comfort in human form.

Ruthie's also the only one who doesn't adhere to the Roadside dress code, claiming years ago that large Black women in their sixties do not wear plaid pearl snap shirts. Which, to my delight, was overheard by my tiny human who demanded an explanation.

I enjoyed watching Ruthie squirm as she backpedaled everything she'd just said about women, skin color, body size, and age.

My mother often has to do the same thing when she comments that I'm *getting too thin* or that I *dress too young for my age.* They're learning though. Lucy is quick to correct them.

"Miss Ruthieeeeee!" Lucy runs in for a hug like she didn't see Ruthie yesterday and every day before.

Ruthie loses her mind with glee, picking Lucy up and spinning her around, my girl's light, strawberry blonde curls flying.

They both squeal and laugh.

I suppose I would run for a hug like that every day, too.

"She's right. We're gonna be late, Bug. Let's go."

We hurry out of the front door and around the side of the building to my truck. I quickly say my daily prayer that the thing will actually start as Lucy throws her backpack on the seat and climbs in behind me. Mercifully, it does.

I hate rushing. I know this is my fault, because I was dragging this morning. Not only because I went a little nuts last night during my shift behind the bar. In fact, I went nuts last night because of this, right now. The sticky, bone-deep dread I feel about going into town. Board meetings are a small price to pay for the salary I receive, but today my father will be present. Okay, so, medium price to pay.

Only a couple more years.

It's a quick drive to the school, during which I study Lucy in the rearview mirror as much as I can. There are days I can see her face change as we get closer to the school. Anxiety is not something one should find on an eight-year-old's face. Especially not over school. I don't see any today, though.

She unbuckles and leans up front to give me a hug and kiss.

I look her over. *Navy school uniform, check. Navy backpack, check. Navy cardigan, check. School water bottle, check. School lunch box, check. Neon pink, light up sneakers that hurt my eyes to look at, also check.*

I love this girl.

"Bye Mommy!" She slams the door and bounds up the sidewalk.

I sit and watch my whole heart gallop away from me. Until some impatient son of a b—*biscuit* honks behind me. I flip him the bird down low as I drive away.

He can't see the gesture, and neither can my child or any teachers or staff, but I know it's there, and that's one small comfort. A little something for me as I drive toward my father.

Maybe I'll stop and get a huge sugary coffee, too. Eh, not worth the money.

His offices have good coffee for free. And breakfast, which I now realize I'm starving for. Not sure I can eat around him though.

I wonder which Dad I'll get today: the serious businessman, the polite former Mr. Mayor, or the real Robert Canton. A shiver passes through me. I grip the steering wheel and sit up straight.

He can't hurt me anymore, not really.

I can do this. I can do this for Lucy, and I can do this for myself.

I don't know what today's meeting is about, which is how I like it. I show up when asked, say nothing, do nothing, and deposit my checks. Occasionally, I have to vote on something, and I try to vote against Daddy dearest as often as possible.

He doesn't say anything because he can't have his one child be an estranged child. He needs me around to make him look like a family man.

Like a Welton. Because the Weltons run this town and, well, the whole country, obviously, since they own AmeriMart, the world's largest chain of big-box stores. But since their headquarters are here in this little corner of said country, almost everyone within a hundred-mile radius works for them in some capacity. Dad included.

But, he'd say, *at least he doesn't work for his brother.*

Stupid, sad, bitter, ol' Dad.

Maybe I'll get to vote against him today.

I smirk as I take my exit toward the newest, biggest, and most expensive office buildings in Northwest Arkansas. Therein lie the Weltons, all the AmeriMart executives, and all of the businesses associated with them. Buyers, distributors, consultants. Thousands of people covering everything from choosing product to designing price tags, all the way to scheduling and driving delivery trucks.

Which is my father's specialty.

I fight a yawn.

This is for Lucy. I can do it.

I pull into the parking spot next to a few designated executive spots marked CANTON. Because they are ridiculous. As if my father and I really need marked spaces by the door. Although, my dad does hate to see my beat-up truck, literally duct taped together in places, in one of those spots...ah, well, I've already pulled in and I'm late. I throw my one black blazer on over my Roadside uniform and head through the gleaming glass double doors.

The vibe is weird the second I hit the lobby.

The receptionist's desk is empty, and I can see people gathered around in the center bullpen. I remember that someone is visiting today, a financial consultant making a presentation or something.

Maybe I should have read the email, since everyone here clearly thinks this is a huge deal. My dad is probably beside himself trying to butter this guy up. They're probably shaking hands and laughing about golf scores.

I scoff as I walk through the bright, empty seating area.

Whoever this fancy schmancy businessman is, I already cannot stand him.

2

Dad's employees part like the ocean for me to walk through the hallway that leads into to the main conference room. The office is done in wood, natural tones, and a ton of glass, so all the staffers can see me coming. They don't quite know what to make of me.

Just the way I like it.

Susan says I am an Enneagram 8. A rebel.

She's definitely whichever Enneagram number is the leader and the rule follower. As the COO of Canton International, the massive greeting card empire started by my grandpa, she kind of has to be. Now the business has a publishing division and a new entertainment department, too.

That's what my cousins tell me, anyway.

I mostly stay out of Canton businesses, both the billion-dollar-enterprise that used to be Grandpa's, now my uncle's, and my father's multimillion dollar totally separate entity.

I don't care about any of it. And I refuse to take personality tests. I cannot be boxed in. If that makes me an eight, so be it.

Nowadays, with my dramatic make up and grungy clothes, I just find people's reactions hilarious. It started as a way to proverbially flip off my father. Small town life was, and is, painfully boring. So, my oddities provide some gossip fodder for my fellow citizens here in the Arkansas Ozarks, and their interest provides entertainment for me.

Like today, my hair is bleached bright white. I'm about to color it again, maybe neon this time, so it needed to be stripped of remaining purple tones. It's pulled up in a high pony, so my plethora of ear piercings are on display. My make up is dark but not too extreme, because my goth looks of old freaked Lucy out. I'm in tight black jeans, combat boots, a black plaid, pearl-snap shirt, and my long blazer. My shirt is open to show a little cleavage or else I'd feel like a nun. This ensemble could maybe be called country-goth, business chic.

I'm giving off a weird energy.

Weird is fun.

Everyone mumbles their awkward greetings at me. I would normally grill Jan, the receptionist, for details about the consultant but I'm already late. She also appears to be in a battle with the copy machine.

My stomach twists at the sound of my father's voice when I get closer.

He's in his smarmy former mayor character today. Saying something about how the interns will come in and get drink orders for everyone.

Awesome, because I need two espressos, at least.

I barge in.

"Ah, lovely. I'll just have a black tea, please," the fancy—British, I guess—consultant says to me, not looking in my direction.

My father's eyes go so wide, I think one might fall plum out of its socket. He looks at me, then the suit, then the door.

My father is... nervous?

I should make him squirm. I should dress down this pompous a-hole consultant in front of everyone. I should make a little scene with the whole board present. But I guess part of me still has a conscience, because seeing my dad rattled... I can't do it.

I'll get the tea and go nuclear after. I turn and leave, just as Jan approaches with some copies. "Where's the intern? I guess they want tea and coffee."

"Mabrey? She's on it, in the kitchen already."

I nod and make my way to the break room.

Mabrey has a tray started with a plate of donuts and bagels, a pot of coffee, creamers, and sweeteners. She mutters something under her breath.

"Mabrey?"

"Oh! You... you're Kat. Hi!"

"Guilty. What's up, can I help?"

She gestures at the countertop. "I don't know how to do tea other than just put the bag in a cup and pour the hot water in. But Jan says the British are very particular about their tea."

I chuckle. "So what? He's in Nowhere, Arkansas, USA. I'm sure he's not expecting the Queen's royal tea service. Just grab the bags and I'll take the kettle."

"Are you sure?" she squeaks.

"What's gotten into you guys? It's just tea, not communion for shit's sake." *Crap! I was doing so well.*

She looks around and whispers, "I mean, I heard he's *wealthier* than the Weltons. Like the billionaire other billionaires go to for money advice or something." She looks down at the kettle which is whistling now. "What if I do this wrong and get fired? I need this internship this semester."

This girl is actually tearing up.

About tea.

"One, break out of the matrix, honey. This ain't that important. Two, are you even getting paid? I can get you a job at the Roadside for actual money." She makes a face, as if waitressing in a small-town grill is her worst nightmare. I get it. "Three, I won't let anyone fire you."

She nods, comforted, then wipes her eyes.

Seeing her, seeing everyone, so uptight almost gets to me. I fight the urge to spit into the tea kettle. And it's a strong urge. But, mature twenty-five-year-old single mom that I am, I refrain. I grab the pot off its cradle and follow Mabrey back to the conference room.

As we enter everyone takes their seats.

And then I can see his face.

This f—*freaking* guy.

Dang it. Just when I thought I had broken the habit.

I clench my jaw tight.

He hasn't looked up from his stack of papers. Good.

Mabrey carefully sets the tray down at the edge of the table, while I stop at the empty chair next to *him.*

"For your tea," I say.

He doesn't even glance up from his laminated, collated hand out. "Thank you. Oh, I didn't get your name earlier, miss?"

I plop the kettle down so hard hot water shoots out and almost hits him in the crotch. *Yes!* Dramatic, but not something he can press charges against me for. Perfect.

He jumps, pushing his rolling chair back. The back of his chair actually rams into the wall, and I have to stifle a laugh.

"Katie." Dad chastises. "Uh, sorry about this, about her, I mean. Well, this is my daughter, Katherine Canton."

"Oh, we've met. Lovely to see you, *Dennis.*" I say his name like it's a disease and watch the color drain from his face. Because no, I'm not the intern.

We've talked to each other, danced near each other. We were in my cousin Samantha's wedding together for an entire week. And he didn't even recognize me.

By the look in his eyes, he didn't know I'd be here. Or maybe he forgot that I exist. That there's a whole other Canton family aside from the perfect one. That there are other Canton women besides just the famous one, Sadie, who also happens to be his ex-fiancée.

The one he insulted in front of her entire wedding party.

"Oh right, of course you've met," Dad starts.

"Kat." Dennis stands and stammers, "I didn't, I mean, I'm sorry, I—"

"Don't worry about it." I squint at him with the fakest smile I can muster. "You're here to present, right? By all means." I gesture toward the projection screen at the front of the room, plop down in my seat, and cross my ankles, resting my dusty combat boots on the shiny glass table.

Who cares if he doesn't remember me?

This isn't my first rodeo. Being ignored, shunned, forgotten, all of it's the same. And it's fine. I can live my little life in peace, miles away from here.

All the hoity toities around the table shuffle uncomfortably as I settle into my obnoxious position.

I just smirk.

Like the employees, no doubt listening on the other side of the wall, the board members are not sure what to do with me.

Shelly, the only female on the board, gives me her standard disapproving glare. Still, she says nothing.

I have the majority share after Dad, so they tolerate my antics.

"Right," Dennis says, still frozen behind me.

My dad shoots me that crazed glare again, before taking over. "Dennis, we really appreciate you taking the time to look over our numbers. You're the number one Crisis Consultant in the industry so whatever you suggest, we're ready to get to work."

Crisis? What?

"It's my pleasure, Robert. And thank you, but you overestimate me. You do not, however, overestimate your current situation." Dennis moves toward the screen as it fills with the first slide of his presentation.

He easily takes control of the room, which is irritating. He's tall and his suit is expensive, flawless. It fits his built frame and wide shoulders in a way that screams *I have a personal tailor.* The fabric pulls against his muscles as he moves. And the movement—the walk—also screams, something like, *and I travel with a personal trainer who works out with me two hours a day.*

He's always been Mr. Tall, Dark, and Perfect. His hair is perfect, his jaw firm. His stupid accent that comes out of his stupid perfect mouth. His teeth have got to be veneers. Not that he ever smiles. But if he did, he'd look a lot like a taller, beefier Richard Madden.

I bet Dennis could pull off actual armor...

I shake my head. Why am I looking at him, anyway? He's a horrible human being and I need to focus on his slides, not him.

"...I own the majority share in many companies that, just like Canton Tracking, partner intricately with AmeriMart. In short, you cannot afford to lose their contract. And you're in jeopardy of doing so."

What?

My smirk is gone.

For the first time ever, I pay attention during a board meeting.

Canton Tracking is a software company that integrates with AmeriMart's trucks. It's the most un-sexy, un-exciting, un-creative business ever—the polar opposite of Canton Cards, run by my uncle, Dad's nemesis—but it's a solid business. Dad made a lot of stupid mistakes before he started this company but now, he's somewhat successful. He learned the ins and outs of shipping goods when he was still working with Gramps and Uncle Jonny.

Before the bitterness of being passed over for CEO swallowed him whole.

AmeriMart's fleet, and thus their contract with Dad's company, is huge. We can't survive without it.

Dennis takes us through graphs and charts and spreadsheets. His presentation is boring and detailed and complicated. It's also clear.

We are indeed in a crisis. Which means I am in a crisis.

Dennis has so much to cover that he talks for almost an hour straight. An hour in which he doesn't look at me once. It is just bizarre. *Hello, I'm sitting right here, dude.*

When we hit the hour mark, we decide to take a fifteen-minute breather. A little intermission to break up the horror show happening in the spreadsheets.

I get up quickly to find some air.

I don't look at my father, who has once again screwed the pooch.

Not only is he a toxic person who has created a toxic workplace. He's also made extremely risky decisions. I've warned him about this, but he can't help himself. Plus, he always responds with the most hurtful string words he can think of to lob at me in response, so I stopped trying.

Now we could lose everything.

I bust out a side door and inhale the cool spring air.

"Kat!"

I roll my eyes as I hear Dennis push through the door behind me.

"Kat, I apologize, your hair is different and—"

"Can it, Dennis. It's not like we're buddies. We spoke like two sentences to each other at the wedding."

He frowns. "Can it?"

"Yes, it's an expression, it means cut it out."

He dips his chin. "I'm well aware of the phrase, just confused as to why you won't allow me to apologize for—"

"For thinking I was the intern and ordering me to get you tea like you're the fucking King of England? Oh, great, I'm back to f-bombs. Perfect, thank you."

Dennis shuffles backward a few inches. "Have I otherwise offended you?"

"Otherwise offended?" I gesture down at myself, now sans-business-jacket. "I am not the Queen, Dennis. You don't have to speak a-hole, you can talk like a normal person."

He squints down at me but doesn't respond. He just watches me.

Also, how tall is he? Six foot three, maybe?

I mean I don't normally feel small. I hate feeling small.

"What?" I shrug and lift my hands. "Shit or get off the pot, dude."

His eyebrows shoot up. "I don't remember you being this foul-mouthed."

"I remember you being exactly this stuck up."

He huffs. "I think you're just very unaccustomed to civility."

I bat my lashes. "Thems words are too bigs for my small-town girl brain, sir. Like I tried tellin' ya, I don't speak asshole!" I am yelling now. Whoops.

I realize after the words fall out that maybe I am more upset with the reason Dennis is here, and not the man himself, but it's too late.

"Oh, I think you're quite fluent," Dennis raises his voice slightly, "but since something is clearly, deeply, *disturbingly* wrong with you, let us agree to simply never speak again, yeah?"

He turns, grabs the door handle, and almost pulls the door off its hinges.

As I watch his large silhouette disappear down the hall, I can't stop myself. "Apology not accepted," I holler.

"Apology rescinded," he calls back.

The door slams shut in my face, and I just stare at it. *Apology rescinded?* Who even says that?

I cannot get over this guy. I've been around Brits. Like Emerson, Samantha's husband. It was at their wedding that Dennis and I met.

Emerson is quiet and polite but he's not pompous. He has become a good friend, surprisingly, and Lucy loves him.

Dennis is supposedly Emerson's best friend.

Or was.

After he got drunk and called Sadie a lying bitch, I think their friendship took a hit.

I can't see Dennis as anyone's friend or best friend, definitely not a fiancé. I could maybe see him as the snooty prince of a small country. That's about it.

Eventually, I catch my breath and head back in.

The presentation drags on and again, Lord Dickwad doesn't look at me. His eyes, a brown so deep they're almost black, skip around the table to everyone but me. Shelly even gets a smile out of him. It's not a real smile, but it's striking.

He is striking.

If only he didn't talk.

"So." Dennis pauses after another hour and a half of leading this meeting. "All that I've just shown you to right this ship can be done in a quarter. I'm excited to dive in and work side by side with Robert for the next ninety days."

My turn for my eyeballs to try and fall right out of their wide sockets.

Dennis DeLane, billionaire jerkoff who forgot I existed before declaring something is "deeply wrong with me" is going to be around. For ninety f—freaking, ninety *freaking* days.

Well, around here.

This is totally fine because I'm never here. I'm in my safe, small-town bubble twenty highway-minutes away. In fact, I probably won't see him the entire time. There will be one follow-up board meeting at the end of the quarter and then he'll be gone.

Okay.

Ninety days from now I'll have to suffer his presence again. Until then, I won't see him or talk to him, so between now and that meeting, I won't think about him at all.

I'm not going to happen to run into him in my everyday life.

He doesn't even know about the Roadside. It's not like he's going to show up tomorrow for an early lunch. Even if he knew about my happy little life, he just said he'd rather we never speak again.

Fine by me, man.

So why is my gut all twisted up in knots for the entire drive home?

3

Because my stomach is f—*freaking* psychic, apparently.

"Reporting for duty, Ethaaan," I call out to my gangly, typical-college-bro co-worker as I step out of our apartment door and into the little lobby of the Inn. Lucy finally fell asleep so I'm exhausted, as usual, but I try to stay cheery. Until I round the corner.

"Oh, Kat, good!" Ethan stammers. "Um, a complimentary rezzy came in and—"

"Kat?" Dennis stands there, looking tall and crisp and agitated. And too much for the little, kitschy space.

The Roadside Inn and Grill is not meant for people like Dennis. It's meant for small town tourists and people who want a tiny upgrade from camping out in nature. Maybe also for social media types who want a certain aesthetic with the hotels they choose.

The motel-bar combo is shabby in an intentional way. It's on the edge of Beaver Lake, one of the Ozark's highly-regulated lakes. The natural lake is huge, yet there are no big hotels, no marinas the size of small cities, no fancy floating restaurants. Coming to this little area is like going back in time, and the Roadside reflects that.

Everything is clean and some of the paint and furnishings are even new. But they're made to look old. They're faded and textured. The ceilings are low, and the walls are covered in fishing, camping, and boating memorabilia.

Dennis is in his dark, navy three-piece suit and light blue shirt, not a near-black hair out of place even though it's nine pm.

He's all wrong in here.

"Nope." I say, breezing through to the desk.

"I was going to ask Miss Ruthie, but she's already gone," Ethan shifts his weight and grabs one of his elbows. Poor kid.

"Ethan, it's fine, you can go, I'll handle this."

"Nice." he says in his fratboy broseph voice before bolting out the front entrance.

After the doorbell finishes its chime, Dennis cocks his head. "You work here?"

"I see why Dad is paying you the big bucks for your fancy consulting. Very smart." He glares but I go on. "There are two very nice hotels in town, go stay at one of them, *Dennis.*"

"Why do you say my name like that, *Katherine?*"

"Just feels right. Now I'm not sure what my dad said to convince you to stay out here but believe me, you don't want to."

"Of course, I don't," he snipes back. "The two aforementioned hotels are full for some boat show."

"Aforementioned?" I mutter. This guy. I shrug. "So find an Airbnb."

"I did." He puts his hands on his waist. "Didn't suit. I tried the hotels. And a few motels. All full."

"What *didn't suit* about your Airbnb?" I match his stance, both of us growing more irritated by the second. "No fine china, was the silverware not actual silver? The nerve of some people, I tell ya."

"The place was fine, the area was… dodgy."

"Dodgy?" I laugh and wave my arms around. "Dodgier than this?"

"Unbelievably, yes."

I squint up at him. "Anywhere around here is going to be too sketchy for you. Rent one of the big lake mansions."

"I plan to. First thing tomorrow."

I realize as he stares at me that I have all the power here. He literally has nowhere else to stay. I grin. "Well. Have you ever slept in a car?"

"Kat."

"First time is a bit weird but if you can get the passenger seat all the way down flat it's not too bad unless you have back problems. Which, at your age…"

"I already booked the room, just give me the key."

"Another option is a hammock between two trees. It's still chilly out, but I would bet my left tit you have a fancyass overcoat in your suitcase."

He makes a shocked noise.

"Shit, I said ass. And shit. Ugh! You bring out the sailor in me, go away!"

His mouth hangs open for a beat before he finds his voice. "I'll pay for it. Your father said he knew the manager but obviously I don't need a free stay."

"Obviously."

"Katherine." He almost growls my name through clenched teeth.

I mimic his grumpy face and tense shoulders right back at him. "Dennis."

He releases his poor, but very trim, waist from the iron grip of his hands and looks up at the ceiling. Then, as if noticing where he is, he glances around at the fishing gear on the walls, the camping signs, the retro Coca-Cola fridge in the corner.

His gaze lands back on me. "Why do you work here?"

I cross my arms. "Why are you consulting for my dad?" He frowns for a second. "Yeah, I'm onto you. There's no way you take on a small client like us for ninety days of your big fancy billionaire life, unless something else is going on. So, what is it?"

Something flickers in his eyes, and he leans in, planting his hands on the counter on either side of the register in front of me. He glares, assessing.

I don't miss that his eyes dip to my open shirt for a second. The realization almost makes me blush. Which is weird as hell.

What is happening here?

"There's no way a board member of Canton Tracking needs a job at a shit little motel. So, what is it?" His low voice, repeating my phrase back at me, brings me back to the matter at hand. That he's a jerk.

Shit little motel?

I really cannot stand this guy. I'm out. I grab the key off the peg board on the wall.

"It's none of your business." I toss the keys at him, hard, but he catches them easily. Annoying. "Enjoy your complimentary stay."

I turn and march down the little hallway, past my apartment door to the office, slip in and close the door. But Sir Snooty Face follows me. He doesn't barge in, though. That would be too un-civilized. No, he knocks politely, making me even angrier.

I fling the door open. "What?"

"Look, let me pay for the stay. I insist."

"It's already booked as complimentary, nothing I can do." I try to slam the door on him, but he stops it with his hand.

"Let me talk to, uh, Ruthie, was it? The owner?" I roll my eyes, but he keeps on. "Will she be in tomorrow morning?"

He's not going to let this go. Ugh.

I sigh. "She will but, hopefully, you won't. I'll work it out with her and make sure you're charged, okay?" I flash a bright, bitter smile. "You'll see it come through while you're sipping mimosas on your new private dock somewhere on the lakefront. Ideally on the *other* side of the lake."

A muscle in his jaw flexes as he inhales. He looks past me into the office. It's wood paneled and dusty and covered in piles of paperwork. Ruthie calls it an organized disaster.

"Are you in... some kind of trouble?" He looks back down at me.

I snort. "If I was, do you think I'd tell *you?* Did I miss the part in between dismissing me, forgetting me, insulting me, and then insulting my place of work where we became *friends?*"

"I apologized—"

I cut him off. "You rescinded that apology!"

"And for good reason. Bloody hell, woman! You are..."

"Shutting the door in your pompous face. Bye!"

This time, he lets me shut the door. I freeze, listening.

He huffs out some kind of grunty sigh, curses, and stomps away.

Good. I hope he hates this whole experience and stays far away.

But since I really, really want him to disappear, I'm not hopeful. Because I am one unlucky little b—*babe*, so if I want him to vanish, I'd bet my *right* tit he's here to stay.

And if I have to suffer his pretentiousness I sure as hell am going to figure out why he's really here. This is a small town. I bet I'll hear by dinner time tomorrow.

4

Clang!

"Kat!" Ruthie scolds me. "I know you keep messing with the schedule so that those two work the same shift. Why do you always stir the pot, girl?" She gestures from the back line of the kitchen to where Ethan has just dropped a tray of plates. His face is purple, and he keeps glancing at Stella, who I sometimes call Barbie in my head because she is the doll in human form. Barbie is oblivious.

"Because the pot needs stirring! He's hopelessly in love with her and everyone can see it but her."

Ruthie levels me with her no-nonsense glare.

I concede. "And I am bored, and they are entertaining."

"Do I need to say it?"

"No." I start to walk away from her.

But of course, she says it anyway. "You need to start datin' again. Stop terrorizing this poor town just for shits and giggles."

"Jar!" I holler back.

She grabs a one-dollar bill out of her ample bosom and puts it in Lucy's kitchen swear jar.

I smile, feeling like maybe my luck has changed after all. No Dennis all day. Not that I've been thinking about him the whole day.

Today was a test day for my Lucy Bug. She was anxious during the drive this morning and had no smiles when she hopped out of the car. She put on a brave front and it almost killed me. She doesn't need to be brave. It's just school, for Pete's sake.

I melt when I see a bundle of navy uniform and unruly curls bound through the door.

She's smiling and skipping, both good signs. My mom steps inside behind Lucy looking frail and sad, as always.

"Bug!" I bend down to hug her. "How was Gramma's?"

"Great. We watched Cinderella with real people!"

"Epic! Let's get you changed out of that uniform. Here." I hand her the apartment key and she runs through the restaurant without a care in the world. I stand. "Thanks, Mom."

"Of course." She smiles. Then, awkward as ever, she nods and turns to leave.

I don't know what to say, so I leave too. I follow after Lucy, avoiding customers' curious eyes as I go.

"Bug, any homework tonight?" I call as I walk into our apartment.

She's already half out of her clothes, of course, because she's never not in a hurry, unless she's asleep.

"Nope."

"And the test?"

"Fine." Her whole body sags.

I die a little bit. I desperately want to press for more details, but I don't. It's over now, we can discuss details before the next one.

I move her bag from the middle of the walkway, onto a kitchen chair. "Hmm, did you have any treats at Gramma's?"

She sighs. "No! Because she said you said she was giving me too many artishfishal flavorings and food dice and I said what are food dice and she said things that make food different colors like red juice or purple grape candy and I said, 'well what about white stuff like marshmallows or ice cream?' and she still said no, Mommy!"

I'm pleasantly surprised. "Well, Gramma was right, and I am right. Buu-uuut you make a strong point about plain white ice cream." Her little face pops up from where she's tying her sneakers back on. "C'mon. Dinner first."

She talks non-stop while we go back out through the restaurant and into the kitchen. She bounces up and down in place while we make our plates of salad and chicken strips. She makes up a song about mashed potato and convinces Ruthie to join in until I worry we're going to actually disrupt business. Not that anyone who matters would care, but you never know when you'll get a testy customer.

Except... I know right now. Why the hairs on my arms are suddenly standing on end. Why Ruthie whispers a *Lawd Have Mercy* under her breath and why all the females stop and stare at the hostess stand. Then I hear his British accent asking for a table.

A table? What?

"No. He's not getting a frickin' table."

"Mommy."

"I said frickin'!"

She rolls her eyes at me, exactly like me. "Who's that?" she says when he comes into view, walking through the restaurant.

"That's Uncle Emerson's friend, Mr. Dennis. You saw him at the wedding."

She frowns. The wedding was a decade ago for her little brain.

I set her up with her plate at the end of the bar. "Eat your dinner, I'll be right back." I leave my plate next to her and storm across the space.

"What are you doing?" I get right to the point as I reach his table.

"Dining," he deadpans. "This is a restaurant, isn't it?"

"I'm surprised you could figure that out, since there ain't any crystal or candlelight or violinist in the corner." He almost smirks, one eyebrow raised. "Or whatever the hell billionaire restaurants are like. Anyway, you aren't supposed to be here, we already talked about this."

"Do you work here as well?"

I put a hand to my forehead in salute. "Yup, going for employee of the month. I get to wear a special pin and everything. Why aren't you at your luxury, far away, mansion rental, *Dennis?*"

"Because, *Katherine*, it's not available for a week."

My head starts shaking involuntarily. "No. Sorry. No vacancy."

"I already booked the room for the week," he says, looking over the menu as if I'm not staring him down. "With my credit card this time."

"Okay, stay here at night. I'm sure you've moved a coffin into your room to sleep in. Great, fine. But you can't eat here."

He slowly looks up at me and lets the menu drop to the table. "Aren't you Yanks always going on about how this is a free country?"

"Exactly. We have the right to refuse service to anyone, especially grandiose moguls who will hate the food and the vibe and then ruin our Yelp score."

"Right to refuse?" He looks me up and down. It got warm in here earlier so I'm in my usual shirt but paired with obscenely short, frayed denim shorts and my combat boots. "And you can make that call? A waitress?"

"Ruthie!" I yell, much louder than necessary. The whole town is going to hear about this now. Ah, well, you're welcome for the juicy gossip, everyone. "Do I have permission to refuse service to this asshole?"

"Sure, honey."

"Jar, Mommy!"

Dennis and me and everyone else, looks at Lucy who is fidgeting in her seat at the bar that is clearly only for patrons twenty-one and older. I pull a dollar out of my back pocket and hold it up high so she can see. She nods once, appeased.

My eyes go back to stare down at the deep mahogany pair staring at my daughter.

"You heard Miss Ruthie," I say, sounding calmer now.

He looks up at me, a little shocked.

"That's Lucy, she was also at the wedding. Did you forget her, too? Were you high that whole week?"

He looks down. "I was... not myself."

"Ha, I think you were exactly yourself. Namely, the dude I really don't want in here scaring off customers and ruining our reviews."

"Mother of f—" He stops himself, glancing at Lucy, who is definitely watching. He calms his face and tone, but grips the crap out of the menu. "I promise not to leave a review at all, *Katherine*. Your father said I couldn't stay here without trying the food. He went on and on about how people drive in from all over the state just for the burgers."

"He did?"

"And you very well know there is nowhere else close by. I will eat and I will leave, you have my word."

I put a hand on my hip. "Your word, huh?"

"What have I done to make you doubt it?"

"Well, for starters, you said you were going to leave and yet, here you are. And—" I stop what I'm sure would be an epic, hilarious rant, because his shoulders hunch and he actually starts to get up.

Hmm. Seeing him deflate is not nearly as fun as seeing him pissed and twitchy.

"Fine," I say before he can stand. But because he's him and I'm me, I have to add, "But you better order extras and leave Stella the biggest tip of her life."

"Stella?"

"Your server this evening." I gesture with my thumb over my shoulder.

She is pretending she's not watching us from the kitchen, loitering next to Ruthie, who is also pretending to be busy.

"Oh, you won't be—"

"Serving you? Over my dead, cold, crusty, lifeless body, *Dennis*."

His nostrils flare. "Are you always this..."

"Lovely? Yes, I am. I warned you to stay away, dude. Now I'm fixin' to go join my daughter and eat in peace." I lean down and get in his face so I can whisper and surprisingly, he doesn't back away. "Don't you dare watch my ass as I walk away."

I turn quickly before I can see his reaction, but I hear it.

He chokes on his own spit. Score one for me!

I fight a laugh as I walk to the bar.

Maybe he should stay around. Torturing him is the most fun I've had in a long time.

But I am tortured right back because I have to sit with Lucy at the bar and not look at him. I know he's probably charming Stella's tiny britches off, and probably asked for some expensive wine we don't have.

I want to know what he orders and how he reacts to his first bite. I want to know if he lets loose and really chows down or if he cuts up his burger with a knife and fork.

Wait, why do I care about any of that?

I'm just bored. And curious. That's all.

Anyway, I don't look. I direct Lucy to the subject of her cheer classes, and she tells me a million different tales about her teammates while I eat. Ruthie keeps eyeing me, and I know Dennis looks over at us at least once or twice, but I stand firm.

We're in the clear, I'm sure. Dennis has got to be leaving soon. Lucy and I finish our dinner quickly and then Ethan brings out two tiny hot fudge sundaes for us. But he winces when he sets them down. It's his special the-point-of-sale-system-is-down-again face.

"The POS says the ticket printer is offline, but the printer has the green light. Can you take a look at it?"

"Sure." I hop down.

And in the few minutes it takes me to unjam the stupid machine, my social butterfly of a child has taken her ice cream straight into enemy territory. She's babbling, of course, and he's just staring at her across the table.

I'm about to go intervene when Ruthie demands to know more about the suited mystery man and Ethan runs in explaining we need to cover his tables because one of the toilets is overflowing.

Fantastic.

It'll just be a few minutes.

Surely Lucy won't blab our entire life story to Dennis in that time?

5
DENNIS

My burger is taking ages. Normally I wouldn't mind but that woman affects my whole being. It's like my body is trying to escape my skin. And my eyes keep looking over at her, and the miniature her, without my permission.

I get out my phone to dig back into my emails but pull up my texts instead.

Dennis: You failed to warn me about Kat
Emerson: Warn you?
Dennis: She is

I stop typing to think. What is she, exactly? Deeply annoying. Strangely captivating. The most irritating, grating human being I've ever encountered. And I simply do not get annoyed. Ever. So, what the hell?

She's rude, uncouth, unusual, unstable...

Dennis: She is highly erratic
Emerson: I didn't think you'd see her.
Dennis: Well, I did.

Emerson: She's a single mom who works herself to the bone. Be nice.

Dennis: I'm always nice

Emerson: Not always.

Damn it.

How long is he going to hold a one-minute portion of one drunken evening against me? A long while, apparently.

Finally, my burger arrives. I dig in, angry, exhausted and starving. I went with the classic and...

Oh.

Wow.

This is the most exquisite mix of flavors I've had in possibly decades. I can't help but close my eyes and savor the bite. Beef, bacon, cheese, and other flavors... I'm not sure. Practically Heaven between two buns. After the euphoria of the food dies down, only slightly, I look back at my phone.

Emerson's reply just hangs there on the screen.

I miss my best friend. Really, my only friend. We live in a small, weird world filled with distant relatives, wealthy business associates, and greedy acquaintances. Emerson's been my best mate since primary school.

I just wish he could understand that I—

"Hi!" Kat Junior plops herself, and her ice cream, down at my table with a huge smile. It's Kat's smile, I think. Not that she's shown her real smile to me.

"Mommy says you're a friend of Uncle Emerson. So, you can be my friend too, if you want. I'm Lucy. Mommy says we met at the wedding, but I don't remember that. Do you? Sometimes grownups remember things that kids don't, like when doctor's appointments are and what month goes in what order and boring grown-up stuff like that. So I don't remember you being there. But if you were, maybe we were already friends. Were we?"

I blink a few times, processing all the words. So many words. "I, uh, don't believe we met."

"Oh. Okay, well, hello, I'm Lucy Canton." She straightens and extends her tiny hand to me. It is so very polite and respectful I cannot believe she's Kat's child.

"Hello." I shake her hand. "I'm Dennis DeLane."

"There, now we're friends!" She giggles. "What's your favorite ice cream? My best friend Ellie loves chocolate, but I like strawberry the best, but Mommy says I can't have food dice anymore so no more red ice cream for me. Vanilla is okay though, especially when you put hot chocolate sauce and whipped cream on it like Miss Ruthie did." I nod, unsure if I should actually participate in this conversation she's having. "This is sad ice cream, though, so it's not as good as normal times." Her little shoulders hunch over.

"Sad ice cream?" I'm intrigued.

"Yeah, Mommy was sad that I was sad, so she let me have a Miss Ruthie Sunday even though it's not a weekend. Normally I only have those on the weekends."

"You're here on the weekends?"

"I'm here every day," she says casually.

"Your mother works here every day?"

"Uh huh, every one that ends in 'day!'"

I press the issue, hell if I know why. "Surely she gets days off?"

"Ohhh, PJs days! Mommy says we can have those once a month. We watch movies all day. I love those days. But sometimes those are the same as today, where the tests make me sad and then Mommy gets sad. And she thinks I don't know that's why it's a treat day, but I do know, and I don't want to be sad and don't want her to be sad... but I also really, *really* like ice cream."

I almost chuckle. Smart girl.

She takes a big bite and stares at her bowl.

"Tests?" I ask, curious what could possibly dim this little light.

"Yup." She pops the p and spits tiny ice cream particles everywhere.

It's disgusting but luckily, I am seated just out of range.

"Spelling tests, science tests, math tests. Math is the worst. I am not smart at math. Well, Mommy says I am smart at math I just have trouble listening to the lesson and so then I don't know the answers when the test comes and so tests make me really nervous. Then, when I'm nervous I can't sit still to take the test and then I have less time and do worser on the test!" She gasps, upsetting herself.

"What is your favorite subject?" I ask, trying to redirect her a bit.

"Social studies! I like the history lessons and sometimes reading, too. For history, lots of time Mrs. Henderson lets us watch movies or listen to audio books, or she tells us the story. She's a really good storyteller, she does all the voices. That's why I like reading time, too. Unless it's student reading time. Mommy says I am a very advanced reader, but I don't like reading time at school because we have to stay in our seats and not make any noises."

"And your test today was maths?"

"Math, Mr. Dennis." She snorts. "There's just one math."

I smile at her correction of the British term. So, a little like her mother, after all. "What type of math?"

She looks away and starts to fidget. "Multiplication." Her voice sounds so sad as she says it that I can't just leave it there.

"Right. What if you made the numbers into a story then?"

She sits up on her knees, then back down. "How?"

Bloody hell. I don't know.

"Hmm. What's something that rhymes with six?"

"Tricks!" She beams at me.

I take a couple swigs of my beer. This feels harder, and possibly more important, than the numbers I scoured through all day.

"Uh, One Lucy had three bags of tricks. Two Lucys with three bags makes six?" I wince and wait for her to... have some kind of eureka moment, I guess?

"Ba ha," she explodes with laughter. Surely the loudest, cutest laugh that has ever been. "Two Lucys?" She snorts and collapses in the booth across from me. Everyone is looking at me now, for the second time this evening. And not in the way I'm accustomed to. "What's a bag of tricks? A trick is a prank, Mr. Dennis! You can't have a bag of pranks!" She squeals.

"What did I miss here?" Kat says, sounding angry as she arrives at the table.

"Mr. Dennis is so funny, Mommy. He is my new best friend. Way funnier than Ellie."

Kat juts her chin out and raises her eyebrows. "He is?" I shake my head. She looks over at Lucy and her face softens. "All right, Bug, take your dish to the kitchen. Time to go."

"Okay," Lucy says, still giggling.

After the tiny thing is a few feet away Kat locks her fiery greenish gold eyes on me, upset, of course. About what, I don't know. Infuriating woman and insane, truly.

"What did you say to her?"

"Say to her?" I cock my head, baffled. "We discussed math. Honestly, what do you think I would say?"

"I don't know, something condescending and you know"— she gestures at my whole body—"uppity." I muster all of my self-discipline and hold my tongue. "Sorry if she talked your ear off, she does that. I'm sure you think she's nuts just like—"

"I think she's brilliant." I cut off whatever rubbish she was about to say. But she squints down at me like even complimenting her child is somehow offensive. So, my tongue flips me the bird and does what it wants. "How such a lovely little thing came from *you* is the real mystery, isn't it?"

"And there it is." She shuffles back a tiny bit. "I hope you have a horrible sleep and a miserable week and please never, ever step foot in here again." Then she turns around and leaves, and damn it all to hell, I do look. I look at her tight, swaying backside the entire time she stomps out of sight.

She wants me to stay away?

Gladly.

Because I cannot survive ninety days around her. I mean, what the bloody hell just happened? And why? Why does someone—who clearly has a heart deep down, and can teach manners and decency to her daughter—why does she insist on pushing all my buttons? Why does her button-pushing turn me into an altogether different person?

Oh. And. Working herself to the bone? A Canton, working hourly, only taking one day off a month? It's all puzzling. She is puzzling.

So, I'm right screwed is what I am.

Because this is not why I am here, and not what, or who, I should be thinking about.

But hell, I love a good puzzle.

6

Buzz Buzz Buzz

Man, I'm tired. I stop my alarm and stretch. Then I climb down the ladder of the bunk bed I sleep on because my child was afraid to sleep on the top when we moved in here a few years ago. The bed is horrible. Last night was awful, complete with a plumbing disaster and a Lucy too excited about her *new best friend* to fall asleep.

I start the coffee pot and get in the shower, all as quietly as I can. *Only a few more years. Stick to the plan.* Eventually she's up and at it, talking my ear off and flitting around our little home while she gets dressed. I smile and nod but it's one of those days where I am just empty. It's beyond physical exhaustion, it's total depletion. Maybe I'm not getting enough iron. And I never eat breakfast. Or maybe I'm about to start my period.

Maybe it's the fact that my pride and joy will not shut up about Dennis.

What is that about? I'll take *Things I Didn't See Coming* for $500, Alex. I shake my head. My mom loves Jeopardy. Weird that my brain just pulled that out of nowhere.

I get Lucy off to school and swing by the hardware store to pick up a part that Ruthie's preferred plumber said we need. By the time I get back to my happy place, Ruthie's there, the music is on, Stella is even early for the opening shift. Things are looking up.

Mostly, my coffee has kicked in.

I'm serving for the lunch shift and the work is fun and easy, since I know most of the patrons. I've been a server here since I was sixteen so I can do this job in my sleep. I almost am today. But the time flies and I'm on my feet, doing work I can see in real time. Every plate I pick up, every table I wipe down, gets me one step closer.

And Dennis doesn't show, which makes me smile with relief.

"What you smilin' about?"

"Just life, Ruthie."

She stops stirring the batter she's working on. "Life in an expensive navy suit and tie."

"What?"

"Don't what me. That man is fine."

I wave her off. "Sure he is, until he opens his snobby little mouth."

"Are you talking about Dennis?" Stella breathes, rushing in from one of her tables. "Because I have tea."

"Well, by all means, spill it," I say, annoyed at how suddenly awake and interested I am.

"It's so crazy! Those ladies at table 42 were just going on and on about Grace Rockford."

Ruthie abandons the bowl. "Grace who?"

"Rockford. I didn't know the name either but—"

"I do. They supply AmeriMart with all their steel. Like how some families are old oil money, they are old steel money."

Stella points at me. "Yes, like, founding fathers' type of money. They live here and, apparently, she's trying to land a husband. So, all these billionaires are in town to impress her! And date her! Like a real life bazillionaire bachelorette. Can you believe that?"

My mouth flops open and I think Ruthie's does too.

"I mean, here, in Arkansas! That's got to be why Dennis DeLane is in town, staying here, right?"

I manage to close my mouth and Ruthie goes back to her batter without saying a word. Ruthie's silence is pointed and weird, like I'm bothered. Like I care why Dennis is here. I don't. But I'm pleased I've caught him in his little charade.

"Yes, Stella. You're right. That is exactly why he is here."

———

"I knew you would come back even though I told you not to," I greet Dennis at the hostess stand. I am only mildly surprised to see him. On the one hand, shouldn't he be wherever Grace Rockford is? On the other, he knows his presence bothers me. So, of course, here he is.

"Honestly I tried to stay away but that burger changed my brain chemistry." He just said something nice, I think and I am taken aback. "Bothering you whilst I have dinner is just an added bonus."

I suck in a breath and bat my lashes. "Right this way, sir."

"What, now I've your permission to dine here?"

"Ugh, if you keep talking like that, I'm going to change my mind." I set a menu down on a booth table and then slide in opposite.

"What are you doing?" He eyes me warily as he sits down across from me.

"Not chowin' down with you, don't worry."

He doesn't relax. He's not wrong.

I continue, "Why are you really here, Dennis?"

"Why do you work here, as your daughter says, every single day that ends in day?"

"Simple. Free room and board." He processes, furrowing his brow and I know more questions are coming, so I answer them. "To save. I am building up my savings. Your turn."

He works his jaw, probably debating if he's going to push me for more details or not. He decides not, sitting back in his leather seat. I watch some emotion flash across his face when he looks away, then back at me.

"Emerson asked me to take on Canton Tracking. This is a favor to him. I hope to repair the... damage I caused."

He looks genuinely contrite, and yet, he's lying to me. Or at least omitting a huge freaking piece of this weird puzzle we're in. I decide to cross my arms and glare silently until he folds. He makes it about ten seconds.

"You heard."

"Big money makes people forget this is a small town. And I mean all of Northwest Arkansas, not just out here in the sticks where I live. It's all just one tiny town. You're the hot goss, man."

He nods and closes his eyes. "That makes sense."

"So, liar, liar, pants a daggum inferno, Grace Rockford. She's why you're here."

"Hey, pardon me, I didn't lie to you. Grace is why I planned a trip to the area. Emerson heard and asked me to take on your dad's business. I did so as a favor to him. Like I said."

Something about the way he says her name makes my internal organs freak the heck out. Probably because it sounds pretty in his accent. Sounds like she's elegant, perfect... *I need a real queen, Kat.*

I'm not sure why Dennis and Grace bring up the bothersome, ancient memories, but they do. I'm bothered.

"So, do you actually like Grace or is this like a billionaires gotta stick together type arranged-marriage thing?" It sounds ridiculous coming out of my mouth, like something from one of Sadie's romance novels, but he doesn't balk.

"Grace is fine." He shrugs. "She's the only Rockford heir and doesn't know anything about business. She needs guidance. Heaps of it. So, her father wants her to marry someone with industry knowledge."

"A damsel in distress. Sounds perfect for you," I tease.

He grimaces. "Don't believe everything you read."

I feel a teeny, tiny bit bad for him. Sadie did write a novel loosely based on their love story, which made her famous. A fledgling Oklahoma writer taken under the wing of billionaire pretty boy Dennis DeLane. The Cantons weren't *The Cantons* yet, but they were after that book. Then she dumped him a few months before their wedding.

"I didn't read it, actually. I saw the movie though." He rubs his fingers along his forehead, perturbed. It's kind of funny seeing him so bothered. At least I'm not the only one feeling a bit rattled. "But c'mon, Sadie was in distress back then, for sure. Then I saw the magazines, you were with two more damsels, the poor artist gal and the royal whats-her-face who had cancer."

"Bloody hell." His face turns tomato-y as he leans in and whisper yells at me. "Would you care to discuss your entire past? Lucy's dad, then? Hm? Where is he?"

"Geez, sorry!" He sits back and I lean forward. "I didn't mean to roast you I just—" He looks up at me, his eyes flashing equal parts fury and hurt. "Okay. I did mean to roast you. I'm sorry. You're just so entertaining. You should see how red your face is right now."

He shakes his head and mutters a string of curses while looking at the menu.

"Don't bother looking, you have to have Ruthie's chicken sandwich."

He just nods and puts the menu down. He won't look up, though.

I think I've poked this bear one too many times. "Welp, good luck with the Great Grace Race." I scoot out of the booth.

"Wait." He puts a hand on the table, almost reaching my fingertips.

I look at our hands—because weird, why am I noticing our fingers—and up at him.

He moves his hand away so fast it's like God set time to fast forward for a few seconds. "About Grace. She would be good. For me."

I shift back to my original position and wait.

He takes a sip of one of the two waters that Ethan dropped off at some point.

"It would be a very favorable match, the Rockford family. As you are so keenly aware, I am utter crap at dating, romance, all of it. This would be a great solution."

"Solution." I snort. "You're right. You do suck at romance."

"What the—" He's back to whisper yelling. "Do you kick puppies for fun? Are you a psychopath? I'm trying to talk to you, here."

I almost laugh. "Why? Why talk to someone you think is so disturbed, *Dennis?*"

"Because, *Katherine,* I think maybe you can help me."

Well.

Stick a fork in me, because I'm done. Shocked. Frozen.

He finally continues. "It's a shock to me as well. But the Rockfords are hesitant about me." He holds up a hand when he sees my mouth open to tease him. I stifle a smile at the fact that he anticipated that. "I realize what I am about to say might provide you with significant glee and ammunition to use against me until the end of time. I am trusting you with it anyway." He raises one eyebrow just barely.

"I make no promises other than that I am dying to know what comes next. Do you need me to promise not to laugh? Wait. No. That's too big a promise. I could flash you or moon you or something."

"Bloody hell, forget it."

"No. Now I have to know!" I hold up my right hand. "I solemnly promise not to use whatever it is as ammunition against you for... a year. Best I can do."

He rubs his temples. "Has anyone told you you cause headaches?"

"Migraines, my dad said it daily. Lay it on me."

He straightens and puts his hands on the table. "The Rockfords are hesitant about me because they feel I am, quote, *too out of touch with the average Joe.*"

I bite my lips between my teeth to keep my mouth shut. But my lips shake. Actually, I think my whole body is shaking now.

"Out with it, Katherine."

"BA HA!" I do let it out. "I mean, *ya think?*" I manage to go off in-between snorts and gasps. "Your suit cost more than people's mortgage payments! Have you ever not worn a tie? Were you born wearing a teeny tiny little baby tie? A bowtie maybe?" I hit the table. "I can't. *I can't.*"

Dennis gives a polite smile to the people gawking at me while I lose my mind. Then he clears his throat. "Are you quite finished?"

"That." I point at him. "*Am I quite finished?* You can't talk like that, Dennis. Seriously. I'm surprised you even know the expression 'Average Joe.' This is just too good." I continue to giggle as I wave over Ethan. "Two of Ruthie's chicken sandwiches, put some spicy sauce on the side for him to try. And let's do both a fry sampler of all types and the onion rings so he can taste them all."

"Will you get in trouble with Ruthie for that?" He frowns.

I take a few gulps of my water. "Nah, she won't care. So," I start to laugh again and then stifle it. "Out of touch, you say?"

"This was a terrible mistake," he says, but he's almost grinning.

I nod. "For sure. The cat can't go back into the bag though."

"Indeed." He looks up from the table finally and for the first time his eyes aren't as black as voids. They're warmer, lighter. It makes me shift in my seat. He goes on, slowly. "Maybe you could... give me some instruction. Help me know what to say, how to say it, to win Grace over."

Again, with her pretty name. Why do I hate that so much?

"Is this about Grace? Because winning her heart is different from winning her dad's wallet. And, I mean, you're already a billionaire, why do you need this partnership?"

"I need *a* partnership. My father has wanted me to settle down for a decade and he's done waiting, apparently. Grace is perfect."

I'll bet she is.

Something sinks down in me, into the bitter part that I try to hide away. *Sorry Kat but I need a real lady.* The smile that's been hurting my cheeks since he started this conversation fades. I have to give myself a second to recover.

"Kat, I don't mean to say you're an average Joe," Dennis stammers. "I only meant you could show me around here perhaps. I could compensate you, if—"

"Compensate me?" I squeak.

"Shit, sorry. I don't know, I just meant like a trade. Surely there's something I could help you with."

I move to get up again. "Nope. I'm good. Best of luck, you're gonna need it."

"Please, just think about it," he says, sounding sincere.

I storm off to the kitchen. And I do think of something. I could use his help, as much as I hate to admit it. But I need to consult the High Canton Council first. I pull out my phone.

> Kat: How do we feel about Dennis these days?
> Sam: Boooooo.
> Skye: ??? Most random question ever?
> Sally: What Skye said.
> Susan: I will defer to Sadie, but yes, also, ???
> Kat: My dad hired him as a consultant.
> Skye: [yikes emoji]
> Sally: [whoa emoji]
> Sam: WHAT! BRB
> Sadie: Dennis is fine. As far as consulting, he's a wizard, just like Emerson.
> Susan: Is CT in trouble?
> Kat: Hell if I know, I try to do as little with the business as possible, you know that.
> Sam: Em says he was going to be in NWA anyway, so he took on your dad's contract.
> Sam: He says CT is in very good hands!!!
> Sam: I still don't like him though.
> Susan: I tend to agree. No one calls Sadie a B.
> Skye: Except for me. LOL
> Sadie: Guys, he was drunk and he apologized. I mean, he's not great. But he's fine.
> Kat: OK.

Not great but fine.

I'm not sure I agree. Fine seems generous for such a giant snob. But I guess, in asking for help, he's admitting that fact. And this idea, this is something he'll surely hate. And Lucy will love it. *Yes.*

I go back to his table.

"All right, Denny." He makes a face. "Oh, good, you hate that. I'll call you that from now on."

He crosses his arms. "Fine, *Katie.*"

"Ugh, point taken. Dennis, I do have a trade." I rub my hands together to build up his dread. It works, as his scowl deepens. "You have to tutor Lucy."

"What?"

"You heard me."

"But I don't—"

"She won't even say the word *multiplication* to me, and she thinks Math Time with Mr. Dennis was the most fun thing to ever happen in her life. I don't care if you barely discuss math, you made her open to the idea of learning outside of school. She needs that. You want hick lessons? You give her math lessons. That's the deal."

I watch and, to my surprise and maybe horror, he smiles. Like a real, happy, relieved smile.

It's disarming.

I am no longer armed.

Defenses melting down into the beat up, original wood floors.

"Why are you smiling like that?"

"Because this is brilliant. Lucy is delightful. And you I can tolerate, for a few weeks at least, to get the lay of the land, *Ce n'est pas la mer à boire.*"

Woah.

Dennis smiling and praising Lucy and speaking French is... now other parts of me are nearly melting.

"It's French." He mansplains to me. *Well, that's one way to douse a girl's fire.*

Good, that was getting weird anyway.

"I knew it was French, as—" I look at the swear jar on the bar top. "*Jerk*hole."

"Of course." We pause as Ethan drops off all the food. Dennis goes on, "It's an expression that means this will be easy. When do we start?"

I cut the huge fried chicken sandwich Ethan dropped off for me in half. "I don't know, you have the big important schedule."

"Nonsense, you're doing me the favor. What's the best time for Lucy?"

"Dinnertime, I guess? I mean, you've got to eat anyway, and it'll free me up to help out during the rush."

His face seems unhappy, but he says, "Sure."

"Not every night," I quickly add, feeling awkward. "She stays with my mom on Tuesdays and Thursdays, and she has cheerleading on Wednesdays."

"Mondays and Fridays, then."

"Just Fridays is fine." Then he smiles again.

I can't stand here next to... all this. I grab my half a sandwich and a few sweet potato fries. "I need to get back to work. Try the spicy sauce."

His smile evaporates as I walk away. Maybe he's realizing the same thing I am. We are going to kill each other if we have to be around each other multiple times a week.

This is a terrible idea.

7

"He's here!" Lucy squawks. I look at my watch. Exactly when he said he would. *Okay, Dennis, six it is.*

"Wait, Bug. I need to talk to him first."

I watch him as I walk out from the back office toward the hostess stand. I'm not the only one staring.

Again, he's in a suit. This time he's skipped the vest. Navy tie and pocket square, though. *Pft, who wears a pocket square?*

He sees me approaching and starts to smile, then stops and looks away.

I remember then, the uniform. I went with a solid black pearl snap tucked into black jeans today, no butt and no midriff, so my shirt is unbuttoned the girls are pushed up and on display. The Roadside dress code is like Hooters Lite, work what ya got, but you can only choose one of the skin trifectas at a time. I guess Dennis is a boob man.

Interesting.

I mean, no. Not interesting. I don't care.

"Hey," I say.

"Hey." He looks around me to find Lucy. He can't look at me. "Am I late?"

I almost snicker. "Nope, just wanted to tell you a couple things."

"Okay?" He finally makes eye contact, concerned.

"Listen, if she's too much to handle, just tell me, okay?" He jerks his head back a bit, offended, maybe? "Lucy has ADHD, heavy on the H. Hyperactive." He starts to nod. "You've seen how she can chat, I'm sure, and fidget. She'll complain about treats and food dye, or dice as she calls it, but she's on a very low dose of meds, and the only way I can keep it low is with none of that crap."

"Understood."

"Also, we didn't talk about when you want your first hick lesson."

He exhales. "Must you call it that?"

"There's a tip for you right there. We don't mind that we're country people. We love it, celebrate it. No one here is going to be offended that I'm giving you hillbilly lessons. Hell, they'll sign up to teach you too." He works his jaw but says nothing. "So?"

"I suppose it would be best for me if we could do those on the weekends. I am actually working with your father every day."

I grimace. "My condolences. Okay, well, we'll figure something out for next weekend then."

He clears his throat.

"Unless it's urgent?"

He looks down at his ridiculously shiny, unscuffed leather shoes. "I have a date with Grace next week."

I become an obnoxious child out of nowhere. "Ooooooo. You have a daaaate!" Worth it though, I think he's actually blushing. "Ok, we'll do something tomorrow. Luce!" Just as I turn to wave her over a large group files in behind Dennis filling the waiting area. "I'll be right with y'all." I say around the suit who I think just winked—Dennis winks?—at my child.

I lead Dennis and Lucy to a small booth at the back of the restaurant.

"Luce, you have to actually eat your dinner and you have to actually do a lesson, okay? You can't just tell Mr. Dennis about all your friends and cheerleading and your favorite movies."

"Yes, ma'am," she says, desperate for me to go away so her happy fun time can begin.

I look at Dennis. "You sure you guys are good?"

Dennis feigns seriousness. "Yes, ma'am."

"Weird. Don't be normal, it's unnatural."

He sighs. "Go away, *Katherine.*"

"Much better. Bye." I kiss Lucy on the head and make for the hostess stand.

It's a busy Friday night.

I forgot it's March Madness. I don't care about basketball, but other people do.

The few TVs throughout the space have games on and there is cheering and chanting. More alcohol flows than on non-sports Friday nights, meaning more mixed-up orders, food sent back, drinks spilled and on and on it goes.

It's past eight before I look at my watch. *Crap.*

"Sorry! Didn't see the time," I say when I walk up to the little table. Lucy is laughing hysterically again, and Dennis seems, well, kinda smitten.

I get it, she's amazing. I just don't often see that look on someone's face who's not either female or related to us.

"No problem, we just finished eating anyway."

"Mommy, I showed him the walrus! He thought it was"—she makes a Dennis face and tries a British accent—"disgusting." She busts up giggling all over again.

"It is kinda disgusting." I shrug. A French fry up each nostril is not the most appetizing joke. I make a sorry face at Dennis, but he waves it off, grinning. "Okay. Well it's bedtime, Bug. Let's go."

"Awwwww!"

"Come now, Lucy. I'll see you again tomorrow. I think," he says, asking me.

I nod. Whatever I decide to do with him, Lucy will join us. We're a package deal.

"And I think I need a stout beer." He gets out of the booth and stretches. His jacket is off and his arms in that shirt... maybe he really does travel with a personal trainer. Still has a tie on though. Weirdo.

"I bet. Just tell Otis you're with me. I'll be back out in a bit."

His head jerks in my direction. "You're coming back to work?"

"More like I kinda... stay on call, since I live right there."

He frowns but I turn away. I don't want to see his disapproval. I like to work hard, and I need to work hard.

He doesn't need to understand it.

Lucy runs ahead, down the hall to our door. The office, supply closet, laundry room, and the restrooms sit in between our studio apartment and the restaurant. It's still only a hallway away, though, so before we moved in, I added extra soundproofing insulation between the studs. It does an amazing job, but I always turn on a white noise machine on the weekends.

Part of me hates this. Bedtime on the weekends.

Lucy doesn't realize or care how weird it is, and before she does, I'll get us out of here.

Soon. Really soon.

These nights, these hours, the board meetings and keys and busted pipes and everything else I can shove into every single minute of every day, they are all going to be worth it.

Once she's truly asleep, which only takes about twenty minutes, I check the camera app on my phone. I can monitor the feeds of multiple cameras on my watch, and motion sensors alerts me if there is any movement while I'm down the hall. One time a raccoon passed by our window on the outside and I lost at least three years of my life. It proved the app works though, so it was actually kind of comforting.

I head out and lock the door behind me.

Normally I'd swing by the Inn's front desk, but we're all full and the phones are forwarded, so there's really no need. Plus, Dennis is probably tired of waiting for me. In fact, why did I tell him to do that? He is probably done with his beer by now. And he's too polite to leave. *Dumb move, Kat. Weird and dumb.*

I see him at the bar when I enter from the back hallway, but I don't head over. Because I catch someone, a dude clearly not from around here, getting handsy with Rebecca. Stella can hold her own, but Becs is brand new. I storm over.

"Hands off the staff, buddy."

"There you are, darlin'. You disappeared." This guy is very drunk, as are his friends. At nine at night. Stupid basketball. He puts his hand on my waist, and I tell Rebecca to get out of here with my eyes. As she goes, Handsy pulls me into him. "Man, I love these uniforms." Ass.

He's definitely moving his hand down to my ass now. Go time.

I pull away with a bitter smile that the guy can't tell is a bit unhinged. He tucks me back into him and I yelp involuntarily. At that, Dennis is up and moving this way.

Ah, ever the white knight.

But I'm no damsel.

"C'mon baby, let's dance," I say in the guy's ear.

He's up in a jiffy and, the second he stands, I knee his crotch so hard the whole restaurant reacts. Drunk Guy doubles over and when he does, I stand on his chair and shove him with my boot so he literally faceplants into the wood floor.

"Three cheers for everyone capable of keeping their hands off underage waitresses. Hip hip—"

The crowd yells, "Hooray!"

I repeat that two more times, up on the chair, guiding the crowd on how to react to the situation. Sadie taught me this back in her theater days.

"Add a little extra to our tips tonight for our trouble y'all."

The guy gets up off the floor. He's angry but his friends are already making their way out. They're embarrassed, as they should be.

I wait to make sure he's nowhere near me before I get down.

From up here I also see Dennis, who stopped dead in his tracks about halfway to me. He looks completely shocked.

This is becoming a regular reaction to me from him. I just shrug and smile when we lock eyes. He doesn't smile back, just shakes his head and opens his hands as if to say *WTF, Kat?*

I hop down and head over to him. "Sorry, I missed our beer."

"Are you bloody mad?"

"Don't say bloody mad on your date with Grace. But yes, I am. I have to be. He was getting handsy with Becs, who is frickin' barely eighteen."

He rakes a hand over his face. "And you don't have bouncers? Security blokes?"

"Blokes?" I snicker.

"Katherine!"

"Dennis!"

He sighs and storms toward his coat hanging on the barstool. What the hell—*heck, Kat, heck*—is he so pissy about?

"Hey," He turns to me, jaw all tight and twitchy again. I explain, "I don't need you worrying about me, we are not friends. I'm fine. It was fine. A couple years after I had Lucy, I took a bunch of self-defense classes. If those don't work, I have multiple shot guns."

His eyes go wide.

"Ha! Yes, Dennis. This is gun country. You really do need that lesson tomorrow... if you think you can handle it."

"Honestly, I'm not sure. You are an actual lunatic."

I just roll my eyes. "Give me your phone."

"What?"

I hold out my palm. Finally, he pulls out his phone and unlocks it for me. I add my number, under Lunatic, obviously, then text myself a message from him.

I am more pretentious than the queen.

I save his contact. "There." I stuff his phone back in his hand. "You decide if you want to hang out with us tomorrow and let me know. I'm going to check on Rebecca."

As I turn to leave him, he calls after me. "Does that happen a lot?"

I start walking. "Only when there are sports on."

"How often are sports on?"

I yell over my shoulder. "Pretty much all the time. G'night!"

I hear him say lunatic, mad, I think bullocks and a few other choice words before I finally pass into the kitchen. He's a pot that is pretty easy to stir up. It makes me smile.

"Why do you look like that?" Ethan asks me when I get back to the little group of staff comforting our newest waitress.

"Like what?"

"Like you're, I don't know, happy."

I make a weird *pffft* noise. "I'm always happy."

"No, you always pretend to be happy for Luce. You're like, really... smiley," he says, totally weirded out.

I wipe the smile off my face. It was only there because I got to knee a moron in the balls. That is the singular reason. After everyone is comforted, coddled, and settled, I tell Otis, our gruff bartender and occasional bouncer, that I'm turning in. When I reach my door, I feel the buzz in my pocket.

His Royal A-hole: I am not. And you are not. A lunatic.
His Royal A-hole: I can only imagine what name you gave me

I'm not telling you. I fish out my keys.

His Royal A-hole: I told Lucy I'd see her tomorrow, so I had best see her tomorrow.

My eyes get all itchy at that. No one ever comes through for Lucy except me. People try, like my mother, but they fail sometimes. There's no room for failure with little kids. If you say you'll be there, you need to be there. I can't believe *he*, of all people, seems to get that.

Kat: Ok. I'll text you in the morning.

I get into my door and collapse back onto it as it closes. I'm tired. And weirded out. Was I *smiley*, really? And why do I enjoy getting a reaction out of Dennis so much? And I have to endure more of this with him tomorrow.

Which means I need to come up with something both quick and terrible for him to do.

8

Buzz Buzz Buzz Buzz
What?

Oh no. That's not my alarm. It's Saturday. Just after five-thirty on a Saturday morning. That's the Inn phone, forwarded to my cell. Someone's toilet is flooded, or they fried the power to their room, or who knows what.

I hustle out of bed, anxious, and go into the bathroom. I shut the door and try to keep my voice calm and quiet.

"Good morning, Roadside, how can I help?"

"Kat?"

Ugh. Freaking kill me now.

"Dennis. What is it?"

"It's... I mean... Forget it. Are you working already?"

I sigh. "I told you, I'm on call."

"There isn't an overnight crew?" He sounds disgusted.

"You're talkin' to her, man."

He sighs now. "I'm sorry, I didn't realize."

"What do you need? Is something flooding? Burning? Melting?"

"What? Heavens, no. It's nothing."

I rant through my teeth, trying not to wake Lucy. "Dennis. You already woke me up, nearly gave me a heart attack with worry, and if something really is wrong, I need to know sooner rather than later, it's Saturday so fixing a—"

"It was just bloody coffee pods, Kat. Go back to sleep."

"Coffee pods?"

He huffs out a long breath. "Yes, I am up working, and I ran out of coffee. That's it."

"Dude, why are you up working before six on a Saturday?"

"Katherine. Go back to sleep."

Beep beep beep

He...he hung up on me? The king of propriety woke me up on my sleep-in day and then he f—*freaking* hung up on me? Oh, heck no. He wants coffee pods? He's getting his frickin' coffee pods.

I storm through our little apartment on tip toe, slip out our door and go to the supply closet. I grab the whole box of pods and hustle across the lobby, down the hall to the last door on the right. I want to pound on the door, but all the normal human beings are sleeping, so I just tap.

I hear him sigh with exasperation before he opens the door.

He is exasperated with *me?*

This guy. He is truly going to be the straw that finally snaps my back right in half.

"Kat, you didn't—"

Before he can finish, I pitch the box at him but it's open, so all the pods fly out. There are probably a hundred pods in this box, and most of them whack his torso before falling to the ground. I don't even care that they make quite a bit of noise when they all hit the engineered wood floors.

He just stands there with his eyes closed, gripping the door-knob, and breathing through his nose. And panting.

His chest is really... a tee shirt. He's in a white t-shirt. And slacks, of course. I bet he doesn't own sweatpants. He is just all wrong in the ski room. There are colorful vintage water skis mounted all over the scuffed, paneled walls. And he looks... like that.

"Coffee pods, your majesty."

"You are the most insufferable—" he starts but then he opens his eyes, and his words seem to get caught when he looks at me.

Oh. Right.

I'm just in my pajamas—a thin white tank and underwear. I don't have much in the way of curves but what I do have is tight and perky. But as soon as he glances at me, ever the gentleman, he looks up at the ceiling. I squelch the urge to cross my arms over my chest.

"Got a problem with our night shift uniform?" I smirk.

He puts a hand up to rub his eyes. "Honestly, what is wrong with you."

"Some pompous dick woke me up on my only day to sleep in for effing coffee pods."

"I didn't know I would be waking you—"

"Then," I cut him off. "He hung up on me!"

"I—"

"Dennis if you say you apologize to me one more time, when we both know you're not sorry and you can't stand me and I can't stand you and you're just being f—*effing* polite... if you say that again, I will have the staff spit in your food and slip spiders in your sheets, I'm serious."

"I can't," he says, the long *a* sound of his accent making the expression even more dramatic. "I can't do this with you. You are absolutely mental."

"Fine, I didn't want to spend my Saturday with you anyway. Deal's off."

"Fine."

"Fine!" I turn and rush back to my room, irritated that I can't stomp my feet the whole way or feel the sweet satisfaction of slamming my door.

Being a grown adult is so lame.

———

I haven't seen his highness for days and that is fine by me. I do know that he's ordering dinner to his room each night, seemingly to try every single thing on the menu. At least he's not out in my space.

He can hole up in that room until he checks out, which will be today or tomorrow. It's been over a week so he should be gone by now.

But I'm not about to inquire.

He's not eager to talk to me either, clearly.

So I'm surprised to see his text come through.

> His Royal A-Hole: I would like to meet with Lucy tomorrow. I gave her homework for the week, it's only right that we go over it
> Kat: Homework?!
> His Royal A-Hole: You asked for a tutor, did you not
> Kat: We said the deal was off.
> His Royal A-Hole: Deal's off with you. Lucy is not totally insane.
> Kat: She's young, give her time.
> His Royal A-Hole: 6pm?
> Kat: Fine
> His Royal A-Hole: Thank you
> Kat: You're so weird.
> His Royal A-Hole: According to?
> Kat: Me.

His Royal A-Hole: Highly unreliable source
Kat: [middle finger emoji]
His Royal A-Hole: Classy as ever, Katherine

The smile that was taking over my face dies a swift death at his last text. I can't really explain either phenomenon.

Well, the first is about Lucy.

Seeing someone support her is obviously going to make me smile. But why do I give one singular... frick if he doesn't think I'm classy?

I need someone classy, Kit Kat.

Ugh. *No.*

I haven't thought about that in forever and now it's suddenly in my head on repeat.

I'm quirky by choice. And I'm not going to think about this anymore. Ruthie said we over ordered on the liquor for the week so I need to help figure out where it's all going to go and how we can get it moving. Time to get to work.

I am a frazzled mess by four, when Tran, my best girlfriend in town, drops Lucy off.

"Thanks so much," I tell her. She's older than me but with her black hair pulled up in a high pony, her flawless skin and bright, bag-less eyes, she looks like the young one. I never get to see her unless our kids play together.

She smiles. "No problem, Ellie loves when we pick her up. But, uh, they begged for snacks and all I had was chips that I'm pretty sure contain just corn solids, sugar, and food dye."

I grab her arm before she can apologize. "Hey, one snack is fine. Thanks so much, really."

"Bye Ellie!" Lucy yells as she runs through the restaurant.

"Slow down, Bug."

Tran laughs. "When's your next Grammy night?"

"Tonight, actually. Can you come back, I'm behind the bar."

She dips her chin and gives me a solid mom glare. "So, it's your one night off from single parenting and you're bartending?"

"It's good money, T."

"Text me the next time you are taking your night off, actually off."

I nod, and then we wave goodbye as Lucy starts yelling for me to join her and unlock our door. After she changes clothes and grabs some activity books and markers, I'm back at the shelves and she's set up at the bar.

I keep an eye on her as I run around but I know Stella will stop and chat with her and Ruthie will color a section of the papers with her.

She hums and works on her puzzles and is happy as can be.

"Mr. Dennis!" she screeches in a pitch that's reserved for dogs. Okay. *Now* she's as happy as can be.

"Four fifty-five, someone must be starving," I say following after my ecstatic child who is sprinting to the front.

He smiles at her, then frowns at my whole person.

"Oh. Unloading pallets today," I say, explaining the sweat, the grungy black cropped T-shirt, and the dust and dirt all over my black leggings.

"That's how she gets her big muscles. Show him, Mommy." Lucy flexes her own biceps like Popeye the Sailorman, and Dennis looks at me, brows raised.

I mimic her pose, unashamed. I do have defined muscles. Tiny ones, but they're there.

"Very impressive," Dennis says dramatically.

"Right? We're so strong. We're like superheroes." Lucy beams. "I'll go to our booth."

"So? What can I get you?" I ask Dennis as we trail behind her.

He makes a face. "I'm not actually eating here. This evening I am otherwise engaged."

"Oh mylanta, Your date." I gush. "What are you going to do? You haven't had any training! You're going to be horrible." I can't help but tease him.

He rolls his eyes. "I have dated before."

I snort. "I don't think you have, actually. I think you've courted and wooed and seduced, maybe."

He finally makes eye contact with me, one side of his mouth quirking slightly. "Seduced?"

"With your money," I quickly add. "But dated? Never." I slide in next to Lucy.

"Mommy," she whines. "I am supposed to have my lesson."

"Yes, Kat, this is quite the intrusion."

I look down at her, serious. "Hey, Mr. Dennis needs our help. We can't let him make a buffoon of himself on his date."

"What's a buffoon?"

"Someone who says things like *this is quite the intrusion*." I look back at him. "What are you doing? For your date?"

He hesitates, looking regal and polished and too tall for the tiny back booth. "Just dinner."

"Dinner where?"

"A steakhouse that is—"

"Nope. Dennis, no. A steakhouse? Snore! Who's your competition in this *which billionaire gets the babe* competition?" I roll my eyes at his sigh, then keep pushing him. "C'mon, you're a strategist. Let's strategize."

"And you say I'm weird."

"It's good to be weird," Lucy chimes in without looking up from her coloring.

I nudge her with a proud smile. "Damn straight."

"Mommy!"

"C'mon damn is hardly a cuss word."

She extends out a hand, so I give her a dollar.

Dennis is watching with an expression I can't read. He's probably appalled that I'm a mother with a swear jar. Jars, plural.

"So? Who are the other guys?" I get out my phone and pull up a new search.

"John Winston," Dennis says softly.

I put in the name. "*Pfft*, he's like sixty. Next."

He leans forward. "Sixty? He's only a few years older than me!"

"How old are you, fifty-five?"

He dips his chin. "I'm not even forty."

"So thirty-nine. Almost in adult diapers. Got it. Still, that guy is in little blue pill territory, next?"

"What's a little blue pill?"

Dennis chokes on his water at Lucy's question. He looks truly terrified that I might explain to her in detail what erectile dysfunction is.

I consider it. "It's like a special Tic-Tac for old men."

"Like Grandpa?"

"Ha, yes, exactly like Grandpa," I say, enjoying that Dennis is fully choking across the table.

He's so rattle-able. He's something else.

"Anyway, next candidate?"

"Wesley Baron."

"Wes, let's see..." This guy is young and ripped. Bald and bearded. I scroll through the images, trying to decide if he's hot-bald, or just bald.

Dennis clears his throat. "He's the youngest, but he's also pretty green. Nowhere near as much experience as the others."

I look up. "How many men is Grace pulling in for this?"

"There wasn't a formal roster made. There are a few other families who have shown interest, but they aren't quite at the same, uh, well..."

"Not billionaires." He nods. "So just Winston and Baron, that's it?"

He sucks on his teeth and looks down at the table. "And"—he inhales—"Benedict."

"Clark?" I gasp. "Emerson's brother?"

Dennis pinches the bridge of his nose and nods. "That's the one."

"Well, then, you're screwed."

Dennis almost chuckles. "You think?"

"C'mon, he's got the money, the looks, he's younger, and he's, you know, fun." I pull up his picture. "I'm kind of surprised, actually, this doesn't seem like his scene."

"I thought the same. But he's only a few years younger than me. And our fathers are cut from the same cloth."

"Bet that is some stiff and itchy cloth."

He lets out a half laugh, like the sound surprises him. "Quite right."

"But what about your friendship with Emerson? Now you're competing with his brother?"

"Emerson is the one who told me about it. Ben thought it would be fun. May the best man win and all that."

"Fun? This is a marriage to a human adult female we're talking about, not a game of foosball."

Dennis picks up one of Lucy's markers and rolls it in his long fingers.

"Grace knew what she was agreeing to when her father set this up."

I cock my head. "True."

"But I am short on time. So perhaps you should let Lucy and I get to work."

"Yeah!" Lucy perks up.

All right, I guess I'm being dismissed. "Okay Bug, Grammy will be here soon to pick you up."

Dennis watches me climb out of the booth. "Are you actually taking a night off?"

"Nope, I'm bartending tonight. You know what that means?" I say to Lucy.

"Bigger pours, better playlist," she replies, as trained. "Mommy is everyone's favorite."

I smile and nod.

"Is she?"

"Yes, but only because of the heavy pours part," I joke.

"And the sing-a-longs!"

"Pardon? Sing-a-longs?" His eyebrows get lost far up in his thick, dark hairline.

I shrug. "Gotta see it to believe it but"—I snap—"Oh darn, you're busy."

"When's your next barkeep shift then?"

"Never," I say, but at the same time Lucy rats me out.

"She does it twice in a month."

Dennis shakes his head and drops what I think was about to be a real smile. "I don't think I've met anyone who works more than you and I am a workaholic surrounded by more of the same."

I ignore his comment, unsure if it's a complement or an insult. "And all of them would take Grace to that boring steakhouse. You want to beat out Ben, you're going to have to go hard, Dennis.

"Drive her down to Fayetteville, and I mean in a car, like, with your hands at ten and two. Not a helicopter or a limo." He starts to object but thinks better of it. "Go to Jim's Pizza near campus. She's an Arkansas alum and I bet she hasn't had it in years. She'll have all the feels."

"Hmm." He looks at the marker in his hand. "Insightful. Thank you."

"Okaayyy, bye now Mommyyyy!"

Dennis joins her in waving obnoxiously. "Yes, off with you."

———

The night is fun, as always. Ruthie stays late, Stella and Becs are killing it, the crowd is happy but not sloppy. Tran does stop by for a free drink, like I hoped she would. Otis comes in with his whole motorcycle club even though it's his night off.

Beau comes in too, looking hot as can be in a backwards ball cap. Too bad I couldn't fall in love with him. I tried, because he is the stuff of small-town, plaid-clad, romcom dreams right there.

But alas, there were no sparks.

Well, there were sparks. Just not in my heart.

Everyone's here. Almost. I think we'll go Full Sign tonight. Whether or not Dennis shows. Why did I think he would come by? I didn't tell him to. Plus, he's on a date. With his future fiancée. Both of them are probably taking turns adjusting the sticks stuck way up the other's tight, snooty little buttholes.

Oh, your stick is so straight, positively lovely.

Yes, jolly good stick you've got in your ass as well.

Gross.

Weird that I'm thinking in a British accent now.

But also, true.

I chuckle to myself as I pull on the Coors Light tap.

Stella collapses dramatically onto a barstool while she waits for me to get the drinks she just rang up. "I just can't get over how dreamy she is."

"Who is?"

"Grace Rockford. Obviously." Stella pulls out her phone. "Just look, look at her feed!"

I look up and down between at her phone and the stein in my hand. "What am I looking at here?"

"Someone created an account just about this whole thing on TikTok and they're not-so-secretly following Grace and all the men around. Look at her clothes. Look at her hair."

I'm not really, until she scrolls to a video. With Dennis.

"Wait, go back," I say, almost dropping the glass. "Let me see."

He looks perfect, as always, but she... she *is* perfect. Huge brown eyes, gorgeous auburn hair, porcelain skin. She looks freakishly like Jackie Kennedy. She doesn't have pores, I don't think, but if she did, they'd ooze sophistication.

I bet she wouldn't need a swear jar because her child got in trouble for dropping so many f-bombs in first grade that said child insisted on cash-producing-habit-breaking mechanism.

"This is tonight?"

"Yeah, an hour ago," Stella says, all breathy. I watch the clip replay.

He listened to my advice, they're in Fayetteville. That makes me feel good, but also... something else. He's opening the door for her and gazing at her across the table and touching the small of her back and like, *not* scowling. He's different with her.

Of course, he is.

Someone classy. She's a queen, Kat.

"Can you even?" Stella pulls her phone away.

"I can't, I can't even." I smile, telling her what she wants to hear.

She holds out another photo from tonight. "I mean, they make Fayetteville look glamorous. I want to go down there right now and take pics for my Insta. That's how gorgeous she is."

The photo does look glamorous in an old money kind of way. I think it's the tailored clothes that do that. Her figure is perfectly hourglass, his looks somehow beefy and lean at the same time.

Grace's long brown locks are so shiny they reflect the lights of the street like a mirror.

That reminds me. Tomorrow morning, I have a few precious hours of me-time. And it's time to do something with my hair. Something unsophisticated, unusual.

Something fun.

9

"Ooooh, Mommy I love it!" Lucy runs out to me. The front door I know so well slams behind her.

I hate this house and all the memories locked up inside it. Lucy doesn't hate it though. She just knows it as Gramma and Grandpa's. And since I make sure she's rarely here at the same time as my father, it's one of her happy places.

"I wanted to match you a little better. It's strawberry blonde."

She slams into me for a hug and talks into my stomach. "Mommy. It's way cooler than mine, can I dye mine?"

"You know the answer to that."

"When I'm eighteen," she grumbles.

"It's... bright," my mother comments from the large, covered porch.

I hitch one shoulder. "Technically, based on the dyes I used, it's neon strawberry blonde ombre."

"I think it's my new favorite, even better than the purple that one time."

I finally let Lucy out of my grip. "Well then, it's my favorite too. Go get your stuff."

"You sure you don't want to come in for some brunch?" My mother tries.

I give her a tight smile and shake my head.

Even the way she asks the question, the way she makes effort, is just so...weak. Like my father's cutting words whittled her down to nothing over time. She's standing there, I can see her, but she's also... blank, empty. Except with Lucy. That's the only time there is any kind of light in her eyes.

"Can we paint our nails to match, Mommy? Neon strawberry?"

"Absolutely we can. Let's go to the store and find the perfect color."

"Yes!" Lucy jumps across the grass.

"Thanks, Mom." I give her a wave before heading to my truck.

I take my time getting us to the store, then I let Lucy take for-absolutely-ever picking out nail polish and stickers and anything in CVS that is the same color as my hair. Every couple of weeks we do this, paint our nails, get a few little tattoos or stickers, and then within twenty-four hours my nails are totally chipped, and I look like I took a half-dried sharpie to my hands and arms. She loves it though.

And right now, for the first time I can remember, I don't want to go home to the Roadside. The realization pisses me off. That's my home. My place.

Mr. Fancy Pants needs to move into his lake rental already.

I might have Ruthie talk to him.

My phone buzzes.

Speak of the devil.

D-Bag Denny: Well, I would like to renegotiate our deal.

I smile. I forgot that I changed his contact name last night after my end-of-shift extra strong Long Island Iced Tea.

Kat: ?
D-Bag Denny: The date did not go well

I start to reply that it looked like it was going perfectly fine on TikTok, then realize how bad that sounds.

Kat: What happened?
D-Bag Denny: Long stretches of painfully awkward silence
Kat: [yikes emoji]
D-Bag Denny: Precisely. Care for a lesson?
Kat: I'm headed to work in a few.
D-Bag Denny: Tomorrow
Kat: Take a guess.
Kat: [I'm working animated gif]
D-Bag Denny: [angry emoji]
Kat: Don't hate the player, hate the game.
D-Bag Denny: What??
Kat: LOL
D-Bag Denny: I am not laughing.
Kat: I am not surprised.

Lucy and I get our gear and head home. We hang out in the office almost the whole afternoon and evening. We paint our nails, do a Zumba YouTube class, and watch a movie on Lucy's tablet.

Mostly I work on the stacks of papers Ruthie set aside for me to tackle today. The one for the grill is the largest, then the one for the Inn, then the others. She is pretty organized, even if I won't be able to find these piles again after tonight.

Luce pretends to be my assistant in between making up cheer routines. She even moved the couch back so she could have more room. She won't say the words to the cheer out loud yet, but she is very into her new moves. Physical activity is great for her, so I just let her do her thing.

Ethan brings some salads and bun-less burgers to the office for our dinner. "Who y'all hiding from?"

I huff. "We're not hiding."

"What you doin' in here, then?"

I gesture around at the piles everywhere. "Working. I'm working, Ethan."

"Weird."

I am not at all hiding from anyone. If I were, it would probably be well past time for that person to get lost. It would probably be a sure sign that I should not help that person on their marital quest. Or let that person continue to bond with my daughter. Or think about him at all.

Get it together, Kat.

Lucy and I go straight from the office to our beds because we are tired. Not because we're hiding.

We wake up the next morning and hustle out the front door to get to church because we're running late.

And finally, after church, we sit singing in the car before it's time for me to clock in for my lunch shift because it's fun.

Not because I'm dreading going inside.

Eventually though, I know Ruthie will text me if we don't get moving.

And, just as I somehow knew he would be, Dennis is here. Eating lunch.

"Mr. Dennis!" Lucy's racing to his table before I can stop her.

"Lucile Canton. You look like a princess," he says in a way that is just… too… I don't know. Too something. But then when I reach them, he does a double take at me. His face twists up all weird and whatever sweet moment lingered, it's sure as hell gone now.

My girl does look like a princess in her frilly pink church dress. We only wear dresses on Sundays, and she loves to be as extra as possible. All my dresses are black, but today's is a touch of little house on the prairie, with buttons up the whole thing and tiny gray flowers in the pattern. Lucy picked it out. I don't think Dennis is a fan.

"Don't you love Mommy's hair? It's neon strawberry."

"Mr. Dennis doesn't like neon, Bug." I decide to rescue him. "Let's go change for our shift."

"Yes, boss." Lucy jumps up. "Oh! Can we get Mr. Dennis the Lucy special? Pleeeease?"

I look at him, and he looks thoroughly annoyed. Shocker.

"Have you ordered?" I ask, trying to mask my irritation at his irritation.

"No."

Where is all that charm you just beamed like the frickin' sun at my daughter?

"Well, sir, do you mind waiting a little bit?"

"Not at all," He replies, but I squint down at him. He sticks his chin out. "What?"

"I mean you *said* you don't mind with your words, but your whole vibe is saying you mind. Like, maybe you mind a lot."

"Maybe you just can't read my vibe for shit."

"Mr. Dennis! Jar!" Lucy gasps.

He sighs the heaviest sigh that has ever been sighed.

"He can have a pass on the jar this time. And we'll hurry. C'mon Luce, let's go change."

We do hurry. Hurrying, though, is always a bad idea. It stresses both of us out, so we yank too hard on her dress, which catches in her hair. Then it takes what feels like an hour to get the tiny curls out of the zipper.

By the time I successfully get her out of the dress and into play clothes, she's almost crying, I'm almost crying and I'm sweating in my dress anyway. Forget it, I can just work in this. I grab a plain black apron from the office as we zoom to the kitchen.

Sundays are brunch days. We still open at eleven, but we serve breakfast food all the way until dinner. Some Sundays we have a line down the sidewalk. Today there's a line, but only in the waiting area.

Dennis must have noticed because he gave up his table and moved to a bar seat. Weirdly considerate of him.

"How do you like your eggs?" I ask him, walking backward into the kitchen while I talk.

"Over-easy?" he says like he's unsure.

"We need a Lucy special, over-easy, please, Miss Ruthie," I holler into the kitchen.

"Comin' in hot," someone yells back.

"Move your butts, we're down a chef. Lonnie burnt his hand."

"Sh—*crap,* is he all right?"

"Yup, he'll be back after he gets it wrapped up."

That's not good. But I can't think about it right this second.

Lucy gets her gloves on and stands in the line, serious.

The Lucy Special is just the special, a bed of hash browns under a waffle topped with two eggs and two chicken strips, no syrup. The only difference is she herself gets to assemble the plate and she makes a smiley face, adding a strawberry for a nose. She takes a while but doesn't drop anything this time, thankfully. She's been in this kitchen since she was a toddler but she's still just a kid.

"All right, you can be the server. You got it?"

"Yup," she says, holding the plate with both hands. She delivers it to Dennis like it is the Holy Grail.

"You made this, Lucile?" he says, again with the full name I gave her. Where did that come from? She nods and shifts her weight back and forth, almost jumping from foot to foot. "It's brilliant."

He's gushing. So what.

Everyone gushes over her. She's adorable.

"No syrup. That's what makes it special. Try it!"

He carves into it, getting a bit of each flavor on his fork. The waffle batter has maple and way more sugar than normal and there's cheese in the hash browns. The flavors together are a sweet savory blessing from heaven.

We watch Dennis take a bite. Lucy keeps hopping and I have to stop myself from actually holding my breath in anticipation. Finally, he closes his eyes and groans.

"Mthfrr"

"Pretty sure that was a jar deposit," I snicker.

"Is that good?" Lucy asks. I motion for her to ask him. "Is it? Is it good?"

"It's better than good. How?" He looks over her head at me. "How is every single thing on this menu so fantastic?"

"Simple. Butter, sugar, white flour. The holy trinity."

Ruthie yells at us from the kitchen and Dennis frowns in her direction as he takes another bite. Lucy runs back to the kitchen saying something about more Lucy Specials.

"Ruthie's is scolding me that that's blasphemy," I explain. "That's another lesson for ya. We're churchy people around here."

He considers that while he chews. "You? You believe in all that?"

"What, I don't project church goer?" I gesture at myself, laughing but he's still waiting for my answer. "I didn't used to."

"And then?"

"And then that little angel popped out of my vagina." He chokes. I knew he would. I laugh. Hard. "Oh, Dennis, bless your heart." I almost put a hand on his shoulder, like I would a friend or a regular, but stop myself.

He still looks a bit disgusted.

"I'm picking up that you and the big man upstairs have beef."

"Can't have beef with something that doesn't exist."

"Ooooo, an atheist," I say in a loud whisper. "Around here you're 'bout as rare as a purple speckled unicorn." I look at Lucy again. "I get it. This world is f—messed up, for sure. But she changed me. Can't see any way around an actual creator who designed all this, versus..." I look at him. "Well, just don't tell Grace you're in *camp big kaboom, everything is happenstance and thus there is no real purpose to our lives.* Not a popular camp here. Anyway, I need to get back in there, we're down a chef."

"You cook too?"

"I've worked here since I was sixteen, I've done everything. Still do, so enjoy."

His face goes back to its usual scowl. Dennis takes his time eating and then stays for a light beer.

I almost think he just likes watching Lucy in the kitchen. She's so serious and so happy, it's hard not to watch. Well, if you're not hustling around like chicken with its head cut off, that is. I am greasy and sweaty and altogether gross when I find Lucy talking his ear off.

"Hey, you're on the clock, Luce. Give Mr. Dennis a break and help me with the boxes."

"Boxes?" Dennis asks.

"Just a few things in my truck I need to bring in. We went into town this morning, so I made the weekly Tim's Club stop."

He stands. "Let me help."

"Can Mr. Dennis sub in for me?" Lucy asks, leaning against the bar top.

"Sure, go watch something in the office, Bug. Great work today."

Her little chest puffs out with pride as she skips away.

Dennis follows me through the kitchen to the back door. "Isn't it illegal, her working here?"

I snort. "She's not actually working, Dennis, she mostly spills powdered sugar in the kitchen and then cleans up her own messes."

"Rubbish, I saw her delivering plates just like the other servers. She's a bloody work horse."

I look over my shoulder at him with a smile as I open the door. "Wonder where she gets that." I move around to the back of my truck and open the bed. I turn to hand Dennis a box but he's stopped a few feet away.

"This is your vehicle?"

"Um, this is my truck. Truu-uuuuck," I say obnoxiously. "Have you never seen a truck before? Gosh, big day for you then."

He takes a few huge strides to meet me at the tailgate. "This is not a truck, this is a damn *disaster on wheels.*" He looks at the truck, then back at me. "That's it."

"What?" I say, but he's already stomping back inside. "Dennis?" He flings the door almost off its hinges. "I want to talk to Ruthie. Right now."

"Wait!" I run after him. "What exactly is happening?"

He doesn't answer he just keeps stalking forward like a madman.

"Oh, boy. Um, Ruthie?" I try to warn her with my tone. When we reach the kitchen, I give her my best *please be cool* face. "Dennis says he wants to talk to you."

He stands tall, hands on his hips, taking up the whole kitchen. "Ruthie, is it?"

She does not like his tone. Not one bit. She takes a step forward, grabs a towel and starts wiping her hands, looking him up and down. Despite what she said about his attractiveness the other day, she looks completely unimpressed.

She finally meets his eyes. "That's correct."

"Listen, I need to discuss your practices and policies here. I don't know what kind of establishment you're running but—"

"Let me stop you right there, honey. I am not the boss. I am the head chef. I manage the grill. I help with the Inn. But I'm not the owner nor am I the complaint and suggestions box, so you can go ahead and see yourself right on outta my kitchen."

Everyone stares at Dennis with wide eyes, me included.

"Then I'd like to speak to him, the owner." Ruthie puts her hand up to her chin and considers it as Dennis goes on, "Just say when and where, I'll meet him straight away."

"Well, he usually has coffee at the Muffin Top in town before he comes out here in the morning. Like nine-ish. I'll tell him you're coming but..."

"But what?" he snaps at her. She changes her stance and raises her eyebrows up into the ceiling until he calms himself. "Excuse me. But what?"

"But you should leave well enough alone, sugar. You're no match for our boss."

He huffs a laugh. It's a little scary. "You don't know me, Ms. Ruthie."

"Your funeral, honey."

"We'll see about that," Dennis says and he storms out of the restaurant.

Oh, sh—crap. Crap!

I am so screwed.

10
DENNIS

I sit down in a cheap little chair with my overpriced mediocre coffee.

I cannot wait to meet this son of a bitch.

What kind of asshole lets a single mother work herself to the bone like that day after day? And to not offer childcare? Not insist she drive a company vehicle? A company vehicle not held together with bloody duct tape.

I cannot remember the last time I was this angry. And of course, of course it has to do with *her.* Katherine Canton is a right whack job. I never know what she's going to say or do but I know it will be deeply irritating. And no matter what *I* say or do she'll be irritated with me too.

Her irritated with *me?*

For being polite and civil. The absurdity.

I cannot pinpoint what exactly has gone awry in her twisted mind but there's something. I don't even know if I want to figure it all out anymore. Why she accepts such meager pay for such hard work. Why she would let Lucy, precious, hilarious, incredible little Lucy, sleep one door down from a bar?

What the actual...

No. I don't care why.

Now I just want to fix it. I want to beat her boss to a pulp—very unlike me—buy the whole place—much more my style—quadruple her salary and find her a house too. Hell, maybe I'll buy the whole tiny town.

I look around the yuppy coffee shop on the edge of Northwest Arkansas' main metropolis.

And this town, too.

Forget the AmeriMart people.

I'm a DeLane.

And this man is about to discover exactly, painfully, what that means. Whenever he arrives. I adjust my tie a bit, tied too tight in a fit of rage earlier as I thought about this meeting. I look up as each patron enters, ready to have a go at them. I'm not sure what I'm expecting, a pudgy middle-aged bloke maybe.

The store front bell rings, I snap to attention.

But it's Katherine.

Ugh. Fantastic.

"Hey, look," she starts, breezing in and sitting down.

"Kat. You should go. You don't want to be here for this."

She rolls her eyes. "Oh really? What exactly do you plan to say?"

"Oh, a whole bloody lot and—"

"Shocker. So maybe don't do this here." She cuts me off quietly, looking around.

"What?"

"Dennis, we're probably being broadcast on TikTok right now with a hashtag like Grace Watch 24/7 or something, so unless you want the whole world to watch you lose your sh—*crap,* maybe wait outside?"

"Is he on his way? Your boss."

"C'mon." She gets up and waves for me to follow.

Once we're outside, I implore her, "Really, you need to leave, Katherine."

"I heard you, *Dennis*," she spits my name in that way that makes me want to... lash out. She leads me around the corner of the building, past all the windows. "And I would really love to know what you're going to say about me."

"Wait, are you afraid I'll get you into trouble?" *Hell, what if I am going to get her into trouble.* "Kat? Am I putting your job at risk? Or is it more than that? Are you in real trouble? Who the hell is this guy?"

She won't stop moving so I grab her elbow. She looks down at my hand on her bony joint. This woman needs to stop and eat once in a while. She tugs out of my grasp.

"There is no guy."

"What? I'm talking about your boss."

She breathes in and out, labored. "C'mon, buddy, you're really smart. You can do this."

"What the hell are you on about?"

She flattens her mouth into a line and raises her brows, waiting.

"Kat?"

She looks down, smiling. "Any second now..." She leans back against the brick wall. I'd say she's snickering, even. Like I've been had.

Oh.

I have been.

"There's no other boss. Ruthie just didn't want to deal with me directly." I clench my fists.

Kat laughs now. "Getting closer."

I study her. She's biting her lip. Now that I notice it, pink and full, I can't quite look away. Something about the sight of her bright lipstick in between her teeth is... I don't know.

No matter. I force my eyes away from her mouth so I can really take her in.

Her all-black ensemble today is worn, like most days. Her neon hair is falling out of her ponytail and the matching nail polish is chipped. She's picking at it anxiously.

Who would push this girl like this?

She crosses her arms.

Kat.

Kat would. Kat would push herself.

"You," I exhale.

"Ding, ding, ding!" She laughs. "I'm texting everyone we know to tell them you are not the genius they think you are. I mean, wow."

"You own the Roadside?" She does a weird bow curtsy thing. "That whole place? You're what, barely thirty?"

"Ouch. I'm only twenty-five, Grandpa. Not that age matters one single hill-a-beans."

Hill of what?

I shake my head, trying to get sorted. "Wow, I thought you only looked young. You're even younger than Grace."

She leans back into the wall again. "Again, not relevant. You're ancient, I don't hold that against you."

"I am thirty-eight, definitely *not* ancient and wait." My mind starts to catch up. "You had Lucy when you were seventeen?"

She looks up at the sky, exasperated. "Should I put all this in a spreadsheet for you?"

I am reeling a bit. An unfamiliar, unwelcome sensation. "I have so many questions."

"I figured. But I don't owe you any answers. Now, you know that I'm fine, Lucy's fine, the business is fine. No one needs any rescuing here." She flashes me her bitter smile, the one I see the most. I do not care for it at all.

"Are you sure about that? Because I checked my accounts for this meeting, and they haven't been charged. Not for the rooms or the dinners or—"

"That's correct."

"What? Why?"

She pushes off the wall. "I don't need your charity. I don't need your business help. I don't need some dude swooping in to mess with my plan. Not my dad, not Beau, not you, not—"

"Who the hell is Beau?"

"Nobody. I don't need your advice or your financial wisdom or whatever else."

She starts to walk off and I follow. "I never said you did."

"It was coming, and we both know it."

I grab her wrist. "Would you stop putting words in my mouth? I never said you needed advice. I also never said that I hate neon, for the record."

She snorts at that and, realizing we are by the window, starts to retreat into the alley. She pulls her wrist away and grabs mine instead, yanking me after her. Her fingers are soft and small and freezing. That must be why my wrist almost burns where she touches me, even after she releases her grip.

"Explain how you providing me a room and me paying you for it is charity," I demand.

"My dad offered you a free room, you weren't supposed to pay. And I don't need you to."

I narrow my eyes at her. "If your business is doing so bloody well that you don't need your customers to pay, why do you drive that?" I point at the barrel of parts she calls a truck.

"I realize you have a lot of questions and concerns. That sounds like a you problem, honey."

I absently rub at my wrist. "Is your ownership some kind of secret?"

She shrugs. "No, but people don't need to know."

"Does your father know?"

Her face twists with disgust. "He does, unfortunately."

I inch toward her again, and she doesn't back into the wall. "Is he... The way you talk about him, should I not be trying to help him, his business?"

Her eyes go wide. "No, yes. Please! What's good for him is good for Lucy. Make him a billionaire. Well, you can't. He'd screw it up. But if you can give him, like, an amazing few years, that'd be perfect."

I rub a hand over my face. "I am so confused."

She chuckles again. "I'm picking up on that."

I open my eyes to lock with hers. They're a fiery hazel mix of colors. "I hate to be confused."

"I'd say that's pretty universal."

"Katherine."

"Dennis."

I push in closer. "Fine, if you won't tell me anything about your life, tell me *why* you won't tell me."

She's panting, and hell, I think I am too. I don't quite know why. Anger, maybe. We are nose to nose, even though I'm much taller. It's those combat boots. And she smells fruity, like a watermelon hard candy.

She shrugs. "It's none of your business." Her voice is soft, breathy, but still agitated with me.

I clench my jaw, unsure what to say, how to get her to just talk to me. Be a normal human being with me rather than some kind of caged animal.

"All this hero energy, this knight in an Armani suit of armor thing you've got going on?" She looks down at my mouth for a split second. "You need to channel alllll of that on Grace." She ducks out from under me and starts to walk away. And I hate it.

I hate her walking away, I hate the idea of her getting in that vehicle, I hate this whole rubbish conversation. "Wait!"

"Ughhhhh, what?" She stomps and turns at her truck door like a child.

"About that. We never renegotiated our deal. I still need *your* help."

She looks genuinely surprised. *Yeah, welcome to the club, sweetheart.* Her face shifts though, unbelieving.

I explain, "I need this. The marriage, the arrangement—Grace. The pressure has only built over the years, and I can't afford another failure." She seems satisfied with my answer, but I ask again. "Fayetteville, the pizza place, that was brilliant. Totally saved me. I need your help, Kat."

"I'm sorry," She makes a show of cupping her ear. "Could you repeat that? Little me, needs to swoop in to save you, Mr. DeLane?"

Hearing her call me that is like a kick to the gut. I grunt. "Mr. DeLane," I mutter under my breath.

"Wait." Her face lights up. *Hell, she's perceptive.* "Dennis, did she call you that? On your date?" Kat shrieks.

I want to ignore the question, but I look up and she is beaming. Her eyes and smile light up so much, she's like a frizzy, bright pink light bulb shining out of an all-black socket.

It's gorgeous.

So I barely nod.

"HA," she starts. And she laughs so long and so hard that she has to double over and put her hands on her knees.

I let her prattle on, laughing and teasing. She takes her bloody sweet time. But I get the sense she needs the laugh, and I quite like the sound. I lean against her horrible truck and wait.

"Oh, man." She sighs, coming down from her giggles. "That is the most hilarious thing I've ever heard."

"Happy to entertain you," I deadpan.

"Okay, okay." She leans against the truck as well, on her side, facing me. "Lucy does love your lessons and even though she won't tell me your methods, she is starting to actually review her multiplication tables with me now. So, I suppose we can go back to our original arrangement. But you have to move out."

"What? Why?"

"Because I said so, and, as you now know, I'm the boss." She bobbles her head at me. "You move out, you stop asking me questions about my life and my business. You stop glaring at Ruthie every chance you get."

I wince. "Right. I thought she was taking advantage of you, I'll apologize."

"No need. She thinks the whole thing is hysterical. She did lie to your face, after all."

I point. "As did you."

"I did not. I said I'm saving up and I am." She raises a hand when I start to inquire about that. "No prying. We're not friends, we're business associates, facilitating a trade. Deal?" She lowers her hand to extend it to me.

I take it, even though I don't like her terms. She grips hard and gives one big shake and then lets go. But I'm still holding on, just watching her. A strong, wild, bright mystery.

She glances down at our hands, so I finally release my hold. But it's definitely the oddest hand shake I've ever encountered. Like I almost couldn't physically break the connection. *Weird.*

"'Kay, well." She opens her door and I straighten. "I'll come up with some helpful hillbilly ideas and text you. Got that whole Inn and restaurant and campsite to run."

"Campsite?"

"Bye." she yells before shutting her door in my face.

Then, even though my toes are dangerously close to her bald tires, she pulls straight out and turns. She flips me the bird, for no reason whatsoever, and drives off in a hurry.

I stand in the side parking lot staring after her an embarrassingly long while, befuddled.

Eventually I snap back to reality and begin walking to my rented Audi around front.

Wait.

Who the hell is Beau?

11

"Why is it such a big deal for him to know?" Janie's face fills my phone that's propped up on a counter.

I grunt at her from my spot on the floor where I'm cleaning yet another mess. This time a pipe busted. "Because. You know how wealthy people are, men even more so."

Janie is Skye's best friend, but since she and Sally and I were all single at Samantha and Emerson's week-long wedding extravaganza, we've become pretty close. She understands my cousins and also understands that while I'm a Canton too, it's not the same.

"You didn't want him to know you're a successful business owner because *he's* the snob?"

I sit up and glare at the screen. "No. Well, yes, because he'll feel this deep need to get involved in things, help, improve, advise, make things better. Which always makes things worse. Ugh."

"Has he? Gotten involved?"

"Not unless you count endless angry looks at me, at my truck, at his food, at the decor, the cash register..." I go back to toweling up the mess.

"I don't count that. Isn't that just like his resting expression?" Janie jokes.

I snort. "True. Unless he's with Luce."

"That's weirdly sweet."

I sit up again. "Right? That's exactly how I would describe it. No one just likes kids, and Lucy is, well, a lot. And somehow, he's getting through to her in math and also not getting annoyed with her. At least not the once a week that he sees her."

"And he moved out?"

"Yup, thank the Lord, he was ruining the vibe."

She laughs. "You and your vibes."

"I'm never wrong about vibes. It's bad enough he still comes in to eat every single day."

"Huh."

I look away. "Yeah, huh. I'm just waiting for his spreadsheet on how I can expand or some shit. Ah, crap."

"Jar," she teases as I gather up a wet towel and swap it for a dry one. "I know you have your whole 16-point plan, but I don't envy you, girl. How much of your time is spent like this, all sweaty and gross?"

"Wow, thanks."

She shrugs, I think. I can't see her whole torso. "What about your lessons for him?"

I gesture around the room. "In all my spare time? All I've done so far is text, answering his questions about the area and sent him reminders like *don't say shall. Americans don't say shall.* Amazing knowledge bombs like that, just right and left."

She chuckles. "He's so lucky to have you."

"I mean, I think I'm giving him an edge. She's dated him more than any of the others, even Emerson's brother." I stand and stretch.

"How do you know that?"

"TikTok. This whole place is deeply invested in the competition. The only thing that could happen around here that'd be more exciting would be the return of the Lord Jesus himself." I chuckle with her. "Well, I know this was longer than my allotted phone call time, I will go back to texts only for the next few weeks."

"Thank you." She bows her head, used to being teased for her introversion. Then she pauses before ending the call. "So, you like Dennis for her? Him and Grace?"

I must make a face because she makes a face. "Huh? It's Billionaire Bachelorette they're all good for her. And she seems perfect for him from the videos I've seen."

"All right," she drawls the word like she has more to say, but then nods.

We say goodbye and I start to gather towels and text the plumber. Again. I need to hustle to get into town for a million errands, get Lucy from school, and then run back by the Roadside before I get her to cheer.

And because I am in a hurry, my stupid truck won't start. At the same time, Ruthie calls. She only calls if there's an issue.

"What's up?" I ask.

"Uh, catering order for lunch today, big one." She sounds weird.

I stop trying to get the engine to start. "Okay, do you need more staff then? Or?"

"I think we can handle it, it's just...it's almost all the food we have on hand. After this I'll have to send Stella to the store. We might even have to close."

"Wait. Order for who?"

"A few floors of offices it seems, was placed by—"

"Oh. Right." I cut her off. She doesn't have to answer because I already know.

And so it begins.

"Let's go girls!" Tran yells beside me.

The kids are hyped up more than usual, and that is saying something for a cheerleading squad made up of seven- and eight-year-olds. This is their exhibition night, to show their parents the routine before they go to their first competition out of town. They even get to wear their uniforms tonight and Lucy insisted on space buns for her hair. She also insisted I match.

Lucy gets my attention, so I wave then she points. But I don't have to follow her finger because all the women are already reacting to his presence.

Dennis DeLane just walked into this cheer gym. In a navy three-piece suit, looking like it's seven in the morning instead of seven at night. Why doesn't he ever look frumpy or wrinkled or something?

I let myself stare because he's not looking at the stands, he's looking at Lucy. He waves and mouths something and she nods. I look away because I know he's coming over to me and I have a pretty good idea what he's going to say.

"Katherine Canton," he starts, sitting down right beside me.

"Don't—"

"Are you..." He ignores my heavy sigh. "Wearing... Is that..." He pretends to be confused. "...pink?"

I flash him a gnarly side eye. "As if you can lecture me about my wardrobe. I'm always in black but you're always in blue. Royal blue, Navy blue. Pinstripe Navy. Really dark navy with a lighter navy shirt."

"Am I?"

"And who wears a suit, with a vest, to a kids cheer exhibition?"

He shrugs a shoulder, almost nudging into mine. "Someone coming straight from the office."

"Okay but it's not 1999, who still wears fancy suits to the office?"

"Fancy people." He keeps staring at me, even though I refuse to turn my head.

I sigh. "I guess Lucy told you about this?"

"She did."

I decide to turn my head at that. "You didn't have to come."

He frowns. "Of course, I did. She invited me." He looks out at the floor. "Not like I can say no to our girl."

What the hell did he just say?

I'm frozen. And now he won't turn his head.

"I like it," he says, but my brain still isn't working. He finally looks over at me. "The pink." He gestures at my bright pink sweatshirt.

"Well then, I'll be sure to burn it later."

He rolls his eyes and looks away as, thankfully, the girls start their exhibition.

The coach talks through all that they've learned this year and the more advanced tumblers show off their newest skills. Lucy lands a back handspring combination perfectly and I'm actually startled when Dennis yells, "Go Lucy! Yeah!"

I didn't even know he could really yell.

He does it again after their routine and I can somehow physically feel women getting turned on around me. Some of them are married. Two of them are lesbians. Doesn't matter. He's that hot, that rich, and he's cheering for my eight-year-old like she's Taylor Swift or something. Or Coldplay? Who would he cheer for? I don't know, because I never in a million years would've guessed Dennis capable of cheering at all.

This is too much.

When it's over, we make our way down to the superstar. She is glowing.

Even more so after Dennis lavishes her with his *very well dones* and *brilliants*. He walks us out to my truck afterward, both of us just listening to Lucy ramble. When we reach it, he opens Lucy's door for her. After he closes it, he looks across the truck bed at me, smug as ever.

"How was business today?"

But I don't take the bait. "Great. You have time for a hillbilly lesson tomorrow?"

"Sure."

"Maybe late afternoon? Can you duck out of work early?"

"Of course."

I mimic him. "*Of course.* Man, what must it be like to be a magnate?"

He scoffs back. "You own your own business; you can also take off early whenever you want."

"Ha, spoken like a true *investor* versus an actual owner. I can't take off a *minute.* Meet me at the Inn parking lot, at the back."

"All right?"

"Great."

I climb in, slam my door and pray like I've never prayed before that my truck starts on the first try. It doesn't.

"Why is Mr. Dennis so mad?" Lucy asks.

I look over and see him watching us from his rented Audi. The driver's side door is open, but he hasn't gotten in yet. I'm sure he just didn't want any barrier between himself and the very sad, very loud sputtering sound.

"He's not mad, he just doesn't like our truck," I explain calmly.

"I don't either," Lucy says, equally calm.

I look over at her, losing the calm. "What?"

"Look at his car. It's new and shiny. Let's get one of those instead."

I say more prayers, desperate ones, and turn the key again. It starts and I exhale at the ceiling. *Thanks, Big Guy. If you feel like smiting anyone with a rogue lightning bolt, there's a lone grump just over there.*

"Luce, where would we put all our bags and boxes? Flour and paper towels and pipes and wood and everything else," I rant, sounding a little crazy.

"Oh. You're right, Mommy. Our truck is okay."

Okay.

The saddest okay I've ever heard.

This is what people like Dennis do to my life.

Now the truck that we've had for years and never discussed is no longer good enough. Now it's a sad truck.

Which is why tomorrow, Dennis DeLane is going to pay.

KELSEY HUMPHREYS

12

I grip the steering wheel hard.

Lucy is in the backseat, giddy about my plan. She promises to keep her mouth shut. We'll see.

Our girl.

Why the hell did he have to say that?

I didn't sleep at all last night. I just kept picturing him saying it, there in his immaculate suit, dark hair and even darker eyes, in the bright gym, surrounded by pink.

My brain replayed it over and over. I don't even think my own parents have said that phrase. I'm sure Susan or one of my cousins has said it when referring to Lucy at some point, but I can't recall any other instances.

This is why I can't let people in.

Lucy is already too attached. She can hardly contain her excitement right now as we pull into the parking lot to wait for him.

But he's only here for a short blip of time and then he'll be gone, back on his private jet, hopping from city to city. Even after he marries Grace, they won't settle down here. Even if they did, it's not like his new wife is going to let him bum around with some other woman's kid once a week.

All of that makes me irrationally sad.

Why? I do not even like Dennis. He's serious and pretentious and his history with the family is too complicated for us to be friends. But Lucy loves him and he's going to leave her. He's got to go sooner rather than later, so I need to shut this whole thing down.

Not to mention the effect he's having around here.

Now that I know that *he* knows I'm the one in charge, I am always on edge. Is his meal perfect? Did he notice how all the parking spots have lost their paint lines? Are my prices too high? Too low?

It's all exhausting my mind while keeping my brain from sleep.

And then there's Lucy and the truck. *Our truck is okay.*

My psyche replayed that all night, too. I remember buying that truck with cash when she was two. I remember the first time I filled the bed with tile to renovate a bathroom. All by myself. I was so proud. Now the truck is tainted.

Stupid, freaking Dennis.

Here he comes now in his sleek black car.

At least this afternoon is going to be fun for me.

"Mr. Dennis, c'mon!" Lucy barrels down the trail behind me before he's even closed his car door.

"Luce, slow down." I turn back to see him frowning at me, as usual.

He locks his car and sticks his key in his pocket, staring at me. It was another hectic day so I'm sure my flyaways are crazy and my mascara is smudged.

"Are you ill?"

"Wow. That bad, huh? You pull up carpeting on your hands and knees all day long and we'll see how you look."

"I only meant—"

I raise a hand. "I know, I look tired. I'm fine. Bonus tip: don't ever walk up to Grace and ask her if she's ill. Now let's go." I turn and start walking before he can respond, but I hear his irritated murmuring as I go.

I make good time getting down the stone steps to where the trail starts. The path to my equipment shed is not long but it's a little overgrown. It's not too muddy right now but it's also not paved or gravel lined. It's just leaves and dirt and probably some dog crap. Definitely deer droppings.

I smile and yell over my shoulder, "How much did your swanky shoes cost?"

"Not sure but I don't have another black pair here. Shall I take them off?"

"Oh, Dennis. What did we say about saying *shall*? I would love to see you barefoot though. That'd be so weird."

"You've seen me barefoot." He grunts. "At the Inn. When you chucked coffee pods at my head."

I stop and turn, confused. "That's right, I forgot. Good times." I laugh, looking down at his shoes; they're not ruined. Bummer. "We're almost there, then we'll hop in the Gator."

"The what?"

I can't help it; I laugh some more. "An alligator, Dennis. We're going to ride on the back of an actual alligator."

"Must you always—"

"It's a four-wheeler. See?" I pause and point to the clearing around the bend, where the small building is. Under the carport is my little utility vehicle with Lucy already in a backseat, legs swinging. "That. And this is why we're doing this. Grace needs someone who knows what the hell a Gator is."

As I walk away, he huffs. "I very much doubt that."

Hmm. I think of Grace. I may or may not have scrolled through a million pictures of her last night when sleep evaded me. He's right, she probably doesn't know what a Gator is. She probably wouldn't even think what I am about to do is funny.

She'd be wrong, though.

"Hop in." I am almost gleeful about my idea as I get the four-wheeler started.

Dennis gets in cautiously, a little tall for the tiny vehicle. "The excitement on your face concerns me."

"Nah, just showing you the campgrounds. And there are rags in the glove compartment for your shoes if you want."

"They're fine." He looks out at the small gravel path ahead. "So, you said campsite the other day, you own this land?"

"Yup." I pull out and start our journey. "The state owns most of the campgrounds but there are a few private ones. Small, but of course the private areas are nicer, maintained much better." We wind around through thick trees that are starting to turn green. It's a bit chilly out but not cold.

"Mommy, can we put on some music?"

"Sure, Bug." I turn on the Gator's radio.

"No, we need to show Mr. Dennis the midnight playlist," she whines from her seat.

Dennis turns to her and asks again, "The what?"

"He's not ready for that yet. That's like ten hillbilly lessons away. Plus, there's no Bluetooth in here." She groans but realizes the radio is playing a song she knows and starts humming along.

I can feel Dennis itching to ask me what the playlist is all about and why he's not ready for it, but I start our little lesson. "Have you ever been camping?"

He just dips his chin and cocks his head. Because obviously he has not.

"Shocker. Okay, so for someone who is elderly and out of touch, you're probably thinking of tents and sleeping bags. And people do that, but not usually. This one on the right is a deluxe site, a huge RV can fit here. There's a big grill instead of just a fire pit, power hookup, water line and it's closest to the bathrooms just over that hill. I have a few of these and come summer they'll be booked every night."

"Booked, like a hotel?" he asks.

"Yup." I drive on to a section that's full. "See, these RVs are smaller, and these sites are cheaper. Closer together, no hook ups, but a nice fire pit and still close to the bathrooms. There's also an extra set of showers over on this side."

His mouth drops open as he watches the sites go by. "You have to maintain all of this?"

As if perfectly timed, we hit a huge bump in the road. "Yes, but as you can see, this is the wild out of doors, not too much maintenance required."

"Bullocks. There is the land, the plumbing, the power, and I'm sure you strung all these lights?" He points to the Christmas lights that line the paths. They're not on yet but they will light up automatically when the sun goes down a little further. I'm surprised he noticed them.

"Well, not me personally," I mumble, but he glares. "Okay, yes I did do them myself forever ago."

"I helped!"

"That's true, Bug, you did." I quickly go on, so he doesn't think I don't know how to scale a business, "But I have a manager for the campsite, now." I point ahead. "Now we're headed into the state side, which is four times as big."

"Yes, I can see the difference here immediately," he says, matter of factly. But him noticing how much nicer my area is... it affects me, like he's just said *very well done.*

My reaction is stupid. Who cares what Dennis thinks about campsites? Not me. Time for the main event. I speed up.

I pull out onto the main road, part of a big loop that leads back to my outbuilding where we started. Off the main road is a turnoff, a drive through with a little pump at the center. Lucy is already giggling.

"Okay, now, we need your help."

"All right?" He hops out, following me and Lucy to the pump.

"Lucy can you pick up the hose?" I ask.

She is trying so hard to keep her cool. I don't think Dennis is picking up on her excitement yet though. She grabs the hose by the handle and hands it to Dennis who takes it, looking at me, ready.

I ask him, "Ok, can you put your hand over the end of the hose for me? Make sure when I start the pump nothing leaks out."

"Okay?" He does it. Jackpot.

"Now. I'm not going to turn it on yet, but you heard me mention some of the sites have water hookups, some have power. But in an RV, there's one more hookup that's really important."

Lucy starts giggling now.

"Am I about to be soaked by a fire hydrant?" He moves the hose away from him but it's too late. He's already touched the end and one of his hands is wet by the way he's flopping it.

"Oh, it's not water. Remember I told you they have those at the site. But aaaaall those campsites, the state ones and mine, we have to have one more hookup. Can you guess what for?"

Lucy starts to giggle, and he looks between us, frowning.

"POOP!" Lucy loses it.

Dennis throws the hose and I laugh hysterically too.

"Mother f—"

"Jar," I yell through my laughter.

"I will give Lucy a bloody hundred dollars! Fucking hell, Katherine, shit on my hands? My bare hands? Really?"

"Really," Lucy yells, falling to the ground by the pump she's laughing so hard.

I wipe tears from my eyes.

Dennis is not laughing. As one would expect, I guess.

"Oh, is this quite funny?" Suddenly he jumps at me with his hands out.

"No! Ah! I'll get you some wipes." I leap back before he can touch me. I run for the wipes and get back to him as fast as I can. "Here."

He turns to Lucy, going at her with straight zombie arms. But he doesn't actually touch her.

"Un-bloody-believable." He grabs the wipes package out of my hands angrily, but he looks over at Lucy who is still laughing.

I'm pretty sure the corner of his mouth would lift up in a half smile if he let it.

"That," I exhale, still fighting off a chuckle, "was for the lunch order."

He freezes and slowly turns his head in my direction. "Pardon?"

"Oh, you heard me. That was to get you back for meddling. I said no meddling, dude. No fancy orders that buy out my entire fridge and pantry. We had to close for an hour to restock."

He takes a small step toward me, still scrubbing his hands. "Oh. Did you lose business?"

"It's fine, your order more than made up for being closed during the dead zone between lunch and dinner. That's not the point. This is exactly what I mean when I said no swooping in. Luce, go get in the Gator. Let's head back."

He waits for her to get lost in her singing before he inches even closer to me. "So, you're punishing me for being a customer."

"Be a normal customer, come in and have meals. I don't punish you for those."

"You don't charge me," he says through his teeth. "What the hell is the matter with you?"

I shrug. "Abusive dad, absent mother, small town mean girls, teen pregnancy, horrible taste in men, take your pick."

He grabs his forehead then quickly pulls his hand away, looking at it like it's still covered in filth, even though he's already wiped it down fifty times. He growls through clenched teeth, taking a few long strides away from me, then back again.

"Why can't I just be your friend?"

"I don't need friends, Dennis. I told you that."

"Yes, and then we established that I needed your friendship, remember that? And you agreed. Lucy and I are thick as thieves, she's thriving, I moved out of the Inn, I patched things up with Ruthie, I think your staff is even warming up to me, and here you are sticking my hand in shit. Because I tried to do something nice. For you."

Well, crap.

Maybe I went too far.

He shakes his head and starts ranting, even more exasperated than before. "Hell, if it's not your weasel of a father pestering me—whom I really don't care to help now, obviously, but don't worry, I wouldn't *dare* ask for you to share anything about that with me—then it's Emerson ignoring my texts, Grace keeping me at a distance, Benedict rubbing my nose in his wins, or you, cutting me off at the knees." He looks up at the sky and I just stand with my mouth hanging open, shocked. "I should not have come out here. I am going to get cut off from my own family after dragging the DeLane name through the mud all over again, like a proper twat."

"Hey, hey, you won't. I'm sorry, I'll help. It was just a prank." He doesn't look down, but he seems to calm a bit. I wait a moment and then add, "It was a pretty good prank, you gotta admit."

He pulls his gaze from the clouds and locks his angry eyes on mine. "And how, exactly, was this supposed to help me win over Grace?" He stalks toward me like a lion stalking its prey, voice low and eyes tight. "What was the point other than to push all my damn buttons." He only stops once he's right up in my space, our chests touching. I can smell him, his breath and his cologne, detergent maybe. He's all minty and clean and towering over me. "Get me so thoroughly bothered that I snap like a twig, pick you up, toss you over my shoulder and carry you off somewhere to teach *you* a few lessons, hmm?"

I...

What did he just say?

And.

His eyes. They were angry, they still are, but now they're heavy, darkened. And he's not looking at my eyes anymore. He's looking at my mouth. He... he's leaning. He's leaning down to... I can't... We can't...

"The Daisy Air Gun Festival," I blurt out. He freezes, and I back up, finally able to move my legs again. "It's tomorrow. It's out here, but she'll love it. Worth the drive. Food, music, quirky booths, a lot more than just guns. It's put on by the museum but it's also a farmer's market and all of the small businesses in the outlying towns set up booths."

He takes a step back and smooths down his tie. "Will the Roadside have a booth?"

"Yeah."

"Will I be allowed to purchase something at said booth?"

I smile, not able to help myself. "You can try." He shakes his head, but I think he's fighting a grin. I wave him to the Gator. "C'mon, let's get you to a sink with some soap."

"And bleach, preferably."

We climb back in, and Lucy eyes us. We did just have a throw down yelling match a few feet away. But she's making a bracelet, always with those tiny rubber bands in her pockets, and humming to the music, not too concerned.

I make much better time driving us back the way we came. *Saturday in the Park* comes on the radio and Lucy perks up.

"Can you turn it up, Mommy? We gotta crank midnight playlist songs!"

"Okay, Bug." I turn the knob and fight a snicker, feeling Dennis staring.

"Katherine, tell me one measly thing about the midnight playlist right now or I will buy every other business in town, every property around yours, every grocery store and market and every last thing until I'm so far up your—" he glances back at Lucy for a second—"your *business* that you'll never be rid of me."

"And you say I'm the crazy one." He inhales, ready to tear into me again. "It's just a playlist."

"I thought it was never just a playlist, Mommy? I thought it was a legend?"

Dennis seethes.

"Okay." I throw my child a side eye. "When I was bartending a lot more, I noticed that about 11:30 people would start to mentally get ready to go. Like midnight was a cut off in their minds. So, I started playing singalong songs, bar songs, but only the best ones. Better and better until midnight, and by then everyone was singing along and having too much fun to leave. It became a thing." Dennis doesn't respond he just stares at me, so I shrug.

"But it's the best when Mommy is there. Everybody goes crazy."

"Lucy hasn't actually been there." I quickly answer the question he was about to ask. "She's heard stories, seen video. We don't do it every night, not even every weekend. Makes it seem even more legendary, I guess."

"Right, then. When is the next one?"

We pull into the carport and climb out. "They're not planned and, like, it's not really your scene, Dennis."

"You think I don't go to pubs? Half my meetings are over drinks, so—" His thoughts are cut off by his phone buzzing. "Ugh, it's Grace. I'm going to be late." He walks quickly up the trail, leaving me behind. He calls over his shoulder, "You're sure about the festival tomorrow?"

"Yup," I say, feeling weird suddenly.

"Text me when the next midnight thing is happening. I mean it, Kat." Then he's gone from sight.

Just like he will be for good, in a few weeks or months.

The thought used to comfort me, so why the hell am I thinking about his threat to buy up the whole town, and maybe wishing it were real? It'd be interesting, even fun, messing with him every day.

"Can I have mac and cheese for dinner?" Lucy asks, waiting by the back door to the Inn.

I just nod. I'm losing it.

I need to focus on my own projects and plans, starting with the booth for tomorrow.

Because now it needs to be perfect.

Stupid effing Dennis.

13

I decide to close, even though it's not my shift. I need to keep busy. But I'm not really busy. The bar is quiet and empty. It's late, around 2 am, when I sense Dennis come in. I freeze at the bar top, back to the door. I know he's slowly making his way across the restaurant.

I should turn and tell him to go.

I could make a run for it, go to my apartment and lock him out. He wouldn't pound on the door with Lucy sleeping inside.

But I don't want to run. I want to see what he's going to do. I don't even bother pretending to wipe down the corner. I just stand still, waiting.

Then I smell him—spearmint. And I feel him right behind me.

"Katherine," he whispers in my ear, and without thinking I tilt my head, exposing my neck for him. He kisses the spot, but lightly. Too light.

I lean back into him, and the motion makes him growl as he grips my hips. He tugs me hard into his front, obviously as turned on as I am.

"What do you want?" he whispers before biting my earlobe.

"A lesson," I whisper back.

He chuckles softly behind me, a deep dark sound that I feel down in my core. He moves a hand, smoothing over my lower back and down until he reaches the hem of my dress.

His hand comes up, and my skirt with it. He shifts to the side and rubs my ass cheeks that hang out of my thong panties. He strokes, squeezes, breathes in my ear, almost groaning. His hand pulls away and I brace myself for what's coming. But he chuckles again and goes back to squeezing while he pushes himself into my side. He's hot and hard and tall and—

Slap!

Holyyyyy...

"Is this why you're so naughty with me? Hmm?"

"Y-yes," I say on a breath, squeezing my eyes shut and sounding desperate. Because I am. I want more of this. More of Dennis.

He smacks me again, then quickly positions himself behind me.

"Are you ready for me, Katherine?"

I hear him unzipping as he says it.

"Yes," I whisper.

"Louder."

"Yes." I open my eyes.

And see my ceiling.

Oh, crap.

Did I just?

I did.

I just had my first sex dream in at least a year.

About Dennis DeLane.

What the hell?

No. *No, brain. No, sad, neglected vagina. We're not doing this!* I am not, cannot, will not think about Dennis like this. He's snooty, rude, old, rich, annoying, complicated. So what if he's hot and nice to my kid? No. Absolutely not.

I throw my covers off and climb down to face the day. I've got a booth to set up, among all my other usual Saturday chores. I have no time for spearmint spanking fantasies. My butt cheeks even tingle as I brush my teeth.

No, butt cheeks! Brain, body, get it together. We are Not. Doing. This!

———

"We should make the samples a little smaller," I say, looking over our tables.

"Will you stop? You haven't fussed like this since our last health inspection." Ruthie slaps my hand away. She is a hit at these things, cooking and chatting with everybody. We're selling beer but the main event is our samples. Tiny cups of chicken and waffle, our signature burgers cut into bites, small cups filled with each of our fries, and cubes of Pig Sooie Pie, which is really Arkansas's famous Possum Pie with red sugar dust.

"I'm just thinking the weather is great today, maybe I should go get more supplies. I don't want to run out."

"If that'll get you out of our hair, by all means, honey."

I nod and head to my truck. I check my texts, making sure Tran is fine with keeping Lucy all day. They'll swing by the festival at some point but in public I can't have Lucy behind the counter handing out beers—exactly what she'd end up doing.

Because I am a stellar mother.

I swing into Tim's Club and keep filling my cart with giant packs of dry goods until I feel more settled. But I never do. I am freaking out about a booth that we've done plenty of times, without issue. Still, in case today is a banner day for attendance, more cups and ingredients and napkins won't hurt.

When I finally get everything loaded into my truck and slam the tailgate, I realize that I may have gone overboard. It's fine, though. We'll use all this stuff throughout the week. I climb in, sweaty already, and turn the key.

But the truck won't start. The engine isn't even turning over. I talk to the Lord above, and the truck and myself but to no avail. I only know one person close by with a spare truck. And a nice smile and an amazing set of biceps.

I watch the road for him to pull in, thinking about his abs and other parts. What is happening to me? Maybe I just really need to have some sex. Get this tension out of my system.

Finally, I see them, two pick-up trucks, old and dirty but much nicer and newer than mine. I hop out to greet them as they park next to me.

"Hey there, little lady." Beau is still sexy as ever, laid back and sun-kissed like a landlocked surfer boy. And he's not subtle about watching me move bags and boxes from one truck bed to the other. But there were no flutters in my stomach, or further south, when Beau and his brother pulled in to rescue me.

Right now, with him biting his lip that he's got pulled in a knowing grin, the kind that says *I remember what you look like naked,* I just want to get back to my booth.

I thank them quickly with promises of free liquor forever and get moving. Beau doesn't mind me running off. They have a booth too, so he gets it. He also would've nailed me in the back of my truck in the parking lot right here and now, I think.

I smile.

I've still got it.

My smile fades throughout the morning. It is busy, and we do go through product fast. Mostly though, I'm watching the crowd. For them. For her.

I'm also driving Ruthie nuts.

I keep moving the price signs and sample set up. I want everything to look nicer, bigger, fuller. I realize in late afternoon that Dennis and Grace might not even come.

Why would she want to come to a small-town street festival? If she didn't want to come out, he wouldn't insist. Because he's too polite and because it's not like he wants to come just for himself. He's Dennis DeLane. I'm sure he'd rather be golfing.

I also realize around the same time that we are crushing it. We have a line for our waffle samples and we're selling twice as much booze than the other food and beverage vendor. Ruthie has made a million new friends, Stella is cheerful and efficient, and I am keeping them running. Before they need a napkin, I'm handing it to them. Before we're down to the last beer can, I'm refilling the ice chests.

I still keep adjusting the tables nervously. Levels. We need display levels so people can see the different options. I go to the back of the tent and grab a couple small crates. That'll work. As I move to set them on the table, one snags on my shirt. I tug, in a hurry for no real reason other than general anxiety, and the shirt rips.

"Oh no, are you all right?" Stella turns into me just as I reach forward to set the crate on table. In between her hands and my body are three pie samples. Were. Now they're on what's left of my shirt. And my exposed stomach and the top of my back jeans. "Sorry."

"It's fine, I got it." I grab a rag and wipe myself, but the rag was covered in something else. Salt and pepper and seasoning mix, by the smell of it. I glance down. I'm a mess of torn black fabric, sweat, white blobs of whipped cream residue and seasonings.

So of course, Dennis and Grace are here now. I don't even see them, I just know. There's a hubbub around us, and a sense of dread in my chest. I peak around Stella and spot them down the street. Stella sighs and I get it.

Just like all their dates, they look like old Hollywood is filming a small-town movie here, and they're the stars. She's in a champagne blouse and tight blue jeans, he's in one of his brighter blue suits, no vest.

And I'm wearing half the kitchen across my ripped AC/DC tee shirt.

Honestly the rip and the spices may be an improvement on this shirt that has seen better days. Plus, I'm dripping in sweat and Lucy talked me into two braids this morning, making me look like I'm about twelve. I jump out of the gorgeous couple's line of sight, and over to Ruthie.

"Ruth, shoot me straight, how bad do I look?"

"What?" She is confused and it makes sense. I've never in my life cared about how I look.

"Pretty rough," Stella answers honestly. And they are coming closer. *Shiiiiii—*

There's nowhere for me to go, our tent is up against a wall, if I run off, he'll see me.

"I'm not here, you guys hear me?" I get down on my knees.

Ruthie starts, "What in God's good name are you—"

Stella gives me an I-understand-this-in-a-deep-way girl-code type of nod and turns Ruthie away from where I am crawling on the ground. To hide under one of the tables. We have long checkered tablecloths that reach the grass. He won't see.

"Miss Ruthie, you're looking lovely as ever, darling," Dennis says, a smile in his voice.

"I look like I've been cooking outside in a tent all day, but you're sweet." Ruthie smiles back.

He asks the big question. "Where's Kat?"

Ruthie hesitates. *Crap.* I should have made a game plan.

"She's not here, honey." Good. Not very creative but she follows instructions, I'll give her that.

"Ah." Dennis doesn't really react. Good. Move it along, buddy. "Grace, forgive me, this is my dear friend Ruthie. And Stella, and over at the griddle is Lonnie."

Dear friend? And Dennis knows everyone's names?

He goes on. "But most of all, here, you have to try this." I hear him take a cup and try not to imagine him finger feeding her. I am positive he chose the chicken waffle hash cup. It's his favorite.

Grace groans with her mouth full. "Ohhh. So good."

"Brilliant, right? I knew you'd love it," Dennis coos back at her.

In this moment I hate that sample. And this stupid festival. And this town and my life and this grass. Which is itchy.

"Right, then. We'll take a couple beers, and can we buy a plate?"

"Not today, honey. Gotta go to the restaurant for that."

Stella gets his beers and he asks her this time, "Is that where Kat is?"

"She's puttin' out a fire," Stella says casually.

"Literally?" He's getting loud and it's even funnier how he says the word with his British accent. *Litraly* in three fancy syllables instead of four.

I hold in a snort.

Stella laughs too. "No, no. No emergency."

I actually hear him sigh with relief and then mutter, "Knowing her, she probably owns an actual fire truck and the wildling would be pumping the water herself."

"Ha," Ruthie laughs. "That's the truth."

"So, she's at the Inn?" He won't let it go and it's getting weird.

"Dennis?" Grace asks, picking up on the awkward.

He clears his throat. "Sorry, darling. Just wanted you to meet her."

"Your client's daughter, right?"

"Right."

Stella says something to the person behind them, and Dennis apologizes for the hold up, I think. I can't really hear over my pulse.

Darling.

Client's daughter.

"You gonna stay under there all afternoon or can you get me some more cups?" Ruthie snaps me out of it with a huff.

"Stella?" I ask the only one of my staff who seems to understand my situation.

"Yeah, they're long gone. I don't see them."

I climb out, grabbing some cups as I go.

"I gotta get out of here. I'll be back later with the last of the beers." I am talking fast and weird.

Stella just nods but Ruthie turns to me. "You know, I've only ever seen you like this about one other person. Hiding and actin' a fool."

I grimace. She's right.

"Yup. Used to only have one Darth Lord, now there are two. Lucky me."

She shakes her head and starts muttering but I turn to go.

I have to stop myself from sprinting to Beau's truck. Once inside I collapse against the wheel. This is bad, like Ruthie said. I shouldn't be freaking out about anyone, let alone Dennis. I don't know if it's loneliness or horniness or his sweet friendship with Lucy, but... Wait, that's it.

He's good with Lucy. Great with her, even. He's filling a hole in our little family, a wound that has remained painfully open, for years.

I need to cut him off, then I can get my wits back about me.

My phone buzzes and before I can think too long about the fact that my knees itch from hiding under a table like a five-year-old, I do have fires to put out. Metaphorical ones. The dryer is out at the Inn, and someone trashed one of our campsites. Welp. All in a day's work.

When I pull up back behind Main Street with more beer, Tran messages me that they're having dinner at the festival. She hasn't hit me up all day, so I know this late message is the Mom Bat Signal for *I'm Done, Send Help.*

I hustle with the boxes, along with Stella and Ethan. He gives me a weird look. I guess I've ventured into scary territory. I didn't have time to change and now my ensemble includes some dirt from shimmying my body between the dryer and the wall. Oh well, I'm only going to get Luce and leave anyway. I take a few steps, but Stella stops me.

"I have an extra pearl snap in my car, seriously, don't go to the booth like that."

I laugh. My employees are worried I'm going to make us look bad. What a great boss I am. I nod and she runs to get it. I am still dripping with sweat, so I just leave it open. I have on a black sports bra that covers more like a crop top and my high waist jeans, so nothing is showing, and the breeze feels heavenly.

I wave Lucy down and cave on some ice cream, feeling a little guilty that someone else took her around to enjoy the fun of the festival. We walk slowly hand in hand back across the big field to where the truck is parked. She babbles on and on about her day with Ellie and I smile and nod and let her get all her energy out.

"Sounds like a lovely day." A deep voice comes from nearby as we hit the lot.

"Hi, Mr. Dennis!" She bounds away.

"Bug, don't drop your ice cream."

"I can buy her another," Dennis says as he bends down to scoop her up in a hug. He lifts her off the ground and squeezes hard, making her giggle. My heartbeat short circuits at the sight.

He puts her down and locks eyes with me. He's intense. "Where were you today?" I almost react, giving away that I know he interrogated my team earlier, but he takes a long step toward me, frowning. "What's wrong with your shirt?"

"Huh? Nothing."

He looks down to my midriff then back up. "It's… open."

"As is yours, actually. No tie?"

"Grace said it was too stuffy for an outdoor festival."

I suddenly have to keep from screaming. Grace? *Grace* is the one who convinces him to loosen up? As if I haven't told him he's too stiff for weeks? "Well, she was right. C'mon Luce, it's past your bedtime." She lets go of his hand and hops her way to Beau's truck.

"Did you get a new truck, er, *newer* truck?"

His tone pisses me off, but Lucy responds before I can. "This is Mr. Beau's truck. He has a boat too. It's huuuuge."

Dennis looks from her to me. "Does he?"

I unlock the doors and she continues as she climbs in, "Yup, we used to have sleepovers there, it was so fun. Like sleeping in a big pool float! But then Mommy said we couldn't sleep over there anymore. It was so sad. He has a dog too. I love dogs. Mommy says we can get one when we don't live in the Inn anymore, but I think the Inn could have a dog, like a mascot and—"

"Luce, what did I tell you about telling our whole life story to randoms?"

She looks genuinely offended. "He's not a random, he's Mr. Dennis."

"Exactly right, Lucile," he says, stiff and twitchy. He moves around me to buckle her in, even though she doesn't need help. "Do you know what a yacht is?"

"Oh, brother," I mutter.

Lucy's ice cream is melting around her hand. "A what?"

"A yacht. It's a very big boat. I have two."

I let out a bitter laugh as I open the front passenger door to get one of the napkins I know Beau keeps in the center console. I hand a couple back to Lucy, ignoring the dark eyes watching my every move.

"Yacht." She tries out the word. "Hmm, I bet they aren't as big as Mr. Beau's boat. I mean, it's really big."

Dennis is visibly bothered by that, and I can't help but laugh. Men and their overpriced, impractical toys.

"Well," he starts, "how many feet is his—"

"Dude, calm yourself." I snort. "Beau has a hundred-foot houseboat. It's old and not a yacht. You win."

He grunts.

"Tell him bye, Bug, we gotta go."

"Good night, Mr. Dennis!"

"Good night, darling girl." He kisses her on the head and then shuts her door.

Darling.

"G'night," I say, walking around to the driver's side in a hurry.

He stalks after me, somehow looking totally different in a button up shirt, without a tie, and slacks with no jacket. But his bitter condescending tone is the same as always. "Kat, wait, is that where you were today? With Beau?"

"What? No. I was working." I get in and move to shut my door, but he stops it with his hand.

"Katherine," he grits out. "I went by the booth, the Inn, the grill, the store?"

"So?" I slump in my seat, annoyed. "Why?"

"Because," he snaps, with a tone suggesting him looking for me is normal. It's not. "I see you every day, it was weird."

"You don't see me every day."

"Almost. And you told me you'd be at the fair, then I looked, and you weren't anywhere."

"False." I grab the door handle again. "I was everywhere today. You just missed me."

He sags into my space a little bit. "I did."

Nope. *No no no no no.*

He didn't mean that like it sounded. He was on a date with his future fiancé. His *darling*, for fu—for Pete's sake!

"Not that it's any of your business, anyway, *Dennis*. And since I was all over Dodge and back again, fixing dryers and hauling drinks and finding a truck and everything under the sun, I am very tired. Good night." I pull hard on the door, and he lets it go.

I drive home, get Lucy taken care of and then drug myself with half a glass of wine and a Benadryl. Desperate times call for pathetic measures. There will be no spiraling thoughts or stimulating dreams tonight.

I fall into my coma with a quick prayer that I don't see Dennis again until his next tutoring session with Lucy.

But I have a feeling this time the big man up there isn't going to listen to me.

14

It's been a few Dennis-free days. I think God is doing me a solid because we have been going to church for months now. Sure, it's also Lucy's school, and she begs me to go. But still, my butt's in the pew. Plus, I've hardly been cussing at all lately.

Out loud.

In my head it's mostly a string of F-bombs in connection with Dennis DeLane.

Even though I haven't seen him, he's still somehow every-where. He orders food, Lucy mentions him, or Stella goes on and on about his latest sighting with Grace. Usually somewhere I recommended to him via text.

I turn onto the narrow gravel road I know so well. This area is even more remote than the Roadside, overgrown with big trees, budding light green now in the spring light. I don't often see this road this early, when some of the dew is still sparkling as I pass.

That's the upside to all this—the What Would the Billionaire Say Effect. I forced myself to leave the grill to my capable staff this morning and go see to my newest headache. I could hear him in his snooty accent saying all manner of things.

Why don't you delegate, Katherine?

How will you scale if you focus all your efforts at the grill, Katherine?

How do you expect to make a return if you don't invest, Katherine?

Do you need a lesson, Katherine?

No.

I am not thinking about that. It was one dream. And he was only looking for me the other day because he's a control freak. I was a duck outside of his perfect little rows.

I hop out of my truck and inhale the spring air. I look at the cute little A-Frame. Well, it will be cute. Time to get to work.

It's always overwhelming at the start, so I bum-rush the beginning, trying to gain momentum as quickly as possible. Soon, I've crossed many items off my list, made multiple new lists, hit my head on a low ceiling beam and burned my hand on an exposed pipe.

Not too bad for a day in the life of a small business owner.

I'm in relatively good, albeit sweaty, spirits when I feel my phone buzz.

"Ruthie? Everything okay?"

"Um, you have a delivery here."

I rack my brain. "Something you can't sign for? I don't remember what that is. How big is the box?"

"Honey, just come see. And don't shoot the messenger."

"Okay?"

"Okay, see you in a jiffy."

She hangs up and I stare at my phone for a beat because... what? She sounded so weird. Like nervous and filled with dread but also smiling.

I better get to it. I race the couple miles back to the Roadside, hustle in the front and go straight to the office.

"It's out back!" Ruthie calls playfully.

I walk faster at her tone, through the hallway to the rear door of the grill. I step out into the bright spring light and...

And I'm pissed.

A little shocked. But mostly just livid.

A glittering, I think literally with sparkle paint, brand new, black Ford F150 truck sits in the middle of the lot. I am about to turn and yell at anyone and everyone about it, but I see the big piece of neon pink paper tucked under the wipers.

KATHERINE,

THIS IS <u>MY</u> TRUCK. YOU CAN SEE THE INFORMATION IN THE GLOVE BOX. I THOUGHT YOU MIGHT WANT TO BORROW IT. I DON'T NEED IT RIGHT NOW SINCE I ALREADY HAVE THE AUDI.

BEST,

DENNIS DELANE

I reread the note a few times, riding an emotional tilt-a-whirl in my brain.

"Well? What's it say?" Ruthie asks, suddenly appearing beside me like some kind of genie. I hand her the note. "Whewy, he knows you, doesn't he. He wasn't here when the dealer dropped it, but I figured as much." She hands the paper back to me. "Keys are inside, I had to stop myself from going for a joyride."

I cannot find any words.

"You like it?" Ruthie asks. I shake my head, because no, I don't like it. "Your smile says somethin' else." *Am I smiling?* "And, baby-girl, it's like the man searched the earth high and low to find a truck perfect for you. Look innit, go on."

I step around to the driver's side. "You looked inside already?"

"Honey, I had the key in the ignition ready to test it out. Go look for yourself!"

The black paint is in fact sparkling up close. I pull open the door.

Oh.

My.

Lanta.

It's all black everything inside except for leather over the center console. It's neon pink. Then I notice some of the leather sections have the same pink color in the stitching. Subtle but perfect. He custom ordered this. I look back and my eyes sting because of course, *of course,* in the cab behind the passenger seat is a small black and pink booster seat that matches exactly.

"Ruthie." I say, dumbfounded.

"I know it."

"I mean, Ruthie, what'n the Sam Hill? Look at it!" I get down and walk around, gawking at the beautiful beast of a machine. It's more truck than I need, but not a gargantuan King Ranch. It's perfect.

For me.

Dennis bought a truck for me.

My smile fades.

That sneak mother f—udge sticks. He left me alone for a couple days only to do the swoopiest swoop-in thing and buy me a new truck?

No.

Hell. To. The. No.

I get out my phone.

Kat: This is a very nice truck.

D-Money: I quite like it.

Kat: But I'd rather borrow the Audi...

D-Money: What?

Kat: It's a text message, Dennis, just re-read it if you're confused.

The typing ellipses pops up and disappears a few times which feels like victory. I bet he is fuming because *no, I will not just roll over, eat my words, and accept your big flashy billionaire gift.*

D-Money: Fine.
Kat: At your earliest convenience?
D-Money: Fine. I'll be there shortly.

"Uh oh," Ruthie says as she walks toward the back door.

"What?" I feign innocence.

"That smile I know full well. God help that poor man."

I laugh and grab the door for her. "He's literally a billionaire."

"Not with you, he isn't."

I just laugh again. She heads to the kitchen when Ethan waves me down to troubleshoot a new Bug in the POS. But we don't get very far before I hear Mr. Fancy Pants peel into the lot. He goes around back, and I head out to meet him.

When I step off the back stoop, he's climbing out of the sedan I'm about to commandeer. He looks gorgeous in a light gray suit, a very blueish gray, no vest. Not a dark hair out of place, scowl firm on his brow. He's pissed. Good. He can join my little club.

But he's... smirking?

"Your chariot awaits."

I put a hand to my chest. "My hero, swooping in to save me like this."

"Mhmm."

As I reach him, I hold out my palm. He pulls the key out of his pocket and looks down. His grin vanishes. He grabs my wrist and takes my fingers in his hand.

"What the hell is this?"

I try to pull away, but he doesn't let go. "It's nothing."

"How?" He demands.

I don't think he will react well to learning I was messing with pipes like some kind of plumbing expert, something I definitely am not, hence the burn.

"It doesn't matter, I'm fine."

He reads me like a book. "Or... is it... a who? *Who* did this? Your father? Katherine, so help me God, I will—"

"It's a burn, Dennis. Will you chill out? It's a tiny burn from an exposed pipe." I yank again but he doesn't let go.

"Did you go to the hospital?"

I guffaw at him. "Really, out of the two of us, *you* are nutso. No, I did not go to the hospital for a blister." He's staring down at my hand, and I am about to yank it away again, but I realize he's moving his thumb back and forth on my bare wrist. My throat closes almost all the way up so I can barely croak out the words. "Dennis, let me go."

He does. He clears his own throat and looks at the truck. The awkward pause helps me get my sea legs back.

"Anyway, thanks for this, I have to go get Lucy and the Audi will be perfect. Plus, you'll get to drive your pretty new truck yourself." I give him the hugest eat-shit smile I can.

"You like it, then? The Ford?"

"Eh, I mean, I would've thought you'd go with cobalt blue exterior and navy leather interior, but it's all right." He looks up to the sky, exaggerating his frustration. I bat my lashes. "Want to run into town with me, pick up Luce?"

He's confused. "In the Audi?"

"Yeah. I'll grab the booster seat out of the truck."

"Sure."

Ruthie was right. Poor Dennis.

———

"Hell, woman, slow down!"

I can't stop laughing as I accelerate around the tight turns. "I've driven these curves since I was fifteen, you're fine."

"I am unwell."

"Eh, you can barf, it's a rental." He makes a growly sound and tightens his grip on the arm rests. "If it were you driving, you'd probably go even faster. You're only losing it because I'm a girl."

He scoffs. "A girl. More like she-devil. A siren maybe."

"A wildling," I mutter.

"Absolutely." The memory of him talking to *her* about me pisses me off. I push the little car harder, even though a truck towing a huge boat is barreling toward us on the winding two-way road. "Katherine!"

"Dennis!" I shriek back as we pass the truck with inches to spare. The guy honks and I do feel a little crazy, I can admit it. But my passenger just brings it out in me.

"You can't pick up Lucile if you're dead," he cries, actually looking a little green.

I slow down and watch him settle. I hold in a snort when he straightens his tie like we're headed to a board meeting. This guy.

After we've traveled a few minutes in silence, safe on wide, straight highway, he pulls out his phone. "Right, then. I'm returning the truck."

"What?" I did not see that coming.

"There is absolutely no way you can drive that monstrosity on those roads. Completely mental. No."

I shrug. "Beau's truck handles just fine." I don't look, but I can feel angry laser beams searing me from my right side. I just drive for a couple minutes, and he continues staring. He's very committed to his glares. Wow.

"Is he..."

"My boyfriend? No."

"I meant is he—"

"Past lover is a more accurate description. Friends with benefits, go-to-booty-call. I'm sure you have plenty of—"

"Lucy's father. Is he Lucy's father?"

"Oh... no." I don't glance over to see what kind of expression is on his face. I know he wants to know more. I throw him a bone. *"He* wouldn't drive a truck. He's not in the picture. Never has been."

"Does he know about her?"

I shift in my seat. "He suspects." I glance over this time. The man next to me is seething. I think maybe his hands are even shaking. Though, that could be the traumatic drive. Still, it's all just too much. He doesn't need to concern himself with Lucy's little life. My life. We're fine, always have been, always will be.

"Look." I inhale. "I appreciate what you've done for Lucy, but I think we're good. You're going to get busier and busier with Grace, and—"

"No." He cuts me off.

"What? What do you mean, no? I'm her mother, Dennis, I—"

"She asked me to come tomorrow morning to pregame for her spelling test."

My mouth falls open. No one has ever pre-gamed with us before. "She... she did?"

"Yes. I intend to be there."

I stammer for a second. "I... I don't... I don't understand what you want here."

"What I said. I help with Lucy; you help with Grace. And you take the damned truck."

"Borrow the truck," I correct and he huffs. "I guess I can handle borrowing it until you leave town and then you'll have to sell it."

He sneers, half-joking. "If it's not asking too much of you."

"I'll live." I smile. "We're here."

I pull into the sprawling campus that holds a huge church and an even bigger school. It's impressive, I know.

Dennis clearly approves as he looks around.

All the buildings are new and sleek, and the landscaping is gorgeous. Wide sidewalks, big trees, flowering shrubs. There are multiple playgrounds, sports fields, even ponds with fountains in between the buildings. We pull into the pick-up line, and I can almost hear the gears cranking in his brain.

"This. This is why you need to fix whatever is wrong with Canton Tracking." I say softly. Dennis nods slowly. Before either of us can say anything else we spot Lucy. He touches his door handle. "No. For the love of all that is holy stay in the car, man. We'll be excommunicated if we slow down the car line. Just roll down your window and get her attention."

"Lucy. Lucile!"

"Mr. Dennis!" She lights up like the Fourth of July as she bounds to the car. Like a well-trained cog in the machine that is the carline, she flings open her door, throws herself inside and shuts it as quickly as possible. "Why are you—"

"No chatting yet. Buckles, Luce, c'mon,"

"Is that really necessary?" Dennis tries to scold me but as he does, the car behind us lays on their horn. The man next to me transforms as he turns in his seat. I didn't think he could go from his default angry to even angrier but as he glares at the truck in the mirror, he embodies a dragon ready to blow. I see him lift his hand; I'm assuming with one finger raised.

"Don't! That could be someone in Lucy's class, if not this year, then next. Respect the car line. This is the way."

"This is the way," Lucy chirps in the back, repeating the famous line from the Star Wars show we like.

Dennis just shakes his head at us.

The ride back to the Roadside is quick and completely filled to the brim with words. Lucy doesn't stop from one parking lot to the other. Surprisingly, Dennis is almost smiling the whole time, just listening and nodding, occasionally asking a follow up question.

When we pull up beside the truck, a small smile appears on his face.

Because Lucy is beside herself.

I try to explain over and over that it's not ours and we're just borrowing it and we'll have to return it, even though yes, it's pink inside and even though, yes, the booster seat matches exactly and on and on. Doesn't matter. This big sparkly new truck is the coolest thing she's ever seen.

And Dennis is beyond smug about it.

"Better than *Mr. Beau's*?" he mutters.

"WAY BETTER!" she yells back.

I can't help but chuckle. "Are you going to buy a houseboat next? One hundred *and one* feet?"

"There aren't any available locally."

"Dennis."

"I'm joking." He gives my stare right back. "Mostly." His phone buzzes. "Ah. Dinner bell, I'm afraid."

"Ok." I toss him his Audi key.

"See you in the morning for the pregaming, then?"

I just nod.

I should hate his cocky smile, his bravado, his perfect stupid suit. I should hate that he's barging in on a special tradition tomorrow. I should hate the truck.

I should *not* hate the fact that he's leaving to go have dinner with someone else.

But da—*darn* it.

I really do.

15

"Good morning."

I am not used to seeing Dennis first thing in the morning. Normally I see him at the Inn or the grill only after taking Lucy to school and grabbing a coffee and doing my morning rounds. And vice versa, I realize, when he does a double take at me. I do look better this early. The bags under my eyes are medium rather than supersized, mascara is still in place, hair is not a frizzy mess yet.

And he looks irritatingly stunning, one hand casually holding on to the hostess stand. I've seen this suit before. I've seen all of them now, I think. It's a navy pinstripe that clings tighter to his noticeable muscles underneath. Either it's tighter or he's getting bigger, but when would he workout? Where? How? I start to imagine him lifting and squatting and grunting and...

"Freezer first," I almost yell instead of saying good morning back like a normal person. Both Dennis and Lucy look at me like I'm losing it.

Which I most definitely am.

But Lucy runs off to the kitchen. I turn and follow. Dennis walks closely behind me. Or maybe it's a normal distance and I'm just hyper aware of him. Even if I shouldn't be. We find Lucy standing in front of the walk-in freezer holding the door open.

'The usual?" I ask her.

"Yeah, but I think let's add sprinkles."

Dennis stops behind me, close enough that I can smell him. "Ice cream for breakfast?" He says in my ear. Or maybe I'm imagining that. I shift away, trying to become one with the freezer door.

"N-no." I'm stammering? *Come on, Kat.* "No. No sugar for breakfast, definitely not on a test day. Or lunch. But we plan out her big after-school super dessert now for something to look forward to."

"Ah."

"For breakfast I think we go Full Sign." Lucy declares.

I smile. "Wow, that hungry, huh?"

"Full sign?" Dennis looks between the two of us.

"It means full out, all the way, like here when—"

I cut my daughter off. "He'll learn when he sees it for himself, Bug."

She deflates. "Okay."

"Why don't you practice ringing up an order for Mr. Dennis?" I say as I start gathering supplies. It cheers her instantly, getting to tap around on the POS screen like an adult.

"It's not coming on," she whines.

"Yeah. It does that." I whack the side of the little black machine that sits under an old iPad. It comes on.

"What'll you have, sir?" Lucy gets serious.

He leans back against the counter where she's fiddling with the iPad, but his eyes watch me. "Hmmm. What's your full sign special this morning?"

"Scrambled eggs and bacon, plus you get hash browns and half a biscuit with butter if you're really hungry. Are you really hungry?"

"Ravenous." The way he says it is... different. But I don't dare look up.

"What's rav... rav..."

He finally looks at her instead of me. "Ra-ven-nous. Desperately hungry. Starving. Might die." I think he's looking at me again by the last word. But I'm busy now, not at all flustered. Only hot because of the burners. "You cook?"

"I told you; I've done everything around here."

"Mommy is a boss. That's what Stella always says. And I thought she was saying Mommy is the boss like in charge, because she is in charge, but then Stella said no, Mommy is *a* boss and she said that means Mommy is awesome at everything."

"Indeed." He takes a few steps into the kitchen that suddenly feels tiny. "Can I help?"

I scoff. "And get bacon grease on your suit?"

"I'll buy another one." He stands next to me, so close our arms are touching. Too close. He's too close.

"Drinks," I say quickly. "You can hit start on the coffee pot, but you won't want that, it's just plain ol' drip. But I'll have some and you can—what, have juice? That'll have to tide you over until you can get a latte or espresso or something. Bug? Can you show him where the OJ is?"

"Yeah," she says, abandoning the iPad.

Again, he's just freaking staring at me. "Are you all right?"

"Yup, just don't want to be late," I say, sounding chipper and squeaky.

He finally leaves my side to help Lucy and start the coffee. When I can feel him headed back into my space, I redirect him.

"Why don't you go sit at a table?"

He frowns.

"That way Lucy can be your waitress."

He nods but he's grumpy about it.

She takes her server job very seriously, only spilling a tiny drop of coffee on the table. Dennis moans about how good the food is but I just shovel the food in. Lucy does, too. Neither of us is a fan of being late.

"'Kay," I say when we've all nearly finished. "Go get your stuff on, quick." She runs off and I stand.

"Are you ever not moving?"

I answer with my mouth full, "I just sat down for a full six minutes to eat. You were there."

He huffs out a grunt of disapproval into his napkin.

I get a barstool set up in an open space between tables. "You ready, Luce?"

"Let's do this," she says in the hall.

Dennis crosses his arms and leans back in his chair. He can't stand not knowing everything.

I wiggle my eyebrows at him. I go behind the bar to where the microphone is. I love the sound system in here and as The Final Countdown starts blaring, I conclude again, yes, it was worth every penny.

Lucy walks slowly, in her slow-motion walk, wearing her backpack underneath a wonder woman cape she's had since she was a toddler. It's worn and faded now, and so is the mask she has on. There are even arm bands that we've managed not to lose this whole time.

I give her my best announcer voice. "Ladies and gentlemen, coming into the ring now, we've got the heavyweight spelling champion of the entire. World. Nay! The entire universe."

She raises her arms and silent screams and Dennis laughs. A real, deep, big laugh that has me forgetting what to say because I can't not stare at him.

His whole face is... he's just... amazing. He looks back at me, expectant.

I inhale and then shake off whatever is wrong with me this morning. "They call her wonder girl. The little lightning Bug. The brainiac. Sixty pounds of pure genius, right here in Deerfield, Arkansas."

She flexes her muscles, still in her hilarious slow mode. Her face is intense.

Dennis cheers as I go on, "She has never met a test she couldn't defeat. Spelling words, be warned. There's nowhere you can run. Nowhere you can hide! Lucy Canton will find you and She. Will. Crush. You!" She breaks slow-mo and runs a victory lap, arms up and I put the mic down to cheer and clap.

Dennis stands up, and claps, even does a fancy loud whistle through his fingers.

Once she's made a full lap and is clearly spent, I fade the music down.

"Did you like it?" she asks Dennis.

"Fucking phenomenal, Lucy," he says, and as she gasps, he laughs again. "I know, jar, I know." He takes some money out.

"No that's the wrong one." Lucy tells him.

"What?"

"That jar is just for Mommy."

He looks at me while he talks to her. "Is that so?"

"Anyway," I say, ignoring him altogether. "You're ready, Luce. We've reviewed every night. You got this. Right?"

"Right."

"'Kay. Let's roll." I walk out from behind the bar. "Miss Ruthie will get this." I gesture at our table full of dishes. "I let the song go a little long. C'mon."

She runs to the door.

"Lucy, get in my car," Dennis calls after her.

The speed with which my child just says okay and changes her path is alarming.

I'm about to object but he steps in *my* path.

He puts his hands on my arms. His hands are on my arms. They cover my biceps completely. His touch is warm and firm and still he smells so minty.

"Let me take her to school?" His eyes plead with me. "Take the twenty minutes. Sit and have a cup of coffee."

Holy hell that sounds amazing. But, what? No. I shake my head.

"She has a whole playlist for tests for the car, and you have to pump her up the whole way and—"

"Katherine," he whispers my name, his voice all crackly. "Let me do this."

"She needs a booster, she's underweight for her age so—"

"I put one in there last night."

"You what?"

He shrugs one shoulder. "You may have wanted to drive it again. She'll be late, just say yes." He squeezes my arms.

"O-okay." I stare up at him, feeling shocked and happy and skeptical and one million things. He's frozen and I am too. "Y-you better go then."

He nods and drops his hands, and I follow him out. Lucy loves the idea of a ride from him and doesn't even insist on a hug or kiss goodbye from me. I am so discombobulated I don't even make a joke about it.

I start to open my mouth to give instructions, but he yells as he gets in his car, "Sit down. Have coffee." Then he slams his door and I watch in awe as they drive away.

In a zombie state, I head back inside and stare at the empty room. I need to clear these plates and make sure Lucy didn't mess up the POS but there are maybe three sips left in my cup. So, I sit.

One sip later, Ruthie walks in. She stops dead in her tracks.

I brace myself.

"Kat Canton. What are you doing, child?"

"Sitting. Feels weird. Feels wrong. Don't love it."

She walks over to me, still shocked. "And who took little Bug to school?"

I stand. "Don't start."

"Oh my Lordy! You let that man take Lucile to school? Are you high?"

"Ruthie..."

Seeing a rare, golden opportunity to tease me mercilessly, she pounces. "Should I call somebody? A doctor. I'm fixin' to call the doctor. Or the news! You've been abducted by the aliens." She follows me as I try to escape with the dirty dishes. "That Elon fella has replaced your brain with his nanos. Are you a robot, Kat? Blink twice if you've been taken over by a robot, honey!" At that she dissolves into laughs and after a full fifteen seconds I join her.

I laugh long and hard and it feels amazing. Then Dennis sends me a text just to let me know she made it to school and was happy as could be when she got out of the car. And that she did not wear her costume in. He even attached a photo of the wonder woman garb gathered in his passenger seat.

It feels like Christmas morning.

Like the best morning ever and that lasts for a couple hours. Until I get another text.

Dennis: Forgot to ask you this morning.
Dennis: I need a gift for Grace. It's her birthday this week.

For reasons I don't want to acknowledge, my mood immediately tanks. Something about the stark contrast between the set of pixels in my palm and our experience this morning. His laugh, his eyes as he begged to help me, his hands on me, squeezing ever so gently.

The response bubbles up in me quickly.

Kat: How does she feel about trucks?

Dennis: Very funny

Dennis: All these bastards will give her the same things, diamonds, cars, villas in the south of France.

Kat: What cheapskates. Poor Grace.

Dennis: You know what I mean

Kat: That Grace is living out every woman's wildest dreams?

Dennis: What?

Kat: What what?

Dennis: Do you want a villa in the south of France?

Kat: Hell no.

Kat: I want you to win this thing and get out of my hair.

Kat: NWA has reached max capacity on billionaire a-holes.

Dennis: OK

Dennis: Any suggestions to help me then?

Kat: Yup, I know exactly what you should do.

Kat: This place. Local art studio. The blown glass figurines are famous and they're blue. Perfect for you. There's one that has two birds together.

Kat: Make sure it comes in the store's gift wrap.

Kat: [Link]

Dennis: It's only $25

Kat: Exactly.

Dennis: Stella is right, you know.

Kat: ?

Dennis: You are good at everything.

I ignore the effect that last text has on me. My eyes are stinging because I'm exhausted. My hands are shaking because my muscles ache from working on the A-Frame the last couple hours. That's all this is.

Kat: I know. [shrug emoji]
Dennis: Good.

I slap my hands up to my face and massage my eyes in a way that will leave me looking like a sad raccoon. Because I am having all the feels about a man who is currently buying a birthday gift for another woman. A woman he hopes to marry.

A woman who is sophisticated and put together. Grace Rockford isn't just wealthy, she emits, well, grace. Just seeing her walk through the market the other day, it was like she was floating.

I need a queen, Kit Kat. You understand.

No. I have spent years getting over all that crap. I'm not digging it up and rehashing it now. I'm so close to all the things I've worked for that this is plain ol' stupid.

I am not going to get off track because of a man, past or present. All they do is swing in from the rafters with grand promises they don't keep and amazing ideas they can't deliver.

No. This morning was fun, and I want more of that. That's all this is.

Tonight's going to be a Full Sign night.

And I am going to have some freaking fun.

16

"Got a lake crowd coming in since it was almost warm today. I think all the stars are linin' up, Boss," Stella says to me at around nine at night.

"Stella, we make the stars line up," I joke. I'm doing this thing whether we have a hot crowd or not.

I didn't tell Dennis I'm bartending. He's a smart guy. I'm sure he put two and two together when I told him my mom would have Lucy for the whole afternoon and night and we'd be skipping her tutoring for the week. I think that was part of why Luce wanted him at our spelling test pre-game session, since she wasn't going to see him tonight.

I'm not going to fixate on why she's so attached to him and what that might mean about the kind of male roles lacking in her life. There are only a couple weeks until her big state tests anyway. Then our weird arrangement will be over.

It has to be.

"Does that mean you want me to post to our stories that it's a sing-a-long kind of night?" Stella asks the next time she breezes by.

"Not yet. Maybe at ten?"

"You got it."

"You're the best." I smile as I get a couple a wine and a beer. Letting my staff tackle social media was one of the best things I changed in the last couple years. The girls like posting and I like not obsessing over every caption and angle and graphic.

I actually got the idea from Sadie who said she had three different social media assistants for her personal author accounts alone.

Sadie.

Dennis' ex-fiancée.

This is all so *effing* weird.

Well, wait. No. Because there is no this. Not really.

So what if I texted Dennis a few local ideas for wooing his bride-to-be? Sadie wouldn't care. My family might think the tutoring thing is weird but not if they know it's actually helping Lucy. She comes first.

It's not a thing.

I turn up the music and try to focus on the drinks I'm pouring instead of my thoughts. It's still early so I haven't switched to my playlists, but this satellite station has a good vibe to it. Business stays steady and I let my very excited server post the teaser to our social accounts a few minutes early.

I've no sooner told her to pull the trigger than I sense him, like that scene at the beginning of Mary Poppins. Like he's brought a storm through the front door with him. I glance up and see his pissed off expression as he strides through the restaurant.

Yup. Storm.

"Where is your phone?"

"Hi, Dennis, how's it going?" I say while filling a stein with beer. We have to talk loud over the crowd. That's a good thing.

"Katherine."

"*Dennis.* It's in the office."

He stands in the tiny space between the bar and the side walkway through to the kitchen. He's too tall for the little opening. When he puts his hands on his hips, he's literally in the way.

"I thought you agreed to tell me the next time there was a singing thing?"

I square myself to him and I don't miss that he quickly looks me up and down. When I changed into my pearl snap earlier, I put my hair in braids and added more dramatic eye make-up than usual. Black shirt with black frayed daisy dukes. I added a studded belt and fishnets tonight, with black cowboy boots instead of my usual combat platforms.

I straighten my spine. "Hey, looks like tonight might be a singing thing night. There, I told you."

"I want to talk to you." He looks around at the hubbub.

I smirk at him over my shoulder and challenge him. "Then grab a rag."

Some emotion flashes over his face for a second, like maybe he's going to run and tackle me just to shut me up. But in the next moment I see him give in with a half-grin. He takes off his jacket to reveal a vest today, of course, and looks for a place to hang it.

"Oh geez. You're hopeless. Come on." I leave my post. "Five, Otis!"

"Yup," he says from the other end of the bar.

"Five what?" Dennis doesn't move out of my way.

"Minutes, so I can get you ready for your shift." I gesture behind his big frame. "Go to the office."

He turns and follows my instructions. But once he walks into the office, he stops. Right. I should have thought about this.

"It's organized disorganization. Don't start." I storm past him to the locker on the side of the room. I pull out a hanger. "You're going to want to ditch the vest too. You can put them in here."

He starts unbuttoning his vest. "You're serious, you want me to tend bar?"

"Yes." I suppress a laugh. "Or else how will you know not to ever say *tend bar* again in your life?"

He rolls his eyes but seems almost happy. Excited maybe? No. Probably not. Except I bet he does love a challenge.

I realize I'm just standing watching him undress, so I turn back to the metal cabinet. "You could put on an apron or a Roadside polo, I think we have a couple spare in—"

"This is fine. You act like I've never soiled a shirt before."

I turn to grab the hanger. "Do me a favor, when you do spill all over your shirt, which you will, will you yell out, *Oh, the horror, I've soiled my shirt!*"

"Funny." He starts to unbutton his sleeves.

Aaand that's my cue. I'm not going to get trapped here watching his arm porn. Because I'm a sucker for forearms and I will stare and possibly start drooling.

"Ok, see you behind the counter. I'll be the one tending bar." I grab my phone from the desk and take a few quick steps to the door.

"Wait," he says and I turn back in the doorway. "What's this?"

Oh.

Crap. I should move this thing. But I don't really have anywhere else to put it.

"That's my vision board. It's hokey, I know, but it keeps me focused."

He steps toward the worn little loveseat that sits under the big cork board. He points. "And this?"

"Just an idea," I say quickly, before he can start trying to figure out where my dream house is and how to buy it for me. "For someday."

"And everything else? What do these mean?" He looks way too closely at what is basically soul vomit, my very dreams and hopes and insecurities—hence the multiple images of women in crowns—all in one three-foot rectangle. Moms and daughters, women relaxed enough to sit by a rainy window and read, recipes, packaging, and a new black truck that is eerily similar to the one sitting in the back lot right now. There are butterflies, symbols, colors, lots of random stuff.

"My plan. All the things I want to do, feel, be. A million random ideas that only make sense to my brain, that is, as you've said, disturbed. C'mon." I rush out of the room, but he follows after, still rolling his sleeves.

"I never said that."

I ignore him. Otis is slammed, so I immediately jump in.

"What can I get ya?" I ask the girl waiting.

"Two margaritas please, Patron?"

"Sure, sugar. Is salt okay?"

"Yeah!"

I turn to Dennis. "You heard her, two top shelf margaritas."

He freezes. The terror on his face is so hysterical and endearing I immediately let him off the hook.

"I'm kidding!" I talk while I start the drinks. "Otis and I will make the drinks. I'll yell to you if it's a can or a bottle you can grab from the fridge. Or wine, you can pour wine, right?"

He glares.

"Just don't over-pour, or a bunch of the women will be drunk before showtime." I shake the margaritas. "You can also restock the glasses as we go. Wipe them down as they are brought out from the kitchen." I look behind him at the clean towels. He grabs one, eyes a little wide as he watches me salt the glasses and pour. I smile at him and yell behind me, "Number one rule for a bar trainee, Otis?"

"Don't get in the way."

I look down at the billionaire's expensive, blindingly bright white shirt as I add the limes. "Just watch out and remember what to say when you spill on your shirt."

"Uh huh."

A few seconds after Dennis starts wiping glasses as a big group comes in. I recognize quite a few faces, college kids who must've been nearby, frequent campers, some of Otis's club, and marina employees. Clearly people were on the lookout for Stella's post.

This is going to be epic. I should do the social media thing every time, even when Stella isn't here to remind me. I pull out my phone and voice-memo a text to myself.

The rest of the hour flies by and to my surprise, Dennis is actually trying. He maneuvers around us and starts to get drinks.

"Two Pino Grigio's, three Guinness. And it's eleven, Kat," Stella calls out.

"Need some limes down here," Otis yells.

"Limes, Dennis," I say, really enjoying bossing him around.

Dennis spins in a full circle, getting stressed. "Where are the limes?"

"Right there."

"Hey, you're Dennis DeLane!" A guy says from a barstool.

I smile. "He is. What can he get you?"

"Three Buds please."

"Got that, Dennis?"

"I still haven't found the limes, damn it!"

All the regulars who know the rule about myself and the staff, to my delight, yell out "Jar!"

Dennis quickly gets the three beers and pushes them to his fan across the counter.

"Where are those wines, y'all?" Stella asks Dennis, also thoroughly enjoying this.

"Dude, this is Bud Light."

Dennis pulls on the back of his neck. "Bloody hell, I'll pay for them."

"Nice!"

I turn to get the wine bottles out, brushing against a stalled Dennis as I do. "Gonna be an expensive night if you do that."

"I'm good for it," Dennis grouses.

"Hear that, ya'll? If fancy man here messes up your order, he's buying!"

Everyone cheers. At this point, the regulars have crowded around the bar. They know the drill. I get my phone, pull up a playlist, and hand it to Dennis.

"Here, get this connected to the Roadhouse Main Bluetooth please."

He does so, then stares at my phone. I move around him and Otis glares at both me and Dennis, annoyed we're slowing him down. But I know Dennis is reading the song titles and I'm interested in his thoughts. Finally, he asks me about it.

"Lot more oldies than I thought. And is this Disney on here? A bunch of grown men are going to sing Lion King?"

"Lion Sleeps," I say and then turn to shout at the crowd. "Dennis is doubting my playlist, everybody."

The cries of boos are so loud it shocks me, even though I was ready for it. I look over to see him raise his arms in surrender.

"So, what's the big number, *Don't Stop Believing*?"

I shrug. "Too long, too slow. You'll see. Two Cab Savs, please, barkeep."

Dennis turns but it's honestly like he's in slow motion compared to me and Otis.

He looks up to the ceiling speakers, just desperate to know how and what, and every single detail. "And this now, these aren't the singalongs?"

I sigh. "Watch, by 11:40 people will be singing without the sign."

"Where's the bloody sign?"

I reach around him for a glass. "Just wait and see, Dennis."

"Why can't—" He lifts his hands and turns to get out of my way and slips just barely on an ice chip. He recovers quickly but still, it's enough to fulfill my rock-solid prophecy. Red wine is all over his shirt. He immediately locks eyes with me, and even though he's got his jaw clenched, I think he's fighting a smile.

I raise my eyebrows.

He shakes his head.

"I'll consider buying the truck from youuu," I sing-song at him.

He turns to face the crowd, spreads his stance and unbelievably, yells at the top of his lungs, "Oh the horror! I've soiled my damn shirt!"

"JAR!" The whole bar yells back.

I die.

I'm dying.

I have to bend over I'm laughing so hard.

Dennis pulls yet another bill from his wallet and shoves it in the jar and the crowd cheers again. He turns to face me, chin jutting out and brow furrowed.

"That was"—I can't contain myself—"the best thing"—I snort—"I've ever seen."

"Oh yeah?" He charges at me, wrapping me in a bear hug before I can even blink.

"Ah, you're soaked!"

"Mhmm. Thanks to you, you little lunatic." He doesn't let go, and I'm still laughing, not hugging back just... being held for a second.

I pull back to look up at him, and he looks down at me, his eyes wrinkled up on the sides.

"Uh, Kat?" Stella says, knocking us out of whatever that was and back into the mayhem.

"Sorry." I turn and get back to taking orders. Dennis sticks to just beers, and he gets a little faster. Otis and I are back into a blazing rhythm of pouring, salting shaking, stirring, slicing.

"Howdy, Kat." I hear Beau yell over the din. People have already started singing, currently the song is *You've Lost that Loving Feeling.*

"Hey, honey," I yell, not looking up from the lemon drop martinis I'm mixing. "Be my knight in shining armor and grab two more cases of Shiner for me?"

He doesn't reply but I know that's because he's already on the move. He knows his way around.

"Where you want 'em, little lady?" Beau smiles.

Dennis does a double take at him, then glares at me, then back.

"Beau, Dennis. Dennis, Beau. Will you put those in the fridge please?" I say to Dennis. Dennis is staring me down, but I don't have time to deal with whatever is happening on his face.

"C'mon Kat," someone yells from the thick crowd. "It's eleven-thirty!"

"Ehhhh, I don't know..." I play along but within seconds they start chanting "Sign! Sign! Sign!" So, I give in. I nod at Otis, who flips a switch down on his end of the wall.

The bar explodes.

Dennis leans over to see the neon sign.

Everybody Sings or Nobody Drinks

"That's it, that's the sign?" Dennis asks, smirking.

"Nope." I call back, reaching down for some shot glasses.

"What do you mean?" He yells.

"I mean that's not the sign! Just watch, baby." I don't think about it as it slips out. I just say it. I'm pouring shots and people are singing loudly now to *Sweet Caroline*.

"What did you just say?" He gets closer to me; his voice different. But I'm leaning forward to hear an order from a girl a few stools down. "Katherine. Stop. What did you say?" He's smiling and he...

He has his hands on my hips.

I move to push his hands away but feel his wrist.

"What is—" I ask, looking down. At least five bright rainbow elastic bracelets, next to a watch that probably cost almost as much as the new truck out back. A bunch of pink and blue, and one solid black.

"From Lucy," he says.

I barely hear it over the singing and talking.

"And you're wearing them?"

"Of course, she made them for me."

I look up at him. I'm caught, trapped, transfixed.

His eyes are different, like he's pleading with me. One hand is a little lower and I feel his pinky finger on my thigh. That tiny bit of contact, his fingertip grazing my fishnets, the bracelets, his open expression... Crap. It's enough for me to shut down the bar and mount him like a derby jockey right this second. But the crowd is losing their mind, watching the wall.

Plus, Stella is back. "We goin' all the way tonight?"

"No, just the one," I answer her, but I'm looking up at Dennis who is still watching me, holding me.

"D? What the hell are you doing, mate?" A British accent cuts through the noise.

"Dennis?" A woman's voice follows.

Dennis turns toward the sound then I watch him blink a couple times and his grip loosens. I jump backwards, realizing who the voices belong to. I follow his line of sight, then glance back at him.

Dennis looks down at his shirt, embarrassed. Then he wipes, using his pants to clean his hands, the ones that were just gripping me. His voice is even different when he finally answers.

"Grace, uh, hello."

17

"DeLane, what is this?" Beside Grace and Benedict are two more of the Great Grace Race contestants. They all look shiny and fresh and do not at all match the already-tipsy crowd around them.

"He got the bad end of a deal." I smile, saving him from all the awkward.

"Kat? So, this is where you've been hiding? Come here!" Benedict, Ben to his friends, is genuinely excited as he rushes around to the side of the bar. I haven't seen him since Samantha's big wedding. Dennis moves out of my way, a bit dazed.

Grace and the other men join Ben at the end of the bar. Emerson's doppelgänger brother reaches down and picks me up into a big, raised hug. Dennis clears his throat behind me.

I catch Grace's eyes bouncing around between the three of us.

"Grace, this is Katherine Canton the manager of the Inn I was telling you about," Dennis says loudly.

"Yes, your client's daughter?" Grace extends an elegant hand to me.

I take it and open my mouth to respond but Ben interrupts.

"Always so serious, just like my wanker brother. This girl is family." Ben puts me in a chokehold like we're kids. "My brother's cousin. She's like our little sister."

"Oh, lovely to meet you," she says, her voice all light and buttery. No Arkansas accent to be found. "I'm Grace Rockford."

"What you are"—I break free from Ben's hold—"Is great for business. I bet a whole team of groupies followed y'all in so thanks for coming!"

She shakes her head, bashful. Graceful. Ugh.

The crowd starts calling for me, only a few minutes to go.

"Excuse me, it's about to blow up like a bad fried turkey in here."

"I heard about this, free drinks at midnight?" Ben asks.

I point to the sign. "Only if you all sing. Don't spoil the fun. Even you, *Dennis*," I spit his name as I shrink back into the bar. He starts to follow. "No, go with them out there, so you can really experience it."

He looks torn for a second, but his posse is calling for him. He leaves, disappearing into the mob of happy customers, most of whom are singing already.

Stella rushes around behind the bar. "So, just *Hooked on a Feeling?*"

"Change of plans. We're doing both."

She squeaks with excitement. "Are you going to pour tonight?"

I hesitate. She knows the only reason I am pausing is because we have a handful of fancy people here, so she huffs in disgust. She looks to our regulars who are watching us frantically prepare pitchers and gather liquor bottles as we talk. Stella digs out the microphone before I can stop her.

"Allll right everybody you know the rules. Everybody sings or no body drinks. Sing to your gal and if you don't have a gal, sing to us. And, if y'all really sing your guts out, maybe we can get Kat to pour tonight!"

All of our friends and favorite customers yell their heads off as Stella turns the music up. The whole crowd looks up at the wall, wailing the "*oogachacka*" lyrics as loud as they can.

Rebecca comes to grab a pitcher, along with one more new-ish gal who hasn't been able to clock out yet because we're that busy.

Which is amazing.

My great-money-night-high is fading though.

I don't look to find Dennis and Grace and their group. I'm sure this looks like a bunch of hillbilly backwater nonsense, like each of us is the bad 90s movie version of country folk—barn-raised, missing teeth and struggling with a drinking problem.

But when have I ever given a flying f—*care* about what people think?

These are my friends, my neighbors. They work hard and about once a month or so we play hard here together. Otis and I serve the last couple drinks before we pause the bar for the big pour. My fellow bartender turns into a bouncer, watching the crowd.

I hear Stella ask Beau for a ride, breaking Ethan's heart. Rebecca hops on the shoulders of her boyfriend, and Ginger, the new girl, climbs up onto Ethan. At certain lyrics, the guys at the bar sing to me, and I raise a hand to my ear and smile wide.

Toward the end of the song, the guys nearby start yelling my name in a chant I'm pretty sure Stella started. She and Becca and Ginger are on their male chariots, standing against the wall, pitchers in hand. Otis lines up additional pitchers along the bar, because they'll be empty quick. Even though the patrons nearby are chanting my name, they're looking up.

The tail end of the song winds down and I yell out, "Clear those barstools for me, y'all!" Everyone cheers again and *Pretty Woman* starts. The crowd is really insane, louder than maybe

I've ever heard them and then I nod to Otis. He flips the switch and the custom neon sign glows bright.

SINGERS DRINK FOR FREE

Holy crap.

Now they're louder than I've ever heard them.

And they're still chanting my name up at the front.

Otis gives me a hand up onto the first barstool with a bottle of tequila in one hand and a vodka in the other, both with our tight spouts. I'll pour a lot of free liquor out but each person only really gets a little less than a shot's worth.

When the lyrics start, we move. Everyone is singing to us, hands raised. Shot glasses, beer steins, wine glasses, up and ready. I walk slowly from stool to stool, able to easily pour from up here on the raised makeshift walkway. The girls are guided around on the guys' shoulders, pouring as they go.

I wobble a bit and people reach out to steady me and the stool.

Because, honestly, I'm not really walking.

I'm strutting, dancing, goading them to sing louder. I pour into mouths, I take a shot of vodka myself, and I put on a really fun, sloppy show. I have to lean to get the people a few rows deep into the crowd, and whoever is close, props up my legs for me like I'm about to crowd surf. When people aren't singing, whistling, or hollering my name, they chug or shoot the booze, then raise their glasses again.

I reach back with an empty bottle and Otis swaps it out. The girls circle around to drop empty beer pitchers on the counter and Otis hands them up fresh ones. Beau already has beer on his shoulders, but he doesn't care. He almost always drinks for free here anyway. He sings up to me as they get situated and I pour a shot into his mouth.

Then they're off again. Girls in the crowd get huge pours compared to the guys, so they don't mind that their men are serenading us. They sing too. New guests file in at the last second, and they find empty used glasses from tables to join in. Gross but fine by me.

It's three minutes of free alcohol and total mayhem. And it's made my little bar and Inn low-key famous.

I continue to strut and smile, never looking for the billionaires. I'm sure they're watching me wade through an ocean of hands and empty glasses.

Alcohol spills everywhere, on arms, faces, down my legs, all over my hands. It's a mess. But a flirty, crazy, sexy mess. At least, I think so. I'm sure I'm smudgy and sweaty too but with thirty dudes singing *Pretty Woman* to me with considerable gusto, I feel pretty good.

When the song ends, I take a bow, and the hollering continues. We make a show of pouring the last of what's left in our grip out to everyone still cheering.

Otis hands me the mic. "Give it up for our chariots tonight; Beau, Ethan, uh, boyfriend guy, you guys come get some shots. Everybody else, order your next round before we start running out of your favorites!" More cheers. I walk back along the barstools as the next song starts. I made sure the next track was *The Lion Sleeps Tonight*, just to show Dennis the magic.

Sure enough, people are still singing. The signs are off now, but people are beyond tipsy at this point. Otis stays vigilant about cutting people off as necessary, so I don't mind.

At the last barstool, I turn to quickly scan the room for them. I just have to know. Did he have fun? Is he impressed? Disgusted? A little shocked or a lot shocked?

I glance around and see Ben, standing and clapping. The other guys are there, but not Dennis. He's gone and so is Grace. They left.

He left.

All that about wanting to be here, wanting to see it, and he bails? What the hell? Why would he do that? Maybe it was too loud. Too uncivilized. Too dirty. The floors are sticky, people are packed in so tight we're all touching shoulders. Maybe Grace was grossed out.

Still, would he really just go, without a word?

And why are my eyes stinging at the thought of that. Without looking away from Ben's booth I let a pair of hands grab me and gently place me on the ground. They don't let go even after my feet hit the floor. I snap my head around, thinking maybe it's Dennis.

It's not.

"Hey, Kit Kat."

18

"He wants to go to lunch, can you believe it?"

"Yes," Tran says, both of us talking quietly as the girls play on the playground in front of us. "Because he saw you chumming it up with a billionaire, then watched your bar explode into song, at you. I mean, I watched the whole thing on someone's livestream. It looked epic, Kat."

I smile a little bit. "It was. It was probably the best Friday night we've had in years, and…"

"And what?"

I don't want to say, *and Dennis missed it.* Why am I still thinking about stupid Dennis? I've got new problems. Well, old problems, back again.

"And then *he* showed up in my face. He offered to stay and help clean. To clean Tran!"

"Are you going to go? To lunch?"

I tug on the edge of my vintage t-shirt. "I mean, shouldn't I at least hear him out?"

She tilts her head one way, then the other, considering. Finally, she asks, "Have you asked the High Council?"

I chuckle. "Are you a *Stories of Loya* person too?"

"Every person is a *Stories of Loya* person. I can't believe you haven't read them."

I gesture around, "During all my free time? When I do have a spare second, I feel like I need to read Sadie's backlist of books I'm way behind on, or one of the many bestsellers by other authors she's sent me for free over the years. I think I have every single-mom-rom-com ever published stuffed into the shelves of the office."

"I get it. But your cousins. Have you asked them?" I shake my head. She bumps her leg into mine where we sit on the back of a park bench. "Because you know what they'll say."

"That he's a slimy a-hole who doesn't deserve the time of day. But this is Spencer we're talking about."

"Yeah. The one guy you get all weird around."

I huff. "I do not."

"He messed you up, Kat. If you decide to hear him out, how can you do it without opening yourself up to all of that all over again?"

"I don't know. But I think I want to try. For her."

"And what about the chummy billionaire?"

My heart starts to race suddenly. As if I have something to hide? Maybe I should take up cardio like Skye keeps saying. For mental calm or whatever.

I school my features. "What about him?"

"What about him? Kat, a billionaire who is trying to win the hand of another billionaire was bartending at your little bar at midnight on a Friday night in the middle of nowhere, Arkansas. What. The. Hell."

I laugh. "Yeah, that does sound crazy. I'm helping him out. He's my cousin-in-law's best friend."

"Samantha's husband, right?"

We both pause to pretend to be amazed at the girls' cartwheels as if we haven't seen them do these one hundred times a day since they were four.

"Amazing, Bug!" I call out then lower my voice again. "Right. He wanted help getting the lay of the land here locally, to win over Grace, and in return, he's tutoring Lucy in math."

"Wait, Samantha's husband's best friend, so, isn't he the older guy, the one who was engaged to Sadie?"

"The very same."

"Ah, okay. So, nothing romantic could happen there anyway. You looked cute together last night but that'd be weird."

Again, I have to keep my face still and my heart calm. I'm not sure I succeed. I need to text Skye and ask if there is a Running For Beginners app or something. My lack of cardiovascular health is ridiculous.

"Yup," I manage to say.

We let the girls run around for almost an hour before I call it. I have a few errands before checking in a couple guests at the Inn.

As we watch our kids run to the car, Tran turns to me. "Text your cousins. About Spence. They were there, I wasn't."

I sigh and nod. She's right.

When we pull into a spot for grocery delivery, I get out my phone.

Kat: So, everybody stay calm, but...

I wait, already snickering. Here it comes.

Sam: ?!?!?
Sam: YOU ARE EVIL! WHAT IS IT!!!
Susan: I agree!
Kat: LOL. It's so easy.
Kat: Well, I have been asked out to lunch.
Sadie: You've piqued my interest!
Skye: Same.
Sally: By whom?

Kat: ...Spencer [anxious emoji]
Sam: WHAT! NO!
Sadie: [thumbs down emoji]
Skye: I hope you told him to [middle finger emoji]
Sally: Context, please.
Susan: I agree on all counts. Context?
Kat: It was a killer night at the bar, and he just showed up. Said he wanted to talk. Offered to stay late and help clean and close. So weird.
Sam: He is the worst!!! When was the last time he came sniffing around?
Kat: Few years ago, when there were rumors I'd bought Roadside.
Skye: You mean another time when you were crushing it!
Sadie: You know the rule: if you're not with me on the bus, you don't get a seat in the limo. I'm with Skye [middle finger emoji]
Sally: Agreed.
Sam: Totally!
Sadie: You knew this is what we would say.
Kat: I did, and the big question is this: What about Lucy?

A couple of them start typing and then stop. It's Susan who comes through first.

Susan: Hear him out. But only for her. Not you. [heart emoji]

All of them like her comment.
I open a different text thread.

Kat: Quick question. Did you see this? [Link]
Janie: I did, I follow like three people and Roadside is one of them! So fun!
Sally: No but I have been buried underneath piles of text-books and sheet music.

Kat: But this, specifically...

I attach a screenshot of me and Dennis from the livestream. It's the last moment we had before his gang of moguls showed up. His hands are on my hips and my hand is on his stack of bracelets and he's looking down at me like, well, I suppose it could just look like two bartender friends laughing.

But it's not. It was a moment. When my heart jumped, and my skin burned, and my smile was huge and real.

Sally: Explain.
Janie: Explain immediately!
Kat: It's weird, I know, but he's helping Lucy with math and I'm helping him win over Grace.
Kat: I've been texting him places for dates, gift ideas, then showing him around out here in the sticks
Kat: Bartending was like homework for him to take the massive stick out of his butt.
Kat: We're friends. It's fine for me to be friends with Dennis, right?
Janie: I have no idea.
Sally: I think so, Emerson has always said Dennis is like a brother to him, and Emerson is family.
Kat: True.
Janie: Is that what we're looking at, though, a snapshot of two family friends? Because...
Janie: [one eyebrow raised gif]
Sally: ?
Kat: Barely friends. Not even. He drives me crazy while constantly calling me insane. He's really great with Lucy, though.
Janie: Then why, dear friend, did you send only us this text???
Janie: [one eyebrow raised gif]

Kat: Because it looks how it looks! I see it. But it's just a fraction of a second where we were laughing instead of rolling our eyes at each other and someone caught it on camera. Right after this he pissed me off and I am not even talking to him right now.

Janie: What did he do?

Kat: Billionaire stick-butt stuff. The point is, I didn't want the Sister Squad all up in a tizzy over it. I don't think any of them saw or they would've asked, probably. Right?

Sally: Definitely Skye would have.

Janie: For sure.

Kat: Okay. Let's keep this *at the single's table.*

They both like my last message, a code phrase that means *this stays between the three of us.* Skye and Janie are still super close, but Skye is married and traveling all the time now.

I hope Janie is happy to have a few more Cantons in her life. I think she needed us, as she tends to go into hermit mode for weeks at a time and Skye is too hermit-like herself to intervene.

Lucy and I get our groceries, sing Disney songs all the way home, and get everything unloaded into the Roadside's kitchen. I get her set up with some dinner in the office while I get guests checked in at the Inn desk. I stick around to work on some record keeping and after a while Lucy joins me in the lobby with her tablet and headphones. It's quiet, peaceful even.

Until I feel him do the Mary Poppins thing again. This time his breeze rushes in from the hallway that connects to the grill side. I guess he's quite comfortable just showing himself around now.

He storms up to me, prickly as ever. "Why do you even own a phone?"

"Hey Dennis, how are you?"

He just makes an impatient face.

"I put it on silent at some point. The notifications from Instagram were driving me nuts."

"You know you can set it so some contacts can still call, even while your phone is set on do not disturb?"

I snort. "Of course, I know that. You didn't make the cut, dude."

"Mr. Dennis!" Lucy throws herself at him, abandoning her tablet and headphones on the little couch.

"Lucy! Last night was rubbish without our lesson. How was the spelling test?"

I inhale slowly. This is fine. It's normal for a tutor to take a vested interest in their pupil. Lucy is his pupil. Just like I'm *his client's daughter. Like a kid sister.* That's it.

When they've chatted for a minute, he dismisses her to turn back to me. She goes back to her device, humming as she goes. Dang, she really loves him. Ugh!

"Kat, last night was—"

"Epic!" I take over this conversation. Because I don't want to have it. I don't want to accidentally go off on him for leaving, demand to know where he was, rant about how he hurt my feelings. Double Ugh!

We're not talking about any of that. Especially since I'm suddenly Kat again, not Katherine. When did that happen?

I go on, talking fast, "You bartending was huge online, I probably owe you a big fat commission. What did Grace think?"

I think saying her name physically hurt my throat. Something is definitely happening in my esophagus. I ignore it. Dennis is grimacing, probably because I'm making a face due to the throat thing. I try to calm my features.

"She thought it was incredible, of course. We all did. Listen, I want to talk to you. Can I take you to lunch? Tomorrow?"

"Tomorrow, we have church."

"Monday, then."

I let out a shocked giggle. "In a very weird turn of events, I actually have lunch plans already on Monday."

His head jerks back as if he was just slapped. "With whom?"

"Your Mom," I say like a child. He sighs and I look at my screen, getting back to work. Or pretending to, that is. I lift a shoulder. "I'll have to get back to you about later in the week."

"No. Tuesday." I start to protest, but his voice changes. "Please. A half hour."

"Fine." I go back to my fake clicking on the computer.

"Have you eaten?"

I don't answer.

"It's almost eight. Did you have any dinner?" I open my mouth and he adds, "A handful of fries don't count."

"I had chicken, Dennis." It's not a lie. I had one handful of fries and one handful of chicken tenders. He just watches me. "I need to get this done and put her to bed so…"

"So, Tuesday."

"Fine." I continue staring a hole into the computer monitor.

He stares, waits, slumps where he stands, but he doesn't push me. He gestures to Lucy instead.

"Goodnight darling girl. Go straight to sleep for your mum, yeah?"

She yawns. "I will."

"Brilliant." I see him glare at me out of my peripheral vision, but I maintain my position. After yet another sigh, he leaves.

When the door shuts, I throw my head in my hands.

Because this is just great.

First, he messes up my excitement over the biggest Friday night ever, then he barges in on a lovely, calm Saturday evening, and now I have to dread whatever he has planned in two days. I have no idea what he might want to discuss, but I'm certain it'll make me angry.

That's good. Mad is fine.

Mad is better than whatever I'm feeling right now.

Not to mention Spencer.

I am tied up in knots all night. And all day on Sunday into Sunday night. But Monday morning, one call turns everything upside down.

Turns out I won't be making it to either lunch date.

19

Kat: WTF exactly did you teach my daughter, Dennis?!?!

He calls instead of sending a reply. I'm surprised how fast he responds during what I'm sure is a busy Monday morning for him.

"Seriously, Dennis, what did you guys do in your lessons, Lucy wouldn't go into details other than to say I'd see when she got her grade." My voice is a wobbly mess. I shouldn't have answered the phone.

"What's wrong?"

Why is it that whenever I want to keep it together, a simple act of concern from someone will make me fall apart? Am I that starved for kindness? That desperate for someone to give a rip about me and my little life? I inhale and try to keep my voice steady. "Nothing. Never mind."

"Where are you?"

"You don't—"

"Katherine. You know I will look everywhere, just tell me."

I sniff. "I'm at the stupid school, but—"

"Don't move. I mean it."

He hangs up and I just stand there in the bright white and gray hallway. I stare down at the sparkly linoleum floors in shock, breathing in a mix of smells: cleaning supplies and frier grease and glue sticks. I suck in the stinky air because I need to get a grip. I don't want the bitches in the office next to me to see me lose it. More importantly, I don't want Lucy to see me get any more emotional than I already have.

There is very little that can prepare a mother for this. Seeing her child weep, and not because of a scraped knee or a dropped ice cream. Because of a deep wound, a real hurt.

I hate this. Feeling powerless and confused about how best to help. I want to burn the world to the ground for her, but also step back and let her learn and grow on her own. I have to be her safe place while also disciplining, molding, teaching.

Daggum it, I'm tired.

She pops out from the office with her things. I can't talk. She can't either. I grab her hand and we start our journey down the hall to the security doors. Her backpack jingles in the silence with a million keychains. By the time we reach the interior set of double doors I can see Dennis outside, rushing up the steps.

His face looks beyond agitated or curious, he's almost distraught. Again, the sight of him so affected pushes me over the edge.

I sniff, begging my eyes and my chest to last a little longer before any sobs break free.

We step out to meet him and he looks us over, clenching his jaw. I'm sure both of us have splotchy faces and red eyes. We're sniffing and trembling. He locks eyes with me and wordlessly bends down to pick Lucy up. She wraps around him like a tiny koala.

He offers me his hand and I take it.

I'm too worked up to care about how this looks right this second, what it means or doesn't mean. Who Dennis is to us in this moment. I just want to climb into his Audi and close off the rest of the world.

I guess he senses that desire because he leads us straight to his car and opens both passenger doors. I get in while he sets Lucy down in the back. When he climbs in, he sighs, his breath choppy, just like mine and Lucy's.

Once we get moving, I sit up straight. "Lucy, why don't you tell Mr. Dennis what you did today?"

Her voice is tiny in the back seat. "I punched Cruz Regan in the face."

I glare at our driver, happy to have someone to be angry at. "She had a pop quiz this morning. Math."

Dennis looks between me and Lucy in the rear-view mirror, confused.

"Didn't go very well. Whatever you guys have been working on, she says she couldn't do it. I don't even know what that means. But what I do know, is she got teased and then"—I turn and look back at her—"Instead of talking about our big feelings, or asking for help, or just walking away like I taught her, she hit a kid. She hit someone, Dennis!"

The man next to me apparently wants to flirt with death today because he smirks.

"Are you *smiling* right now?"

"I feared much worse."

"She's suspended for three days. It's pretty bad!"

He looks over, growing irritated again. "And the little prick that teased her?"

"I'm sure he got a scolding but that was just words, he wasn't the one throwing hands." I slump back in my seat, feeling the weight of failure. "Where are we going? What about the truck? I wasn't even thinking."

"It's fine. Let's just take a moment and regroup. Did you all have lunch already?" He looks down at my legs that are exposed, because I'm wearing a dress. On a Monday. If he's fishing for information about my date, I'm not giving it to him. I cancelled on Spencer the second the school called.

"Lucy just ate, it was recess after lunch when it happened. I didn't, but I can't eat right now." He grunts in understanding and Lucy whimpers behind me. I take in a deep breath, and I notice Dennis does too.

"What exactly did he say?"

"Wait." I stop him from going there. "I want to know what happened with the test, the math, because that is what started it, right, Bug?"

"Yeah," she says, barely talking above a whisper.

"All right, so what happened?" I look between my child and Dennis.

He clears his throat. "Lucile made up a cheer. A couple different routines. To memorize her math facts."

"She did?" I turn. "You did?" That is a really good idea. *Why didn't I think of that?* "How come I haven't seen it? When did you practice it?"

"You're always working, Mommy."

My stomach takes a sharp turn like the road we're currently on. The guilt is so real, I have to put a hand on my stomach. Good thing it's empty.

Lucy goes on. "And I wanted to surprise you with the hard ones, like eights and nines. But then today was the surprise quiz and I couldn't remember, I was trying to move my arms to think through the moves and say the chant, and Mrs. Henderson kept telling me to sit still," her little voice gets frantic. "But I was sitting still it was just my arms! I didn't get up out of my chair once!"

Dennis huffs, "You're not allowed to get up during a test?"

"She can't disrupt the whole class."

"What kind of fancy school doesn't have provisions? Exceptions? Standing desks? What's the point of private education if not for flexibility, creativity?"

I huff this time. "Fancy schools care about grades. Period."

We pull off the main road that will eventually lead to the Roadside and dead end at the edge of the lake. I figured he found a rental around here and I was right. The lake view houses are huge and nice but all kind of log cabiny. I wonder if that's his vibe—an old money lodge. I also wonder why I am going to his place right now.

We pull up to a big house that looks exactly like I predicted. Stone, wood, huge windows, probably four levels of balcony on the back. I'm sure it has a pool and even though we're up in the hills, I'm positive there's a boat and dock that comes with the house.

"Come on. There's a pool, sauna, library, theater room—"

Lucy gasps. "Can we swim? Can we watch a movie?"

"No, Bug. You're grounded. You can read in the library while I talk to Mr. Dennis. Then we're going home."

"Okay," she says as we get out. She looks like she is filled with guilt.

I know the feeling all too well. I watch Dennis as he leads us into the house but can't quite read how he's feeling. He doesn't seem agitated at this particular moment. Refreshing.

We follow him into the entryway which has high ceilings and an antler chandelier. There is a grand split staircase leading up to a balcony overlooking the front door.

Lucy bounds up the steps. "Wow! This is the biggest house I've ever seen!"

"Luce!" I call after her. "You can't just run wild!"

Dennis smiles at me and says softly, "She can, though. If she wants."

"I found the library!" she calls back with glee.

I shrug. "Okay, come down if you need something, don't just yell. No electronics. And don't wander around alone."

Ugh, I am such a mom right now. A failing one, at that. My shoulders sag and I look to Dennis, wondering what exactly I am doing here.

"Would you like a tour?"

"Not really. Maybe something to drink."

"Right. This way." He starts forward into a formal sitting area that looks like it could hold monthly hunter meetings. All the mounted heads freak me out. The view out the windows is amazing though. The lake, rolling hills, wide open blue sky.

Off the living room is a big dining area that flows directly into the kitchen. The heavy wood table has twelve overstuffed chairs around it, complete with another antler light. The kitchen is big and updated, but still in browns and greens.

He pulls out a heavy upholstered barstool for me. "Sit."

I look around. "This place is, uh…"

"Bit ghastly, isn't it? But it had the pool, sauna, gym in the basement." He shrugs and turns to get a cup out of a cabinet.

Once his back is to me and we have a lull, a moment without a crisis or conversation or anything at all, I exhale. It's a heavy breath coming from somewhere deep. It brings up a million emotions that were buried, sealed. I put my head in my hands on the counter and shove my palms into my eyes. I don't think that will stop the tears that threaten but it's worth a shot.

"Hey, hey, hey," Dennis says quietly over the sound of his footsteps. I feel his hand on my back, firm and warm, up and down. "Kat, this is not a big deal."

"It is, though!" My voice breaks. "It's me. She is me. After all I've done to keep her from taking on my baggage, the anger, the pain, it's the exact same. I've worked so hard her whole life and then failed. Just like my mom, I'm failing her."

"Katherine, look at me." His voice is rough, and my body is frozen. I don't want to move my palms from my eyes. "Look at me." Slowly, I sit back and lower my hands. Once my face is free, he takes it in his warm grasp.

"You are a fucking phenomenal mother, and you very well know it." I close my eyes and try to disagree, but he tilts my head up, placing his thumbs under my eyes. "You are. And you run a business, an impressive one, and still you've raised that beautiful girl without help, without a partner, without support. It's bloody incredible, Katherine. You are incredible."

The sob finally breaks free and he moves closer, holding me to him. My head is cradled against his firm warm chest and it's possibly my new favorite place in all the world. Even though it shouldn't be. Even though I can't stay. For now, I just let it out, the tears, the thoughts.

"You don't understand."

"Tell me then."

I talk into his chest. "Today, they said...they called her Little Lucy Canton Can't. Lucy can't sit still. Lucy can't be quiet. It's just a matter of time. Then it's high school and it was Kat can't smile. Kat can't keep a boyfriend. Kat can't keep her legs closed. Which wasn't even true." His hold on me tightens, one hand cupping my head and the other arm locked around my back. I sink into him even more. "I was so hurt and so angry. All the time. I didn't want that for her."

"Shh, Shh." He rests his chin on the top of my head. "She's not angry. Hurt maybe, but not like you're describing. Not hurt that comes from"—his voice cracks—"abuse."

The word hangs there for a moment, like a looming storm. I decide to answer his question. "It was verbal. The vilest things I've ever heard about me, the worst things ever said to me, and they came from my father."

Dennis starts breathing faster, his heart rate picking up under my ear. "I'm sorry," he finally says.

I pull away and he releases me, moving one hand to the back of my stool and the other to the bar countertop. I wipe my face.

He studies me, intense.

"And you?" I ask. "I'm sure your high society parents were a couple of winners?"

He scoffs and tilts his head then pushes off to go fix some tea. "They were uninterested. My father had my older brother to mold and my mother was very ill all my life."

"Oh no, is she...? Because I made a *your mom* joke and if she passed away then I'm a real bitch, aren't I?"

He almost laughs. "No, she's not dead. But still sick to this day."

"I'm sorry."

He pours the hot water into the cup. "It was actually you who put the pieces together for me, more than anyone else ever has."

"What? What pieces?"

He doesn't look up at me. "The bit about the damsels."

"Oh." I realize what he's saying. "*Oh.* Like you're still trying to save your mother?" He nods. "Dang, that's heavy."

He brings the teacup over to me, still not making eye contact.

I decide to lighten the mood. "Doesn't explain the suits, though."

He looks up. "What do you mean?"

"Dennis. No normal person outside of books and movies wears a suit every single day. Not even billionaires, I googled it." He rolls his eyes. "Seriously. You never just want to wear jeans and a t-shirt?"

He dips his chin. "You don't ever want to wear pink and lace and, I don't know, polka dots?"

I raise my hands. "Point taken. No, I don't. Not anymore."

"Since...?"

I think back, remembering the horror that was high school. "The girls in polka dots, if you will, were so fake. Like, stab your back the second you walked away. When they stabbed me, starting all kinds of rumors about sex and blow jobs under bleachers—total lies—just because I was the new girl, I rebelled against all of it. Bonus was, it made my dad so angry. He wanted me to be perfect little Katie Canton." I scoff at the memory. "So, a therapist would say my all-black-all-spikes-everything get up is my armor against any of them hurting me ever again. Are suits your armor?"

He looks out the window, thinking. "I was invisible growing up. When I left home, left our small bubble of society where my kind of wealth is normal"—his words are slow, thoughtful—"I remember getting out of the car and walking up to one of my first meetings. I was in a suit that cost thousands of dollars, quadruple what all the other executives had. I wasn't invisible anymore."

I stare at his profile in disbelief.

He is stunning. A firm brow, sharp nose, sharp jaw, sharp everything, kind of. Except for his full lips, soft and free from even a hint of stubble. There is no way he could ever be invisible. Especially like this, open and honest and not frowning.

Why isn't he frowning? Frustrated? What is even happening right now?

"Well, this is weird. Quick, let's start arguing."

He smiles a small grin and faces me. "I'm sure I'm doing something snobbish you can scold me for."

"Uh, yeah, this." I point down at the black tea. "Where is the cream? Sugar? And, you know, the best part, the coffee?"

He lets out a little laugh and starts rummaging. "I can make coffee."

"I'm actually hungry now. Do you have anything in that massive fridge?"

"I've no idea. Let me order us something in."

"Ha! This is the sticks, honey, there isn't any place to order from."

His head jerks up, with an expression I'm afraid to name. He's just barely biting his lip and his eyes are hooded, like he's hungry too.

"Just, um, take us home, I can eat there."

The heat in his gaze morphs back to his usual irritation. "If you go there, you will just get to work on something urgent and forget to eat altogether. Stay." He twirls around quickly, opening both fridge doors. "Look, this thing is chock full."

I hop down and walk across the kitchen to survey the situation. When I get close, he drops an arm.

I lean forward to inspect the professionally organized shelves and drawers. No ready-to-eat meals but plenty of ingredients. I can work with this.

"Well?" he asks in my ear, close, hot. I straighten and turn. His hand is back on the far fridge door. I'm trapped between his big warm body and the freezing cold shelves. And his face is so close to mine, lit blue in the fridge light.

I stare, looking into big, dark eyes with heavy lids. I fight the urge to look down at his perfect mouth. I fail.

And he leans. He's leaning...

"Lucy!" I yell, having some kind of mental break. "Y-you go check on Lucy, and I-I'll make us something."

He doesn't pull away, just watches me, almost smirking. I think he likes that I'm trapped. I think he loves it. And I hate it, and I think he knows so, and loves that too. Finally, he agrees with a nod, pushing off the fridge doors.

I slump as he retreats, feeling cold metal shelves digging into my back. I try to think about what I can make for lunch. But all I can think about is that I'm here, in that man's space, not leaving, not retreating to safety.

I pull out bread, lettuce, meat, but it doesn't matter what's in my hand. This afternoon is a recipe for total disaster. And there's always been something else *Kat can't* do and that's what's good for her.

20

"Is she all right?"

"Asleep, actually."

I do a double take, because of the words he just said and the clothing he's wearing. Or not wearing. He's abandoned his jacket and tie and unbuttoned his shirt a couple buttons. It's like the bar the other night. The night I thought maybe there was something, something big and crazy and unsaid happening, before he up and left.

"That, uh, that's weird. She never naps." I turn back to the cutting board. "I guess crying will do that though."

He slides up next to me at the kitchen counter. Close. "It smells divine already. Can I help?"

"No, it's just BLTs. Nothing fancy." I don't look up from the cutting board where I'm slicing a tomato.

"I can make sandwiches, why don't you just sit? Rest?"

"I did." I gesture over my shoulder to the barstools. "Over there on that uncomfortable stool. It was terrible." I ignore him when he huffs. "And it's too quiet in here, it's weirding me out. Can I connect my phone to those?" I point at one of the speakers mounted in the corners of the all the rooms.

"I'm sure." He extends his palm and I pull my phone out of my dress pocket and carefully hand it to him, trying not to get mayo anywhere.

"Code is Lucy—5829. In Spotify, I have a cooking playlist."

He taps around until a quirky Louis Prima song starts.

"Mr. DeLane? Seriously?" He asks, feeling a bit prickly at my side.

"Currently. You were D-Money for a while, oh and His Royal Ass—er, *a-hole*."

He puts my phone on the counter and chuckles softly. "I suppose I should set up a jar for us here."

My hands stop moving, holding up slices of bread in mid-air.

Us.

A swear jar. For me, for Lucy, here, at his house.

I go back to my task, trying to keep my breathing even.

"Why not just Dennis?" He's inched closer to me, almost touching the front of his entire body down the side of mine.

"You were just Dennis for about thirty seconds." I shrug. "Before you did something to piss me off again, then I changed it."

"Hm," he says, his voice so low is sounds more animal than human.

I inhale and try to think. This is insane. Because I want him to lose it on me. To grab my hands, shove me up against the counter. To touch me, take me, swallow me whole. I want to feel his fingertips like I did the other night.

The night he left, Kat, with Grace, his girlfriend!

"So," I say, shifting away and gathering back all my wits. I finish assembling the two sandwiches on plates I found. "You, uh, didn't like the singalong."

"What?" He furrows his brow and shifts backward in surprise.

"It's okay, it's not for everyone." I cut a sandwich in half. "I don't know what I expected you to think, it's not really your scene, like, at all."

"I already told you I thought it was incredible. I think you're a bloody genius," he says, but he sounds angrier by the syllable.

That makes two of us.

"You didn't even stay to watch Dennis, just admit it." I put the knife down and reach for the pickle jar.

"No," he says. but I barely hear him.

"What was it?" I pop open the jar and fish out two pickle spears with a fork. "I can take it. It was too loud, too crowded?"

"No, it—"

I drop a spear on each plate and slam the fork down, then reach for the lid for the jar. "You were grossed out, probably."

"No! I—" He grabs my wrist and pulls, forcing me to turn and face him but I don't make eye contact.

"Maybe you had some kind of secondhand embarrassment then. You were uncomfortable—"

"I was angry," he yells and yanks me into him. He's panting, I realize, because I am smashed up against his chest as it pumps air violently. He's still holding my wrist and his left hand has moved to my hip where he holds me flush to him.

And he is fuming.

He goes on speaking through his teeth, "You were pure, hot, delicious sex up there on display for *everyone else.* Flirting with *everyone else.* Smiling at them. Laughing with them. I was so angry I think I blacked out, Katherine. I couldn't see, couldn't breathe, couldn't think. All I wanted was to yank you down and drag you away. Out of sight." He lets go of my wrist and puts his hand on my cheek, his thumb grazing under my bottom lip just barely. His gravelly voice dips even lower. "And out of earshot of another living thing."

"W-what?" I somehow say.

"Exactly. What the hell is this power you have over me? That I think about you all day long. That I want to bite this lip." He presses with the pad of his thumb and tugs. "How I want to hear you scream my name, frustrated with me for an altogether different reason." He slides his hand from my waist back and down, squeezing. "I want to suck the words straight from your filthy mouth. Make you forget everyone else, all of them saying your name, reaching up to touch you, to catch a glimpse of you. I was murderous, Katherine. That's what I was."

I try to say words but all that comes out is a cracked gasping sound.

"Tell me you want that. Tell me you can hardly think of anything else."

I look at his mouth, so close to mine. I do want it, all of it. I want him, right now. But I can't make a sound pass through my throat. I'm frozen.

All the heat in his face, the fire, it shifts, just for second. There's a longing, an uncertainty in his eyes that I've never seen before. He leans in so our mouths almost touch and whispers.

"I'm going to kiss you now, and you, wildling, are not going to kick me in the groin." He straightens and keeps talking just out of reach of my mouth.

My lips follow, waiting and hoping.

"You're going to open up and let me in, let me take you over, let me ruin you like you've ruined me."

Yes, yesyesyesyes. My head is all the way back, my mouth hanging open, desperate now. I'm throbbing everywhere with the anticipation.

"Hm?" he asks.

Oh, he's asking me. I begin to nod but just a fraction.

The sign of movement is all he needed.

He...

Holy...

He is doing exactly what he said, owning me with his tongue, in huge, fast strokes. He holds my head and moves it as he pleases, changing the angle. Because I am putty in his long, warm fingers. He sucks on my tongue, he bites my lip, he does whatever he wants. He moans and leans down further to reach me.

I grip his shirt, pull back and jump onto the island counter. I pull him into me, hard. I do what I've secretly dreamed of doing a hundred times, twisting myself around him like an unruly vine. I grip his shoulders and put a hand up into his hair. I pull hard.

His hands latch on to my hips again like they belong there, like they never should've let go. He groans and I shiver at the fact that he's coming undone. Because of me. We kiss for an instant and an eternity. I lick and bite his neck. I wrap my legs even tighter around his waist and grind myself up into him.

"Yes, yes, Katherine," he says moving his mouth to kiss at my jaw and nibble down my neck. He kisses all over my chest and back up, pausing under my ear. "You smell like candy"—he inhales me, causing goosebumps to erupt all over my skin—"and I have to know, do you taste like candy too?" I moan as he bites on my earlobe. "Do you want me to find out?"

I rock into him, grip him tighter, moan louder.

He smiles into my ear and his deep voice is scratchy, but playful. "Do you?"

"Y- yes." I breathe.

He squeezes my hips and holds me still. He exhales a sigh in my neck, then kisses under my ear again before his hot whisper is back. "Ask nicely."

I make a sound that I would consider a squeak. They are the hottest not-hot words to ever be whispered in my ear. I'm not sure if I should be mad or play hard to get or do anything other than obey him. Which is what I'm going to do, so I don't actually die of arousal right here on this kitchen counter.

"Please."

"My name, Katherine."

"Dennis. Please, Dennis."

He whispers a string of filthy words down my whole body, peppering me with kisses on my skin and over the thin fabric of my dress. Then, like a man possessed he throws up my skirt and gets down on his knees.

He spreads me wide and moves in immediately to torture me, just breathing at center. He starts to move, softly kissing my thighs, barely touching me, until I beg him again. At the sound of my voice crying his name he moves my panties out of the way and…

Totally.

Destroys.

Me.

I can't see what he's doing under my skirt. I can only feel and hear. It's erotic, the noises, the sight of his head covered in fabric. I grip the counter for dear life, repeating his name until I combust. It's an explosion that is unlike any I've ever had before.

He stands, grinning like a little boy who just won a prize.

I breathe and work on staying upright, watching in shock as, like some kind of barbarian, he uses my dress to wipe his face. Who even is this man?

"Holy fff—" I can't think so I just let the f sound sit there.

"I agree." His mouth goes back to my neck and, coming back to earth, I remember to look past him for any signs of Lucy awake and wandering the house. I don't see anything. I reach for his belt, but he moves his hips away.

"I have to go," he says into my skin. "I have already canceled twice." He kisses my neck again, and I think he may be trying to give me a hickey. "I gave my word I wouldn't reschedule." More sucking. Until I realize he is probably on his way to Grace.

Grace.

What the hell am I doing?

"Oh, uh, okay." I yank myself back, but he puts his hands on either side of my neck.

He looks into my eyes, serious. "It's a marketing presentation. They put in hours of work for it. That's the only reason I'm not taking you upstairs, locking Lucy in the library and ripping this dress off this instant." He kisses my forehead. "I like it, though. Probably best not to rip it apart." He takes a few steps to the table where he's put his jacket and tie.

He comes back quickly, kissing my head again. "Stay. Read, swim, watch a movie, or, my vote, just do nothing for a bit. I'll be back in two hours at the most." He puts a finger under my chin and kisses me, a hard peck that makes me lean back. "Damn it. Just two hours, yeah?" I nod.

He grabs half a sandwich off the counter and takes a huge bite as he rushes out. I hear the side door slam shut and the start of his car. Then he's gone and it's just my erratic breathing and very soft music.

Ow. I'm still gripping the counter so hard my hands are white.

I slip off the bar and I'm slippery. Because I just had the orgasm of all orgasms... with Dennis. The snooty, grumpy bane of my existence, not to mention my father's current right-hand man. And, oh yeah, my cousin's ex-fiancé who hopes to marry a local billionaire debutante.

What was I thinking, exactly?

I wasn't.

I was feeling.

I am lonely. That's what this is. I'm lonely and horny and he is kind to me, to Lucy.

Lucy.

What if she had walked in on us kissing? I can't do this. I cannot have flings in vacation rental kitchens with her upstairs. I can't accept non-gift trucks from a nosy friend.

He is that—a friend. An annoying, overbearing, unbelievably hot friend. Who played my body like a fiddle just now.

Well, I got my fantasy. That has to be the end of it. No more friends with benefits, and I should even go easy on the friends part.

Lucy is already too attached.

My hands tremble as I start to clean up the kitchen.

I made a mistake in a moment of weakness. I've done that before. While it gave me the brightest joy of my life, it cost a lot too. This time I know better.

I dump the sandwich I can't bear to eat into the trash and send out a 9-1-1 text to the Singles Table group chat. I need to talk this out, so I don't let it happen again. I also start looking around in the drawers.

I grab the paper and send an SOS text to Stella, asking her to pick us up. Just a few minutes and then I'll wake Lucy.

We're getting out of here before he comes back.

21

DENNIS

This is another one of those painful moments where I glance around during a presentation I could give shit-all about and realize how little I like my life. It's a familiar wave of grief and irritation. But I have been having a lot less of these lately.

I have been distracted. Like I am now, hardly able to even feign interest. Robert Canton sends me an inquisitive side eye.

Robert.

I am not a violent person, but his face is putting all my restraint to the test. I don't need to know what he said to Katherine as a child because she was a child. His child. Just hearing her voice crack earlier, feeling her sob in my arms...

I grip the ridiculously over-engineered designer pen in my hand so hard that the metal frame makes a snapping sound.

The only thing stopping me from effortlessly destroying this man's professional life is that it could affect her. Oh, but I have thought about it. In detail. Buying his business and all the competitors, then shifting the whole market to make his life's work take a long, slow march to death. It would be brutal. Painful for his wallet and his ego.

But she asked me to continue to help.

I'll continue until I figure out where her money goes and why her shares here are so important, then re-evaluate.

There's Emerson to think of, too. He at least answers my texts now. And I always liked Jon Canton, apart from my relationship with Sadie. He is a good man and I believe, though Emerson didn't say so explicitly, that he is the one who wanted to help Robert, his brother.

I absently play with the little plastic bracelets tucked under the cuff of my sleeve and look at the time. Again. I've endured an hour of this now. I am beyond restless, a new feeling for me.

I am having a lot of those lately. Foreign sensations and urges. I've raised my voice; I almost flipped that driver the bird in the carline. DeLanes do not do such things.

But Katherine, she...affects me. She intrigues me. It's fascination at this point, really.

I have been able to think of little else than provoking her, talking to her. My thoughts progressed quickly to kissing her, touching her, tasting her. Now that I have, I am a man consumed. I stopped to turn my car around twice on the drive here. I had to force myself out of the car when I reached the garage. Every minute since I left that kitchen has been an hour. And we're about to hit number one hundred and two.

I let my mind wander to her lips, her neck, her little noises. I adjust my position in the conference room chair.

Okay, perhaps I shouldn't let my mind wander just now.

I was so sure she couldn't stand me; thought I was old and stuffy and unbearable. But she's started to smile more, to let me in. When she called me baby behind the bar the other night, something snapped in my psyche. A far-fetched idea became a nagging obsession.

Not to mention her sexy little show. For all those other men.

I put my pen down before I actually break it.

When the meeting concludes, with no idea what I just sat through, I simply agree with the marketing manager. She's whip smart and could have handled this without the fanfare. Marketing people do love their fanfare, though. So, I congratulate her, give Robert a nod, and almost run to the elevator.

I speed the whole way back to the house. I take the tight curves filled with genuine curiosity. What have they been doing? Did Katherine finally rest? How's Lucile feeling now?

When I walked up to the school and saw them, the fiery siren and the beautiful cherub, with red eyes and quivering lips, I felt as though I'd been stabbed. It was physically painful to see them like that. I wanted to stomp inside and scream at someone. Again, surprising myself.

What are these girls doing to me?

I mean, what was all that earlier about my mum and my suits?

Just being around Katherine makes me want to, I don't know, open up? Maybe because she's so shut off. She won't tell me about her business, her goals, that weirdly pretty dream board thing in her office, or who the hell got her pregnant and then disappeared.

A shiver runs over me.

Hm. Perhaps it's best I don't know who he is. But when it comes to her, for some reason, I want to know anything and everything. I want to figure her out.

Starting with how I can make her come apart again.

I feel almost giddy getting out of my car. I bound up the steps, desperate to see them both even though it's only been a couple hours. I fly through the side door and back into the kitchen. It still smells heavenly in here, but it's clean. No sign of them.

"Katherine? Lucy?" I walk through to the kitchen but stop short when I see a piece of paper taped in the doorway.

DEAR JUST DENNIS,

THANKS FOR THE... SANDWICH. WHILE IT WAS INCREDIBLE, MAYBE THE BEST I'VE EVER HAD IN MY LIFE, WE CAN'T HAVE ANY MORE SANDWICHES TOGETHER. EVER. THAT WAS A ONE-TIME MEAL. FOR A MILLION REASONS YOU KNOW AS WELL AS I DO.

Wait. What? No.
I rip the paper down.

I HOPE THE SANDWICH DOESN'T AFFECT OUR FRIENDSHIP, BE-CAUSE LUCY AND I REALLY LIKE HAVING YOU AROUND. NOT JUST AS A TUTOR BUT AS A FRIEND. A SNOBBY, IRRITATING, ELDERLY FRIEND, BUT A FRIEND ALL THE SAME. ;)
- KAT

The hell?
This woman.
The second our lips finally touched she was on me, climbing my torso like it was a tree. I've never experienced anything like that. She left fingernail marks, bites, and I think she pulled out some of my hair.

Of course, I've been with women who are responsive, fun, but not wild. She's wild. And if it's the best sandwich she's had in her life, how the hell is she saying she doesn't want anymore?

I grab my keys off the counter.
She wants more. I know it.
And I sure as hell do. I want a lot more.

22

In a half hour or so Lucy and I are back at the Roadside, holed up in our apartment. Neither of us love staying cooped up in here, but I am claiming it's because she's grounded, not because I'm hiding. We talk through her feelings again, her punishment. We also go over her cheer routines. They are both adorable and seemingly effective. She doesn't miss a single math fact.

Eventually, I let her rest. She flops on her bed with a graphic novel, and I escape into our tiny bathroom. I pull up the messages, because a new one finally came through.

> Janie: Sally is still at her audition, what's going on?
> Kat: We need a group FaceTime STAT.
> Kat: I repeat, 9-1-1!
> Janie: Sally, get back to us when you can!

I look at the newest text.

> Sally: How about now?
> Kat: Too close to little ears. We'll have to text.
> Kat: Everybody sitting down?
> Sally: Yes.
> Janie: Yep.
> Kat: I kissed Dennis!??!?!!?

Sally: You're not sure if you kissed Dennis?

Janie: Let me pretend to be surprised really quick. [surprised emoji]

Kat: No, I'm sure. He kissed me, I kissed him back.

Kat: What do you mean pretend?!

Janie: He's gorgeous, he's tutoring your child, and he gets under your skin...I'm betting literally.

Sally: Wait. Did you sleep with him??

Kat: No! Technically I guess he was under my skin? Eww. We made out, he did other things. To me.

Janie: And how are we feeling about it now?

Sally: I am glad that I did sit down.

Kat: We are feeling bad. It can never happen again. How do I get away from him?

Janie: Maybe just... stay away from him?

Kat: He knows where I live, where I work, where Lucy goes to school. He's with my freaking father every day! There's no escape!

Sally: Is he stalking you?

Kat: [eye roll emoji] Again, Sal, you're losing it with your crazy mafia romance reader brain. No, not stalking me. He just... is around. All the time.

Sally: If you ask him to stay away from you, will he respect that?

Kat: Maybe, but what about Lucy's tutoring? Our deal?

Janie: Deals can be cancelled. He's a businessman. Your arrangement has run its course, just tell him so.

Sally: Is he being a jerk?

Kat: No, he's fine, annoying, intrusive, maybe. But he's not an a-hole.

Janie: What about his bazillionaire girlfriend?

Kat: She didn't exactly come up.

Sally: Kat! Are you the other woman?

Janie: [yikes emoji]

Kat: As I understand it, she has four boyfriends at least, one of whom is Dennis. They're not exclusive.

Janie: He said that?

Kat: Again, we weren't really chatting!

Janie: Maybe it's time you chat then.

Kat: Ugh, maybe.

Sally: This is too weird. I mean, he's Dennis.

Kat: I know.

Sally: Just a couple years ago, at Sam's wedding, he looked at Sadie like an abandoned puppy.

Kat: I remember.

Janie: Also glared at her like he might kill her.

Kat: Yup, I was there.

Sally: So how does he look at you? How can you ignore all of that? Their past? He was going to marry her, Kat. What if you just remind him of her? What if he's just using you to get to her, get to our family?

Sally: I am NOT on Team Dennis.

Kat: I gathered that.

Janie: I'm on team you need to have a conversation with him and nip this in the bud. Before Lucy picks up on whatever is going on.

Kat: Roger.

A rope of anxiety ties tight around my stomach. And my chest. And my eyes.

I'm glad I didn't bother eating or reapplying the mascara I cried off earlier. I look at Sally's message, re-reading the paragraph over and over until everything blurs. She makes points I didn't want to stare in the face, but there they are.

I've barely stepped foot out of the bathroom when I hear a knock. It's polite and urgent at the same time. I wipe my eyes. Time for that chat, I guess. I open the door.

"What is this?" He holds up my note, now a crumpled wad in his fist.

"It *was* a note, communication from the olden times, I thought you'd appreciate it given your advanced years," I snipe, but there's no bite behind the words. No playfulness. Just fatigue.

"Funny. Can I come in?" He has his one long arm propped up on the door frame as he glares past me into the room. The room that is a mess right now, overstuffed and much too small for him.

I shake my head. "Lucy, I'll be in the office for a minute."

"Okay, Mommy."

His features soften for a second. "How is she doing?"

"She's fine," I say ducking under his arm quickly to go down the hall.

I push into the office and walk around behind my desk. Having a massive piece of furniture between myself and Dennis seems like a good idea.

"So?" He shuts the door and tosses the paper ball onto the desk. "What the hell is this about no more sandwiches?"

I almost smile at the silly metaphor. "Look, we clearly have a lot of chemistry in a weird love-hate kind of way. I'm not denying that. But *you* can't deny that we cannot do that again."

"Why not?" He steps into the room, like he's about to round the desk and...

"Stop! Dennis, I'm serious. Surely you don't need me to make you a list."

He does stop. "Enlighten me, please."

I throw my head back in frustration. "Fine. How about we start with your girlfriend? You know, Grace?"

"Not my girlfriend."

"What is she then?"

He gives a tiny shrug. "That's just business."

"Business? You really are heartless. She's a person. What does that make me?"

His eyes darken. "Pleasure. Definitely."

"No. Don't do that sexy growly thing. I mean it."

He starts to move again. "I'm always serious."

I hold up a hand. "Stop. Really. I mean, what, you want to be sex buddies? I can't do that because Lucy will catch us and then the whole of Arkansas will know about it. Plus, that's too confusing to her, you're only in town for a little while."

He huffs. "I could give you another *sandwich* right here and now and she'd never know."

My mouth falls open. "Wait. Is that what this is? I owe you one? Will you let this go if I drop to my knees right now?"

Now his mouth falls open. Then he shuts it and rolls his lips in his teeth, his eyes drilling into me. Clearly, he's considering it as if it were a real offer.

I start to laugh at the absurdity of it, but he shakes his head. "I don't think that would result in me letting you go."

"Well, you need to."

"Kath—"

"Dennis! You're my dad's right-hand man, you're too old, too uptight, too controlling, and too complicated, and come on, just admit it, all of this must just be about Sadie."

He takes a step back and shifts his shoulders. It's like his whole body becomes a disgusted grimace. "W-what?"

"Maybe I remind you of her. Maybe you're trying to get back at her or something."

"Tell me you're joking. That was a decade ago."

"Still, I saw you at Sam's wedding. She is my *cousin*, Dennis. More like a sister, honestly. The woman who crushed you."

"No, she crushed my pride. She embarrassed me. End of story, full stop."

I sigh. "Even if I believed you, it's all too complicated. If I could have a casual fling with someone—and, again, I can't—it wouldn't be with you."

He flattens his lips into a line while his nostrils flare. At least he's stopped arguing.

I go on. "I also think we should end our arrangement. You really did help Luce with her memorization, but I can take it from here."

"Wait"—he steps forward and puts his fingertips on the desk, looking like he's gone into negotiation mode—"What about staying friends?"

"I just—"

"I'll back off. No more sandwiches. Don't... don't shut me out."

I exhale and let my lips flap in the big huff of air.

His eyes watch mine, looking sad, almost desperate.

"No flirting, no touching, no staring at me, no more brand-new trucks." He blinks hard, like it's a painful idea. "That's the deal, nothing other than friends."

"Can I still see Lucy?"

The question, the sincerity of it, guts me.

I nod, unable to say anything. I know it's just his genuine interest in her, rare though that is. It's just my loneliness and exhaustion. Still, I have to blink a few times to keep tears from gathering on my lashes.

Dennis catches it. He clears his throat. "Can I hug you?"

"Dennis."

"Friends hug."

"No. Just go, will you?"

He lets out a heavy sigh, nods, and goes to the door. He stops with his hand on the knob and looks back at me. He opens his mouth to say something, stops himself, and leaves.

I collapse into the chair. It was the right thing to do, to stop whatever this is before I get carried away, let my guard down, let my life get off track. I have a plan. I need to remember that.

Lucy and I are well on our way.

Plus, if there's one person I should maybe think about letting into our safe little bubble, into Lucy's life and heart, it's not the man who's older, British, complicated and moving back to San Francisco with a new bride at the end of his ninety-day contract.

It's the man who has texted me five times since lunch.

23

"I could've come to the Roadside, you know I'm always out and about," Spencer says as I join him in the restaurant lobby. He leans forward to hug me and, stunned, I just kind of stand there.

"I am, uh, always out and about too, actually," I stammer.

He is still a handsome guy. I know he bleaches his hair from red to blonde. It's working for him. Kind of like a Viking. Well, a dorky, khaki Viking in a golf polo and cheap sneakers. He's relatively fit though, remainders of the athlete he used to be years ago. I'm only a couple inches shorter than him in my platform boots, so I'm able to look into his bright blue eyes. They are starting to have tiny wrinkles around them, but they look so much like Lucy's it's freaky.

"You look amazing, as always," he says quietly.

"Th-thanks." I kind of laugh.

As always? Before he showed up at the singalong a few nights ago, I hadn't seen him in probably two years.

Well, I've seen him, of course. He hasn't seen me.

We get seated in a big corner booth. This new Chili's is bright and nice, in a chain restaurant kind of way. Not my favorite but he said the location is convenient and he's right. We order water and the hostess leaves us for a minute.

"So, uh, everything okay?" He fumbles with the menu. "Yesterday you said it was an emergency and then, nada."

"Oh. Sorry, yeah, everything is fine now."

"Good, okay. Good," he mumbles.

We both look at the menu in tense silence. The server comes and we are happy to give her our orders. She takes the menus, leaving us without any barriers.

I watch him, waiting, and almost chuckle again when he sucks down water like he's a fish flopped up into the sun.

"I'm nervous." He finally chuckles.

I don't comfort him. I want to see what exactly he's up to.

"I've wanted to see you for a long time I just..."

"Waited until you saw online that I am crushing it now?"

He lets out a shocked laugh. "Wow, already back to bustin' my balls and it's been, what, a whole thirty seconds." I just shrug and he grins. Then his smile vanishes, and he looks away. "I saw that and yeah, you are, but that wasn't it."

"What do you mean?"

"I saw her. With your mama in the grocery store. Just turned a corner and there she was." I keep myself totally still, even though my heart is pumping hard in my eardrums. "You never post pictures, not since she was little. She... she looks just like..."

"You. She looks just like you."

He exhales. "So much. And like you too. I mean, she"—he locks eyes with me—"looks like *us.*"

I narrow my eyes. "She's looked that way the whole time, Spence. When she was born. When she was a baby. A toddler. A preschooler."

"I know, dammit, I know. I was young and scared, okay?"

"Ha! *You* were young and scared? That is just—"

"Wait"—he holds up his hands in surrender—"I was wrong. I know. I should have stayed, helped, been around. She... When I saw her in the store, she was talkin' a mile a minute, lit up about cereal. She grabbed some box and read every word, even the crazy ingredients. Hell, I probably couldn't have pronounced them. She... she's so smart. Just like you. She's incredible, Kit Kat."

"She is," I say, still angry. "She has been, this whole time."

"I know." He leans forward. "I know it. I made"—he stops so the server can drop off our food—"I made a lot of mistakes, Kat. I want to try and fix what I can now."

"Fix what, and how, exactly?"

"Whatever and however you want," he says quickly, then his eyes dart past me.

Some bro, also in khakis and a dry-fit polo shirt, walks up to our table.

"Hey man, this is Kat Canton, Kat this is Pete Sutton."

I offer a small smile and watch the men exchange pleasantries. I guess Pete is a long-time client of his.

"Anyway," Spencer restarts after the guy leaves. "I've just, you know, thought about you. About her. Us."

"And yet you never once called, texted. Came by. Sent a check."

His eyebrows shoot up. "I offered you money right at the start, Kat."

"Your *parents* offered me hush money that I didn't want. And I don't want a cent from you now either. I'm just saying you have never showed an interest. Now, suddenly, when my business is doing well and she's thriving, when we're not a bother or a burden, here you are. Forgive me if I don't believe a word coming out of your mouth."

He sinks back into the booth. "I have come by the bar over the years, but you've never really seemed, uh, happy to see me."

"True. Why the persistence this time? Why the texts, the lunch?"

"I don't know." He puts a hand up to his forehead. "Figured maybe you were ready to forgive me."

"I forgave you a long time ago, Spence. I'm not mad at you. But I'm not about to let you waltz back into her life. We are amazing, she and I. We have a happy little life up there."

"I don't doubt it," he interjects.

"So, I'm not going to let you mess that up. You can't be kinda sure. You can't hang out with her for an afternoon and then decide she's annoying. You're her *father*, Spencer."

"I know." He puts both hands up again. "I'm not asking to waltz in anywhere. You're in charge, whatever you think. Maybe I can meet her, later, when you decide I can."

I take a big angry bite of salad.

He watches me like he's a little afraid of me. He should be. Just the idea of how a father can really screw up their little girl's brain, heart, soul... all that she will *already* have to sort through with a therapist. He's lucky I don't lob this fork into his eyeball. I've got pretty good aim.

"Does she know about me?"

"She knows she has a dad out there somewhere. One who couldn't be a dad to her because he had his own problems."

He nods.

I'm surprised he doesn't correct me or defend himself. For a while we eat in angry silence. Well, I'm angry, he's watching me like a spectator watches a lion in a zoo. An angry lion. An angry lioness with a cub in her enclosure.

After I've simmered slightly, he gathers up his bravery. "Will you tell me about her?"

Luckily for him, she is my favorite topic of conversation. I indulge him in talking about her quirks, what she's great at, how funny and kind she is.

As I talk to him, he laughs and gets animated, and I see Lucy. I see her expressions, her excitement, right there on his face. We're interrupted again. And again. I am reminded just how small our town is, and that everyone in it is probably one of his clients. And as he says my name over and over, people are probably remembering me. Remembering my dad and the other Cantons in Oklahoma. The famous, successful ones.

Some of these people in the restaurant might even put two and two together, recall that Spencer and I dated back in high school. Before the golden boy went off to play basketball at Arkansas, and the punk girl with the anger problem disappeared into the hills.

Still, he introduces me every time, apologizes when they walk away, then jumps right back into his interest in Lucy. Our daughter.

This is so weird.

Not weird bad, though.

It's easy for us to talk, to laugh, to gush over Lucy. I show him photos, he asks a million questions. He is still the goofy, happy guy I remember. Only now he's gone on to build his empire, like he said he would.

The empire a baby and a teen bride would've ruined. Can't be a star division-one basketball player with a baby mama on the side. No, he needed a proper southern lady. I sit back in my seat, suddenly full.

"What does Chrissy think about this? About Lucy?"

"Oh, Chrissy and I broke up a while ago. For good this time." He studies me for a reaction.

I try my best not to give him one. I don't care about her, about them. I did, but that was a long time ago.

"Well, this was interesting." I put some cash on the table. "I have errands to run before I get Lucy from school."

"Can we do this again?" he asks as I stand, and he stands too. I blink, again stalling out in surprise. "Maybe."

"Please. Just think about it. I was serious before, she's incredible *like you,* Kit Kat."

Seeing that look in his eyes snaps me back. Back to when I was an infatuated little outcast, reveling in the praise of a popular, superstar boy who was in awe. He looked at me like I was the hottest thing he'd ever seen. It was intoxicating.

Back then.

This is now.

I just bobble my head in a weird nod and back up. I almost take out a server, so I turn and walk the rest of the way like a normal human being. I never felt quite normal around Spencer Taggart.

Guess some things never change.

———

"What's this?" Dennis sneers from the doorway.

Lucy runs in to grab her tablet and then runs out. I guess the two of them are done eating and working already.

"Those are flowers," I explain.

"From?" he asks, stepping in and looking irritated.

Man, he's hot when he's bothered. Which is always. Especially since Monday. He's still come in to eat but I think it's just so he can glare at me. I think he knows that his glare is sexy, and he's been wielding it as a weapon.

He's stuck to our rules though, refrained from so much as a lingering stare at my legs or my cleavage. Not that I've displayed any more than normal.

I did think about wearing a dress today but realized I just wanted to torture him. That's not what friends do.

And it would've been torture for me too. I would've remembered his head under the fabric. His mouth...

"Katherine? Who is this eyesore from?"

"Oh, a friend."

He inhales slowly. "Well, it's cheap and hideous."

I laugh. "They're pink roses. Like three dozen. It had to cost hundreds."

"Right. Pink roses. So, the *friend* clearly doesn't know you." He pulls out his phone.

"Dennis, don't."

"Don't what?"

"Don't order some giant f—some giant *freaking* arrangement of who knows what that is too big for my tiny office. These flowers are too much in here as it is."

"I concur. Let's toss them in the bin."

I laugh and throw my head in my hand. "Can I help you with something?"

"Not at all. I came to ask you if *I* can help." He looks down at my piles of paper but I'm already shaking my head. "Not with your precious papers. I meant I could take Lucy for some sugar-free frozen yogurt or something, give you another minute."

"Oh." I was not expecting that. "She's fine."

"I know she is. How are you?" He moves closer, resting a hand on the desk.

I shrug. "Also fine." He cocks his head a tiny bit. "What, do I look ill, as you would say?"

"You look delicious." His response is deep and quick. And he's almost smiling.

"Hey, we said no flirting." He rolls his eyes, but I shoo him with my hands as I stand. "Go. Thank you for the tutoring session. You are relieved."

He puts his hands on the vase and turns to the door.

"Don't you dare."

I cannot believe it, but polite, respectful, Dennis DeLane dares.

He moves fast. I call after him, following at almost a run to keep up. In a few long steps, he's taken my giant bouquet of roses and thrown them upside down in the supply room's large trash can.

I stand in the doorway, stunned.

"You're welcome," he says walking back to me. "You hated them, they were too big for your desk, and the smell was too much for your office." He pauses in the doorway, our bodies almost touching. "Just being a good *friend*," he says in a husky voice reserved just to awaken neglected vaginas. Then he leaves.

What just happened?

I don't have long to think about it because my phone starts going off on my desk. I walk back to the office to check it, even though I know what it will be.

Yet another text from Spencer.

The guy is relentless now. Those weren't even the only set of flowers he's sent since Tuesday.

I slump down into my chair and stare at the empty spot where the roses were. It is better in here without it.

You look delicious.

Let me ruin you like you've ruined me.

Ask nicely.

Ugh. As if I need another one of his scorching hot lines to haunt me at night.

I shake it off. I can't think about it. Not even in the bathroom in the middle of the night, frustrated as all get out, rummaging to find an old vibrator in the back of a storage bin.

It was a weak moment, but I stopped myself. Because I am not going there.

I am, however, going shopping. Because after many texts and bouquets and even a few handwritten notes, after double checking that all my secrets are still secure and out of his grasp, I said yes to Spencer.

For the first time in years, I have an actual, proper date.

24

"You look so pretty, Mommy."

"Thanks, Bug." I smooth my hair again. I am not sure about a low bun for my hair, especially not without any free pieces hanging around my face. I'm also not sure about this modest dress. I wanted black, obviously, but not edgy or sexy. That ruled out all the dresses I owned. I do have a few formal gowns, but this is not a gala.

This high neck, mid-calf length plain black number seemed to fit. I feel like I actually look like a successful twenty-five-year-old.

I kept my make up minimal. The look feels weird but also appropriate. I feel like the right version of myself for this thing. Probably?

It's just a benefit for a local cause, not a huge soirée, but there will be people I know there. A lot of them. Because this is a big, tiny town. There will be people from high school, regular patrons from the grill, friends of my father. I actually checked with him to see if he'd be there, but he won't, thankfully.

"Are you nervous?" my tiny, sweet human asks me.

"Um, maybe?"

"Your hands are jiggly so maybe you should sit on them, but whenever I have to sit on my hands, my jiggles just move to my legs and then my legs are jiggly, and they make noises on the floor or the desk and then Mrs. Henderson says *Lucy!* in her grumpy voice."

I really try not to hate people, but Mrs. Henderson is overdrawn on her grace account with me. One more revealing side comment like this from my child and I'm going to start googling things like *how to secretly, completely total someone's car without accidentally killing them.*

"I'm sorry you have to sit on your hands, Bug. That's annoying. Tonight, I might see a lot of people I haven't seen in a long time, so I guess I'm just a little jumpy."

I know what else this is. Anytime I dress up this happens. Memories of all the hateful things my dad would say about his *mediocre* family whenever we had events. His *disappointing* daughter who couldn't muster the class and grace of the other Canton girls. His *mousy* wife.

I've trained myself to recognize this for what it is: past trauma, false narrative BS, and to mute the angry replay in my mind. Tonight, though, the play button seems to be jammed.

Lucy lights up. "Want to actually be jumpy? Jump around?"

"Umm, duh. Absolutely I do." I pull up *Jump Around* on my phone. We jump for a minute or so, then I fix my flyaways. I also put on my amazing heels from Sam's wedding.

They're nude sandals, in keeping with my non-sexy choices for tonight, but they have some studs and tiny leather straps that lace up my calf. The straps will be mostly covered by the asymmetrical skirt of the dress, but I'll know there's a little bit of Punk Kat hiding under there.

"Okay, ready to go to Gramma's for the night?"

"Yeah!"

"Let's roll." I follow her out our door into my office to get my keys.

I can't help but smile when I look at the new addition to my desk. Because I really do love the black and deep blue roses Dennis sent, or technically they were sent from *I'd rather give you a sandwich but at least these aren't pink.*

They're Infinity Roses that last a year, have a very faint scent and they come in a cool square box. They have a hint of glitter in some spots but it's only noticeable in certain lighting. It looks more like an art installation than flowers. So freaking cool.

I get Lucy settled with my mom and then drive over to the museum. Spencer hated the idea of meeting here, but he also understood he couldn't exactly pick me up for a date at the Roadside.

I pull the truck into a spot at the edge of the packed full parking lot. Nerves bubble up within me again.

This is a small local fundraiser, not a big AmeriMart gala. It's not even black tie. This will be no big deal, we can walk around, make an appearance, and then maybe go get a big juicy burger somewhere.

When is the last time I ate? I was bouncing back and forth from the A-frames to the Grill to the hardware store and back; I don't think I ate anything other than a roll. I need to remember that if there's champagne.

I text Spencer and see him walking through the parking lot shortly after. I get out and meet him in the middle.

He looks excited and handsome, in a white shirt and a gray dress jacket with jeans.

"Wow, Kit Kat," he says, looking me up and down. "You look incredible."

"Thanks." I smile awkwardly. This is just so totally foreign.

He offers his arm and escorts me in. Inside we make our way to the crystal bridge part of the Crystal Bridges Museum, a gorgeous space with curved wood ceilings and wall-to-wall windows.

As soon as we enter the ballroom, I understand just how I right I was. I know most of these people, some by name, some just their faces. I don't know how many of them remember me. They all know Spencer though.

He leads me around to everyone, always introducing me, gushing about the Roadside. He gets us drinks and even brags about me to the bartender. It's so different from our past, where we could hardly be seen together in public.

There is a not-small part of me that wants to remain bitter and angry about the contrast. But this is Lucy's father and honestly, the praise, the doting, it feels pretty wonderful. I'm not used to it, however, and I'm pretty sure it shows in my awkward greetings and lack of eye contact.

Since I'm looking down and away a lot, I don't see *him* approach.

"Katherine."

"Oh, hey there. Dennis DeLane? Uh, that's right! You know my Kit Kat," Spencer says, suddenly giddy.

Dennis looks to Spencer then at me, then back at him. The resemblance is clear as day once you have the context. Seeing Spencer and me side by side, it's undeniable who he is to me and to Lucy.

Dennis starts, "You're..."

"Yeah, Spencer Taggart, you've probably seen my mug all over town on benches and whatnot." Spencer beams at Dennis as he extends a hand. "Would love to talk to you about your real estate options if you decide to stay in town."

Oh.

I see it now.

I am an idiot.

My face burns at the realization.

Spencer didn't see my success and reconsider me. He didn't see Dennis and get jealous. He saw me as a connection. To a billionaire.

I inhale a deep breath, hoping it calms my rage and settles my blazing hot cheeks.

"Oh, Kat. How lovely you all came out for this. It was a great idea Dennis had for us to get involved in more local grassroots causes." Grace's voice is syrupy sweet, but I don't look up or smile.

My eyes are not focusing on anything really. My mind is focusing on not screaming.

"Hi, Grace, you may not remember me, we've met before," Spencer launches into his spiel.

Dennis grabs my elbow. "Can I borrow you for a moment?" Before I can answer he announces to our dates, "Excuse us, I have an investor chum who wants to talk to her about the Roadside." He's already pulling me away as they mumble their replies.

We make quick work of exiting the ballroom and as soon as I get into cooler air, I feel better. I needed that reminder of who exactly Spencer is and why I used to—should now, and most definitely will from now on—stay very far away from him.

I don't quite register my surroundings until Dennis closes us into a supply closet.

"What are you doing?" I ask.

He drops my arm and takes a few steps away. He's panting, I think, with one hand on the back of his neck.

"Dennis?"

He turns, nostrils flared, lips in a hard line. He takes a step back toward me and makes a show of looking me up and down.

"What. The hell. Is this?"

"A dress?" I raise my brows and almost smile, but he seems to be having trouble even breathing. And I get the feeling it's not because he's overwhelmed by my beauty. "Listen, if you're about to tell me I look tired..."

"You look like someone else. Like you're hiding in all that... fabric."

"It's—"

"It's all wrong, is what it is." He takes a long angry step away and then back again, closer. "Where are your boots? The holey tight things? The neon? The fire? I saw you across the room and did a double take because your smile was small and shy. I hated it. I hated it because it wasn't you. I didn't even recognize you."

"Wouldn't be the first time," I mumble.

"Oh, will you stop prattling on about that? You didn't recognize me either until we saw each other face to face."

"I remembered who you were, though."

He inches closer to me. "Oh, I remembered. I remember those sexy little shoes you're wearing right now, traipsing through the sand at the reception. I remember a stack of plastic bracelets on your wrist that didn't match your bridesmaid dress. I vividly remember the line of butterfly tattoos that snake up your spine."

"Y-you do?" I shake my head. "You must've seen those at the bar."

"No, believe me, I've been waiting. None of your shirts show them off. It's killing me, honestly." He puts his hands on my hips and leans down so his face is inches from mine. "All your dresses should be backless, black as night and dripping with studs and spikes and diamonds. Black diamonds everywhere." He is whispering and I'm trying to stay upright, stay conscious.

His mouth, saying these things, I can't... I...

"Okay. Yup. We're doing this." I drop to my knees and grab his belt.

"Wait! No."

I look up from under my lashes at him, my hands gripping the buckle.

As he looks down at me, his face changes color. His mouth has fallen open, and he looks beyond shocked. "I mean, yes. Absolutely yes, but, not in here. Not with you in that. Come on, let's get out of here."

He pulls me up and my consciousness resurfaces as I stand.

"Wait, what are you going to tell Grace?"

His eyes roll. "She has three other dates with her, she'll hardly notice. What are you going to say to *him?*"

I huff out a bitter laugh as he opens the door for me. "I have some colorful ideas."

"Splendid." Dennis smiles, offering me his arm in the hallway.

"No, Dennis." I look around. "We can't leave together. You go, and I'll go, and we can meet at the truck."

"Fine." He sighs.

I stomp back to my stupid date in his stupid jeans with his stupid bleached hair. "I'm leaving, Spence."

His plastic smile melts into confusion. "What?"

"You met him. Dennis. My work here is done, right?"

"Kat, I—"

"Do not contact me ever again, Spencer."

He steps toward me, looking around since all eyes are on us now.

"You are not welcome at my bar. Don't even drive by, not after what you did to me." I let the words land. What he did to me, technically, was abandon and shun me eight years ago. But now, all these onlookers will draw one million conclusions and spread rumors about him like a virus. Fine by me, as long as the focus is on him and me and not Lucy. I keep the last threat vague.

He'll know what I mean.

"And if you ever even *think* about contacting anyone in my family, I will have so many lawyers so far up your ass you won't be able to sit on one of your stupid bus bench billboards."

Don't be petty, Kat. Walk away.

Walk... Nope.

Petty it is.

"And for the love of all that is holy quit bleaching your hair, dude. We all know the curtains don't match the drapes." I turn and walk away, head high, no eye contact with anyone. I'm sure Grace watched that display in horror. It was not graceful or proper but wow, that felt good.

I cannot believe I ever wanted to impress those people, led by that idiot. To make him proud, to be his. Gross.

I hustle out of the building. I really have to keep myself from sprinting when I see Dennis leaning against the big black truck. His dark suit and tie, his almost black hair, all of it just... goes. And it looks like heaven.

When I reach him, he grabs me, turns us, and slams his mouth onto mine, pushing my back up against the driver's side door of the truck. Both of us moan and become unleashed, lips and tongues and hands everywhere. When his hand goes under my skirt my eyes fly open.

"Dennis! We shouldn't be doing this here. We're outside, someone could see."

"Best not to strip you naked now then?"

"Right. Stop."

"I hate outside," he growls in frustration as he pulls his mouth from my shoulder. Where I think he may have just nibbled at me through my dress.

I chuckle and watch him grab my clutch purse in a hurry to fish out the keys. He drags me by the wrist to the other side and I have to almost run to keep up. He opens the door for me looking genuinely pissed. I laugh.

"Go ahead and laugh, wildling." He buckles me into my seat and then moves his mouth to my ear. His hand travels under my skirt again. He sighs and moves his fingers, up, up, slowly. Way too slowly. "We'll see who gets the last laugh." Then he abruptly pulls away and shuts the door.

Okay. He wins. I'm no longer laughing and already close to combustion.

He climbs in and holds the key in his hand, just staring at the wheel.

"Hmm." He looks all over. "How does one start one of these big truck things?"

I snort. "Tell me you're joking."

He glares at me, putting the key in the ignition.

"Oh, my word, you were joking! You joke! Am I dreaming? Am I dead?"

He grins as he puts the truck in reverse. "You will be later, I assure you. I am going to have you reeling you for hours. *Hours.* But first a little torture." He glances my way, serious. There's no negotiating with him.

I swallow.

"You, Katherine, are going to talk to me."

25

"Do I have to?"

"That," he almost shouts. "That bumbling blond idiot wanker is Lucy's father?"

"Yep." I sigh. "You have to imagine him as the star basketball player, the king of the high school...the town, really."

He keeps looking between me and the road. "I cannot imagine that smarmy tool as the king of anything."

I almost laugh at how true that is.

"And you? In this, acting shy? Explain."

I think about that as we pull onto the highway. "I wasn't shy, I was uncomfortable."

Dennis huffs in agreement.

"He rejected me, obviously, Me and Luce, so I guess I just wanted to, maybe, prove him wrong? I don't know."

"You told him you were pregnant with his child and he just what, said, no thank you, have a nice life?"

"Among other things."

"What other things?"

I shift in my seat. "It's stupid now, Dennis. It doesn't matter. We were scared teenagers."

"You *were*." He glances at the mirror and changes lanes, flipping the indicator like he's trying to break the lever. "What about since then? He hasn't tried to see her? Tried to help you?"

"I don't need help. And"—I point at one of the annoying Spencer Knows Northwest Arkansas billboards right off the highway—"since then, he went on to build his real estate kingdom, like he always said he would."

"Real estate. Hmm," Dennis says quietly.

"No, no, no, no." I start getting loud and my eyes go wide. "I can see you plotting his demise in your bazillionaire spreadsheet brain. Do *not* do that. Don't do anything. Lucy and I are fine."

"You're more than fine, Katherine, you're spectacular." He spits the words, passionate and furious. "But he is a coward and a prick and, as he'll soon find out, a very small fish in an even smaller pond."

"Dennis, don't, please."

He grips the steering wheel like he's trying to juice the leather. "Did he offer to help you at all? Even once?"

"His parents offered me money, but my father refused, and I didn't want it anyway. They just wanted me to keep Lucy a secret, make sure not to tarnish their basketball star son's reputation in any way."

"Uh huh, and what are their names?"

I laugh. "You know you keep saying I'm the crazy one but I seem saner by the minute here compared to you. I am serious, don't get involved. It's ancient history."

He takes a deep breath, and I do too.

"What about *Robert*?" He says my father's name with unbridled disgust.

I put my elbow on the arm rest and hold my head to the side with my hand. Reliving it all makes me tired. And sad.

"First was the cursing up and down, claiming that I was a trashy brat. I had only been with one guy before Spencer, as if it matters. But no, I was a slut and a whore and then he said I was a conniving little witch who got pregnant on purpose to make him look bad. After a while he sort of just never spoke about it again. Didn't Bug me about college anymore, didn't try to engage. It was like Lucy, well really both of us, just didn't exist. I moved out not long after she was born."

He clears his throat. "Into the Inn?"

"Not yet. I was working there, but I got a tiny rental nearby. My mom helped a lot, surprisingly. She wouldn't stand up to Dad, but she was there, at least. And Ruthie, even Otis. All the staff kind of took us in."

He studies me, looking over to my side of the cab more than the open, straight highway ahead of us.

"So, this—the nun dress. Was that you back then? You were... *demure*?" Dennis says the word like it's offensive.

I laugh. "Heck no. I was even more of a little bratty, punk rock, angry hornet girl then than I am now. I've really, you know, mellowed."

Ignoring my joke, he presses, "What were you trying to prove then?"

"That I *can* be, if I want. Demure." I shrug. "Spencer said we couldn't stay together because he needed someone like his mom, a southern lady, *a queen,* he said. Someone classy to go to brunches with him and play tennis at the country club. I think my exact reply was eff you and your country club."

"Do you know which club he belongs to?"

"Dennis. You are not. Getting. Involved." I laugh, and he almost smiles, though he's still red faced and steaming.

"I am going to rip up that dress. Then we're setting it on fire."

"You are unhinged, you know that?"

He pulls the truck off the highway and onto a small road that winds through the lakeside hills. "Only with you."

I smile, but something about his reply snaps me back to reality. The idea of him *with* me. Or maybe it's the fact that we're getting so close to my home, to my real life.

"You should just take me home, Dennis."

"We'll have to be quiet there. Plus, you'll get sucked into some crisis and end up working all night."

"No, I mean drop me off at the roadside. Alone."

He laughs, surprising me. "Absolutely not."

"What are we even doing? All the reasons I had before still stand. We can't do this."

He turns onto the windy road that leads to his rented home. I sigh but he doesn't answer me until he pulls into his driveway. "We can and we are. Repeatedly. All night long."

He gets out and walks around.

I open my door, but he still takes over, pushing it all the way and offering his hand for me to climb down. I take it but I look into his eyes, trying to get him to listen.

"Seriously. What about your freaking fiancée?"

"She's not my fiancée, you know that."

I pull my hand out of his grasp, forcing myself to talk to him before going inside. "She will be though, even if you're still totally heartless about the whole arrangement. She's an actual human person and you're definitely her favorite."

He sighs and I can't tell what kind of sigh it is. "No. I am just the wealthiest."

"Does that bother you?"

"What? No."

"If you're in love with her—"

"Bloody hell. I am most definitely not in love with her. I tolerate her. Heartless, remember?"

"You…" I look down. "You call her darling."

He scoffs. "I call everyone darling."

"Not me." I look up and he frowns in thought. Maybe he didn't realize that. "Have you kissed her, or..."

He opens his mouth, then shuts it.

I turn around. "Yeah. This is dumb. Take me home."

He puts out his hand and grabs my wrist gently. "I barely kissed her at the very start, once, and no, Katherine, I haven't slept with her."

"But, I mean, you will, obviously, when she's your *wife.*" I try to go to the truck again, but he tugs me back.

"I'll drop out."

I actually look up at him. I can't really read his expression. It's open, maybe. Waiting.

"What?" My brow twists up in a confused knot. "No, you can't drop out. You'll lose everything. Your Dad, your reputation. I mean, she's the whole reason you're here."

"Not the whole reason, your father—"

I cut him off. "Dennis. C'mon."

"Fine, what do you want, then? Just friends? Because I don't think that's working very well." He squeezes my wrist.

"I don't know."

He tugs me the tiniest bit closer and his voice changes. "You do."

"O-okay." I straighten and nod. Because I really do want him. Even if it's just for a little while. But it has to be on my terms. "Okay. I want you to tell me the second there's some kind of arrangement reached with her. I *will not* be the other woman, so once you have to really try to date her, kiss her or anything else, we're done. Promise me."

"Fine. I promise."

"And nothing—I mean not even a wink at me—in public. Including at the Roadside. We'll ruin everything for you. Bartending together was bad enough, we had our own conspiracy hashtag for a while."

He wraps my arm around him and envelops me in a hug. "What was it?"

"'Dennis likes' and then the cat emoji, but you know that cat emoji also means something else, so maybe it wasn't really about me at all."

He chuckles before kissing my forehead. "It was. Especially if those little internet shits saw you at midnight." His voice turns growly. "All right, absolutely nothing in public." His eyes darken. "What am I allowed to do in private?"

I start to smile. "Whatever you—ah!" My smile turns upside down as he throws me over his shoulder and bounds up the steps. "Dennis! Put me down!"

He does, eventually—on his bed—after ignoring my laughing and yelling and whacking his butt all the way up the stairs. The bedroom is huge and woodsy to match the house. It's tidy and sparse, hardly any sign he's even staying here.

He flops down too, on top of me, and I start to laugh but his mouth takes the noise from my lips. He kisses me hard. I can't help but whimper with the way his tongue completely owns my mouth, reminding me of what he did the last time I was here. His right hand moves over the silk fabric to my chest, and he pulls back.

He sucks in a breath and tucks his finger under the fabric where the neckline forms a shallow V. His eyes flash up to mine.

"I'm going to destroy this thing now. Lie still."

My voice is all breathy. "I don't like to be bossed around."

He smirks. "You will."

I don't argue. Because I kind of think he's right in this particular moment, and because I can't look away from his hands. Slowly, he traces his fingers up my whole body, on top of the dress, then puts both hands on my neck. He leans down and kisses me, holding delicately around my throat. I hold my breath as he sits back and moves his hands to the neckline at the shoulder seam, both sets of fingers tucked in against my skin.

Then he rips it down the entire side seam.

I cry out at the feel of it. The strength of his hands and the shock of tearing, the cool air on my skin.

He pushes the sides of the dress open, exposing my body. He's still in his immaculate suit, sweating and salivating and a total freaking animal. Over me.

"Bloody hell, just look at you." His eyes take me in, and he bites his lip. All that's left on me are nude lace panties, since the dress had little cups sewn into the top.

I pull him down and his mouth goes everywhere.

He licks, bites, groans, sighs into my skin, all while I pull at his tie and tug on his shirt. He gets to work on undressing, without his mouth leaving my body for more than a breath. It is hot, but inefficient.

"Clothes off, Dennis," I whine.

He smiles, gathers me up, and straightens, so we're both sitting up. Then he extends his arms out at his sides, waiting.

"Are you going to order me to undress you?"

He grins. "Do I need to?"

"Ugh!" I start on the few buttons still fastened in his white shirt. "Why is that so hot?"

"Because"—he leans and kisses my collar bone as I unbutton his sleeve—"you have so much to think about all day long. So many worries." Kiss. "It's too many decisions." More kisses up my neck. "Taking care of the grill and the Inn and Lucy. Now you can stop thinking and just let me take care of you." He pulls back. "Take off what's left of that dress and lie on your stomach."

I narrow my eyes at him but damn if I don't quickly do exactly what he says.

He's in an undershirt now, but still in his pants.

I only got them unzipped before he took over. I push up on my elbows and look back in time to see him stand and pull off his pants, then his shirt. And the man is ripped.

"Wait." I sit up. "What the heck is this? You're a secret body builder? How? When?"

He laughs. "Early mornings. Late at night if I can't sleep. It relieves stress." He shrugs as he moves back to the bed. He puts his hand up into my hair and tugs at the pins, letting my hair fall free. His voice takes on that low, gritty sound and his words are slow. "Much better. Now, wildling...Lie. Down."

I do. I can't really see him lying this way. He's not touching me yet and the anticipation is brutal. Finally, I feel his breath on my lower back.

"It is obscene how much I've thought about these." He kisses my pebbled skin. On my tattoos. He kisses each butterfly that flies up my spine. Then he moves his mouth to my ear. "I have to have you like this. Right now. Don't move."

I don't respond. Because I don't think I can. I'm just aching need at this point, desperate and beyond ready.

He smooths a hand over my back and down, squeezing. The sound of foil tearing sends an expectant chill over me.

He teases my center with his hand, then I hear him chuff with satisfaction. He kisses my back again and lies his whole body on top of me, heavy. His mouth comes back to my ear.

"I am desperate for you, Katherine. Absolutely mad. Tell me you want me too."

I croak, "I do. Right now. And I have an IUD, so..."

He freezes. And because he'll probably ask, and I'm about to die, I go ahead and beg. "Please. Please, Dennis."

He doesn't torture me. He just tosses the condom aside and nudges himself in, and... oh. No wonder he's so confident.

I tense up and he kisses my neck, rubbing a hand along my tattoos.

"Relax, there's no rush."

I do. After a few minutes of his hands all over me and his voice in my ear, praising, cursing, sighing, he slides home. I scream his name, and he grunts mine. He takes me like he kisses me, thoroughly, fully, all the way in, all the way out.

I grip the sheets, and he puts his hands over mine. I see the bracelets, one stack on my hand, one on his. Something about it makes my eyes water.

He senses the change somehow and pulls out to flip me so I can see him. He keeps our noses together and our eyes locked as he pushes into me. His intense eye contact is only severed for more smiling, kissing, biting. I suck eagerly on his bottom lip and his eyes roll back into his head.

"You are astounding." He keeps a hand cradling my head watching every emotion on my face. There are many. I watch his face too. Pleasure, awe, a cheekiness that is uniquely Dennis.

It is deeply intimate.

Again, he works my body like an instrument. When I'm close his hand goes from my head elsewhere, coaxing not one but two releases out of me, the second in tandem with his. He calls my name and squeezes his eyes shut and I blink mine furiously.

Because I want to cry.

Because that kind of felt like a lot more than two friends enjoying some benefits while they happen to be in the same town at the same time.

And we can't be anything more than that.

26

He pants. "That was..."

"Wild?" I smile.

"Yes. Stay put," he says before kissing my nose. He goes out the bedroom door and comes back with two waters.

I blush like a silly girl at the sight of him naked and just walking around.

"What?"

My mouth falls open, but no sound comes out.

He loves this. "Lovely. I've done it. I've figured out how to keep you from grousing at me."

I take a water. "Normal people don't say 'grousing'."

"Ugh. Jinxed it." He climbs into bed and sits with his back against the headboard. Then he pulls me to sit in front of him. He runs a finger up my spine, connecting dots between the butterflies.

"You really like them, huh?" I ask.

He hums, tracing the outlines of the largest butterfly at the bottom.

"That one was the go-to tramp stamp I got as an act of rebellion as a teen. But then I added more."

"I love them," he says, just casually throwing the l-word into conversation.

My pulse quickens. I start to push up off the bed. "I should probably go."

He wraps an arm around me, so I lean back into his chest. "Did you not hear the repeatedly and all night bit?"

"I really like to sleep in my own bed."

He sighs. "Sleep? I still feel like you're not understanding my plans for you." He puts his glass on the wooden nightstand and straightens. Then he moves me forward by the shoulders and starts massaging.

"Oh," I moan. "That feels good."

"Keep making noises like that and give me ten minutes."

I relax completely into his hands and moan again. "M'kay."

"Make that five minutes." He kisses my shoulder. He is very good at this. I kind of think maybe he is good at everything. "So, did you love him then?"

"Really? We're doing pillow talk now?"

"Probably pillow arguing. For about, eh, three minutes."

I laugh and he moves my hair to kiss my neck.

"Did you?"

"Love who?"

"The khaki Viking."

I twist to look at him. "Did I tell you that? That nickname?"

"No?"

"That's what I call him in my head."

"Fits."

"Yeah, just... freaky." I turn back and he restarts the kneading with his thumbs. "I thought I did but I was seventeen. We didn't date long, and we didn't even really date."

"Hm. And Beau?"

"You really want to do this? You want me to start asking about my cousin?"

His hands slow. "If you want."

"I don't want. Too weird. And no, I didn't love Beau."

"Good. I think I kind of like the bloke now. I had one of my execs make an obscene offer on his marina and he said that it was a family business and would stay that way."

"You what?" I turn all the way around and get up on my knees. Dennis gets distracted so I set my water on the nightstand and cover myself with my hands.

"Dennis! What is wrong with you?"

"You already told me all my issues. Damsels, et cetera." He pulls my hands down and puts them on his shoulders.

I snicker. "I bet you would turn to freaking steel if I pretended to fall down and cry for help."

"No need." He urges me up and then positions himself, apparently already steel, below me. He puts his hands on my hips but doesn't yank me down.

Slowly sinking, I raise my eyebrows. "New terms to our arrangement here. No meddling in anyone's businesses because of me."

"No."

"What do you mean, no?"

He starts kissing the base of my neck. "I don't agree to your terms."

"I feel like I have all the negotiating power here." I lift up but he holds me still. Then he thrusts upward.

"Do you?"

I cry out at the size of him, and he smiles. A full, confident blinding smile. It's so gorgeous, and he feels so good, I forget what I am trying to say. We actually stop arguing and opt for kissing instead. And sucking and anything and everything we can.

He bosses me around and teases me mercilessly and calls me wildling and I can't get enough. So much so that we finish together, get a snack and more water downstairs, and then start all over again in the kitchen.

After he finds me a solid black t-shirt and his smallest pair of boxers, I restart the earlier conversation.

"I really do like to sleep at the Roadside. I just like to be there in case of something." He narrows his eyes and cocks his head, unsure. "Please Dennis, I want you to take me home now."

"All right."

On the drive over, I clear my throat. "I was serious about Spencer and his business. At some point, Lucy is going to start asking about him and I don't want her to have a dad who lives under a bridge like a troll, bitter and broken and hopeless. I've had that dad. Minus the bridge."

He reaches over and grabs my hand. "Fine. I will not ruin his life."

"Good. Plus, I fight my own battles, Dennis. No swooping. I'm still mad about this truck." He grunts in protest. "I am!"

He pulls my hand to his mouth and kisses it. Then he pulls the offensive non-gift into the farthest parking spot in the back lot of the Roadside, like I always do. He gets out and comes around, but I've already opened the door.

He helps me down, though I don't need it, and then shuts my door. "Did I mention I very much like seeing you in my clothes."

I can't help but smile. "Three times now."

"Shall I replace everything I own, bought solely in black?"

"You only brought like ten suits here."

He stops walking. "Someone's been paying attention."

"They're suits. They're ridiculous." He reaches for the back door. "Wait! You can't walk me in, what if someone sees us?"

"In the middle of the night?"

"People get up. Guests take walks to the ice machine at all hours." He huffs and puts his hand on the handle. "You cannot walk me to my door."

"That wasn't my intention," he says slowly.

My eyes go wide. "You absolutely cannot stay the night. Besides the fact that someone would see you sneaking out in the morning, I sleep in a tiny twin bed."

"Sounds cozy."

"A bunkbed. Above Lucy's."

"Okay. Too cozy."

I nod, thinking I've won but then he goes for the door again. "I'll sleep on the couch."

"Mr. DeLane?" I say his name all breathy, and he freezes. "I *knew* saying your name like that would get your attention."

He puts his hands on my hips. "You have it."

"Listen closely. I will dress in an outfit, act out a whole scene and give you the craziest, filthiest blow job you've ever gotten in your life tomorrow if you turn around and go home as quickly as possible."

Like a cartoon, I see his face go from completely frozen with the flood of thoughts, to shock at what I said, unable to compute, finally settling on determination like I've never seen before. He drops his hands and literally sprints to the truck. I can't help but laugh.

"Good night," I call, but he only waves, climbing into the truck in a frenzy. Then, making me double over and snort, he peels out of the lot.

Who knew Dennis DeLane could be so fun?

Kat: Don't freak out.

Janie: You boinked him.

Kat: ?!

Janie: You only texted me, Sherlock. No Sally = You did the dirty with Sadie's ex!

Kat: Good point, guess that was obvious. I'm tired. Because I didn't sleep. Because we were...boinking. lol

Janie: What exactly are you thinking here?

Kat: Enjoying benefits with a friend while he is in town. That's it.

Janie: Okay...

Kat: Cheer for me! I am back in the saddle! I'm out exploring the wild blue sexy yonder.

Janie: Okay...

Kat: No "..." just okay and give me a bunch of !!!!

Kat: Okay! Maybe some clap emojis, please?

Janie: Are you sure you're not developing any feelings?

Kat: I'm sure. I did this with Beau just fine.

Janie: Beau didn't spend any quality time with Lucy.

Kat: That's almost over.

Kat: All of this is. Soon he'll have to actually be with Grace, or he'll go back to San Fran.

Kat: Until then, I'm just going to have fun.

Janie: Fun that you don't want Sally or any of your sister-cousins to know about.

Kat: Yes, because it's just a fling. No need for them to get invested, and you know they would.

Janie: All right then! [clap emoji]

Kat: Thank you. [confetti emoji]

Janie: How was it?

Kat: Life altering. I think we may have shifted the space/time continuum of the universe.

Janie: lol. Just a fling though. No big deal.

Kat: Correct. There was also a lot of biting.

Janie: I'm good without the details. I am happy for you.

Kat: You need to get back out there too! Dust the cobwebs off.

Janie: Bye ttyl
Kat: [blowing off dust animated gif]

[Janie has notifications silenced]

Pfft. I tuck the phone away and reach for another wad of napkins. Refilling the napkin dispensers is an easy task Lucy can do with me. It's one of our Sunday, post-church rituals, one of the things we can do around the property together. It also requires very little work or thought since I am tired and sore.
But my phone buzzes again right after I slip it into my pocket.

Just Dennis: If your plan was to render me completely useless until I see you again, you have succeeded.
Kat: About that...
Just Dennis: yes?
Kat: I didn't really think through that today is Sunday. No school. My mom dropped Lucy off and she will be here with me all day.

He doesn't respond for a few minutes.

Kat: Are you mad?
Just Dennis: More like absolutely devastated.
Just Dennis: She will go to sleep later, yes?
Kat: Lol. Yes, but I'll be here at the Roadside. A no-zone.
Just Dennis: The truck I bought you has heavily tinted windows.
Kat: I thought that truck was for you...
Just Dennis: I'll send the truck to the Pope if I can somehow see you tonight.
Kat: lol. Probably not room in there for the outfit or role playing that I promised you.

Just Dennis: I'll settle for a kiss, wildling. Just let me come over.
Kat: Okay. I'll text you tonight.
Kat: Late.
Just Dennis: Good.
Just Dennis: Also, I'm sending you something. Don't be angry.
Kat: [unamused emoji]
Just Dennis: It's not a gift!
Kat: ...Sounds swoopy.
Just Dennis: No, I expect to be paid back.

As I am typing that I will absolutely not pay him for anything with sexual favors, he texts again.

Just Dennis: Paid back in US Dollars, just to be clear.

Then we text at the exact same time.

Kat: With interest.
Just Dennis: Without interest.

I smile and huff at the same time.

Kat: Ugh, you are the worst!
Just Dennis: I believe you said I was the best you'd ever had...
Kat: I said *one of*
Just Dennis: I'll have to rectify that straight away.

"Kat, uh, delivery!" Otis yells from the front.

I have to stop myself from leaping up and sprinting out of the storeroom. Lucy picks up on the excitement I do show though, and she follows behind me. Normally, restaurant deliveries are not exciting.

I am confused when I see no boxes and just a couple of dudes.

"Yes?" I look between Otis and the two guys.

"You're Katherine Canton?"

"Uh huh."

"We're here to install your new Point of Sale system."

All the air leaves my lungs. "The what?"

He hands me the order paperwork.

It takes me a minute to digest what I'm reading. Dennis ordered the absolute best of the best. The software, all new iPads, new registers, new scanners, everything. The equipment is way better than what I would've chosen if I had the cash in the business account to do this upgrade right now. It is also way more expensive.

"Can we get started? We can start on the Inn side. Won't interrupt your current restaurant service until this evening when we make the switch."

I look at the nervous man in the company polo. When I see the logo for the software, I'm reminded how terrible their customer service is.

"How are you here, doing this on a Sunday?"

He chuckles. "I don't really know, ma'am. Never happened before."

"I'm sure. Yes, go ahead." I open my arm to welcome them. "Sorry you're having to do this on a weekend."

The second guy laughs, too. "Oh, we're not mad about it."

"Right, you're probably getting paid like quadruple overtime or something?"

He doesn't answer, just hands me another set of papers. The top page has a note.

KATHERINE,

I AM HAPPY TO INVEST THIS SMALL AMOUNT INTO MY FAVOR-
ITE LOCAL BUSINESS. ATTACHED IS A CONTRACT THAT EXPLAINS
YOU'LL NEED TO PAY ME BACK OVER THE NEXT FIFTY YEARS. NOT A
GIFT. NOT A SWOOP TO BE SEEN HERE.

DENNIS

P.S. QUEENS DON'T DO JACK SHIT. AT THE VERY LEAST, YOU'RE
THE PRIME MINISTER.

"What's that say, Mommy?" Lucy asks, probably wondering
why I'm blushing, swaying and probably glowing, staring down
at a boring piece of paper.

"It says... It's says I'm a boss."

"Oh. This is boring."

I laugh. My hands are shaking. This is so not boring. But she's
eight so I get it as she runs back to the storeroom. I'm frozen
here, however.

Dennis listened to my story, really heard me and how I felt
when Spencer said I wasn't a *true southern queen.* Not only does
he hear me, he also sees me. Because I expected, maybe foolish-
ly, a post-sex gift like more flowers or maybe black diamonds.
Something dumb and romantic that I'd immediately send back.

This is something else entirely.

He saw a need in my business, something that drove us nuts
and slowed us down.

I am irritated he is trying to help when I asked him not to, I
am. But, wow, it's hard to be mad about this. I will pay him back.
I need to sit and go over some numbers about when and how
I can start making payments. I'm still standing at the hostess
stand when my phone vibrates again.

Just Dennis: In my defense, swooping is bloody good fun. You'll see one day when you have the expendable cash.

Kat: What I won't see is your face tonight.

[Incoming Call: Just Dennis]

I ignore his call.

Just Dennis: I am canceling the order. They'll start packing up shortly.

Kat: NO! No. They can stay.

Just Dennis: Not if it affects the kiss I have planned later.

Kat: OK. One kiss.

Just Dennis: Two!

Kat: DENNIS.

He stops while he's ahead. Or behind. I don't know what he is.

I definitely don't know what we are. The new iPad in my hand doesn't have friends-with-benefits vibes. It has...

I decide not to think about it.

For as long as I can.

Which doesn't turn out to be very long.

27

I am feeing nauseated. A sensation that began the second the high from the kiss wore off. It's weird, feeling so twisted up in my head and my gut and so glorious further south.

That man.

"I didn't say anything about kissing your mouth."

So freaking smug. So unbelievably hot.

Until we climbed out of the truck.

The crawling guilt and paranoia crept over me with each step away from him. It doubled when I slipped in the back door of the Inn and had to start vigorously scanning my surroundings for other human beings.

I couldn't place why it all felt so wrong for a second. Then I remembered taking the same type of steps my senior year in high school.

I think through it as I get changed for bed. I know it's different this time. I'm in charge.

Dennis seems completely fine with being out in the open about our arrangement. He's not ashamed of me or trying to hide a thing.

But shouldn't he be?

I climb up into my bed and pull out my phone. I have an urge to text my cousins, my go-to helpers. Except obviously, I can't.

And even Janie will just scold me and tell me to end it. If I can't talk to anyone about this, that is probably a bad sign. A sign that the *this* in question shouldn't be happening.

I pull up TikTok and start to comb through the Great Grace Race photos and videos. I am instantly reminded that people have way too much time on their hands. I can scroll through weeks of Grace's life, in vivid detail. Local accounts—a mixture of Things To Do in NWA types, fashion bloggers, hot UArk girls who lip-sync badly for their one million followers, and Welton Watch pages—open my eyes.

Grace does not want this marriage. It looks like she gave every dude three cursory dates. After that, the theory goes, she begged her dad to end the tournament.

He clearly denied her request. He also, it seems, started going on her dates. Group dates, with all the men. It's weirdly comforting, knowing Grace is not invested or hopeful about getting married. To Dennis.

I yawn. I am not sure how much time has gone by, but I am deep in the rabbit hole now. I'm pausing videos, screenshotting, zooming in. I grabbed my headphones so I could listen to background audio. I'm switching between twitter, Instagram, and TikTok so much my hand is cramping. I'm obsessing.

Dennis looks incredible, always. Literally spectacular in every clip I find. He's got that older, wiser, richer thing going on, among a group of already rich men. He's sophisticated and serious, but not aloof. He's always engaged in conversation, most often with Grace's dad.

I notice, to pathetic inner glee, that he's not usually next to Grace or touching her or talking to her like some of the guys.

Dennis isn't concerned with Grace at all.

Grace doesn't want a husband.

So, what the heck?

I switch over to Google.

New DeLane rabbit holes appear before me, and I can't help but dive in. More scrolling, more hours, more thumb pain. Soon, the answer becomes clear.

And I am livid.

In the UK, Dennis is basically a meme. *Dennis DeLoser. DeLusional. DeFeated, DeFunct.*

I have to put my phone down to keep from screaming and waking Lucy below me.

As far as I can tell, the reasons for the garbage spewed about him are only that he is the second born son of a billionaire lord. That he had a lot of horrible coverage by London paparazzi in his teens and twenties and that he moved to the US to "escape" said bad press.

There are rumors that go along what Dennis alluded to with me. Because of the ongoing embarrassment, and inability to settle down with a proper wife, his dad is threatening to cut him out of the family.

As much as I can tell, it's not about money. Dennis would still be beyond obscenely rich. It means he'd be ex-communicated, perhaps even required to change his name.

Change his name?

I would've fled to another country, too.

I keep scrolling. Paparazzi still followed him around New York, of course. But he wasn't all that exciting to them, other than his high-profile girlfriends. And fiancée...

This part is going to suck.

I take a deep breath and pull up a fan site for "America's Paramour" one of the media's nicknames for Sadie. This blogger catalogued their entire romance and I force myself to take in every word. I look at them in photo after gorgeous photo.

Dennis and Sadie.

In New York City. At museums, seeing Broadway shows, at the ballet. Kissing in front of Rockefeller Center. Getting engaged on some rooftop patio that looks like a movie set. They're beautiful, unreal. Celebrities.

They're both so much younger. Dennis seems guarded, much more so than I know him to be now. Sadie is, well, wasted. I can tell she was high in a lot of the photos. *Total damsel. Called it!*

The gossip site goes into theories about the real stories within the book Sadie wrote loosely based on their relationship, and the subsequent film. Before the movie came out, Sadie called off the wedding. The blogs and magazines in the UK had a field day with *Dennis DeDUMPED!* headlines, meanwhile the US rags went on and on about how stupid Sadie was to let him go. Stateside he was portrayed as jilted, heartbroken, and stunned.

I vaguely remember Sadie saying he wasn't stunned at all. She claimed they had been having problems for months, but their romance had become a press op for the movie, so everything got complicated. Of course, the man himself told me she only hurt his pride and nothing else. That seems hard to believe, especially seeing the way he looked at her in a lot of these pictures.

I can see how pride would be a big part of it though.

Dennis is a confident man. He's obviously good looking, stays in unreal shape, and he holds power and influence that comes from wealth. Not to mention what the man can do with his tongue. Also, he's hung like a prize stallion.

Who wouldn't be confident if they were him?

Being publicly jilted must have thrown him for a loop. He's a lot more than his public persona though. Lucy can tell you that. As can all the women who watched him walk into her cheer exhibition. The bracelets on his wrist, the new POS system a few rooms away. He is genuinely thoughtful.

He clearly cares about what he does, too. He's a master at his craft, which I now know—after reading every article ever written about him, even the ones behind subscription gateways that I will surely forget about and pay for monthly, for months—involves financial crisis management, for companies, trust funds, private investors, and non-profits, too. He saves his clients from bankruptcy and recalibrates them so not only do they survive, but he also totally turns things around so they usually go on to dominate their markets. I saw it in his presentation for my dad's little multi-million-dollar business. He's smart and he cares.

He's done an almost unfathomable amount of charity work too. *Almost* because he's a billionaire. Millions donated here and there make sense within the bigger DeLane picture. It is a huge picture, actually, lords and ladies spanning back generations, alongside the actual British crown. The DeLanes kind of make Emerson's family, the Clarks, seem like small-timers, even though they're also some of the world's richest billionaires. I can't even comprehend that kind of wealth.

I yawn and look at the time. It's four in the morning.

In light of it all, Dennis seems, surprisingly normal.

He also seems completely amazing. It gets me angry all over again, thinking about how his countrymen treat him across the pond. No wonder he never moved back to London.

I want him to win this contest. His dad is not going to cut him off. The idea is criminal. Dennis has to win.

I will have to just block out that the prize of said contest is a wife. I mean, I don't want to be his wife. I'm A-okay with him marrying someone else. I guess I'm just bummed to think about our friendship ending. And by friendship, I mean earth-shattering orgasms.

I put my phone down, stretch my cramping fingers, and sigh.

I feel better. Dennis was being honest about Grace, there's nothing between them. Having a quick fling with him while he is in town and still single is no big deal. As long as no feelings get involved, a problem I think I just solved tonight, by staring at him and my cousin for an hour.

This thing with us is just fun. The other conditions I've set in my brain tonight are that Lucy doesn't get too attached to him, my family never finds out, and that Dennis wins the weird bachelor competition. Which means the focus, our focus, since I am re-committed to helping him, is no longer on Grace.

It's time to woo Mr. Rockford.

28

Kat: I'm outside.
Dennis: So come inside.
Dennis: Pun intended.
Kat: No, we're going somewhere.
Dennis: I am naked in here.
Kat: Then put on some clothes and come out.
Dennis: Take off your clothes and come in.
Kat: In three minutes I'm leaving, with or without you.

At the same time, we have the same thought.

Kat: I'll be coming with or without you too...
Dennis: As long as there's no coming without me...

I can't help but laugh.

Kat: Two minutes twenty seconds!

He stops responding and stumbles out the door soon after, in a dress shirt and slacks without a tie. He's irritated, a fact that makes him even hotter in my twisted brain. Maybe because that's just what we do—drive each other nuts.

He stomps around to my door of the truck and flings it open.

I open my mouth to tell him that I can drive but he's already grabbed my face with both hands. It's been days and every time he's like this. Kissing me like it's our last—maybe all of humanity's—last kiss. Always urgent, hard, purposeful.

I moan into him, like I do each time.

His hands start to move, and I pull away. "Nope, we're leaving."

"Out then, wildling."

"I can drive."

"I don't much feel like vomiting just now. Maybe later." He glares.

I laugh and climb down, enjoying the feel of his hands on me as I go.

He pulls me into him once I'm on the ground. "You're sure you want to leave? I had grand plans."

"I'm sure. This is important." I jerk myself away and run, giggling as he mutters under his breath. I know he was going to try to grab me and keep me tucked into him. I hurry around and climb into the truck on the other side.

He watches me, wary. Eventually he climbs in and adjusts the seat.

"Where to?"

"Town."

He turns the key in the ignition and the truck simply starts, a glorious new-vehicle phenomenon I'm still getting used to. "Care to elaborate?"

"No."

"Tell me honestly"—he hits the brakes at the end of his driveway—"will this end with feces on my hands?"

"Ha!" I let myself laugh at him. "Feces? *Feces,* Dennis?"

He shrugs and looks behind him to turn the truck onto the road. "I'm trying not to curse."

"What?" I frown. "Why?"

"For Lucile, obviously."

My chest does a weird squeezy thing. "You don't need to do that."

He glares over at me, then back at the road. "You have enough jars for the both of us, Katherine."

"Yeah, but, I mean, you'll be gone soon."

He checks the road before making a left turn out onto the two-lane highway. "Still, we've weeks until then." He sighs. "Weeks I'd quite hoped would be spent in my bedroom."

"Oh, get over it," I tease. "I'm helping you out today."

"Again, I'm worried about the substances I might come in contact with."

"No feces, calm down. Just a shopping trip."

He perks up. "Are you going to let me spoil you, finally?"

"Never."

He sighs again but I just laugh and turn up the radio. He grabs my hand from the dial and holds it. I look down at our inter-locked fingers, resting on the neon pink leather console. My nails are chipped and dirty, my hand has one scabbed scrape and one band aid. His hand looks like he gets those Satin Hands treatments my mother used to get at, like, Tupperware parties when I was tiny.

Still, how natural it feels, our hands, resting there is... It's *un-natural*. I try to pull away, but he doesn't let me go. I look over, but his face is neutral. Stunning, but blank, just driving. I don't think he minds me trying to pull away because he simply won't allow it. For now.

———

"Tim's Club, really?"

"Yes, really. I'm guessing you've never been inside one or its younger sibling, AmeriMart. We're going big right off the bat." I gesture to the building. "Do you know how it works?"

"Of course, I know how cash and carries work."

I tilt my head, "Cash and what?"

"Tim's Club. It's a cash and carry. That's what we call them in the UK." I wait until he goes on. "Pay cash and carry out."

"That's literally how all stores work. Are there places you pay cash and don't carry out what you bought?"

He sighs. "I don't know the origin of the term, Katherine. I just know it's bulk purchasing without having to order from a catalogue."

"Okay, well, we will be googling that term later. You've never been in one, right?"

"No, and I must say my plans to be inside—"

"I know, I know, you are pouty because you didn't get your afternoon delight. You'll live." I open my door.

"Debatable," he grumbles as he gets out. "Why won't you let me get your door for you, woman?"

"Because it's too slow," I call over my shoulder. "Look I'm already almost to the door and you're still faffing back there."

"Did you just say faffing?"

I turn around and smile. "I heard Emerson say it once."

"I am not faffing. But I do like hearing you say it." His eyes are so warm and gooey as he walks toward me, I stay frozen in place on a grassy median. "Once I convince you to switch from coffee to tea we'll be set." He reaches me and extends his hand.

"Put your hand down," I shriek. "We're in public, I'm not holding your hand,"

"Yet another reason we should've stayed home," he huffs.

I wave my unheld hand. "*Pfft*, come on."

He follows me inside. I see the surprise all over his face.

Not only is this a Tim's Club, which are huge anyway, this is *the* Tim's Club, down the street from AmeriMart Headquarters. When an actual Welton could walk in at any moment, stakes are high. The employees greet us happily at the front, and there's not a spec of dirt on the floors.

"Bloody hell, this place is monstrous."

"Right? And so bright and clean. My cousins didn't believe me that AmeriMarts here are better than any Target in the rest of the country until they saw for themselves. Tim's is even bigger and better. Come on."

He has trouble comprehending what he's seeing, as I expected. Giant TVs next to gazebos next to massive amounts of chips and then women's tights, then paperback books and on and on. Then he starts looking at the prices, usually in disbelief at how cheap things are. I snap some photos and videos of him as we move through the store.

"How do you normally shop?" I ask.

He's looking up, mouth hanging. "I, uh, I don't."

"Ever?"

"I used to go to the tailor to pick out my suits, but eventually there was no need, he sends them to me."

"Groceries?"

"Chef, personal shoppers. Assistants."

I laugh. "Well, just look at what you've been missing out on!" I open one of the refrigerators.

"What's that?"

"This"—I flop the bag down into the cart—"is five pounds of shredded cheese." His face twists up, disturbed. "I know, bulk quantities are kinda gross, but can you imagine how much cheese the Roadhouse goes through? We don't have time to hand shred all of it. Help me get a couple more."

"More?" He gapes.

"Of just the shredded. Then we'll have to get cheese blocks and cheese slices too."

"You're joking."

"I never joke about cheese. Wait until you see how much butter I get." I waggle my eyebrows at him, mischievous. Mischievous and flirty. He reaches for me, trying to cop a feel. I give him my best threatening eyes-wide look, but he just shoves up beside me, pretending to reach around me for something on a shelf.

He whispers in my ear. "If you didn't look so fantastic every single minute, maybe I could keep from touching you." I shudder and he inhales. "And smell fantastic. And taste fantastic." His need becomes obvious, pressing into my side, and I can't help but lean right back into him. "Ugh. Let's get out of here."

"Not yet." I shift away and he slumps, gripping the shelf for support. "There's so much more to see, and I actually am stocking up for the Roadside, so we need to finish my list."

He inhales, a little shaky, and I can't help but laugh. Dennis the billionaire with a visible hard-on in the middle of the dairy aisle at Tim's Club.

"Do you need a minute?"

He sighs but he's almost smiling. "Why do you hate me so?"

"I think I showed you just how much I don't hate you yesterday afternoon. And the night before that." His heated gaze comes back to me, this time with a real grin. "Just stand behind the cart and try not to look at me."

He huffs but we do move on. I get short video clips of him almost yelling about how great the prices are, even on items no one needs. We reach the pool area, and he holds up a massive orca whale pool float that has a tiny motor to move around the pool and spray water out of a spout on the top.

"Look at this! Doesn't Lucy need one of these?"

"We don't have a pool."

He looks like a little kid, holding a new toy above his head. "Buy a pool and have it installed, just so she can have this. It's bloody brilliant."

"True," I say, making sure to get our conversation on camera. "Aren't you getting kind of hungry?"

"I suppose, why?" he says, finally putting down the whale.

I enjoy watching his muscles shift under his tight dress shirt. The viewers of this clip will too. Something about that makes me a bit pissy but I move on. "Because now we need to go try the free samples."

"Samples? Of what?"

"Everything, Dennis. Dips, crackers, meats, desserts. Everything."

He raises his eyebrows slightly. "I'm starting to quite like shopping."

I laugh and put my phone down. *Perfect.*

He steps up to me, curious. "Why are you suddenly playing paparazzi, wildling?"

"Why do you call me that?" He frowns and lifts one shoulder. "Why not wildcat?"

His expression changes to concern. "Do you want me to call you wildcat?"

"No, just curious. I mean, my name is Kat."

He shakes his head. "Your name is Katherine and it's beautiful. Like you."

I clear my throat, which is starting to close up on me. "Don't be nice, it's creepy. Let's go find some free snacks."

"Only after you take a photo *with* me."

"Okay?" I step toward him, weirded out by his request.

"I know you're up to something." He pulls out his phone, then grabs me and tucks my back into his front. He shifts us so you can see the stupid whale above our heads in the background. His arm is locked around me in a way that is way too intimate for the middle of this store.

"Dennis!" I try to shift to a more platonic position, but he won't let me budge. He chuckles, ignoring my rules and pushing my buttons. So I decide to push back. I pose with a smile and the peace sign but reach around with my other hand as he gets the photo set. Right as he puts his thumb on the capture button, I grab his crotch. His eyes go wide, and he makes a weird noise. He releases me so I can double over with laughter.

"Every now and again I forget that you're totally loony," he huffs.

"Let me see it," I say between bellows.

He pulls up the picture on his phone and rolls his eyes but he's grinning. He turns it around so I can see. I'm smiling like an angel, and he looks like he's going to vomit. It's amazing.

"This is the best photo that has ever been taken since the beginning of time!"

"You're quite easily amused, you know that?" He pulls his phone back and shoves his hands into his pockets.

"I do. A cheerful heart is good medicine, Lucy says the Bible says. Between you and her making me laugh, I'm going to live forever."

He sets his jaw and angrily adjusts his pants. "Not if I kill you first."

I laugh again and wave for him to follow me to the samples. I get great footage of him groaning with delight over a new Ranch dip. He made the employee blush and then put three jars of it in our cart. I mean, Ranch of all things! I couldn't have planned a better America's Heartland Husband Material type of purchase if I tried.

We hustle through the rest of the shopping and back to his house so he can get his car and return to work. After a quickie, because he was a really good sport in there.

Once I have all the supplies and groceries unloaded, I sit down in the office with my phone.

"Stella," I call out.

She breezes in through the door and plops on the couch. "You rang?"

"You have a TikTok, right?"

"Of course."

I smile. "How would you like to get some inside scoop for the Great Grace Race?"

She gasps. "What? Yes! How? Who, Dennis?"

"Yes, you know he's tutoring Lucy and we've become friends. We need to help him," I explain, she nods and scoots forward, absolutely giddy. "I got some photos and videos of him in Tim's Club for the first time, you work your magic putting it all together. Here, I'm air dropping them to you."

She accepts the photos and starts scrolling. "Oh my gosh, love it. Yes. So cute."

"Just make sure you can't see me or hear me in anything, okay? Keep the focus on Grace."

"Got it." She starts watching videos, stopping and starting and switching between her apps already.

"Also, are old rich white men on TikTok?"

She grunts. "I hope not."

"What about LinkedIn?"

She looks up at me, totally confused. "What is a Link in?"

"Ha. Exactly. If you don't know what it is, that's where Mr. Rockford is. So we need to figure out how to post all the Dennis and Grace stuff over there."

She thinks. "I'll ask my dad."

"Perfect." I pull up the TikToks about Grace that I've already seen a million times. "Maybe come up with a new hashtag just for Dennis or maybe for Dennis and Grace, like their would-be wedding hashtag or something?"

She looks up. "Wait. What about just hashtag Grace DeLane? Like they're already a done deal?"

I nod. Because I can't talk. Or breathe.

Grace DeLane.

It sounds perfect.

Which is the whole point. I cannot get upset about this. I don't want to marry Dennis and wear beige polka dots and become some Stepford billionaire socialite wife out in San Francisco. I really don't. Dennis really does need to win.

So *hashtag Grace DeLane* it is.

Tim's, step one, was a success. Now on to step two.

29

"Boss, we got a problem." Stella barges into my office.

"Another one?" I collapse back into my wobbly desk chair.

Ruthie cuts in before Stella can start. "Honey, you've been working on this one for months. It'll sort itself out."

"Unless you've got a mattress full of cash somewhere, I don't see how, Ruthie. They keep outbidding me. Out of freaking nowhere."

Ruthie huffs. "You know who it is."

"How did he find out? I have been so, *so* careful."

"I don't know but, in this town, if it walks like a duck and talks like a duck..." she starts.

"Then it's probably Spencer," I finish.

Stupid, sneaky Spencer.

Stella waits, listening, trying to figure out what we're discussing. She won't. It's cute to watch her try and puzzle it out, though.

I straighten. "Well, nothing I can do about the duck right this second, so what do you have for me, Stella?"

"Well, it's about Dennis."

"Okay?" I ask as Ruthie huffs again on her way out.

She doesn't think we should be involved in the arranged marriage situation in any way. She claims we're helping Dennis cheat in a game that they shouldn't even be playing.

I think she might have other reasons for her protest but I'm not going to ask about them.

Stella sits down in front of me with her phone. "He lost a lot of popularity points today."

"What? He was doing so well."

Dennis has been crushing it, thanks to me and my multi-step plan. We've gone to all the local hot spots, where I've gotten shots of him buying this or raving about that. We went on a hike with Lucy where I captured not only gorgeous shots of him by the lake, but I also got hilarious footage of him buying all new clothes and gear from Bass Pro Shop for said hiking trip.

We went to a giant chicken farm, an eye-opening experience for all of us. We're all considering becoming vegetarians now.

My whole staff went to volunteer at the local food bank, and he came along and just happened to be the only one photographed. Stella even figured out how to get a local business influencer to post a lot of the photos onto LinkedIn. Each step has gotten him closer and closer to being Mr. Rockford's top pick.

So I can't believe what Stella just said. I suck down my afternoon iced coffee and wait for her to go on.

"Well, he was caught messing around with another woman, and he's getting roasted for it."

I spit coffee everywhere.

Great.

"Kat? Are you okay?"

"Yes," I croak. "Tickle in my throat." I cough and try and cover up for the fact that I just spewed iced mocha all over my desk like a well-caffeinated fire hydrant. She helps me dab everything dry with paper towels before she continues.

"See? It's pretty obvious."

I take the phone from her hand. It's a meeting between Dennis and Mr. Rockford. I should be excited about that, that's a good sign. But I'm irrationally bothered at the sight of Dennis eating at a nice steakhouse in town. *As if he can only eat at the Roadside, Kat? Come on!*

A waitress passes, coming into view on one side of the screen and walking toward whoever is filming. Her face is pretty, but her curves steal the show. She has the hourglass of hourglasses. So much *cake*, as Stella says. I'm not sure if cake is boobs or butt, either way, this chick has it.

When she passes Dennis, he does a double take, then stares. It looks like he watches her walk away. And bites his lip. He also gets up and, from what we can see, follows after her. The person filming tucks their phone away so all we can see for a moment is the fabric of the tablecloth. Then when it pops back up, we see them both disappear into a hallway.

My eyes sting. Must have gotten some coffee in them.

Stella is right, it does look bad.

"He could have just been going to the bathroom," I offer weakly.

"Could have, but have you ever seen a guy look at a girl like that and then follow her and them *not* end up goin' at it in a supply closet? I meeeannn..." She says *yikes* with her facial expression.

"Right. Well, what about the fact that Grace is dating four other men? Isn't this kind of unfair?"

"Totes. But she hasn't been spotted anywhere at all lately so it's out of sight out of mind. Plus, he was sitting there with her dad. It's like" —she switches to a low, dude voice—"Hey, can I have your daughter's hand in marriage, oh wait, gotta go hook up with this hot waitress, brb, bro!"

I watch the clip over and over, growing angrier and angrier. I shouldn't, because Dennis and I never said we'd be exclusive. I only specified I didn't want to be a side piece when things with Grace became real. We didn't discuss anything or anyone besides Grace. Without that conversation, I shouldn't have assumed. Plus, why would I care about exclusivity in this situation, one that revolves around his future wife?

Yet here I sit, beyond pissed.

"When was this?"

"Sometime today, not sure when it was filmed but it was posted a few hours ago."

I hand her phone back, swiveling my red face away from her. I pretend to sort through some papers.

I cancelled on Dennis today because I had to powwow with Ruthie about the battle going on with Spencer. I only have so much time each day. Dennis and I have been going at it so hard, metaphorically and literally, that I felt the need to go get my IUD checked, just to be sure. Another appointment I barely had time for.

Dennis and I usually meet up once during the day while Lucy is at school and then again in my truck after she falls asleep. It's beyond hot, beyond nuclear, even, though it's almost always rushed. I think we've used every surface of his rental house except his bed. I push him to push me further and crazier, so we haven't had any slow missionary sex other than that first time.

Take off your shorts and bend over the couch.

Tie this over your eyes.

Crawl to me, wildling.

Now my face is red for a different reason. So many *lessons*, too, since I told him about my dream. One day I couldn't sit down the whole evening.

And Dennis wants more. He asked to come stay at the Inn so he'd be down the hall. He has been begging me to ask my mom for a Lucy sleepover so I can stay the night at his place. The man is insatiable.

But maybe it's not for me. Maybe he's just insatiable, full stop. I mean period. Insatiable, period.

I suck in a deep breath. This is not a huge deal. In fact, I knew he and I wouldn't last long. This is the thing about flings, one person moves on to the next fling, then the next.

Stella sighs behind me, bringing me back to the issue at hand.

I swivel back around. "What do you suggest he do to save face?"

"I think at this point he needs to do something for Grace, with Grace. Be seen with her."

I nod. "Makes sense. I'll tell him."

She studies me. "You're, like, a really good friend, Kat."

I let out a bitter little laugh. It sounds a bit broken. "Thanks."

She leaves and I get my phone out to look at the video again. But as often happens, Dennis and I have some kind of ESP connection. We call at the same times, say the same thing, or text the same comment at the exact same time.

In this particular instance, he's texting me while I am imagining kicking my boot into his groin.

Dennis: All good now? What was the emergency?
Kat: Yup.
Dennis: ??
Kat: It was nothing.
Dennis: I sincerely hope you didn't cancel on me for nothing.
Kat: I'm sure you have backup booty calls for occasions like this.

The typing bubble pops up and goes away and pops up again.

Dennis: Do you? Have backups?
Kat: It's unladylike to talk about such things...

> Dennis: Since when do you give a damn about being a lady??

Well, that stings.

I move my thumb to put my phone on DND mode but knowing him, he'll just show up here. It's not the healthiest of traits, his deep-seated control issues. Good thing we're not actually dating.

> Kat: Ha. GTG, I'll see you at the first float tonight.
> Dennis: You will?
> Kat: Of course. It's tradition.
> Dennis: You have a boat?
> Dennis: Or whose boat?
> Dennis: Beau's boat?
> Dennis: ???

That, I don't answer. Let him squirm. He hates not knowing things. He still doesn't know quite a few things about my life. I don't tell him where I'm coming from or going to when we meet up. He knows I have projects I'm working on but doesn't know what they are.

I can see that the mysteries bother him. Even though he gets all twitchy and short with me, he doesn't pry. Because we're not really dating. He's not going to push for personal details with a fling. If I were his girlfriend, he'd probably insist on knowing all the minutia of my business and daily schedule and Lucy's life, top to bottom.

Good thing I'm not.

This is casual.

People fling around with multiple people.

I'm not people. I've never felt right about seeing more than one guy at a time because there was always a clear winner. I usually know if we're vibing right away. But beyond that, what working, single mother has the time to date around? Not me. But Dennis doesn't need to know that.

––––

Susan: Happy First Float!
Kat: How do you remember such things?
Susan: ...I know how to use a calendar.
Skye: [Animated gif "What, like it's hard?"]
Sam: Wish we were there!!!!
Sadie: Send pics!
Sally: What is first float, again?
Kat: Our town's official start of lake season, a cookout at the marina and then all of Beau's rental boats form a parade and most of the boaters in the marina join in the parade.
Sam: You're underselling it! It's so fun!
Skye: Are you sponsoring again?
Kat: Yup, selling food and launching the new line I told you guys about!
Sadie: Such a boss!
Sally: PEAK KAT

I smile at that. It's a phrase my Aunt Sandra, their mother, coined and we all use it now. It makes me emotional. They all add a heart reaction to Sally's last message before Susan continues.

Susan: I need a Lucy pic! It's been over a week!
Kat: [photo]
Sam: OMG your twin
Sally: [heart eyes emoji]
Susan: [heart eyes emoji]
Sadie: Adorable
Skye: I see she's entered her blue era! [blue heart emoji]

What?

Wow, I am the worst mother ever.

I look at the photo I snapped a few minutes ago when we arrived at the edge of the lake. She was beaming in the low sun, standing at the water's edge. I guess most of the time she's wearing long sleeves so maybe I can give myself a pass. A small one.

But there they are.

There are two black bracelets for me, our one matching neon pink bracelet, a purple one for my mom, a yellow strand, Ellie's favorite color, and at least four blue bracelets.

I know who they represent. I also see she's wearing a neon blue marina shirt, that's just a coincidence. But blue socks and blue fingernails and a blue bow, too?

I swallow.

This week is her test. Then it'll be over. I'll end my arrangement with him too if I have to, which would be fine.

I am not falling in love with Dennis. But I fear Lucy might be.

30
DENNIS

I force myself to ease my car into the marina parking lot like a civilized human being and not a madman coming unglued at the seams.

Backup booty calls?

What the f—hell? No. Heck. What the heck?

I take a breath before opening my car door. I am headed to meet everyone on the Rockford's boat, meaning Grace and her father, Hal—and all the townies with their phones and their Grace Race obsession—wait outside this car.

And my obsession is here somewhere, likely with Beau. At least that is my guess, as the little brat didn't clarify for me. I exit the Audi and merge into a throng of people.

It's cool out but people are in swimsuits anyway, carrying coolers and buzzing with excitement. The crowd weaves through the cars toward the main gate that leads to the floating gas station and gift shop. I can smell food grilling and hear music, chatter, and laughter.

Her laughter.

I pick up my pace.

By the water's edge I spot her from behind, unloading something from her truck. So she's working. Of course, she is.

By the time I reach the truck, she's already across the gangway, so I decide to wait. She'll come back to move her truck out of the main thoroughfare. My eyes find her neon hair bobbing in and out of the crowd as she runs around. I can't tell what she's doing but she's quick about it, as always.

Finally, she starts moving back to me. All I can see are glimpses of pink braids. At last, I can see her face. Then her body comes into view, clad in a black bikini top under an open shirt and her barely-there shorts.

My breath leaves me.

This woman will be the death of me.

She has consumed me whole.

I know this can't last. Just look at her—all tight, lively, hot. Fun.

I'm too old for her. Too set in my ways. Too different. Our lives are too different. And she's too free, too wild, too vivacious to be slowed, especially by someone like me. That fact likely explains why she keeps me at a distance.

The little wildling continually pushes me away, toward Grace—or Grace's father, anyway. She really seems to care about this contest for me, for my standing within my family. Over and over, she makes it clear she only sees me as a friend.

Well, a friend who makes her combust three times a day. And vice versa. She makes me feel like a randy teenager again. Her little bikini isn't helping matters in that regard.

I look away from her lithe body back up to her face, trying to redirect the blood that was rushing south of my belt. Her smile twists into a scowl when she spots me. I smirk at first, until I see she's not playing with me. The frown is genuine.

"Hey," she says in a light, happy tone that is a total farce.

"Are you all right?"

"Never better. Just one more load." She doesn't look at me, focused instead on the open truck bed. I didn't even notice the packages. I was totally focused on her.

"What's this? Can I help?"

She grunts, pulling on a crate with a bunch of bags inside it.

"Nah, I got it."

"Katherine, let me." She starts to fight me, until I yank the wooden box from her. The bulky thing is much easier for me to manage, but she rolls her eyes and slams the tailgate closed.

"What are these?"

"Use that big brain of yours and read the labels, *Dennis*," she snipes, turning away and waving for me to follow her.

"You're angry with me."

"Nope, just busy," she lies over her shoulder. She's clearly upset, I just have no idea what about.

I haven't told her any of my ideas for her business, haven't bought her any gifts. I look down at my cargo. I can't speak at first, trying to process.

Products.

She's created a line of products. I scan the bags, all labeled "Roadside Secret Ingredients." Sweet Waffle Mix. Best Burger Marinade. Rib Rub. Pig Sooie Pie Filling.

"Katherine... When... How did you?"

She doesn't answer me. In fact, she's not even near me anymore.

I'm barely walking, staring instead at the stellar packaging, with the roadside logo in bright red and white. There's a typeset design like a stamp that gives simple instructions to "just add" meat, butter, water, and so on to the mixes. I chuckle at the sticker that has a quote attributed to Ruthie saying, "Honey, if it don't taste right, add sugar."

I have so many questions. Like I've had since I arrived in these hills months ago. I know she won't want to answer them, but I can't help myself. I rush to the table where she's adjusting some samples. I set the box down, in shock and so utterly proud.

She won't look at me, but I also know she'll put up a front with all the people around.

"When did you do this?"

"They just arrived day before yesterday, thank God above, or I would've missed this."

I touch her arm. "Katherine." She pulls away but looks at me. "It's brilliant."

"I agree, hopefully everyone else will too." She shrugs. Not even a smile.

Uh oh. I am right screwed for sure.

"They will." I inch closer to her, but she gets back to work next to one of her employees—Rebecca, I think. "What's next? There's a parade or something, I heard?"

"Yup. You're at the wrong side of the marina though," she says, back to refusing to glance in my direction. "This here is where the employees and vendors will be. Normal townsfolk. You'll want to go to that far end." She points. "Where the *yachts* are. The cruisers filled with champagne and linen and expensive leather boat shoes." She looks down at my feet. "Yeah, those. Just keep walking until you spot some *ladies.*"

Oh.

I texted that when I was in a cloud of rage. Clearly, I still have work to do. I am a patient, level man, until I'm not. Then I tend to explode without thinking, a trait that cost me my best friend not too long ago, and the respect of a family I still care about.

One member in particular.

The thought of her with someone else made me drop my teacup earlier. Then again, on the way here. I almost smashed the car whilst closing my eyes to block out the anger.

"Katherine, I—"

"Mr. Dennis!" My second favorite female voice cuts me off.

I smile and bend down to scoop Lucy up as she runs in my direction. She leaps up into a hug, warm and happy. The polar opposite of her mother at this moment.

"Lucile! Where have you been hiding?"

"I got to help Mr. Beau with the party barges."

I put her back down. "Is that right?"

"Yes, he even let me drive."

"He what?" I startle.

Katherine waves me off. "He's sitting right there with her, it's fine." She turns to her miniature twin. "Bug, I need you to stop running around, okay? You could slip and fall in or get bumped over by the crowd. Come sit back here."

"But this is boriiiiiing," she wails.

"Lucile." I say in a tone she knows well.

In some of our math sessions, toward the end, she gets tired and puny and tries to whine at me. I told her whining makes terrible tasks take longer and that she's old enough to simply state what's bothering her. I added, without thinking, that DeLanes do not whine.

She'd replied she wasn't a DeLane and the statement made my lungs collapse. Or at least that was how it felt.

Bizarre.

Lucy straightens and calmly objects. "Mommy. I don't like sitting still behind the table. Can I please go back to Mr. Beau's boat?" The little angel looks at me. I give her an encouraging nod and try to hide the host of other feelings bubbling up. Namely the desire to sink all the boats and take both of these beautiful girls out of here immediately.

Katherine hands Lucy her phone. "Here, set a five-minute timer and when it goes off, we'll head over there together, okay?"

Then they are both going to Beau's boat, as I expected.

Now I want to sink the entire marina too. I need to get a handle on this. As if she's going to remain celibate after I marry and move away? I realize I'm staring. And gritting my teeth so hard my jaw is throbbing.

"You'd better get moving or they'll leave without you," Kat says to me, still not looking up. "And you need to dance with Grace. It's been too long since anyone has seen you two actually together."

I keep staring. I don't want to dance with Grace. I don't want to anything with Grace, she knows this. But she's walked away, and Lucy after her. Now I'm just gawking at the booth, probably looking like I'm ogling the teenage waitress.

Great.

Even with their backs to me, it takes all of my focus to turn my body away from the mother-daughter duo. They're both like magnets to me. Again, a totally foreign and somewhat frightening sensation. Like I'm not meant to be apart from them, and yet here I go, walking away.

I shake my head and pick up my pace.

There are long floating sidewalks connecting the docks. I can see the boat slips get larger and larger as I go. Makes sense Hal's boat would be at the very end.

I start to see familiar faces, all, as she claimed, in pressed linen and the damned Sperry shoes. No crocs or flip flops here, though I can't say I mind that. I don't understand why or when it became acceptable to just publicly display one's toes. Disgusting.

I do mind these people though. Not all of them, but many. Suck ups, phonies, leeches. Waiting for just a minute to "pick my brain" or tell me how their invention or mission or startup will "change the world" *...if they could only get an investor.*

All these wankers clamoring for my time, money, and attention. Meanwhile almost every one of them holds one of Kat's samples in their hand, or a beer wrapped in a Roadside koozie. Or behind them, in the galleys of their massive boats, I can see her new products on the counter. I'd clear out one of my funds for her in an instant, yet she hasn't asked me for help once.

"Dennis! C'mon mate," Ben calls down to me from the bridge of what must be Rockford's vessel. It's a large cabin cruiser, still small compared to my yachts. It seems a little silly for this lake, though, since it's an ocean vessel meant to easily cut through large waves on rough seas. "Seriously, we're going to miss it."

I climb over the short wire railing. I nod at one of the catering staffers as I climb up the narrow white fiberglass staircase on the back of the boat. At the top I move across the stylish open seating area to join the group.

"Miss what?"

"We're not sure, actually," Grace says, half laughing. Right. Grace. "But we know it starts soon."

I cross over to her, and she greets me with a hug while the other blokes watch awkwardly.

"I'll get us fixed up, don't y'all worry," the hired captain says.

I suppose Hal can't drive his own boat. Not that I can drive mine but they're much larger with multiple engines and thrusters and things.

Everyone looks at him, curious, but he just offers a sheepish smile. "We put the radio to a set station, all the boats do. You'll see."

We do, shortly after, and a voice cuts through the static in the speakers. Katherine's voice.

"Welcome to the third annual First Float, everybody!"

HONK!

All of us jump out of our skin as the entire marina, some three hundred boats, honk their horns. The captain laughs at us.

"Y'all know the drill, Lost Lake Marina's fleet will lead the way out of the no wake zone, remember all these pretty party barges, ski boats and jet skis are available to rent every day of the week all summer long so tell your friends who wish they had a boat of their own. To jam with us for the entire parade, keep your radio locked in on this station, with an epic playlist provided by..."

There's a pause and then a tiny voice comes on. "The Roadside Inn and Grill. Next time you're out this way come by and see us for lunch!"

My chest aches at the sound of Lucy, clearly smiling, and, if I had to guess, hopping from foot to foot, trying to contain her excitement and keep her voice level. A feat she just did, beautifully. She sounded so much like her mother.

Kat's voice is back, "Alrighty lake bums, start your engines in five, four, three..." As she finishes talking, The Beach Boys fill the radio and *Good Vibrations* begins. At the same time, all the boats start their engines. The noise, and actual vibration, is unreal.

All of us are stunned, looking around.

Wesley pipes up first. "This Beau guy is a freaking genius."

"Wasn't his idea, though," Benedict says, smiling. "It was Kat's."

Of course, it was. I move to the edge of the top deck so I can see the boats that are supposed to lead this grand parade. So I can see her. I'm only half aware that they keep talking behind me.

"Kat from the bar?" Grace asks.

Ben nods. "Yeah, the marina and the grill both struggle through the early spring so she started this to get lake season started a little earlier, remind people they're out here."

"Hal, you need to hire that girl before the Weltons do," Wesley says. "She should be running someone's marketing department."

"Ha, she'd hate that. Still, you're right," Ben says.

Hal agrees and then they start talking about some marketing plan that sounds utterly dull.

But Wesley is not right. She shouldn't be running someone's anything. She's already running her own thing, and she's a force of bloody nature. I've got to tell her so. And tell her the thoughts I keep having about the grill. After she gets pissed at me for trying to help, I think she'll like my idea.

"D? You coming?" Ben interrupts my thoughts. "We're going down below to eat."

"Yeah, I'll be down just now," I say quickly before twisting back to look for the first few boats. Of course, she's on the first one. It's a large pontoon boat, more of a big floating two-story deck than a boat. But I can see her, and Lucy, Stella and Rebecca and some of the marina staff I recognize vaguely.

They pull out of sight and I can't seem to stand the loss. I turn to the captain, a young kid, college age maybe.

"What do you get paid for a gig like this, mate?"

"Uh, Mr. Rockford pays five grand for the night, ten for a whole day."

"I'll make it fifteen for tonight if you stay by the front boat, that first party barge."

He shifts awkwardly. "Like, cut the line in the parade?"

"I don't care how you do it, but I want to be able to see that boat at all times." He starts to nod. "And not just within sight. I want to be able to make out the people."

"Uh, all right," he says, looking uncomfortable.

I put a hand on the railing to head downstairs and turn back, realizing I sound a bit mad. And I am. That woman makes me absolutely looney. "Actually, uh, be subtle about it at first. Don't want Hal to be cross with you. Or Beau, either."

"I can ease up to them once the parade starts to dissipate. When the boats link up to party at the end, I'll make sure we're right by them."

"Good man."

I step down the shallow fiberglass staircase to the group. They're standing and sitting in a lounge area off the galley, eating something that smells amazing. I am too agitated to eat but I grab a beer and head toward Hal. Then Katherine's voice in my head stops me, and I head and sit next to Grace instead.

I can't tell how Grace feels about me. I don't much care. Her father loves me more by the day, thanks to Katherine. And I...

I just don't want this to end. I don't want to leave these hills. I definitely don't want to marry and go back to my life in San Francisco. Not anytime soon, anyway.

I nod and pretend to listen to the conversation around me while I scan around us for Beau's boat.

This lake is truly stunning. Kat said it's like going back in time here, and she's right.

I quite like my view from the vacation rental, even though there is nothing but green and blue.

Not a single building to be found out those windows.

Basically, the opposite of my apartment out west.

I keep waiting to miss my old life and all its routines. I love my calming, high tech penthouse with its automations and sweeping views. I loved my chef, my driver, my office.

Yet, the longing for home never comes. In fact, I'm starting to think it wasn't home to begin with. That I've actually been homeless, at least since I've been in California. Maybe even before that. Maybe since I left Mum in London.

I've thought about negotiating some long-term agreement with Hal. A delayed merger of sorts. But I don't think he'll go for it without a ring on Grace's finger. And a ring on her finger means no Kat.

"That Lucy really is adorable," Grace says, her voice sad. I wonder about her tone for a millisecond but then violently snap my attention to the scene they're observing.

"Oh, they're doing that with the song. Cute," Ben says.

Ben is standing, looking across the water over my head. I turn fully to see the sight, the whole party barge singing and laughing on the top deck. The radios are all blasting that oldies song, *Higher and Higher.* Katherine is dancing with Lucy on her back. As the song goes on, she moves Lucy onto her shoulders, and they dance for a bit that way. Beau stands next to Kat and as the song shifts to the chorus Lucy moves up onto his taller shoulders. Lucy and Beau dance, he holds her hands out and she laughs.

I love her laugh and hate the sight of it at the same time. That she's over there and I'm over here. This is all wrong.

Their friends around them sing and cheer and help get Lucy higher. The next set of shoulders I think is Beau's brother, who's a bit taller.

I know I'm taller than them both, but Lucy doesn't stay on shoulders for long. The song keeps its driving rhythm and I watch the group lift Lucy up onto the top of the little canopy that covers part of the top deck. I clutch my glass, because that does not look safe.

But it also looks like they've done this a million times. Katherine climbs up too and sits beside her, singing loudly. Beau stands to the side, holding the frame of structure and watching over them.

And I hate all of it.

They look like a family.

He even has a bracelet on his wrist. He's in shorts and flip flops, hat on backwards. They're all in brightly colored logo-clad staff shirts. Kat's is tied up to show off her smooth, flat midriff. Even Lucy has on a tiny Marina shirt. They look good together. Even though it feels terrible.

Or, well, I feel terrible.

I feel wrong over here. My clothes are wrong, my shoes are wrong, this boat is wrong, the people surrounding me... I'm going to be sick.

"D'you see TikTok then? No wonder you look ill." Ben sits down next to me and shoves his shoulder into mine. Of course, he's smiling. He's a bit of a younger brother to me. He certainly annoys me like one.

"What?"

"You do know what TikTok is?"

I sigh. "Yes, Benedict, I know what TikTok is."

He pulls out his phone. "You're getting roasted today mate, since you made off with that waitress."

"Made off with what?" My pulse picks up like the wind around us as the boat leaves its slip. He hands me the phone with the clip playing. I watch myself talk with Hal at lunch earlier today, already angry that I am always being filmed no matter where I go. Then I see her, the waitress from earlier, walking by.

Shit, this does look bad.

"I don't blame you, she's a bloody hot shag, for sure. Should've been a bit more subtle though, yeah?"

I shove his phone back to him. "I didn't touch her, you idiot," I say through my teeth. "I got up to ask her a question. That's all. I wouldn't do that to—"

I stop myself.

Ben frowns. "I don't think Grace would care, mate."

Aha.

Right.

Suddenly, I must stop myself from smiling.

Katherine isn't upset or irritated or mad.

She's jealous.

Because she cares. Because I'm not just a shag buddy. Or a friend who scratches an itch. She's possessive *of me.* This is fantastic news. I look around for the boat again.

My growing smile dies when I spot her. I leap up from my seat and murmur something about needing air. I head up the steps for a better view.

I walk to the side rail of the boat, gripping so hard my fingers pale. Because she's dancing with Beau, but I don't know if that even qualifies as dancing. She's basically grinding on his leg to the music, and his hand is too close to her ass.

But.

She's looking at me, or at least in this direction.

I get out my phone so fast I almost drop it into the water.

> Dennis: I didn't touch her.

I look up. She gets the message on her watch. I see her read it. Still, she doesn't pull away from him.

> Dennis: She had a butterfly tattoo on her back.

Again, she reads it. No change in her behavior, still.

> Dennis: Katherine!

This time she does shift. She says something in that asshole's ear and then gets her phone out. She still grips him with one hand around his neck, but she texts me back with her other hand.

Katherine: I don't care.
Dennis: You do.
Dennis: And you're killing me.
Dennis: Consider me punished.
Dennis: Stop before I do something rash.

She looks up at me. The driver, as promised, keeps moving our boat closer to theirs. I can see the smirk in her features now as she basically humps another man's thigh.

Katherine: Like what?
Dennis: I will jump in and swim to you.
Katherine: Don't! It's freezing.
Dennis: Then quit riding him, ffs!!

She doesn't. I set my phone down and quickly rip my shirt over my head. I take my watch off too. Finally, she pulls away from him. I hear my phone buzzing, so I reach for it, staying ready to jump anyway.

Katherine: DON'T!
Katherine: Are you crazy?!
Katherine: Put your clothes back on!
Dennis: I want to be over there.
Katherine: Duh, we are way more fun.
Dennis: I'm coming.
Katherine: NO! You need to be there with Mr. Rockford.
Katherine: Keep your eyes on the prize, man.

I look up. Lucy has come up to her side to ask her something. Katherine puts an arm around her, saying something I can't hear because we're not close enough.

I stare, and she finally locks eyes with me. I try to tell her everything I want to text but won't. *I am. My eyes are on the prize. You two. You are the prize.*

She rolls her eyes and turns away. I lose her in the crowd of people and then she heads below, out of my sight. I think she was smiling, for a second. I think she was blushing too.

But like always, she turned away from me.

What did I expect? It's why I call her a wildling. Katherine Canton is a blinding, sparkling, shooting star, sprinting across this universe. As if she'd ever settle down long enough to be with someone like me. She's a young rainbow and I'm old, stiff... beige.

That girl will always be running.

But why, for the first time in my adult life, do I desperately want to give chase?

31

"Well? How was it?" I wince, waiting for my mini-me to start crying or huff in frustration or deflate in defeat after her state testing today.

"Great!" She says as she finishes getting herself buckled.

"Really?" I look back at her in the rear view, she's beaming.

"Yeah, Mommy. I could move my feet. I remembered everything!"

I smile and happy tears gather on the edges of my eyes.

She asks me to turn up the radio and I do. My girl was so bummed this morning that Dennis couldn't pregame with us. He could have, in fact he begged more than she did. But we can't incorporate him into our rituals. He's leaving.

Dennis is leaving.

Even if he seems to be making himself at home. That's the only way to describe it. He comes to eat but sits in the back and then clears his plates. Walks into the kitchen and jokes with Lonnie like it's always been this way.

I merge onto the highway, absently humming along to the song while I picture Dennis everywhere.

He shows up just to take Lucy to school so I can sit and have coffee one morning a week. He also brings me coffee whenever I see him, overpriced sugary goodness from whatever coffeeshop is closest to him. And something to eat too.

He's in the office, at the Inn, waiting in the parking lot, he's in the truck.

One Sunday, he even showed up at church. He didn't get to sit with us or hug me or anything beyond a polite greeting, so—after teasing him about bursting into flames when he walked past the threshold, of course—I asked him what in the world he was doing. He simply shrugged and said it was his only chance to see us that day since we had plans all afternoon. The same thing happened on two more Sundays.

The only place he doesn't venture into is our little studio apartment. He stepped in once and was so visibly bothered, I never let him in again. I think he just wants us in a bigger, brighter space. So do I. He's just less patient than I am in that one area.

Elsewhere, I'm the impatient one. I take a hand from the wheel and touch my neck where the latest hickey showed up. The man is some kind of sex expert. Has to be. I've never been needy like this, as if twice a day isn't enough. Some days it isn't, and I call him late at night and stay silent while he talks dirty to me from his bed a mile away.

It might be the hottest thing I've ever experienced.

Well, hard to say. There's been a lot. I am still not over last week, him staring at me across the water in that cruiser, ready to kill someone. Kill Beau, probably.

When I asked Beau if he'd be up for helping me make someone jealous, he was eager to help. Not eager for me, either. It was obvious the way he was looking around that he had someone to show off for, too. Made the whole thing less dirty.

Until Dennis was ripping his shirt over his head and throwing his watch off like a barbarian, ready to jump in the freezing water. His muscles went taught in the cold breeze and his body glowed in the low sun. He looked like a fantasy man. An angry fantasy with sex eyes, totally rabid. For me.

And then at the end his eyes were different for a moment. I'm pretty sure I was imagining it, probably hormonal or tipsy. But for a second it was like he was watching me and Lucy across the water with something deep in his gaze. Something like longing.

Yeah. It was probably the wine cooler.

But I didn't hate seeing that look. I even wanted more. For a half second, I wanted to jump in and swim to him. Which is insane. And is precisely why I can't let Dennis barge in on our rituals.

Including the singalong tonight.

After celebratory ice cream and a dance break in my office, I pack Lucy up and deliver her to my mom for the night. As always, because I'm out anyway, I make my additional stops. Main Street. The A Frames. I don't drive all the way across town, but I would if I had time. But I am expecting a new shipment of product at the Roadside. So I head back, excited.

I'm not the only one who is giddy.

"Boss, these are *so* cute," Stella calls as I walk into the office. There are boxes everywhere, some of them open already.

"You think?"

"Yes. People will buy them. For sure." She holds up one of the new t-shirts. They have cheeky phrases on the front and a vintage illustration of the Roadside on the back. There are tea towels and coffee mugs and tumblers. Coasters, shot glasses, koozies.

Beyond our designs for our brand, I also got some wholesale fishing, camping, hunting and boating merchandise too. It's all kitschy and weird. Eventually, I will build out and combine the front of the Inn and Grill to have a quirky gift shop kind of like Cracker Barrel. I want to have a whole line of Canton Cards and

Sadie's books and Skye's art, which I'll get at cost. It's going to be epic.

Ruthie sniffs as she pulls out a mug with one of her quotes on it.

"Like seeing your name everywhere?" I tease. She can't answer, though, and I understand. I just hug her. "C'mon, enough wallerin', Ruth. We've got work to do."

"I was not waller..." she tries to say but she's too weepy to get it out.

We both laugh and I hug her hard.

We work hard for a few hours but don't make much of a dent. We simply don't have the display space, or the spare storage, meaning the office will just have to be even more cluttered for a while.

Ruthie heads home and I get started behind the bar.

It's a warm night so we're busy. It's starting to feel like summer. Plus, Stella is posting teasers online already. If people stay a while and invite a few friends, it'll be a hot crowd all the way to midnight. That is good. Better than good. But I feel a bit weird about the fact that I didn't tell Dennis.

I haven't decided if I'm going to pour later or not. Not that I need his permission, obviously. Just seems like I'm hiding things from him. Or maybe, *I'm* hiding from him. And I'm a little disappointed he hasn't come looking for me.

We'd normally be deep into a text conversation by now. Since he didn't come in for dinner, we would have discussed our meals, him whining about how inferior his dinner was to mine. We would have talked about our evening plans and maybe weekend plans. He would have insisted on a set time to show up in the Inn parking lot.

I head out to said lot with a full trash bag. I throw the bag into the dumpster and realize I'm huffing like a kid. I'm legitimately pouting. Over Dennis. Ridiculous. He's about to leave for good, and I'm fixin' to go right back to leading singalongs and running my business and parenting my child without him. Surely, I can make it through one measly Friday night.

I should be able to. So, it's concerning that my lip is quivering, and my shoulders are slumped as I head back inside. I give myself a minute in the hallway to get reset before going out to the customers.

"Katherine? What? What's wrong?"

"Dennis?" I look up in shock. "Where did you come from? And what..."

He's wearing one of the new shirts.

I got them for the guys, but seeing him there in slacks and a fitted, black, screen-printed tee that says *Pretend this is a sexy pearl snap shirt*. It's too much.

Dennis wraps his long, firm arms around me. "Hey, hey, I was trying to surprise you in this ridiculous shirt but then I saw you in the hall upset. What is it?"

"I'm just tired," I say, burrowing into his chest.

"You're a sh—a *crap* liar, Katherine." He moves one of his hands so he can lift my chin with his fingers.

I close my eyes and smile at the feel of him all around me. "I'm fine now." He grunts but I poke him playfully. "Especially at the sight of you in a cheap t-shirt."

"It's like sandpaper."

I laugh and push him away. Someone could have seen us. Plus, I can't be sniffly and pissy over a man. Over freaking Dennis, of all people.

"Are you here to *tend bar?*" I tease him.

"If you'll have me."

I move past him and wave for him to follow. "You were good for business last time, so I'll give you a second training session."

"Wait," he says.

I turn and see a million emotions in his face. Oh. This is about later. He doesn't want me putting on a sexy little show. I both love and hate that.

Finally, his face morphs into determination. "Let me carry you around—at midnight. I'm plenty tall and more stable than those bloody stools."

"Oh, it's the stools you're worried about, huh?" I can't help but smile.

He seems a little nervous, but I can't let him get filmed holding me on his shoulders, not with the sexy way he'll look up at me and grab my legs and glare at other men. It's a recipe for disaster.

"I won't pour tonight. I'll be too busy fixing your mistakes behind the bar, c'mon."

He melts with relief. It's adorable.

He's adorable all night, really. When I make him change into an Arkansas shirt to score points in the photos and videos, he pouts and asks if he can at least keep the crappy employee shirt. He's adorable as he genuinely works hard to get better at bartending. He's fumbling drinks, filling the swear jar, paying for people's orders left and right, and watching me.

It's just like last time. Except it's not. He's different, we're different. It's like he's supposed to be here, like he's a part of us.

He. Is. Leaving, Kat.

I push through the night, trying to keep my emotions from bubbling up to my face. We have a stellar sing along, with Dennis just watching the madness with a grin. I pour from behind the bar like a normal bartender, except stretching to get to everyone as they crowd around.

He texts me that my ass looks fantastic. Followed by a vulgar message detailing all he would like to do to it.

It's hot, flirty, fun, and fine. It's fine if I just keep moving. So I do. He does, too.

At two, we shut the party down. I tell Otis to go home, and he eyes us but doesn't say anything. I doubt he will. He knows all the town gossip but he's not a spreader, just an observer.

I stop sweeping to pull my phone out of my pocket and turn the music down. It seems crazy loud now that everyone has cleared out.

"So, what songs do you listen to for yourself?" Dennis asks, surprising me.

I don't look at him. "Eh, I like everything I pick."

He stops wiping down a table and walks over to me. "Avoiding eye contact. I'm going to guess angry girl bands."

"No, I like everything."

He darts at me like a ninja and pulls my phone from my back pocket. I try to grab it, but he holds me off with his other arm.

"Katherine." He stops his scrolling and looks up, the gloatiest of gloaters. "Are you a Swiftie?"

"How do you even know what a Swiftie is, you geezer?"

He laughs. I love the sound. "Defensive. You are a Taylor Swift fan. Why so cagey about it?"

"Because it's so basic twenty-something of me." I grab the phone from him, and he uses his other arm to quickly trap me.

He pulls me into this side. "Nothing about you is basic." He murmurs before kissing my forehead. "What's *the* Kat Canton song? Your own personal theme, play it for me."

I can't resist. I get out my phone, and he rolls his eyes the second the beat starts. I picked *Crazy* by Gnarls Barkley.

"No, c'mon," He scolds as I pull up another and he knows before I hit play, like he can read my mind. "Not *Wild Thing* either. Give it." I scoff and try to keep it away from him but he's too big and strong. "It's the one about the hair."

"What?" I ask, but he's scrolling and tapping. Then he sets the phone down and takes my hand.

Once we're moving away from the table, he taps play. It takes me a second to recognize it as he pulls me into him and starts swaying. It's *Drops of Jupiter* by Train. It does start with a lyric about the woman's hair, but the rest of the lyrics make my eyes burn.

It's painfully sweet—the words, the sentiment. As he gently rests his chin on the top of my head, we slow dance in the dim lights of my happy place.

I can't...

This is...

"Dennis," I whisper.

"Hmm?"

"Quick, say something to piss me off."

He chuckles. "Okay. Let me stay the night here."

I pull back to look at him, glaring. "That'll do it."

"Come stay the night with me."

I shake my head and then burrow into him, hiding from his eyes that will see straight through me. I want to stay with him. I want him to stay here. In Arkansas. With me.

I shudder.

His hand goes down to play with the fraying edges of my shorts. "Let me have you here and now then." I start to protest but his fingers slip under the denim. "Do you know how many times I've thought about that? Your dream? Seeing you light up around me like your sign, in your bar, your little happy place. Please, Katherine."

I whimper at the way he says my name.

At the sound, he shifts to lift me, wrapping my legs around his waist.

"Is that a yes?" He kisses my neck. "Hm?"

"More lights off," I say, already pulling his hair and rocking my center into him involuntarily. We move over to the wall where there is a set of switches.

He slams me into the wood paneling and uses his knee to hold me up so he can rip my shirt open. The pearl snaps pop free.

"That might be my absolute favorite sound," he says into the soft skin bulging out of the top of my bra. I let out a squeal and remember what I'm doing, fumbling on the wall to turn all the lights off except a few strands of twinkle lights at the opposite end of the bar from us.

As soon as they're off, he turns and sets me on a bar stool, kissing my neck and chest while I scoot my shorts and panties down. He pulls at my shirt and keeps kissing everywhere while I get his pants off, too.

Like every time with him, I'm desperate. He grins while I pull at him. Normally he is in just as much of a hurry as I am, and we go hard and fast and crazy. When he thrusts into me, I brace for him to unleash himself. But instead, he stills and kisses me, and talks into my lips.

He puts one hand on my face. "Is it like your dream?"

"Better," I whisper as he absolutely wrecks me.

He groans and works me like only he seems to know how. He stops again, resting his forehead on mine. "You are my wildest dream, Katherine. I don't want to wake up."

I close my eyes to keep the tears in. I moan to keep myself from sobbing.

Because this is all a fantasy, a dream.

And soon we're going to have to wake up.

Very, very soon.

32

"This is the best day eveeerrrrr," Lucy squeals as we take the exit that leads to her school.

"Because *I'm* coming on your field trip, right?" I joke.

She laughs. "Yes, you and Mr. Dennis."

"It's all right, I know when I'm singing back up, Bug. Dennis is clearly the rockstar today." I watch her jump up and down a tiny bit in her booster seat. "I still don't get how Mr. Stuffy Suits is your new best friend."

"He's funny. He says all his words weird."

I chuckle. "That's true. What else?"

"He listens to my stories; he laughs at my jokes." She taps out her thought on her fingers. "He really likes you."

I almost hit the curb turning into her school. "He what?"

"He stares at you all the time and whenever he says something nice about me like I look pretty or I'm so smart, he always says"—she makes a serious face and tries her best British accent—"just like your mother."

"Huh. Well. I like him, too."

"I know. You stare at him the same way." She states it simply as she gets unbuckled. She plops a kiss on my cheek and hustles out of the car when I stop at the line, as trained. "Bye Mommy, see you later!"

I think I say bye before I drive away in a zombie state. I run my errands that way, too. Seemingly a few minutes later it's time to meet Dennis and Lucy and the rest of the third graders at the Natural Science Museum. I'm running late, of course, and Dennis *would never.* I pass his Audi as I scurry to the door.

Inside the lobby, kids are lined up while teachers go over instructions. It's loud and echoey. Dennis is standing with a group of parents watching the mayhem. He's talking to one of the dads. They have their backs to me, but their voices carry in the marbled space.

"I'm glad they are doing this with these kids, don't tell my wife this but this school is just too stuffy."

Dennis displays his perfect Greek-statuesque profile to reply. "You think?"

"Yeah, man, they barely let the kids take bathroom breaks. I get the focus on academics but, geez, let them live a little, ya know?"

"Hm."

The guy keeps talking to Dennis as if they're buddies. "They're just kids. Able is my son, by the way. He's got the blue glasses there in front." He points. "He's autistic. Total genius but struggles with some of the rigidity around here."

Dennis nods and points at Lucy, I can tell he's smiling. "Mine is the one hopping from foot to foot. With the stack of bracelets up her arm."

The guy cranes his neck.

Mine.

I can't...

I...

"Katherine?" Dennis turns around.

I try to smile, although my brain is having trouble firing off commands.

He tilts his head. "Your phone is ringing."

I look down. So it is. I clear the call.

"Hey," I say. The handsome billionaire, in his three-piece suit, starts to try to hug me, but I pull back, eyes wide. "So, Lucy is beside herself excited, but also remember the goal, here. We need to get a few photos of you walking around, admiring the exhibits."

"Yes, yes, I know." He sighs, and my phone rings again.

Except it's not a phone call; it's a forwarded alert I set up for my camera system. I pull it up and lose my breath.

"What?" Dennis grabs my arm.

"Fire at the grill, looks like everyone is fine and it's almost out but there was enough smoke to set the sprinklers off. Everything is soaking."

He gives my bicep a squeeze. "Katherine, they can—"

I look up into his dark eyes, growing stormier by the second. "I have to go, Dennis."

"You can't be serious."

"There's a literal fire. I need to—"

"You don't, though. You have a team of people there."

I lead him to the side of the lobby and lower my voice. "Remember how I still owe you sexual favors with a whole show and a costume and stuff?"

"Vividly."

"That. Later. If you'll just stay with Lucy and get the photos."

He exhales.

"Oh, also I was going to bring her straight home from the field trip, but I could maybe drive back—"

He squeezes my arm. "Go, Katherine. I've got her."

"Thank you." I hug him. It's quick and light, and he barely hugs me back. I understand his lack of warmth right now, since I'm abandoning him with a bunch of eight-year-olds.

I pull away to explain the situation to Lucy and her teacher. I also say a quick hello to Tran and ask her to help with the discreet photos. Then I run to my car and drive like a maniac all the way home.

It's not too bad, thank the Lord. The mess is only in the back section of the grill, the kitchen, storage, and one corner of my office. It's a pain to clean and we will have to run some fans for hours.

Though, since everyone was close by and rushed over to wipe, move, and separate what was still dry, we only lost a small amount of paper goods and dry ingredients. Hours pass quickly as we move into my office, sorting and separating papers.

When my stomach growls, I remember to look at my watch. A pang of anxiety rushes through me at the time. I really need to get better about managing myself, but one disaster always leads to another and next thing I know the whole day has gone by. Every dadgum day.

"Sh—Crap! I gotta go get Lucy from Dennis."

"Honey, she's in a booth just outside the door." Ruthie chuckles.

"She is?" I say, already leaving the room.

Sure enough, there they are, the unlikely duo. I hustle over to them, drawn to the sound of Lucy's little laugh.

"I'm sorry." I scoot into the booth next to Lucy. "A bunch of paperwork got wet, so we had to separate the pages and reprint stuff."

"It's fine, Mommy. We had *the* best day," she says as I mouth a thank you to Dennis.

He is half smiling but doesn't really respond. I can't read him.

"Oh, yeah? Here, why aren't you eating?" I gesture at the plate filled with fries, a grilled chicken sandwich and fruit.

"We got that for you," Dennis says, pushing the plate to me. Pushing the plate to me using his bright blue hands. Lucy giggles. My eyes snap up to meet his. "We made slime."

"You what?"

"We saw a big tub of glue at Tim's Club, and I said I could make so much slime with it and he said, 'You can't make slime you have to buy slime in a container' and I said no, you can, it's easy. And then we got all the things and made it at his house, but we didn't get the ruh... the?" She looks at Dennis.

"Ratio."

"The ratio right and then we were both stirring so hard that the bowls dumped over and now"—she has trouble talking through her giggles—"his whole kitchen is blue with food dice!"

My eyes are wide as they lock onto his, which are amused.

"Just the counters. It will come off."

"Did you say thank you, Bug?"

She nods and says it again.

"Thankya," I add, with my mouth full of chicken.

His eyes dip down to my mouth, and he answers softly in French. *"Tu me rattraperas."*

I frown but I don't ask him to translate. If he's speaking in code in front of Lucy, I can guess what the subject matter is.

I eat while Lucy tells me all about their adventures at the museum and Tim's Club. The latter seems to be a new favorite spot for Dennis. I can only imagine how much he's spending there each time he goes. I watch my child vibrate with giddiness as she recalls the day, and I'm not sure, but I think Dennis just watches me.

My phone buzzes us out of our happy bubble.

"Right." I shuffle out of the booth and stand. "I'm on front desk duty tonight. Go get your tablet and headphones, Bug." I hand her the keys to our place. As soon as she turns, I look at Dennis. The moment I open my mouth, he does too.

"What did you say?"

"I said 'you'll make it up to me.'"

I let out a weird half-laugh-half-whimper. "That, I will. But much later, I have to rework the reservations for the Inn on the new system, so I figured I could handle the front desk for the night while I work on it."

He exhales but it's through his sneaky sex grin. It's probably my favorite of his grins. He nods so I turn and head out of the back of the grill. But he follows.

I stop and look up at him towering right behind me. "Where are you going?"

"Wherever you are."

"Don't you want to change? Shower? Clean your kitchen?"

He gestures beyond me, for me to lead us onward. "No."

I shrug. "Your loss. It's going to be quiet and boring."

But it isn't. He and Lucy play games on her tablet. I answer the Inn phone and try to maintain my composure—a cranky guest is upset about the humidity while staying at the lake in late spring—while reading vulgar texts Dennis keeps sending to distract me.

I go to deliver new towels to that same guest and when I glance into the lobby on my way back, I stop short in the hallway. Dennis is sitting on the couch, jacket off, with his fancy dress shoes propped up on the small chair. In his right hand he's reading a business book.

Lucy is using his thigh as a pillow, propping her tablet up on her knees so she can watch her show. She's got her headphones on so it's dead quiet, other than the hum of the ice machine behind me and the air conditioning running over head.

It's so peaceful.

So… right.

Mine is the one hopping.

This is too much. I've got to do something. But I sniff and he looks up and sees me staring. The smile that greets me isn't a sex smirk or a sneaky grin, it's just happy.

"Is that my book?" I say, trying to play off my near-weeping experience just then.

"It is."

"Is it any good?"

He chuckles. "You haven't read it?"

"I like to buy business books to help me with my business. But my business is doing so well I don't have time to read them. I figure I'll get to it when things slow down."

"Novel idea, what if you slow down but the business doesn't?"

I roll my eyes. "Said like a true cazillionaire consultant." I point at the book when I get back to the computer. "Better idea. You read the books and tell me what they say."

"This one is about subliminal messaging in marketing, quite clever." He looks around. "You've already got it handled though. Your music, the colors, the brand you've made."

"You mean my vibes."

He lets out a small laugh. "Sure, your vibes."

"Is it interesting enough to distract you while I put her to bed?" I lower my voice. "There's a room open for us right now."

Something flashes in his eyes for a second. "Nothing can distract me now. I thought that was against the rules."

"It is, but I owe you big time for today."

A different emotion passes over his face. "You don't, wildling, I mean it. You don't have to compensate me for spending time with Lucile."

My voice is scratchy. "Why do you call her that?"

"It's her name."

I glare so he will answer the question.

"She told me you named her after Lucile Ball, a gorgeous, fiery red-head who changed the world."

"You know she was the first woman to run a major television studio?"

"I do." He sets the book down on the arm rest. "But you didn't need to name Lucy after someone remarkable, Katherine. She already has you; she needs no better example or reminder. I'm not sure one even exists."

I snap my mouth shut and blink hard a few times. "How many times do I have to tell you not to be nice? So cringey." I walk over to them and reach out to pull Lucy's headphones off of one ear but Dennis stops my hand.

"Cowboy boots."

I was trying to avoid eye contact, but I look at him, confused.

His smirk is back. "Tonight, for my little show. I want those damned cowboy boots."

I try to act offended. "You think you can just tell me what to do?"

"I can, and I will, because you love it."

I think I manage to mutter some kind of objection as I herd Lucy away, but he is right, and we both know it.

Hours later, when my cameras have been checked and the hall of the Inn is clear, we sneak into the empty room. I wear the boots and proceed to have the hottest night of my life.

When we sneak back out, Dennis is beaming. I am too. Just like Lucy was when I tucked her in. Happy.

We are all happy.

For now.

There's no way this can last, and I need to remember that.

33

"You've promised to be a good sport, remember," Dennis says to me, wary in the driver's seat.

Unfortunately for him, I am in a foul mood. A spring storm blew shingles off of two of the A-frames, Ruthie has a stomach Bug that she may or may not have given to all of us, and worst of all, I just lost the big battle in my ongoing war with this town and its realtors. And by realtors, I mean stupid Spencer.

I slump in my seat. "Well, I lied. I hate all sports. You've clearly done something swoopy, and I'm already pissed."

"Bloody f—" He stops himself and instead just hisses out a breath.

I laugh a little. "I'll try."

He glares at me with a grin starting on one side of his mouth. I turn up the radio and he quickly snatches my hand like a ninja.

I don't pull away because I don't know how many little hand grabs I have left. Probably only a few.

I shift and look outside instead of at his perfect fingers.

I know this road. This is the back road that runs behind Main Street.

Wait a minute...

"Wait. No. *No.*"

"No, what? You don't even know what we're doing."

But I do. I yank my hand away.

How did I not see this coming from a mile away?

"You! It was *you?*"

He pulls up to the backside of the lot I know very well. "Could you at least listen to me for one second, woman, I haven't even—"

"I can't believe this. Except. Of course, I can!" I throw open the door of his car and get out so I can pace and rant and yell. He gets out but stops before rounding the car and entering my personal space.

"What?"

"You. I was in a bidding war with you! Who do you think was fighting you so hard to get this lot, Dennis?"

His mouth falls open and his blinks get weird. He takes a small step back.

"Yes. It was me. Let me guess. You thought, wow, this is an amazing location for a second Roadside grill. Am I right, *Dennis?*"

He grabs the back of his neck and looks up at the sky.

I pace. "Yup. It is. It is an amazing location, which is why I have been secretly stalking it for months. Months waiting for Mrs. Abernathy to finally list it. Weeks of plotting, planning, bidding. Then, out of nowhere, I'm in a bidding war with some asshole who I thought was Spencer but no, it was you." I let out a howl of frustration.

"I'll pull out, obviously."

"After almost quadrupling the price? I'm not even sure I can swing it now."

He steps forward, barely. "Obviously I can fix this, calm d—"

I cut him off. "Did you just try to tell a woman—clearly losing her mind because a man has swooped in and royally screwed her, yet again—to CALM DOWN?" I screech. "I can't even stand to look at you right now, just go." I turn away and stare at the prime commercial lot that he just took out from under me.

"If you'd just open up, if you'd only—"

I wave my arms like a crazy person. "I am a private person. Deal with it."

"No. You're a scared person," he spits.

I turn around slowly. "Excuse me?"

"You've been wounded before, so your armor is on. I understand that but for fuck's sake, Katherine, I was trying to help."

"I didn't ask—"

"You didn't have to ask. I wouldn't expect you to. You don't want help, but people want to help you. I wanted to. Because I believe in you, because I believe in the Roadside." he slumps. "Clearly, you do too. Why can't we be on the same side here—be a team?"

"A team? You bought a huge piece of land without even consulting me. How is that being on a team?"

His mouth closes.

"Exactly. This is the problem. You don't want to be on a team, you want to *lead* the team."

"I don't. I'm sorry, I only thought—"

"You thought I wouldn't think of it, wouldn't dream as big, or plan as strategically, or envision far enough ahead? Like you— your cronies in your suits and your board rooms? I'm too young, too female? You know what Dennis? I'll show you. Get in."

"What?"

I stomp past him and open the passenger door. Then I go around to the driver's side. "Get in the car."

He looks genuinely afraid, but he obeys.

After a couple minutes he gets brave and dares to speak. "Are you, uh, sure you're in the proper emotional state for driving?"

"I'm sure I will take off a boot while driving and throw it at you while still driving."

He sighs and I look over at him. He looks so defeated.

I'm sure he expected me to be thrilled, moved, a bunch of sappy crap. And underneath I am moved, that he believes in my business that much. Even if he the way he showed it was all wrong.

I decide to throw him a tiny bone. "Have you been through my dad's financial history?" I ask.

"A bit."

"We moved here in my teens, that was after he bet the house on one of his business ideas. Literally. We lost our house. He also lost his reputation as mayor, so we moved." I grip the wheel, remembering. "Never said he was sorry or admitted he was wrong. Just up and moved us. Since we've been here, he's almost lost the house and the business multiple times. You saw that, right?"

He looks concerned. "Yes."

"In my teens, I learned I had a trust fund from my grandpa. Guess who almost cleared it out?"

Dennis exhales.

"Yeah. Dear ol' dad. Again, no apology. I finally moved everything out of his reach. My salary from Canton Tracking is deposited directly into an account and then immediately moved out to a fund he doesn't know about. That's where the stipends from Grandpa are, too. That's what paid for a house and the Roadside and what's left pays for Lucy's fancy school.

"He can't be anywhere near anything. Everything my father touches dies from his blinding greed and bitterness. I can't believe Canton Tracking has lasted this long. When he heard I bought the Roadside"—I take a breath—"he never said anything to me, just went to a bunch of slimy lawyers. Even though I was twenty-one, he tried to claim it, because he wanted to leverage it for a loan extension."

"You're kidding."

"No. He's poison. That's why you didn't know it was me you were bidding against."

I take an exit that's technically in the next town over from Rogers. I pull into the shopping strip. It's small and quirky, dirty even. It's not new and fancy like the Main Street lots. But it'll be busy once it gets dark and that's what matters. I steer the Audi right up to the door and point.

Future Home of The Roadside Bar & Grill

"Wait, so you—"

"I was bidding against *you* for Roadside number three. Number two, this spot with a smaller menu and a full bar, opens in a couple months."

I watch Dennis's face start to light up. "Can we go in?"

"No." I put the car in reverse. "I'm sure you're wondering about cashflow. Don't worry, little me thought about that too." He sighs and starts to protest but I keep going. "One thing I learned from stupid khaki Viking is real estate. His dad handles residential, Spencer expanded into commercial. They really do know the area, so after Lucy was born and we were renting, I saw their signs around. I started paying attention."

Dennis nods, watching me, processing. Keeping his mouth shut for once though.

"The first time I tried to buy something was the first time I saw Spence again, he was all 'it's so cute you think you can get approved for a house all on your own but that's not how it works, Kit Kat.' I think he kinda forgot about my last name. We do keep things low-key around here, but my cousins definitely don't, as you know. He didn't realize I had a trust fund. Still, I didn't want him knowing my business. I found a lawyer to help me set up the business entity for all this."

"All this?"

"You'll see."

Dennis clears his throat. "You realize how exceptional you are, Katherine? I mean it, love, you're only twenty-bloody-five."

Love.

Love?

No. That's just a British thing. Like darling.

I have to clear my throat, too. "I was on my own with a baby girl at seventeen. In soul years, I bet I'm older than you, geezer."

He chuckles. "Quite."

"I did have help. First of all, I am a privileged rich kid with a generous grandpa. I still get mad at him sometimes for messing up the way he did, pitting Uncle Jonny and my dad against each other, but he has always taken care of family.

"Ruthie, though, she's my partner. It was her dad who owned the Roadside. They were going into foreclosure on it, and it was my home then, both literally and figuratively. She and I worked together to buy it and then she wanted some cash a couple years ago, so I bought her out. She still helps me with paperwork and organization."

I pause my story, feeling naked and exposed, and turn off to-ward the A-frames. I glance over at Dennis, and I can't read his expression. After we make eye contact, he bites his lip.

"Are you... Does this turn you on?"

"Everything you do turns me on."

"Focus, you sicko. We're here." I pull onto a gravel road.

He looks out all the windows, expectant like a kid on one of those Disney tour rides.

I smile at my first little house. An uneven walkway of stone pavers leads to a triangle shooting up out of the ground with a little porch. It's tiny and freshly painted and surrounded by flowering shrubs and shaggy trees. It looks like one of those Thomas Kincaid paintings my grandma used to love.

"What's this, then?"

"My first house." My voice is scratchy. I have never shown these to anyone other than Ruthie. My cousins and Janie, even Tran, they have only seen photos. And some video calls while I was working inside.

"It was a dump when I started renting it. But there is a whole row of these A-frame houses. They're small and cute and once Airbnb became a thing out here, I realized they were little gold mines. I flip them, rent them, take the profit from one and buy the next. Now they're residual income, building up nicely." I sound shaky so I finish the thought quickly. "I own the whole street."

I put the car in reverse and back out of the driveway without looking at him. I make my way up the hill, and we pass my four little A-shaped hobbit houses, as Lucy calls them.

"Katherine." His voice is weird, too.

"Don't," I say, not sure what I'm telling him not to do. I only know I'm dangerously close to crying. I can't even pinpoint why. Am I proud? Am I exhausted? Low blood sugar, maybe? We get to the top of the hill, and I turn.

"Wait. Stop!" *Oh, crap.* He points to the modern mountain house on the corner. "You said that house on your dream board was an idea?"

"Vision board. And it is."

He glares at me. "That's the exact house, it's the same."

"I don't want that exact house, Dennis. And so help me, if you try to buy it for me I will never, and I mean *never*, talk to you again."

"But—"

"No buts. The developer bought up this whole hill years back with a plan for huge lots and more of those. The project stalled out but eventually they'll start building and I'll get one. That's what I'm saving for. That's our finish line, me and Luce. Moving into one of those that I buy for us." I give him a look. "That *I* buy for us. We're still at the Inn because I want to put at least fifty percent down. I am, uh, still pretty uncomfortable with debt."

I start the ten-minute drive back to the Roadside.

Dennis doesn't say anything. His silence is weird but he gets out his phone after a while. I relax, thinking he's moved on to checking his emails.

"They're adorable."

"What?"

He shows me his screen. He's looking at the A-frames on Airbnb. "Did you do all the renovations yourself?" I shake my head, but he points at my latest injury on my pinky finger. "But a lot of it."

"There are some things I can do just fine. Plus, out in these hills you'll find the nicest workers, good at what they do but, boy howdy, they're slow. Could be weeks just to get a light fixture installed. I can't stand waiting."

"That's true," he says, dipping into his sex voice for a second. I roll my eyes and he goes back to scrolling.

After just a couple minutes of soft music and him muttering about how incredible I am under his breath, we pull into the Inn's back parking lot. Next to the truck.

Which reminds me.

The swooping.

"Now you know everything, including how you royally screwed up my plans on Main Street." I open the car door. "Bye, Dennis."

He gets out in a hurry. "No, not bye."

I storm off toward the back door. "Yes, bye. I'm fff—freaking furious with you."

"Well, nothing new there," he mumbles.

I let out a frustrated growly sound as I throw open the back door and stomp through the hall.

"Katherine, wait."

I make a beeline through the bar and the side of the restaurant to the office. He follows, and I can hear him smiling and saying hello to onlookers as we pass, and he stops to let Stella through with a tray. Always prim and polite. So annoying.

I go in and shuffle a few boxes out of the walkway in the office.

He comes in behind and stands in the tiny open space between the desk and the couch that's not covered in piles. "Listen, I'll fix the price with Mrs. Abernathy, it will go back to the price you had before, I promise you."

I turn and stand up. "Yeah, but you've ruined it now. It's tainted."

"That's the first childish thing you've said so far. It was a misunderstanding. I'll fix it, your plan goes on just as before."

"Fine. Whatever." I huff. Because he's right. The plan can go right back to how it was, no matter how irritated I am. I'm not going to let pettiness get in the way.

"Good. Now can I tell you how amazing you are?" He tries to step closer to me.

"No. I don't need it, Dennis. Don't you get that? Have I not made it clear?"

"It's clear you're angry but—"

"I'm not just angry. I'm fed up with this, with having to repeat myself. There's no damsel here, as I've said a million times. I don't need your cheerleading, even. I. Don't. Need. You."

"Oh, no?" he says, frowning. "Sure as hell seems like it. Seems like you need me to remind you to eat, to rest. When you want someone to use, to yell at, or laugh with. Or when you're feeling particularly *needy* in the middle of the afternoon or the wee hours of the night."

"Seriously? As if I didn't eat and laugh and everything else without you before? You arrogant—"

He starts yelling too. "And don't forget when you need me to fill in as an uber driver and chaperone and tutor and fucking babysitter-on-call for Lucile!"

A tiny gasp freezes us both dead in our tracks. I crane my neck as he turns around. But it's too late. Teal eyes are wide with shock above tiny lips that tremble. I hear a little sob escape as Lucy runs into our apartment, slamming the door hard behind her. She doesn't like anyone to see her crying.

"Luce," I start, stepping toward the office door.

Dennis moves too. "Lucy, I—"

"No." I grab his arm and talk through my teeth. I'm vibrating with rage now. The sight of her like that, the sound of her little whimpers. I can't remember the last time I was this angry or hurt. "Not. You." I look in his eyes, serious and lift a shoulder. "This is it, Dennis. We knew we were going to end. Turns out it's today."

"W-wait. What?" His eyes search mine.

"Congratulations," I croak, my eyes filling with tears. "You've popped off and hurt not one, not two, but three Canton girls now."

"Please, shit. I'm sorry. Just let me talk to her, I—"

I straighten my spine. "You don't talk to her, anymore, Dennis. Or me. I mean it. You were always leaving; she was going to be disappointed either way. We'll just rip the band-aid off now."

"Katherine don't do this, please." He reaches for me, but I shift around him pausing in the doorway to look back.

"If you care about us, just go."

He pleads with me, "You can't ask me to leave her like this. Let me make it right first, please, with both of you."

I shake my head. "She'll be fine. I'm not going to drag her through some emotional rollercoaster of an apology just so *you* feel better, right before you leave her for good anyway. I'm asking you, Dennis. If you truly want to part with me as friends, just go. Don't eat here. Don't stop by. Just, don't."

I turn and walk away before he can say anything else. I slip into our apartment and shut the door, breathing deep. I gather myself as I walk to where Lucy sits at the table.

I don't cry. Because I'm the mom. Moms keep it together, so everyone else can fall apart. Tonight, when she's asleep, I'll let myself feel all the feelings. Not now, though.

My girl needs me.

34

Janie exhales a heavy breath. "And that was a week ago?"

"Yup," I say, sounding about as empty as I feel.

"Why didn't you call me sooner?"

I give up on trying to get the curtain rod out of the plastic packaging. "Ugh. Why do they package stuff like this? There are no nuclear codes hidden inside a curtain rod, just make the plastic pop right off. Seriously!"

Janie stares, blinking at me on my phone screen.

"Sorry." I calm myself. "I didn't call because I didn't want to face the music yet."

"What music is that?"

"Mostly the tune of you saying, 'I told you this was a terrible idea.' Not catchy. Would not put it on any of my playlists."

She chuckles. "Well, I won't say that. I will say you seem upset."

I shrug. "I'm upset that I didn't listen to my intuition. I knew he'd get all up in my business and spread, like a nasty little fungus. And, surprise, that's exactly what he did."

"But he fixed the deal with the lot, right?"

I pick up the curtain rod again. "Did he unscrew me after he screwed me? Yes."

"And he let you buy the truck from him?" She interrupts.

"Um, correct he allowed me to pay him a huge chunk of cash for the truck I didn't ask for. *But* he hurt Luce, Janie. He broke her little heart. He's dead to me."

She makes a face.

"What?"

"Is he dead to her?"

"Of course not, she misses him terribly and since I did my job very well—explaining he was upset with me, not her—now she says it's all my fault and is mad *at me*." I sigh. "I love being a parent."

Janie laughs. "Yeah, seems like a really great time."

I hold up the stupid curtain rod in triumph, sans its devil-spawn packaging. "Just living the dream."

"Do you? Miss him?"

I look away. "Nope."

"Not even the times you were, how'd you explain it? Shifting the earth's axis or—"

"It was the space-time continuum and no, not at all." She snorts and I concede. "Okay, fine, obviously that was nice. But it was time consuming. I'm getting a lot more done here at this last A-frame and with the new products. I'm a machiiiine!"

"Uh huh, have you ingested anything besides coffee today?"

Her question makes my mouth go dry. Not from hunger. Just because I'm used to another voice asking those questions. "I had a massive bite of scrambled eggs."

"Remember your child needs you to eat. In order to live. Okay?"

"Okay, Mother." The Ring doorbell lets out an electronic chime. "Oh goody, another obscenely well-packaged decorative accent. Got to go."

"Bye. Eat something."

I wipe the sweat off my face and keep my screwdriver in hand. I should get the air conditioning fixed. Only a few more weeks and then Lucy will be out of school and helping me in here. I can handle the heat but not the whining about the heat. I open the door and call to the delivery driver.

"Thank y—Dennis?"

"I won't come in and I won't stay long, I just need a second."

"Pass."

"I spoke with Mrs. Abernathy again," he blurts before I can shut the door.

I set my jaw and cross my arms. He waits, so I raise my eyebrows.

"She was cross with me that I had gotten her hopes up for such a high bid, then I explained everything." He looks out into the trees off the side of the porch. "When I finally quit my rambling, she was actually more furious. She's a bit off, honestly."

I let out a quiet mini snort, because I've also thought that about her.

His eyes jump back to me at the sound, and I look down. "She wasn't fussed about the lot, Katherine. She said I was a fool for walking away, just because you said to go."

I look up, confused. But I shouldn't have. His gaze is so intense, like he's begging me to listen, it's heart breaking. I look away but he inches closer. I back up.

"I said to go because you hurt Lucy, Dennis. What are you even doing here?"

"That was an excuse to push me away and you know it. She would've forgiven me in a heartbeat. You just wanted to shut me out, and"—his voice drops to almost a whisper—"I can't take it. I can't sleep, I can't work, I can't think without you, wildling." His voice shakes and it takes all my strength not to look at him. "I can't eat food that's not yours, I can't stand nights without your voice on the phone."

I shake my head. He's lost it. He can't... We can't...

"Katherine, look at me, please."

I do. I hold back the tears in my eyes, but I have to sniff.

He reaches his hands out but stops short of touching me. "This isn't over, we're not over."

"We are, Dennis. It's just, what, a few more days until Rockford chooses, anyway."

His jaw twitches. "He already chose. I won. Thanks to you."

I exhale, as if punched in the chest. My breath turns into broken coughs. I put my head in my hand and rub my temple, shielding my wet eyes from his line of sight. "Well, then, what are you even doing here? What are you even saying?"

"You know exactly what I'm saying." I look up but it's too much, all that can I see in his big brown eyes. I step backward. "I'm saying I've never felt this way in my life. I'm saying I can't live without you. I'm saying I—"

"No. Dennis, no. Are you crazy? We were a fling. It was a fling, and it's over now."

"Yes, so you said, keeping me at a distance with short texts and quickies in the kitchen and fake dates for Grace and yet here you stand, crying."

I suck in a deep breath to try and calm myself but it's terribly shaky and he notices.

"Why are you crying, love?"

"Because you're my friend and I don't want to hurt you."

He puts a hand up on the door frame near my shoulder, I think to stop himself from touching me. "I'm not your friend, wildling. You know that. And I'm asking you. Let me stay here. With you, with Lucile."

"You're insane."

"I'm not. I'm seeing clearly for the first time ever."

"Dennis, get a grip! Everything that is ass backwards and upside down about us is still true. Our lives are completely different."

"Forget my life. I hated it anyway."

"Well, sorry, man but I loved my life. And you don't fit in it." He flinches like I've just hit him. "Come on, you know I'm right. You need to be in control."

He laughs, surprising me. "*I* need to be in control? You've heard of projection, yes?"

"You think I'm projecting? That I'm the control freak?"

"Katherine, you don't let anyone else do anything. It's not enough for you to remember everything, think of every tiny detail, you must execute, too. All by yourself. You think a teenager couldn't hang curtains for you? Wipe down the kitchen and separate dampened papers? You honestly think you're the only one who can stock shelves, order supplies, pick them up from Tim's Club?"

"I—"

"Did you know Ruthie wants to watch Lucile?"

"W-what?"

"She mentioned it—Lucy did—that Miss Ruthie wanted to watch her sometimes but that you always said no. How do you think that makes Ruth feel? How do you think all your employees feel? Your friends? That no one is good enough to lift a finger for you?"

I try to respond but I'm shocked. "That... I... That's not it at all."

"I don't care about your business, love. You really have thought of everything on your board. You go for your goals and if you want to keep me out of them, fine. I'll never ask again. I won't buy you any more gifts, I won't give you any more loans, I just want"—he lets out a sad, shocked chuckle. "Hell, I just want to be near you."

"Y-you're just confused. We just confused things." He shakes his head, but I go on. "You're still too old, too stiff, too fancy, not to mention, uh, ya did feel all this before, Dennis. With my cousin, remember that?"

"I've told you I'm willing to explain all about that, about my whole past, anything you want to know."

"I don't want to know because it doesn't matter," I start.

He cuts me off. "It does matter because I assure you, not once in my life, not ever have I felt anything even *close* to this, Katherine. Every day this week has been agony without you. And Lucy. I can't function without you both. I belong with you."

I let out a bitter cackle. "You belong with Grace Rockford. The billionaire heiress who you came here for? Because of your dad? Your title and name and status? Oh yeah, and Emerson, your best pal who you are trying to win back? Because my cousin broke your heart and then you lashed out at her? Just like you lashed out at me last week. Come on, Dennis, we had some really hot sex, we did, but that was it. This was a stupid, complicated mess and it's over."

He drops his hand and whispers, "That was it?"

I nod, maintaining eye contact.

He has to go. This is insane. "I know I have a problem with the lashing out. I promise you I'll work on it."

I don't respond.

"You... you really want me to go, Katherine? Honestly?"

"Yes. I want you to marry Grace."

He sniffs once, nods, and straightens. He smooths his tie, a habit of his that would normally make me smile. Right now, it makes my eyes throb.

"For the record, if I've a heart in me at all, only one Canton has ever stolen"—his voice falters—"and broken it." He turns quickly and stalks away as soon as the last tiny word leaves his lips.

I watch him for a moment but the urge to run after him becomes so strong I have to back up and shut the door. I sink to the ground.

Broken it? Broke his heart? What?

No.

I was right, in what I said. He's just confused.

We aren't serious. We never have been.

He has a big, grand, fancy penthouse type of life eighteen hundred miles away. He's got board meetings and private jets and... and he'll lose all of that if he doesn't marry Grace. As planned.

I cough, trying to keep my sobs at bay.

Hashtag Grace DeLane, right?

Okay, I hate that. I can admit it.

I will die when I see them married, stopping by our little corner of the world to visit her father or meet with AmeriMart. Yes, I'll miss him and so will Lucy. Yes, this will suck at first, but change is hard. This is my fault for letting him change our life and now we're going to have to change back. I loved our life before, as I said. I meant it.

I stand, needing to get back to work, back in motion. I am not a control freak, I just have a strong vision, a plan. And I'm sticking to it.

And my plan never involved Dennis. His plan never involved me.

Both of us just need to move on.

I just need to keep moving, period.

So, I do.

35

"Hey, why the frowny face? No frowny faces on Fridays!" I say to the rearview mirror with fake enthusiasm.

"I don't like Fridays anymore," Lucy says, her sad tone and slumped posture stabbing me in the gut.

"Come on, tonight you get to hang with Miss Ruthie. I bet she'll let you bake something filled with sugar and food dye and probably put icing and whipped cream on top, too."

"Yeah," she offers with a smile. But the grin doesn't reach her eyes.

This is the third Friday like this, without her tutoring sessions. And just like last week, her little fingers absently drift to her wrist, where a stack of blue bracelets remain.

We go through our drop off routine as usual, but I can tell she's still sad.

Part of me wants to tell her I'll get to see him today, *Mr. Dennis.*

He'll be at this last board meeting to present his results. I can't believe it's already been ninety days. But then at the same time, it's like he lived here for a year or more. He definitely left a void behind, much larger than ninety-days' worth.

The seat at the end of the bar looks wrong without him. The spot next to my truck needs a little black Audi in it. The truck itself—a machine that makes me sad every time it starts right up without issue—still smells like him, but the passenger seat is all wrong, filled with boxes of stuff instead of kept clear for him to climb in.

I sigh as I merge onto the freeway that crosses town. I knew Lucy would miss him. I knew I would too. I just didn't expect to cry so much. It's only late at night when I've stopped moving, planning, working. It's only long after Lucy and the rest of the world have gone to sleep. But the actual quantity of tears has been so alarming I almost googled it but wasn't sure what to search for.

The black I always wear seems to fit perfectly lately. But I couldn't help it, I had to wear this dress today. I know Dennis likes it and I know I could use the help.

Because I look like crap. Not only am I tired, teary, and disheveled crap, but I'm also banged up, bandaged up crap, from working myself to the bone the past two weeks. If he sees me looking so pitiful...

Well, I don't know.

I would've said he'd grab my hands and glare murderously at the horizon, as if someone needed to die because I have a blister. I'd also guess he'd shove a coffee and something containing protein into my hands. Or maybe he'd just roll his eyes and hold me to his chest for a minute, if no one else was around.

Now, though, maybe he'll refuse to look at me. Maybe he'll glare or sigh. Most likely, he'll be painfully, perfectly polite.

I sniff as I pull into the Canton parking space.

He's going to be polite.

And it might ruin me.

I inhale and check my reflection one last time. Still crap. But it'll have to do. I head inside, chin up, back straight. I brace myself for the emotional arrows about to fly at me from those dark brown eyes. I greet the front desk staffers quickly, deciding to just dive in headfirst. I throw the conference room door open and search for them, the dark eyes I look for everywhere lately.

But they're not here.

Dad starts, "Great, now that you're here, Katie, I'll begin."

"You? What, where, uh, where is Dennis?" I stammer.

"He was called away urgently, but I assure you all, he left us in—"

I step toward my father. "Called away when? To where?"

"Uh, he didn't say. It was almost two weeks ago now."

"To the Rockfords? Like, for the wedding? Or?"

My dad looks around the room and then pulls me to the side. I'm not sure if he's awkward or if I'm being awkward. I'm sure I do not care.

"Katie? What's this about? I need to start this presentation."

"Dad, listen. Where is Dennis?"

"He didn't give me an itinerary. He said he was needed back in California. He'd already well over-delivered on his contract with us anyway. Why, did you bother him?" That familiar flash of hatred passes over my father's eyes. "You did something. What did you do?"

Well, that's it. I'm out. Not going to stay here and listen to him for an hour. I turn to the table of board members.

"If there's a vote today, I vote whatever Shelley votes." I nod and almost run out of the room. I hear murmurs behind me and my dad apologizing on my behalf. I keep up my fast pace all the way through the lobby and back to my car.

I pull out my phone and almost tap on the TikTok app but think better of it. No time for scrolling, I have to know now. I call Stella.

"Boss, you're alive! I swear I haven't seen you in weeks."

"Hey, Stel, how have you been?"

"Bored as hell, same as always. What's up, need me to come in early tonight?"

"No, uh, I wanted some scoop."

She laughs. "Yas, queen, you came to the right place. Is this about Otis?"

"Otis? What about him?"

"Nope, nothing. Otis is just boring ol' Otis. What were *you* saying?"

I almost smile. "You can bet your a—butt we're circling back to whatever news you have about him. But this is about the Great Grace Race."

"Oh." She sounds disappointed. "What about it?"

"Well, I figured you'd know about the venue, has she picked a wedding dress, florist, have they chosen a caterer? Maybe we could cater for them." I try to hide my true motive.

"Kat. There ain't a wedding to cater. You work too much, lady, honestly. This is old news."

My heart jerks inside my chest. I think it's still pumping. "Wh-what?"

Okay, yes, still beating, since I can talk. Kind of.

"I thought you knew since you guys were friends. Dennis turned Mr. Rockford down. That's the story, anyway. Now it's down to the other dudes but apparently Grace's dad is pissed."

"He said no? Dennis said no?"

"Kat? Are you still there?"

Oh. I dropped my hand, and with it the phone. I'm just thinking out loud to my car. I put my phone back to my ear.

"Where did he go?"

"Dennis?"

"Yeah," I squeak, sounding a bit frantic.

"I don't know, I woulda thought *you* would know."

"Right. Yeah, no. He didn't tell me."

Stella seems surprised. "Oh. Guess you guys aren't that close."

I have to close my eyes. Because we were. We were that close. When he came into the grill for dinner, I could see on his face the kind of day he'd had. I guessed the suit he'd be wearing correctly almost every day of the week. I could read in his text messages if he was grumpy or happy. Usually grumpy. Well, at first. Later they were almost always happy. He only bothers with punctuation if he's happy.

Now I don't even know where he is or what he's doing.

"Thanks Stella, see you later."

"No prob."

I drive home in a weird haze. I probably shouldn't be driving. The thought makes me remember the time Dennis asked if I should be driving. Which doesn't help with the haze.

I do make it back in one piece, miraculously. I slip in the back door and head straight for the coffee pot. I had planned to have coffee during the board meeting, and I can feel the beginnings of a headache.

"What you doin' back, honey?"

I spill coffee on myself at the sound of Ruthie's voice in the silent kitchen.

"Crap."

She hands me a towel with a curious look.

"Dennis wasn't there, Ruthie. He didn't, he's not, he..."

"Sit a minute, why don't you?" She herds me to the bar and a moment later she's back with cream and sugar.

"He didn't marry her, Ruth."

"Girl, he never was gonna marry her. I swear you are mighty slow for somebody so smart."

I finally stop staring into space and look at her. "I know you know about... That he and I were, uh, together. I know you picked up on that, but we were just a fling, Ruthie. He was supposed to marry her and keep his inheritance, his last name. His name for Pete's sake."

She rolls her eyes. "I think he'd've given up his first name, too, when it came to you."

"No, it wasn't that serious, he's all wrong for me. And I'm all wrong for him."

She puts a hand on her hip and dips her chin. "Oh, is that so?"

"I'm an excellent judge of character, Ruthie, you know that."

She throws her head back and laughs. "Honey, you picked the town's worst sperm donor. You tried to set me up with my cousin, Lord help you. Oh, and Stella and Ethan? You keep trying but that dog won't hunt. Stella's as gay as they come."

"Stella's a lesbian?"

"Correct. And you're a fool."

I throw my head into my hands, unable to take any more thoughts. I groan.

Ruthie laughs a little bit.

I look up, serious. "Maybe I am. Maybe I should've listened, he asked to stay, but"—I sit back in the bar stool—"he's gone now. He left. Dad said California. I guess he went to San Francisco. Went home."

"So? He has to come back for that big vote next month." She starts to wipe at a stain on the counter.

I shake my head. "That's over, the thing with my dad. He's not coming to any more Canton Tracking meetings."

"I'm not talking about your awful daddy I'm talking about the school."

"W-what?"

She huffs. "Maybe it wasn't him, but if it's not him, you can butter my buns and call me a biscuit because it has to be him."

"Ruthie what the hell are you talking about?" I'm exasperated now.

"My friend Betty said the headmaster said someone bought the school. Not just like some donation to get on the board, either. Lock, stock and barrel."

My mouth drops open.

"And!" She gets excited. "First thing he changed was standing desks. And I said 'Standing desks, Betty? You sure?'—because surely the first thing you'd change would be the bathrooms at the back of the sanctuary that the kids use for chapel, 'cause they're as old as the Bible itself and smell something awful— and she said, 'Oh yes. He said kids need to be able to move while they work and take tests.'"

"Standing desks," I mutter out loud while she's still talking. "Lucy said she could move her feet for her state tests, I just thought she meant, like, her teacher didn't get onto her for once."

"Now, c'mon Kat, use that big ol' brain of yours and—"

"Dennis bought *the school?*" I jump up, yelling.

"Don't take that tone with me, I didn't go and buy a giant private campus the size of a small town for the baby mama I'm having a *fling* with."

I sit back down and grab the bar top for dear life, like my stool might take flight at any moment.

"I thought maybe that was why you sent him away. Since you get mad as a hornet over the silliest things."

"Silly? *Silly?*"

"Yes. Billionaire man buys you a truck? Mad. Man buys us a new POS system? Mad. Tries to buy you a big ol' piece of land for your business? Guess what?"

"I gotta go hammer something," I say, getting up again.

"Mad. Always mad."

I roll my eyes and breeze past her. "I am not always mad," I scream, sounding furious. Ruthie laughs and I grunt another frustrated animal noise as I shove the back door open. I stomp and huff all the way to the truck. I get in and let it all out with a long, wild scream.

He bought her school!

I wasn't lying. I really do need to hammer something, as soon as possible. I start my truck and make for the A-frames. There are some rotting planks on one of the back porches that I've been meaning to rip out. It'll be perfect. I'm not even going to change.

I turn off of the main county highway that leads up into the hills.

I look up and I slam on my breaks.

No.

He didn't.

Did he?

With shaking hands, I grab my phone and call the number ahead of me in bright block print.

"Jenson Development, this is Mandy."

My voice is so shaky it's pathetic. "Hi Mandy, I just saw your new sign, on Lakeview Lane, about Lakeview Estates? Did... did you guys get bought out? New owner?"

"No, uh, not exactly." She switches to a whisper.

I'm grateful in this moment that I live in a town of gossips. Mandy is probably about to tell me everything I ever wanted to know.

"New landowner."

I put my truck in park, losing all my faculties, including the ability to keep my foot on the brake. "So, Mr. Jenson doesn't own the land?"

"Well, between you and me, Mr. Jenson still owns some of the land, but half the land was purchased by some rich big shot. I think he was in the Great Grace Race. I can't know for sure, but don't you think so? Don't you think the Rockfords would want one of those pretty lake view lots if they don't already have one?"

"Totally," I say, pretending to love the gossip.

"Anyway, he said get the houses going and up for sale as soon as possible. Very anxious to make his investment back, I guess. Mr. Jenson is giddy as a schoolgirl in summer with a popsicle— got a great offer and finally has the cash to start on those houses."

"Uh huh, so did the big shot buy any of the lots for himself? Or a house plan or anything?"

"No, and we thought that was odd, surely he'd want that top lot with the best view for himself or one of his mogul friends, right?"

"Right," I say, tears filling my eyes so badly I'm glad the truck is already stopped. "Did he say anything about the prices, or who to sell to, any kind of stipulations?"

"Nope, just get the houses up for sale as planned. No more delays."

"Thanks Mandy," I say quickly and tap the end call icon before a sob breaks free.

He didn't buy my house. He made a way for me to buy my house.

But the school.

It's insane, of course. He's out of his mind. Who buys a school to help one child with testing anxiety? Actually, it isn't to help just one child, obviously, or he would've just interfered with her class, her teacher. Instead, he instituted a school-wide policy.

I can't...

I don't...

I...

HONK!

Oh. Right. I'm stopped crossways in the middle of the street.

I wave and pull over to the side while mouthing "Sorry." After the car passes, I pull onto the road and head to the A-Frame. I don't need to hammer anymore, though. I need to talk.

I need to talk to my cousin.

I just have to carefully figure out what, exactly, I'm going to say.

36

I somehow get myself over to the last A-frame, out of my truck and inside the front door. I'm shaking and struggling to breathe. My thoughts are spinning through my mind so fast I can't sort them, can't process.

I sink down onto the tile floor in the tiny entry space and get out my phone. I tap on the FaceTime icon next to Sally's name. I don't have great service here without the signal booster that I've installed in the other rentals. Luckily, I get the call out, though, and she answers promptly.

"Hey!"

My voice is wobbly. "Do you think I'm a control freak?"

"What?" she asks.

"Well, Dennis said I am the control freak, not him."

"Kat? What's wrong sweetie?" Susan's voice comes over the line, and the warmth of it, the deep concern, is too much. I can't hold the sobs back any longer.

"Suze?" I manage to get out.

"What's wrong? Is it Lucy?" Sadie's voice. The connection is bad so I can't see them, but I hear Sam and Skye, too.

"No, she's fine. Is… is that Sadie?"

Sally explains. "We are all together at home. We're all here, Kat."

"It's a long story." I try to speak through the cries crashing out of me, but I kind of sound like a dying whale. Or a donkey struggling to breathe.

"Did she say Dennis?" Sadie asks, then Skye whispers something.

"Emerson!" Two of them say in unison. Then there is some shuffling and mumbling and yelling in the background. My tears subside as I try to decipher what they are doing and saying.

"We'll be there in an hour and a half." Susan suddenly says.

"What? No. I'm fine."

Skye scoffs. "None of us have ever seen you cry like this."

"And we were there when you were in labor, sister," Susan adds.

I shake my head. "You're insane. You can't just get on a plane, guys."

"Oh, hell yes we can," Sam says. "What's the point of being able to up and fly if we can't up and fly to family? We're coming."

"Sam, don't—"

"I said we're coming," she yells in the background, clearly smiling.

"Don't fight it. This is happening," someone—either Skye or Sadie—says.

As soon as I tap to end the call I'm sobbing again.

This. This is why Lucy's middle initial is S. This is also why people say rich people are crazy. They are. They do things like drop everything on a Friday morning and fly two states over, just because they want to. They buy trucks, land, entire freaking schools...

I lean my head back and try to weep it all out. Try to sort my thoughts and feelings. I'm confused, angry, anxious, tired... heartbroken?

Not like my heart just broke or is currently breaking.

More like it's been holding itself together with movement and goals and caffeine, and it simply can't hold out anymore.

Like maybe my heart has been broken for a really long time.

Since I was alone with a newborn in the middle of the night.

Since I was a scared teen, shunned by my new classmates.

Since I was about seven years old, listening as I was called a *cheap copy of a real Canton girl* by the man who was supposed to shield me, support me, love me.

I suck in deep breaths as the tears fall. I am able to stand after a while and wipe my eyes enough to leave and close up the A-frame behind me. My feet take me to the truck, and I climb in and manage to hold back any more weeping on the drive back to the Roadside.

I slink in the back door and hustle to my room. I try to fix my disaster of a face, smeared and red and snotty. At least wipe off all the mascara residue. I don't bother reapplying because I know the second the girls attack me with hugs, I'll cry again.

Thank God I never blamed them for the way my father treated me. I'll never forget when we were little and Skye said, "So, your dad's kind of a dick, huh?" I couldn't believe she'd just said dick out loud like that, one of my picture-perfect cousins.

Yes, I still get jealous or bitter that their dad is Captain America, and their mother was a saint. But those thoughts don't lead anywhere helpful, so I always shut them down.

The older we got, the more my mother wasted away before their eyes, the more they stepped in and stepped up. Then of course, once Lucy was born that was it. Game over, not just family but best friends for life.

Said best friends start blowing up my phone with announcements that they're pulling into the Roadside parking lot. I head out to meet them, keeping my head down so as not to worry the customers, the ones who know me well. To see me weepy like this, they would probably gape, dropping food right out of their mouths.

"Oh, Kat." Sam sighs as she sees me.

"Thank goodness we came when we did," Skye teases. I flip her off and she returns the gesture.

Susan doesn't talk. She just envelops me, gripping me hard. She's been a mom to her sisters—and me too, really—since her mom died.

"Why didn't you tell us what was going on before it got to this point?" Sadie says as she wraps her arms around me and Susan both. Sam and Skye join. Sally is last to get out of the big black SUV, with Nate, her boyfriend, and Dean, Sadie's bodyguard, who I guess drove them.

"Yeah, holding out on us is so *not* Peak Kat, Kat." Sally smiles as she joins our group hug.

"Facts." I sniff. "I see you brought the assassin." I nod at Nate behind her, her giant, dark haired, brown-eyed, tatted bodyguard boyfriend. He's staying a few steps behind and scanning around us, as he does.

"Canton Six." He dips his chin at me. They had a death threat in the family last year and he and his security detail called each of the Canton sisters by number. One is Susan, the oldest, through five, Sally, the youngest. Somewhere along the way he added me to the official roster.

He pulls Sally back and hugs her, then kisses her like he'll never see her again. I understand the intensity, given their history. He releases her and heads inside to 'clear the area'—as if we'd have a security threat in the middle of this forgotten little corner of the world.

Dean studies the exterior of my building, gives us all a little wave and climbs back in the shiny vehicle. Weird. Private security, having it, and actually needing it, all very weird.

"Come on, time to spill your guts and fill ours. I dream about your waffles," Skye says.

Susan *tsks*. "It's lunch time on a Friday, you're probably busy."

I huff. "Not too busy for you guys. There's a big corner booth with our name on it."

"Literally?" Sally asks. We all snicker.

"No, Sal, not literally. Though there is that sign from Shep hanging above it."

"I hope Matthew doesn't notice that," Skye says, referring to her husband, as we file into the booth. "He'll send you some obnoxious Texas Longhorn signs to hang in here."

All five of us tear that idea totally apart with hilarious, deep disgust as we slide into the booth.

"So, what's going on, Kat?" Sadie starts.

"Y'all want to order first or—"

"No," all five say in unison.

My throat closes up. "This is a weird vibe."

"We're sister-ventioning you. Don't fight it." Samantha smiles wide.

I nod, again, starting to cry as the beautiful women stare me down.

Sally leans in. "You asked if I thought you were a control freak before you started crying, right?"

"R-right," I answer slowly, trying to figure out where to begin.

"Well, you definitely are," Skye says into her drink.

"Skye," Susan scolds.

"What?" She extends her hands out. "It's a sister-vention. I'm vention-ing."

"You have a lot to control, is all." Susan takes over. "You're a single mom, a business owner—a not-so-small business, too. The grill, the Inn, more locations, your new products—it's a lot."

"It's a ton! You're a badass," Sam gushes.

"Jar," I joke. They laugh but then just wait, pushing me to explain. "I guess I just really keep people out. Ruthie had wanted to watch Lucy more, I never delegate, I don't trust my employees with very much. I haven't shown anyone the A-frames, Tran doesn't even know about the new locations yet and she's my best friend."

"Your best friend *here*," Sam corrects.

Sadie narrows her eyes at me. "Get to the real story, Kat."

I glance up at her, into those teal eyes I've been afraid to look at.

She raises her eyebrows. "Dennis. On the phone, you said Dennis."

My eyes start to water.

"I think I hate that man," Sam says while Susan mutters something under her breath.

"Wait, just hear her out," Sally says, causing all four of her sisters to look at her suddenly.

Ethan comes by and gets our orders.

The tension around the corner booth could be plucked like a guitar string. Very bad vibe. Hate it.

Skye glares at Sally again once Ethan leaves. "Will you just listen? He was helping Lucy."

All the pretty pairs of eyes snap over to me. I swallow. Here we go.

"That's true. He needed help winning over Grace Rockford, I'm sure you all heard about that? The arranged marriage thing?" They nod, leaning in. "Yeah, so he was so stiff and formal and polite and ridiculous." I have to stop and breathe. "So, I offered to help him get the lay of the land here and in exchange he started tutoring Lucy in math for me."

"Dennis DeLane," Sam thinks out loud. "Was tutoring a child?"

"Our child?" Susan gasps.

I nod. "He was great with her. She won't talk to me about school because she gets upset and then I get upset then she gets *really* upset."

"If you let him tutor Lucy—a choice I am not sure about, by the way—that definitely doesn't sound like a control freak to me." Sam crosses her arms, still upset.

"Valid point," Sally says.

Sadie tilts her head, waiting.

"He wanted to help out more. He tried to buy me a truck, a new POS system. I told him I wasn't a damsel who needed saving, but he couldn't help himself. He even tried to buy that lot on Main Street that I was bidding on, he didn't know it was me he was bidding against."

Four of my cousins look to the expert.

Sadie nods. "He does that. Gifts."

My chest aches as the air leaves me. I knew in the back of my mind that he had done this before. Fallen for a Canton before. Showered someone just like me with gifts, praise, affection. It wasn't real. Somewhere along the way I guess my heart got confused.

"Ugh, I'm such an idiot."

"What do you mean?" Sally asks.

Skye says softly, "You fell for him."

"I don't, I—"

"Hey, you're not the only one to get swept off their feet by a rich guy and his extravagant gifts. It happens all the time," Sam offers.

"They weren't gifts. He let me pay him back for all of it." My voice cracks. "Even the land."

Susan frowns. "What land?"

"Doesn't matter, the only thing that was really a gift was the school."

"The what?" two of them ask in unison.

I'm staring at the table through thick tears so I'm not sure which two.

I inhale. "He bought Lucy's school."

All five of them sit back in the booth like a gust of wind just pummeled them.

At that moment, Ethan brings the food. He looks around awkwardly and decides not to ask if we need anything else.

I catch him running away from the table in my peripheral vision.

"I'm gonna need you to keep talking," Susan finally says, still aghast across from me.

"I didn't know about that, the school. He didn't tell me. Lucy struggles with sitting still in class and especially for tests. You all know she gets anxiety, not about the test but about sitting silent and still for the test. Well, he—" I can barely say it now, shocked again at what he did. "He bought the school to enact a campus-wide policy for standing desks at the back of each classroom."

"Okaaayyy, so you were definitely having sex then," Skye adds.

"No, she wasn't," Sam says. "Wait, were you?"

Skye talks out of the side of her mouth. "No man is buying a kid's school without getting some action."

"I thought he was dating Grace?" Samantha is beside herself. "What were you then, his dirty little secret?"

"No man is buying a school for a secret, either," Susan says, confused.

"I agree," Sally says, clearly still processing.

"I wasn't a secret," I say. "Well, I was. But that was my choice. Grace was just business; she didn't want the marriage. She stopped dating the guys, the final choice came down to her dad.

Dennis spent his time with Hal, not Grace. We were just a fling; I made that clear."

"And now he's dropped you like it's hot so he can marry Grace," Sam spits.

"No. *No.*" I start to get angry. "You're wrong about Dennis, Sam. I just found all this out this morning, about the school. He turned Rockford down. I tried to tell him he should go be with Grace. She's perfect for him and his dad is cutting him out of the family. He won't even get to be a DeLane anymore. But he came to me weeks ago and asked me if he should stay. He wanted to stay here in podunk lake town middle America with me and Luce, and I said no. I... I turned him down."

Five mouths hang open around the table.

Sadie eventually snaps out of her shock. "Back up, he's losing his inheritance?"

"Not just the inheritance. His dad is cutting him out of their quasi-royal family. His lordship or whatever? I don't know how it works." I shrug.

"Dennis only ever really cared about one thing when I knew him. And that was his name. Being a DeLane. I mean it was all he'd ever say: DeLanes do this. DeLanes don't do that. He begged me to take his name."

Again, we all sit in stunned silence for a while.

"So," Sally says slowly. "He loves you."

I shake my head. "No, it was just a fling. Just sex. Janie warned me this would blow up in my face, but I didn't listen and now—"

"Janie knew?" Sally asks.

"That bitch is in deep trouble," Skye says, already getting out her phone to rage text her best friend.

"Don't blame her, I needed someone to talk to who had some context about us—our family, Dennis, all of it."

"Not that you listened to her anyway." Sally smirks and shakes her head.

"Sadie, what do you really think?" Susan looks over, concerned, but Sadie looks totally befuddled, so she turns back to me. "Well, Kat, what do you think, does he love you? Actually"—she shakes her head a couple times—"forget that. Do *you* love Dennis?"

"I can't... I..."

"Emerson," Sam says.

At first, I look over at her, confused but then see she's looking at the door. There is her husband, billionaire Ken Barbie and Dennis's best friend.

He is tall and lean and has light brown hair and icy blue eyes. He has the same billionaire British vibe as Dennis, formal, stiff.

Shep, Sadie's husband, next to him, does not.

Shep Riggs, former football star, is shorter, blond and tan like only a tv personality can be, a lot more muscular, and has a small-town vibe that's hard to shake. I would know. I don't see Matthew or Adam behind them. I guess that's where Dean went, to get these guys from another flight or something.

I'm about to ask about the logistics, but Nate walks up to join them.

He just appears out of nowhere from wherever he was hiding like a creep. A protective, giant-former-soldier-who-makes-you-feel-very-safe kind of creep.

Shep leads the band of good-looking guys over to us. He's energized, like he's about to go run laps or something.

"All right ladies, what's the game plan here?"

"Shep? What's wrong with you?" Skye asks. "And why are you carrying a bat?"

He slaps a wooden baseball bat into his hand. "Emerson here said dickwad DeLane struck again and this time he messed with

Lucy. Just point me in his general direction, we'll take care of it."
He smiles wide like a madman and slaps the bat again.

I think I'm going to be sick.

"Shep, put the bat down." Sadie sighs.

"Listen, that scum of the earth, ass-wipe, piece of—"

"Stop it, Shep. Stop. He's not scum." I almost yell.

"Em, we need to talk to you about him—about Dennis," Sam tells her husband, who looks very uncomfortable.

"We don't need to talk about jack crap," Shep says, "We just need to know his location."

"I tend to agree," Nate says.

"You can't beat up Dennis," Susan says, also irritated.

Shep retorts, just as loud, "Why the hell not?"

"Because"—Sadie gives him a look—"Kat is in love with him."

I drop my head in my hands and take a deep breath. Tears are bubbling up again, because what the actual f—heck? What the heck is my life? Why did I fall in love with my cousin's ex, who my family hates?

Susan rubs my back and shushes me. The affection from her makes the sobs spill over.

"Kat? Loves Dennis? Our Kat? And Dennis *DeLane*?" Shep babbles.

DeLane.

A name he is willing to give up. Because he doesn't want an arranged marriage anymore. Because he wants to be with me. Me and my daughter, who loves him and misses him. Whom he loves in return and even bought a school for.

Hearing it all out loud, hearing Sadie say it so plainly, is like the permission I need. Of course, I love Dennis. Obviously, I want Dennis. But now I realize the hardest, deepest truth of all. I need him.

I think back over the last two weeks. Two weeks that were the same but totally different. Like a dark cloud hung over my little family.

Because someone was missing.

Dennis was missing. He is missing, from the grill, from Fridays, from my life.

I just hope it's not too late to tell him so.

37

"Clarky, did you know about this?" Shep asks Emerson, using his silly nickname, as the men sit down with us.

"No," Emerson says.

Samantha loops her arm through his. "He didn't say anything?"

Emerson frowns at her and says softly, "I wouldn't keep that from you, angel. You know that."

She nods. "It's just so weird he wouldn't talk to you about it. I mean, she's my cousin and you're, like, his only friend."

"Shocker," Shep snorts.

"Shep, can you put the bat down now?" Skye rolls her eyes at him.

"Not ready yet."

"Shep!" Sadie tries to rein in her husband.

"Bambi, I'm not going to be friends with your ex-fiancé. Ever. Sorry, not sorry." He looks up at his sisters-in-law. "And it's not my fault nobody likes the guy. He's the one who got drunk and called my wife names."

I feel my chest puff out as I inhale, angry. "And you are so cocky you can't see straight sometimes. If you didn't have Sadie, you'd be a total douche bag."

"Kat," Emerson warns.

"And you never talk at all," I snap at Emerson, too.

Susan touches my arm. "We get it, Kat. No one's perfect. You're right."

Sally nods. "Would you just hear her out, Shep?"

"He did apologize," Emerson offers.

"Oh, okay, well then, all's forgiven," Shep says in a mocking voice.

I start to go off again but then shake it off. "I, uh, didn't let him off the hook either." I almost laugh at the memory. "I actually kind of tortured him. I made him get poop all over his hands."

Shep raises his eyebrows. "Now I'm listening."

I start from the beginning. The more I talk, the surer I am that Dennis and I were never a fling. Not since he showed up with the truck. Not since the pink bracelets on his wrist and black roses on my desk and the new iPads throughout the Roadside. And especially not since he kissed every tattoo along my spine.

I don't share that part out loud, but something changed that night, the only time I was in his bed.

That's when I really started to feel, to get scared. He knew it and deep down I probably knew too. Something in his soul connected with something in mine. Two beat up, determined, workaholic control freaks who just get each other.

I keep talking through it all until I get them caught up to the land for the neighborhood and Lucy's school.

"I mean, I guess he earns a couple points for what he did for Luce," Shep says.

"See? He's not all bad," Emerson says to his friend.

Shep grunts and Sadie shoves her shoulder into his. "I am happy for you Kat, and for Dennis." Shep gives her a side eye, but she wraps her arms around his bicep. "And my very mature, big hearted, totally secure husband is happy for you too."

"Now that I know the whole story, I am totally on team Kennis," Sam squeals.

Skye chuckles. "You're official now, Kat. She's given you a couple name."

"There's no Kennis." I slump in the booth. "He went back to San Francisco."

"So, go get him." Nate shrugs like it's obvious.

Sally nods.

Susan winces. "Well, are you sure? Because it's not just you."

I sigh. "I know, it's Lucy too."

Sadie cocks her head to the side. "Dennis is sure. If he asked to stay here? To give up the DeLane name for you?"

"She doesn't have to involve Lucy yet; he didn't ask to marry you or anything right? Just to give it a real try?" Skye makes a good point.

"True, he was just asking for a chance, and I rejected him. I was not gentle about it. He may have some new arrangement with his father by now. He may renegotiate with the Rockfords."

"*Psh*, no. He loves you. Hello! He bought a school. He'll come back if she asks, right, Em?" Sam looks up at her husband.

He frowns. "He's had a rough go of it for years. Hard to say how he'll react to—"

"Another failure," I finish his sentence. "That's what he said. That he couldn't take any more failures. Ugh."

"Listen, obviously you're going to grand gesture the crap out of him," Skye says, surprising me.

I look up confused.

"I've been there. I screwed the proverbial pooch with Matthew, remember?"

"Oh yeah. Where is he, by the way?"

"Big Ted Talk type thing he couldn't get out of." She rolls her eyes but she's clearly very proud of her husband, who I sometimes call Elon Musk, Junior.

I look at Susan next.

"Adam is home with the kids." She quickly redirects us. "If Emerson can feel Dennis out, do you want to grand gesture him? Do you want to really try it?"

"I do." I nod. "I really do."

"Well, dammit, it's like Nathaniel said." Shep sighs. "Go get him."

"Do you have any ideas for your big third act moment?" Sally asks.

"He put a lot on the line, the gesture's got to be good," Nate thinks out loud.

"Hence the term grand," Shep teases.

Sadie laughs. "I would just like to point out that I haven't said any romcom stuff. This is all you guys."

Shep kisses the side of her head. He also has his hand on her thigh under the table.

Nate has an arm around Sally and absently draws circles on her shoulder.

Sam is almost sitting on Emerson's lap, and he has both arms around her, even though it looks awkward and not at all comfortable for either of them.

It's weird how little I've thought about romance, affection, love. I've been so focused on my goals and my plan and Lucy, I never slowed down to realize how lonely I was. I look at the sweet smiles and gooey eyes around the table and I want that. All of it. With Dennis. Right now.

"I do have some ideas," I say and then smile when literally all of them lean forward. "Emerson, text him and just ask how it's going. Something generic."

Emerson nods and gets out his phone.

"Obviously, I'll need the jet," I say, and everyone nods even though it's really only Emerson's plane. It's like the Cantons have commandeered it. "I also think I'm going to need your particular set of skills, Assassin," I say to Nate.

"Oooh, I can't wait to hear this." Skye rubs her hands together like a movie villain.

"I can." Susan looks very concerned. She's always thinking about protecting the Canton name and brand.

I'm about to comfort her but Sam erupts. "He wrote back. What did he say?" She leans over to see her husband's phone. "Oh, Em asked him how he was, and he just replied, *Fine, mate, and you.*"

"But was there any punctuation?"

She furrows her brow. "No. Not even a question mark at the end."

"Yes." I smile, but they all look at me like I'm a crazy person. "He only bothers with punctuation when he's happy."

"Hmm," Emerson says, scrolling. "I thought he just never used it."

My throat spasms. "Try looking at anything within the last couple months?"

"I'll be damned," Emerson says softly. "He used an exclamation point a month ago."

"He did? Let me see. He did!" Sam loses it.

I exhale with relief. "All right. Now I know what I want to do. Let's see if all you fancy pants people can help me pull it off."

With spirits lifted, everyone starts eating. In between all the groans and exclamations about how great the food is, I go through my ideas.

Skye texts Matt about the technical details. Emerson agrees to his portions of the plan. Nate assures me he can help with the big picture logistics in the city since he has a team there.

Shep and Sadie don't say much but I'm happy to see them grinning and nodding.

I look at my watch before I go through a quick overview of everything one last time.

Nate looks at me, a little afraid. "And this is your plan for someone you *like*?"

I shrug. "He bought the school and that land. He went against my explicit instructions about swooping. He needs to suffer a little bit."

"I approve," Shep says sitting back and man spreading in the booth like he's some kind of king.

Sadie rolls her eyes while sinking into his side at the same time.

I guess she doesn't mind that he's an arrogant punk just like I don't mind that Dennis is a pompous snob. To each their own.

"Great. Boys, you get started; girls, you're coming with me to give my baby girl the surprise of her life."

———

"Well, what do you think, great day?" I ask Lucy, knowing that having all her "aunts" around for the afternoon and an early dinner was possibly the best surprise she's ever had.

"Amazing day. Most best day ever," she says raising her hands up above her head in her bed. I poke her armpits. Because how can I not?

"I have a question for you, Bug."

She calms down, catching my more serious tone.

"I, uh, miss Mr. Dennis." My eyes burn for the trillionth time today.

"Me too, Mommy."

"I was thinking maybe I should go find him in California and tell him to come back, what do y—"

"Yes! Yes, you should. Can I come? Please?"

I smile. "I think you should stay with your Aunt Susan for a sleepover while I go there and find him and talk to him." She frowns, shocking me. "You don't want to go see your cousins? You love playing with those boys."

She takes a deep breath, serious. "Are you going to be nice?"

"What?"

"Sometimes you're not very nice to Mr. Dennis. You yell and stomp. And you pranked him with the poop."

I slow blink, processing. "You're right, Bug, I wasn't. But I will be." I take one of her blue bracelets and slide it onto my own wrist. "I promise."

She looks at my wrist and gasps. "Mommy. I have the best idea. He will love it. He will definitely come back."

"Okay," I say, tentatively.

But I shouldn't have been tentative at all. My child is a genius. I kinda can't believe I didn't think of it myself. It's a brilliant addition to my master plan. It's a lot to pull it all off, especially in just a few hours.

I hope it'll be enough to bring him back. Bring him home.

I need it to be enough.

Because I need him.

38
DENNIS

"Good meeting, sir?" Albert asks me, as is my long-time driver's habit. I didn't used to mind it, but I very much mind it now. I just nod and slip into my seat in the back.

The leather is cool and smooth. The texture bothers me. In just a short time I got used to the leather of the Audi and the truck. The seats were always hot and sticky from sitting out in the sun during the day. No parking garages, no personal drivers.

I frown. At the leather beneath my ass.

Perhaps I'm having a bit of a mental break.

I look up and out, instead, trying to enjoy the city views I once loved. San Francisco is peculiar with its steep hills and winding streets with narrow lanes. I can see the ocean even now, past the traffic and…

Wait, what the f—

I crane my neck around to watch a truck pass us. Another one. Early this morning I swore I saw the exact same truck as Katherine's. This one too, just now. But no, it's not. Is it? I twist around in my seat, but I can't see it anymore. Still, big black Ford trucks are not the norm here. And that's twice in one day.

I turn back around and settle into my seat watching the throngs of people pass by on the sidewalks. I just need to try and get back to my old normal. I've had to reset my life before; I can do it again.

Except it was never like this before.

Bloody hell, I miss her.

I swear I can smell her watermelon scent right now. I'm scanning the crowd outside for flashes of neon pink. Looking for those fishnet things she wears on her legs. I can hear her playlist in my mind. *Higher and higher...*

Wait, no, that's in the car.

"Albert, do you have *music* on?"

"Yes, sir," he says, like we've ever had music on in the cab before.

I glare. "Well, can you turn it off, please?"

"Oh, sure," he says, but he changes lanes and takes his bloody time turning the song off.

That song feels like a punch to the jugular. Reliving that moment where Kat and Lucy looked totally happy and complete without me.

I suppose they are.

They might be on Beau's boat right now. It's a Saturday evening after all. And I'm in my damned navy suit and vest going to damned meetings in one of these d—

Wait, there's another one.

Another black Ford truck.

No. Cannot possibly be. The same one must've circled around.

Or I really am having a breakdown.

"Albert, more air please," I croak out as I roll down my window.

I grip my phone in my hand, but I don't look at it. She hasn't texted, not once. I thought—hoped—that by now she'd hear rumors about the school or the land and call to curse at me. I think in the recesses of my mind I wanted her to show up angry.

Angry I can deal with.

Toying with me, evading me, teasing me mercilessly. All that was fine. Would be fine. But the silence, the distance. I don't know how I will...

Wait.

Wait just one bloody second.

"You've got to be joking."

"What's that sir?"

I point. "That truck. The side with the advert. It's for a Train concert."

"Uh huh."

"It says *Drops of Jupiter* on it. That song is twenty years old."

Albert smirks at me. Why the hell is he smirking? "Sir, are you quite all right?"

"No, I'm not quite all right. I'm seconds away from having you drop me straight at hospital."

He snaps his mouth shut. His brow twists up and I realize he doesn't know what I mean. He's a good chum, as far as drivers and bodyguards go, but I don't tell him about my personal life.

I don't tell anyone anything, really.

Except for her.

"There's another one. It is a bit odd, isn't it?" He points up at a billboard on the side of a building. I see the same Train ad for a second but then it switches. My heart stops at the sight of a commercial for hair dye. The model's hair is the exact neon pink color as Katherine's. And she's wearing it up in two buns.

I'm going to be sick.

"More air. I'm serious." I lean back and shut my eyes. I grab my chest, still twisted up at the sight of a hair dye ad.

What has that woman done to me?

And how will I survive without her?

Food is bland. Silence feels weird, but music sounds wrong. The city is too gray. Too hurried. I can almost hear Kat yelling at the crowds of businesspeople to break out of the matrix. And a little voice mimicking her. I miss that little voice.

It kills me that I never got a proper goodbye with Lucile. Not one last hug around my neck, one more bracelet to add, one last kiss on her head. Nothing.

I fuss with the bracelets on my wrist and try to calm myself. But my deep inhale brings with it the smell of jolly ranchers again. And now even a hint of the Grill smell. Kat's food.

Last night before going to bed I actually prayed to the ceiling and today I'm smelling scents that aren't there. And seeing imaginary trucks.

This is truly concerning.

"Are you sure you have the right address, Mr. DeLane?"

Mr. DeLane.

I wonder how much longer I'll answer to that name. I've ignored my father's calls, but I can't avoid him forever. There will be lawyers and paperwork when things start to materialize, so I'll have some warning.

Warning, or not, though, I'm probably going to lose it all.

Fine.

I couldn't marry someone else.

I won't.

"Sir?"

"Oh, sorry, yes. It's a club. The guy's eccentric, wanted to have an *interesting* dinner meeting, he said."

Albert nods and pulls us into the valet lane outside the night club. He gets out and escorts me in. I didn't need him in Arkansas, and I didn't realize how odd it is to have personal security until I lived without it.

My bodyguard does sweeps of vehicles, buildings, rooms. He drives me everywhere and escorts me from the car to wherever I'm headed. In this city, I'm truly led around like a child. I'm also watched and talked about everywhere we go. The paparazzi is real here, so much so that I miss the *lookieloos,* as Katherine called them, from the Ozarks.

I miss everything about the Ozarks. Well, apart from the bugs. Bloody giant, ghastly things everywhere. Lucy loved them, though. Again, my heart burns in my chest. I rub at my sternum as Albert leads me into the club.

It's a small space, but posh. And packed already. Clean and dark with neon lighting around the bar. House music thumps through the air and I think a server just walked past covered in body glitter?

Well. This is weird. So is the man I'm meeting, however. Josh Jazir is the kind of billionaire who gives the rest of us a bad name. Garish outfits, sunglasses indoors, and, apparently, dinner meetings at night clubs that I'm positive don't serve a full food menu.

I am led by a hostess to a seat at the bar. Albert disappears into the shadows somewhere and my phone buzzes. I look at the message. Great. Jazir is going to be late, and I already have a headache from the noise in here. They must have a stellar happy hour deal to be so full so early on in the night.

"What can I get ya?"

I look up and am taken aback. "Otis?"

"Huh?"

No, it's not Otis. But hell, this guy could be his twin. And what the hell is an old, stocky biker type doing in a place like this?

"Sorry, just a beer please."

He nods and disappears. The club music changes to something else, a completely different vibe, as she would say. Some peppy oldies song saying get ready, I'm coming over and over.

I think this was on one of her playlists.

I could be imagining that, though. Like the trucks.

"Happy hour freebie," Not-Otis yells as he slides a small plate to me before turning back to the beer taps.

What. The actual...

I look around. Someone, somewhere, namely here, is trying to kill me.

"The happy hour special is chicken and waffles?" I call to the bartender, my voice high and sounding a bit deranged.

He doesn't hear me.

I'm genuinely afraid to taste the food. It's a fancy little hors d'oeuvre with a garnish. A long toothpick spears through a bite of waffle and chicken and something else. I think it's hash browns. But I'm not sure I can even trust my thoughts at this juncture.

Either this will taste like rubbish and make me sad, or it'll taste exactly like Kat's and I'm going to have to commit myself for psychiatric evaluation.

I decide not to eat it. I'm not sure what that says about my mental state, either, that I'm panicking over an appetizer.

The music gets louder as Not-Otis passes me my beer. The genre of song changes again, this time to some horrid boy band.

I drink the beer and stare at the offensive plate in front of me. I check my watch. It's only been a few minutes. Maybe I should cancel. Get up and flee.

At least the crowd chatter has died down now. But that's because people are humming. Some are singing along.

I recognize the song now. Timberlake or the other guy, I'm not sure. I am sure the song is *I Want You Back*.

It's annoying. Everything single damned thing is annoying.

I've got to get out of here.

I push my stool back to get up and the music changes again, abruptly. I don't care. It's still too loud and too annoying. I'm out of here.

Wait.

That bartender just clapped.

Everyone in here is clapping to the beat.

I look down at the plate. I must know now. If this is what I think it is—all this happening around me. I lift the food by the toothpick and put the whole bite in my mouth.

Yes.

It's hers. It's her.

She has to be here.

I start to stand again but the waitresses, who are singing loudly now, shove me back down into my stool. I look all over; I twist around but I don't see pink hair anywhere. I do notice now that most of the crowd in here is wearing pearl snap shirts, though. And they're all women. I don't see a single bloke in here.

But I also don't see her.

I turn back around to ask Not-Otis and all the air leaves me.

She's here.

In blue.

Her hair is bright blue. Her torture shorts are blue denim. Her sexy, holey stockings are blue and her pearl snap shirt—tied up showing her whole smooth, soft, midriff—is blue too. Even her combat boots.

She's singing and smiling and dancing like before. Like a cheeky sex goddess up there—a blue one. She holds a vodka bottle in her hand but there's no one to pour for. I'm the only one in here.

I look at her gorgeous face, and she frowns for a second. I finally pay attention to the song. She mouths the words, putting a hand on her chest. It's an oldies song about giving one more chance, she mouths "to show you that I love you."

My mouth falls open. I realize the song now. *I Want You Back,* this time by the Jackson Five.

I want you back.

She wants me.

I smile and stand and, as soon as I'm up and reaching for her, she sets the bottle down and jumps off the bar and into me, onto me, wrapping me tight with her whole body. I think I hear her make a noise, I know I grunt in relief, gripping onto her like she's another figment of my imagination that could disappear in an instant. But I can't hear anything over the singing of the entire bar. Who sound bloody good, actually.

She pulls back and holds my head in her hands.

"Yes!" I shout.

"You don't know what the question is, dummy."

"I don't care, whatever you're asking, yes, wildling. Yes."

She laughs and then kisses me hard.

I sit back down in the stool and settle her in my lap so I can kiss the ever-living shit out of her.

The crowd cheers around us and she pulls back.

She narrows her eyes at me. "You bought Lucy's school."

I wince a bit.

"And the land for my house."

"I'm sorry?" I try.

She shrugs. "It's okay. Albert said you looked really sick earlier."

"Albert?" I say, then I realize. "Did you put up that Train billboard?"

"And sprayed Al's car full of my body spray." She smiles. "And all the other really diabolical sh—stuff."

I glare, but I am grinning too. "You know I actually prayed, wildling. I prayed last night for you to come find me. Then by this afternoon I was thinking about committing myself to an institution."

"Be careful what you pray for, I guess." She laughs.

I close my eyes to exhale and chuckle and to just savor this.

Her giggle, her hand in my hair.

Her tight bum is in my lap and my hands are holding her. So I don't much care about the rest.

I open my eyes when I feel her hand playing with my bracelets.

"You're still wearing them." Her eyes are teary.

I pull her in closer to me. I know we're being watched, even though the music is lower now and the singers have stopped. I don't care, though.

"Of course I am. I couldn't bear to take them off. I even showered with them."

She sniffs. "Guess what?"

"What?"

"I'm in distress, Dennis."

I tilt my head, unsure. I also check her body, as if she would have a wound or something, a physical ailment I may have missed.

"Without you. I'm distressed." Her voice quivers. "I'm so sorry. I *am* a control freak. I *was* just scared, like you said."

"Shhh." I wipe the tears from under her eyes. "It's all right now."

"It's not. I'm not. I'm sorry I hurt you. I miss you. Lucy misses you. We are freaking damsels without you. I want you to come back, come home."

"Done," I say, my voice thick. She cries out with a shudder, and I kiss her softly, slowly. When I pull away, I look around. "Where is she?"

"I didn't bring her, in case..."

I pull my head back. "You thought I might say no?"

She pouts her lip out and lifts one shoulder.

"You still aren't sure how I feel about you? And Lucile? Love, I bought her school."

"Yeah, about that," she says. "I'm changing the swooping policy. Moving forward, I'm gonna need my boyfriend to talk to me before he purchases entire campuses or half the county, okay?"

My eyes burn. "I only heard one word of what you just said."

She laughs and grabs my neck. "Yes, baby. Boyfriend." She leans down to kiss me, and I can't help but groan.

"Call me that again," I say into her mouth.

She smiles. "My boyfriend?"

"No."

"Baby?"

I nod, kissing her neck and she breathes into my ear.

"I missed you, baby."

I groan again and grab her perfect ass cheeks in my hands.

She whimpers as I kiss her, suddenly very ready to leave. She rocks into me once and then stops us. "I want to go to—"

"Yes, let me get the plane." I get out my phone.

"No, wait," She laughs. "I want to go to your apartment." She bites her lip and lets her blue hair fall in front of her face. Then she looks up at me from under her long black lashes. "We have the whole night."

"Fuck me," I mutter.

"That's the plan, baby."

A tremor runs through me, and I stand, holding her around me.

She laughs. "Wait, put me down. That's the plan *after*."

"After what?" I slowly set her down, hating the separation.

"After dinner."

"Okay?" I frown.

But she's off and away now, climbing up on a barstool.

"Thank you, San Fran Singers, for your flash mob singing services, Dennis here will be paying all of you triple your usual rate."

The crowd cheers and she winks at me. The little gesture sends a shot of heat straight to my groin. It takes all my strength not to snatch her down from the stool immediately and drag her to some back room in this place.

She turns around. "Gene, your bar is fantastic, thank you." Not-Otis nods and smiles. "Albert, we're ready to go to dinner."

My bodyguard appears out of nowhere, as they tend to do.

"Flash mob?" I ask when she climbs down and links her fingers with mine. I squeeze her thin, cool, calloused hand.

"You also owe Emerson for the use of his jet, Matt and Skye for the billboards. Nate hired the trucks—the subliminal messaging torture was all very last minute and super expensive but I told them you're good for it and you love buying things for me."

"I am and I do." I kiss her head and let go of her fingers so I can put my arm around her. "So, dinner? Like our first real date?"

"Um, not exactly," she says as we step outside of the front door to the club. We walk right into a group huddled outside the door. I look over to apologize to the man I just accidentally shoved.

And there, scowling, stands Shep Riggs.

39

"Shit, sorry," Dennis stammers.

I pull myself taller trying to bolster him up.

Shep grunts. He didn't love this part of the plan, but he did agree to it.

"It's fine," he says to Dennis. All the warmth and charm that is Shep Riggs is gone. It's like he's a different person.

"Dennis," Sam squeaks, making up for all the grace Shep is currently lacking.

My man, who seems genuinely nervous, looks to her husband.

Emerson extends a hand, keeping one wrapped around his wife.

I can't help but smirk.

Samantha is taller than me, gorgeous big eyes and long, wavy, blonde hair. She and Emerson really do look like Ken and Barbie.

But Dennis and I are actually twinning with them a little bit right now. Well, the Ken dolls are twinning with their stiff posture and thousand-dollar suits. Each with an arm around their girl.

With my tall boots on, Sam and I are the same height. But while she's regular Barbie, I'm more of like, rockstar Barbie. I kind of love that for me. Maybe this dinner will be okay, after all.

"You've been quiet, mate," Emerson says.

Dennis sighs, so I jump in. "That's my fault, like I told you all already. I was the one who made him mums the word! Let's go eat!"

"Chill, Kat," Skye says. She smiles at Dennis and Matthew extends a hand beside her.

"Hey man, hope you weren't too freaked out by the billboards and stuff."

"Oh, I certainly was."

Nate chimes in with a grin, "I drove one of the trucks past you. Looked like you broke your neck trying to see. I'm Nate."

"Good to meet you," Dennis says as he shakes Nate's hand and then nods at Sally. She offers a silent wave.

This is definitely awkward. I don't love the vibe. Maybe tonight is going to be terrible.

Sadie chimes in as she walks up beside us. She looks up at Dennis and then back to me. "I know this is weird but according to my friends, and readers—who have filled me in on dating their ex's brother or their sister's best friend, et cetera—it's only awkward at the beginning, then everyone just gets used to it."

Shep huffs at the far end of our group.

"*Everyone* gets used to it, Shep," she yells over her shoulder.

I link hands with Dennis, who had to shift away from me to shake hands with someone at one point.

He looks like a scared deer stuck in a highway.

"Sally, all of you guys, why don't you go get our table. It's that restaurant right there across the street.

"Why didn't you tell us that before? We could've waited inside instead of out on the dadgum sidewalk," Shep snaps at me.

Dennis stiffens next to me, nostrils flared.

"Sorry. I was distracted," I yell at their backs. I also yank on the hand held in mine, before Dennis starts his second fist fight with my cousin-in-law. He's still glaring in their direction, so I hug him hard. "Sorry. I probably shouldn't have sprung this on you."

He puts his arms around me and sighs.

I look up at him. "Are you okay with this?" I continue to *not* chill. "We can cancel, I just... I already told them about how great you are and how much Lucy loves you and that I never needed anything or anyone but, turns out, I need you, and I wanted to win you back and do a grand gesture and all of them helped. Susan too, she had to go home, but everyone's on board, even stupid Shep."

He swallows and his voice is soft when he finally answers me. "You need me?"

I smile a little bit and nod. "I really d—"

He kisses the words out of my mouth. It's a sweet, soft kiss, much more reserved than I'm used to.

We are on a public sidewalk, though. We're in public. Kissing.

The realization thrills me, and I start to kiss him as if we *aren't* in public.

He grunts and pulls away. "Let's just be quick about this."

"Deal."

We go in and join my family at the table. Surprisingly, it's not that awkward.

Dennis gets to know Nate better as he and Sally share their crazy story with him. Dennis and Matthew and Emerson know a lot of the same genius tech people, so they chat for a while about nerdy things. When that topic wanes, the two Brits talk about soccer in very few words.

All the women, including Sadie, ask questions, teasing both me and Dennis, and laugh and nod.

Sam loses her minds when she sees the fifteen bracelets Dennis is still wearing. They ask about his tutoring and all my pranks and buying the school. Before we know it, the food is eaten, and the server is about to bring the check.

Unsurprisingly, Shep has said very little the whole time. He hasn't grimaced or glared, just sat, sort of waiting. Not happy, but not upset. When the bill comes and Dennis grabs it, I widen my eyes at Shep in a silent plea. He rolls his eyes, but he sits up.

"Listen," Shep says. Everyone stops what they're doing and looks at him. "Sadie says you're a good guy deep down and I trust my wife's judgment."

Sadie leans into him a bit more. None of us miss that he kind of emphasized the words *my wife.*

"Also, we all love Kat like our own sister-cousin, obviously. But one, I'm not going to be your friend."

"Didn't you tell me that right before you bought us Best Bud t-shirts?" Nate teases.

"He did," Matt says.

Shep ignores them completely. "Two, I am absolutely going to call you Denny from now on."

"Shep." Emerson sighs.

I start to speak up, but Dennis squeezes my thigh.

"And three—and I can't overstate this—do not, and I mean *do not* fuck this up."

"I won't," Dennis answers plainly.

Shep narrows his eyes. "We'll see. I didn't drag my baseball bat here from the airport, but I brought it on the plane with us."

"Shepperd, no one was gonna let you go at the man with a bat," Nate says.

"Shepperd?" Dennis asks.

Shep glares, dipping his chin. "Don't."

Dennis raises his hands in surrender but he's almost smirking.

Nate laughs. "If you're going to call him Denny, I mean, it's only fair."

"I've never liked Clarky," Emerson mutters.

"Now, that's just a bold-faced lie," Shep says. "You love it."

Emerson rolls his eyes, and we all laugh.

Sadie and I look at each other at the same time, thinking the same thing. Let's quit while we're ahead.

"Okay, I want to go see Mr. Billionaire's fancy penthouse apartment now." I stand up, and everyone else stands too. "Thank you, guys, for coming."

"Thanks for dinner, Dennis," Sally says.

"Of course."

"That's number four, actually. You're paying. Indefinitely." Shep is smiling now. I have a feeling he will add numbers forever.

"Yup. He's fine with it. Bye now!"

I grab Dennis's hand and he happily follows.

Albert materializes out of thin air and walks us back to the valet stand across the street.

My big glass of tall, dark, and handsome doesn't say much as we wait, but he does keep both hands on me at all times. Once we're in the back of his swanky Mercedes, we relax.

"Are you okay?" I ask.

He tilts his chin down to lock his warm eyes on mine. "I'm fantastic."

I reach up and run a finger along his stubble. "You kind of... Well, baby, you look like crap."

His laugh fills the backseat and I love the sound of it. "Someone really f—messed. Someone really messed me up the last few weeks."

"Someone is really sorry."

He kisses the top of my head and tucks a lock of hair behind my ear.

His lips move to my forehead and he talks into my skin. "Someone is forgiven. She also looks breathtaking. I forgot to say so."

I smile up at him. "You like the blue?"

"I love it." His voice changes. "Very much." He looks at the front. "Albert, step on it, man."

I laugh. "It was Lucy's idea."

"Of course, it was. She's brilliant. Like her mother." His left arm is around me and with his right he takes my right hand and squeezes it.

I reach up and link my left hand with his on my shoulder. For a few minutes, I just nuzzle into him, and watch San Francisco pass us by.

He kisses my head, rubs his fingers along my hand, inhales my hair, and lets out happy sighs.

Finally, we reach his high-rise.

Albert takes the car down below to park and then escorts us into the elevator. Naturally, Dennis has the penthouse, so we shoot all the way to the top and exit straight into his entryway.

It's like something out of a movie. Modern white marble and light wood and stainless steel. Low couches and plush rugs and sleek chrome LED lamps. Huge windows on all sides displaying the whole twinkling city and the ocean beyond.

I lead myself around and he follows.

Eventually, I find his room in the corner, all windows and a huge, low bed in the center with one small end table. There's nothing else in the space, but with the view, I can understand that choice by his interior designer.

"Wow."

"Indeed," he agrees, but he's staring at me.

I walk up to where he leans in the doorway. "I'm sorry I put you through the wringer."

"It's okay, love," he says softly.

"It's not, but I'm about to make it up to you."

He swallows and his eyes grow dark. "Oh?"

"Everything I'm wearing is blue, baby."

His lips part.

I reach down to untie my boots. I look up at him as I work with the laces. "Want to help me?"

"No." He smolders.

"K." I shrug. I kick off my boots and point to my blue socks.

He smiles.

I tug them off, then my shorts.

He can't quite see my blue lace underwear because my shirt is long now that it's untied, so I rip the pearl snaps open. He's still leaning, stock still, exhibiting remarkable patience. And restraint. He has his arms crossed but he's gripping his own biceps hard. And his thin dress slacks don't hide how I'm affecting him.

I walk up and uncross his arms.

He moves off the door frame and looks down at me with an awed expression on his face.

My matching blue lace push up bra shows, now. I get started on his tie.

"You wanna know something?"

"What?" he whispers.

"My vision board is all wrong."

He frowns, obviously not expecting me to say that. He helps me slip off his tie.

"My whole plan, really. I had every step, each big milestone." My voice starts to shake. My hands tremble, too, as I work on his shirt buttons. "But there are a few pieces missing. You said I'd thought of it all, but I left off some really important stuff."

He grabs my face and wipes a tear with his thumb.

I go on. "I forgot about having a partner, having someone to talk to, to laugh with, someone I can dance with and sing to. Who will remind me to eat and put Band-aids on my fingers. Someone to share it all with." I take in a deep, shaky breath and look into his eyes. I put my hands on his forearms. "I forgot about love, Dennis. I forgot about love."

He kisses me, moaning, then lifts me up so I can wrap my legs around him. He walks us to the bed, both of us kissing like we've never kissed before.

Our moves are softer, slower, gentler. Like the last few weeks were agony, because they were.

I reach up into his hair and he grabs my ass and both of us tremble. At the edge of the bed he stops, and I understand why.

I slide my feet down to the ground and smile up at him, but with how he looks at me—with so much warmth, with the way his eyes are misting at the edges—it makes my tears start up again. I reach up to wrap my arms around his neck and he puts his hands on my waist.

"Dennis." I burrow into his neck, feeling a little overwhelmed.

"What, love? Katherine, what is it?"

I lean back and look into his eyes, and the concern there, the way one hand holds my face. The way he suddenly doesn't care about the raging need in his pants.

He's worried about me because my voice is cracking.

That confirmation is exactly what I need. "I love you." He takes in a shaky breath, and I add. "And I want you to make love to me."

He kisses me, switching back to the hard, long motions I love, as I work at taking off the rest of his clothes. Once he's naked, keeping my eyes locked on him I take off the shirt and bra and underwear too.

His eyes go up and down and lock with mine, hungry. He's only seen me fully naked a couple times.

I sit down and lay back, scooting up on his glorious, silky sheets. I'm emotional all over again at the sight of his face, tired and bleary eyed, looking amazed and desperate at the same time.

I reach up and motion with my hands for him to come down to me, but he's still frozen. "Dennis?"

He shakes his head. "I just can't believe you're here, looking like this, in my bed. I fear I'm just dreaming. Maybe I've lost the plot."

"Want me to make fun of you for saying 'lost the plot'? Like, what does that even—mahhhh!"

He collapses on top of me and grabs my wrists. He pins them above my head and rubs his nose along mine.

"Fuck, I missed you."

"I missed you too, baby," I whisper.

He looks into my eyes, serious. "I love you, Katherine."

I smile and a tear escapes me as a sniff comes from him. "I know, now start bossing me around."

He makes a low growly sound before commanding me, "Don't move." He gets up and then is back in a flash, presenting his tie. "Bite."

I bite down on the tie, and he ties it around my head, essentially gagging me.

"Now," he says, smirking. "I intend to torture you. I will take my time kissing you all over, slowly." He kisses my head and then moves to my neck. He whispers into my ear while his hand starts exploring the rest of my body. "I'm going to tell you how beautiful you are, and how brilliant and incredible." I fight the urge to roll my watering eyes, but he leans up to lock his gaze with mine. "And I'm going to tell you I love you over and over, as much as I want, and you're going to lie there and take it, wildling."

I pretend to object, and he chuckles.

He kisses each of my cheeks before moving down my body, doing everything he claimed, saying everything he wants, as much as he wants. It is heavenly torment.

By the time he finally positions himself over me, I'm shaking with anticipation and a million happy emotions. He takes the tie off my mouth to kiss me long and hard as he thrusts home.

Both of us moan and shake and smile until I erupt right when he tells me to, in sync with him.

Aside from a few favorite moments with Lucy, I think this might be the happiest I've ever felt.

Maybe this time, the feeling will last.

40

"Do we need to talk about the fact that there's nothing in this giant room except a bed?" I raise my eyebrows at Dennis as I cross from his bathroom back into his master suite.

He looks like a porn star, naked and spread with the sheets all twisted up around him but not covering him at all.

"Apparently." He glares at me.

"I mean, no lamps, no chair, nothing? Is this a sex den?"

He sighs but it turns into a grunt when I jump onto him.

"Admit it, you film amateur porn in here."

He grimaces. "No. No one comes here."

I waggle my eyebrows, holding myself up on my arms against his firm, warm chest. "I see what you did there, and recent events—two of them—beg to differ."

His face melts into a gorgeous, relaxed smile before he pulls me down. "I stopped bringing women home in my twenties, when photos of my bed ended up in magazines."

"Are you saying I shouldn't have posted that photo of your amazing shower to Instagram?" I joke, nuzzling further into his neck.

"You like it?" He plays with my hair.

"The shower? Yes. The massive apartment that is so empty, it's creepy? Not so much."

"I wasn't living here, you'll remember."

I hug him. "Right, and, you think you can handle coming back to the sticks with me for a while?"

His hand freezes. "A while?"

"Well, I mean, what about your dad? Your name and inheritance and all that?"

"I don't give two shits about that." I sit up but he goes on. "I don't want to sneak around anymore. I want to be with you, wildling." He tightens his arms around my lower back.

"I still don't quite understand why you call me that."

He frowns. "You don't?"

"Am I that wild?"

"You're a force of nature." He tucks a hair behind my ear. "And not just bright sunshine. You're an entire season wrapped up into a person."

"Which season?"

He grins. "Whichever one has all the tornadoes."

I chuckle, "Oh, good. I'm destructive and terrifying."

"Yes. You scare me and you have absolutely destroyed me. And I want you to be all mine."

He pulls me down, but I only kiss him once.

"I am yours. But I still want you to fix things with your dad." He rolls his eyes and I poke him. "Seriously. It'll bother me forever if I feel like I cost you your name, your legacy and all that."

"Fine." He tries to pull me down again, but I resist.

"We need to take this slowly, Dennis. I have to think about Lucy."

He huffs. "Lucile loves me."

"She does. All the more reason for us to be smart. She and I can't move in with you. And you still can't buy me my house. Or any other swoopy things. And no one is proposing or getting married. I don't want any of that. Those are my new terms."

He frowns. "We need to come to an agreement about the definition of *swoopy*." I start to huff, and he flips us, so he can lean over me. "I am staying at the Inn." He kisses me quickly, before I can object. "And I get to kiss you whenever I want, no matter if Lucile or anyone else is around. And I'm going to surprise my girlfriend. Lavish her and her daughter with ridiculous gifts."

"No, you're—"

"I am. I won't interfere with your business or your plans. But I am going to royally spoil you both and there's nothing you can do about it."

"I can dump you." I sass at him, so he pins my wrists down again.

"You tried that. And here you are, delicious and naked in my bed, with blue hair and blue bracelets and lovely little blue panties."

I laugh. "Did you just call my underwear lovely? *Lovely,* seriously?"

He collapses on top of me. "Bloody hell, woman, you're impossible."

"True. But you're the idiot who loves me anyway."

He sits up and glares. "I do. Now turn over and let me see them."

I obey and he hums in satisfaction at the sight of my tattoos.

"Have you figured them out yet?"

His hand, tracing the butterflies, stops. "What?"

"One butterfly for me, one for Lucy, one for when I bought the Roadside…"

He continues. "Then four little A-frames," he whispers before clearing his throat. "The waitress with butterflies on her back, the TikTok video, you remember?"

"Yeah?"

He stops and chuckles. "I got up to ask her where she got hers. They looked a bit like yours and I—"

I twist around so I can look at him. "You what?"

"I wanted to get one. A tiny one on my wrist, maybe? Or two, one for you, one for Lucy. I don't know where. But I realized then, chasing after a waitress to ask about butterfly tattoos, I knew I was fully done for."

I get up and he lets me. I take his gorgeous face, twisted up with emotion, in my hands.

"We both know the truth and it's that you can list any terms, Katherine. Whatever you want. I'm yours."

I wrap myself around him and kiss him everywhere. I'm a crying snotty mess and he just keeps his eyes closed and breathes, both of us overwhelmed. I make love to him, sitting in his lap and holding his face and gripping his hair.

He doesn't cry but I think that's a feat that takes significant effort for him.

"You're my dream too, baby," I whisper to him when we're both almost spent. "Let's never wake up."

———

I climb down the narrow steps of the DeLane jet gingerly, since my legs resemble Jell-O. Dennis and I didn't really sleep at all the entire night. When the sun rose, kissing the tops of the hundreds of glittering buildings outside his huge windows, we looked at each other and agreed. We just wanted to come home.

So, we did.

"Mommy! Mr. Dennis!" Lucy squeals at us on the tarmac. She just arrived on the Clark's jet a few minutes ago. Weird how normal this all seems to her.

To me, too, I guess.

Dennis kneels down to scoop her up. "Lucile, how have you grown up so, in only a few weeks?"

"Vegetables," she says.

Both Dennis and I laugh but I can't help but roll my eyes and mouth *Grown up so?* At him. He flips me the bird behind her back, and I chuckle even more. Proper Dennis DeLane, flipping me off. I love it.

"Quite right."

"I'm glad Mommy got you to come back. I missed you," she says, gripping his neck for dear life.

I watch his face turn purple.

It takes him a while to respond.

"I missed you too." His voice is all garbled. I sniff, and he locks eyes with me as I smile wide. He shifts her to his left hip and extends his hand to me.

I link my fingers with his gladly.

We walk to the truck together, as a unit. Lucy babbles a mile a minute about everything she did during her sleepover at Susan's. Dennis just smiles and listens as he drives us from the small private airport back to the Roadside. I stare at him, and he grabs my hand.

When he squeezes my fingers and sniffs, his eyes misty, I'm sure.

I begin plotting.

Time for a new vision board. A new way of living that's not scared, secretive, tired and alone. Time to start on a new plan that incorporates all the precious things I forgot about.

EPILOGUE

MONTHS LATER

"This is just so exciting I can't stand it," Samantha gushes as she adjusts one of the apron displays.

Skye chuckles. "You? Overly excited?"

"Not, overly," I correct. "Appropriately."

"That's just what I was gonna say." Susan straightens from her spot where she was squatting on the floor to grab some microscopic piece of lint or plastic or something.

"Agreed. Obviously, the book nook in the corner is my favorite, but all of it is so dreamy, Kat. Like a modern, lake-y twist on Cracker Barrel," she says as she joins us after wiping down the huge new front windows of the renovated lobby.

Just like I imagined, the big porch connecting the Inn and the Grill waiting areas is bright, funky, and welcoming.

"Quit pulling," Shep yells to Dennis from the far side of a huge piece of furniture before spotting his wife. "Bambi? Are you lifting stuff, because so help me, I will—"

What I never would have imagined is Dennis DeLane helping set up the space alongside Shep Riggs.

"No." She puts one hand on her very pregnant belly. "No lifting."

"Good." Shep shifts back to his task and glares at Dennis.

"I am not pulling," Dennis says calmly.

"Just shut up, both of you. On three." Nate leads them in moving a massive, antique armoire into place. As the three of them grunt, Lucy and Susan's three boys barrel through the space.

"Slow down boys!" Susan hollers.

Behind the boys walks an amused Emerson, and behind him Matthew joins us slowly, eyes wide. He walks over to Skye like she's an oasis in the desert. "Tiger, we're never having children."

She laughs and he kisses the sound from her mouth.

"Quit making out and come tell us if this is centered," Shep barks from the wall. All the men converge to glare at the very heavy, apparently very offensive bookshelf.

"What a great group of butts." Samantha sighs, looking at the five men.

Sally, who was wiping down shelves with me, chokes on her own saliva. "Sam, don't be weird."

"She's not wrong." I laugh and Dennis immediately looks up to lock eyes with me. He is sweaty and gorgeous in a fitted black t-shirt and what we've agreed upon to be his *casual slacks.*

"So, how has it been, the whole takeover?" Susan asks me, eager to divert attention away from the group of men, of which her husband Adam is noticeably absent.

I smile. "Great. Dennis was driving all of us nuts at first, here all the time and wanting to help. Bless his heart, he really belongs in an office."

"And your dad? How did that all go down?" Skye sets a decorative plate on one of the shelves.

I shrug. "He knew it could have been a lot worse. I mean, Dennis could have destroyed the whole business if he wanted, so instead, taking over Canton Tracking and forcing my dad to retire was a gift. I think my dad is grateful that Dennis sort of let him off the hook."

"Tracking trucks," Sam grunts. "What a snooze fest. Emerson says Dennis is geeking out and that the two of them could talk about logistics and growth for hours."

"Could but won't. At least not Clarky," Skye teases Emerson, but only because she's almost as introverted as he is.

"I'm with you," I say refolding the cleaning rag to a new position. "I'm just glad *he* doesn't think it's boring."

Samantha clears her throat, trying to seem casual and failing. "Em also mentioned that Dennis sold his unbelievable penthouse in San Francisco?" She poses the statement like a question and all five of my cousins pause to look at me.

"No comment," I say, but I'm starting to blush.

"You're planning something," Skye whisper shouts.

"I'm not," I reply.

Sadie glares and Samantha makes a squeaky sound. Susan and Sally raise their eyebrows.

"I'm thinking about planning things."

More squeaks and whispers.

"Shh! He's been down this road before. I can tell he wants more kids, he's not exactly subtle about that. I'm just not sure about the engagement and marriage part."

Sam frowns. "Oh, I think he still needs to get married."

"Really? The thing with his dad is still an issue?" Skye asks.

"He says it's not but doesn't go into details." I answer for Sam, who nods. "It's a sore subject. Hence my hesitation, I mean I don't want him to marry me because he has to, I want him to want to."

"Has he dropped any hints about proposing?" Sally asks.

I wince. "Well, I've explicitly told him multiple times that I don't want him to propose because I don't want to get married."

They all groan.

"I know, but I wanted Lucy and I to propose to him. I've been working on ideas, basically since the big grand gesture out in California. But I've done such a good job throwing him off the scent that he's even stopped asking to help buy the house. We're both just kind of tiptoeing around the assumption he'll move in with us when they're done building."

At that exact moment, Lucy runs up to Dennis and jumps on his back without warning. He shifts down and lifts her so she can get a better hold. She asks him something I can't hear, and he heads off in the direction of the Grill. All the men chuckle at whatever she's just commanded him to do.

Skye moves closer to put a hand on my shoulder. "Kat, I love you, but you're an idiot. That man bought your daughter's school, took over your dad's business, and lived for months in a tiny hotel room just to be close to you. He will do whatever you ask, so just ask him to marry you already."

"You think?"

"I agree." Sadie nods, moving closer.

"Same," Sally adds.

I smile. "Okay, I'll start on my master plan."

He and Lucy come back, both of them chewing massive wads of bubble gum. He pops a huge bubble and winks at me before rejoining the men.

I continue quietly, "I just hope the general idea of marriage isn't ruined for him. I mean, how weird is the whole billionaire arranged marriage thing?" I ask.

Everyone nods and chuffs, except for Susan.

"Well, uh, about that..." She says, sounding weird. We all turn and look at her. Sadie cocks her head. Skye frowns. "I think it's time I finally told you all the whole story of exactly what happened between Adam and me..."

THE PROPOSAL

Read about Kat's grand proposal in the swoony, steamy, hilarious extra scene, from Dennis' point of view.
Get the bonus epilogue:
kelseyhumphreys.com/thingsiforgotabout

If you enjoyed this book, please consider leaving a rating or review online right now before, if you're like me, you close this
book and immediately forget everything you just read. Thank
you so much for reading!

MORE CANTONS

Read the Canton parents' quick, swoony
love story for **FREE** in *Things I Always Wanted, A Best-Friends-To-Lovers Romantic Comedy*

Skye and Matthew: *Things I Should Have Said, An Introvert/Extrovert Romantic Comedy*

Samantha and Emerson: *Things I Overshared, An Extrovert/Introvert Grumpy Sunshine Romance*

Sadie and Shep: *Things I Wrote About, An Enemies-To-Lovers Second Chance Romance*

Sally and Nate: *Things I Read About, A Grumpy Bodyguard Romantic Comedy*

Susan and Adam: *Things I Remember,* Coming Soon

**Find links, playlists, photos, and more
Heartlanders goodies at**
kelseyhumphreys.com/heartlanders

STORIES OF LOYA

Read the epic fantasy romance series the Canton sisters are obsessed with! Think *Hunger Games* meets ACOTAR. Written by Kelsey Humphreys under the pen name Kay Humphreys.

storiesofloya.com

FREE BOOKS!

If you loved Things I Forgot About, would you like all of Kelsey's future releases in advance and for free? Become a Book Bestie:

kelseyhumphreys.com/besties

ACKNOWLEDGMENTS

I wanted to dedicate this book to so many; the rebels and the black sheep, the single moms, the entrepreneurs, and all of you who weren't blessed with a family as wonderfully supportive as the Cantons. I see you and I hope you felt seen in this book.

And yes, y'all, Susan is getting a book. The last book in a series needs to be an anchor, a powerhouse title that lives up to all the favorite moments in the whole series. That's what I'm working on. Susan and Adam's story is a long, gripping romance that will be meaty and breathtaking and of course hilarious. And worth the wait!

As for thank-yous, my first thank-you will always be to Jesus for my salvation, my sobriety, and my creativity.

My second thank-you will always be to Christopher, my high school sweetheart, and the inspiration for all my hot, sweet fictional men.

To my family, thank you for your unwavering support through all my many creative endeavors. To my early rom-com readers: Mom, Anita, Mattie, Morgan, Courtney, and Andi. To my team on this series: Shayla Raquel, Karin Enders, Meredith Tittle, Theresa Oakley, and Shana Yasmin.

To my fans and followers who have been with me through my nonfiction writing and speaking, my YouTube talk show, my musical work, and finally my comedy sketches, and most recently "The Sisters." Your love and support for those comedy sketches brought this series to life.

ABOUT THE AUTHOR

After tens of millions of video views, comedian Kelsey Humphreys has captured her hilarious, heartwarming characters in book form. Her steamy stories dig into deep truths about love, identity, purpose, and family. When she's not writing romance or creating comedy videos, she's reading, running, moming and wife-ing in Oklahoma.

Ask your local bookstore to host her for one of the most fun —and funny—book signing events you'll ever attend!

Follow her funny posts on Facebook, Instagram, and TikTok **@TheKelseyHumphreys.**